**Rhys Bowen** is the *New York Times* bestselling author of the Royal Spyness Series, Molly Murphy Mysteries, and Constable Evans. She is a recipient of the Agatha Best Novel Award and an Edgar Best Novel nominee.

WITHDRAWN

Praise for Rhys Bowen

'The latest addition to Molly's case files offers a charming combination of history, mystery, and romance.' *Kirkus Reviews* on *Hush Now, Don't You Cry*

'Engaging . . . Molly's compassion and pluck should attract more readers to this consistently solid historical series.' *Publishers Weekly* on *Bless the Bride*

'Winning . . . The gutsy Molly, who's no prim Edwardian miss, will appeal to fans of contemporary female detectives.' *Publishers Weekly* on *The Last Illusion*

'This historical mystery delivers a top-notch, detail-rich story full of intriguing characters. Fans of the 1920s private detective Maisie Dobbs should give this series a try.' *Booklist* on *The Last Illusion*

'Details of Molly's new cases are knit together with the accoutrements of 1918 New York City life. . . . Don't miss this great period puzzler reminiscent of Dame Agatha's mysteries and Gillian Linscott's Nell Bray series.' *Booklist* on *In a Gilded Cage*

# RHYS BOWEN

# Naughty in Nice

Constable • London

CONSTABLE

First published in the US in 2011 by Berkley Prime Crime, The Berkley Publishing Group

This edition published in Great Britain in 2016 by Constable

Copyright © Janet Quin-Harkin, 2011
Published by arrangement with The Berkley Publishing Group,
a member of Penguin Group (USA) LLC

1 3 5 7 9 10 8 6 4 2

A CIP catalogue record for this book
is available from the British Library.

ISBN 978-1-47212-076-2 (paperback)

Typeset in Berthold Baskerville by TW Type, Cornwall
Printed and bound in Great Britain by CPI (UK) Ltd, Croydon CR0 4YY
Papers used by Constable are from well-managed forests and other responsible sources

MIX
Paper from
responsible sources
FSC® C104740

Constable
is an imprint of
Little, Brown Book Group
Carmelite House
50 Victoria Embankment
London EC4Y 0DZ

An Hachette UK Company
www.hachette.co.uk

www.littlebrown.co.uk

*This book is dedicated to Marie O'Day,*
*whom I have elevated to the ranks of royalty for this story.*

# Chapter 1

London
January 15, 1933
Weather forecast: showers turning to sleet later. Outlook:
depressing.

The Riviera had never looked more inviting. The sun
sparkled on a sea of deepest blue. Elegant couples
strolled beneath the palm trees on the Promenade des
Anglais. The scent of mimosa blossoms hung in the air
while a seagull soared lazily overhead. . . . I gave a con-
tented sigh.

"'Ere, watch it, love. You're slopping soup all over.' The
gruff voice brought me back to the present with a jerk.
I wrenched my eyes away from the poster on the wall
and down to the scene in front of me. A long, gray line
of shabbily dressed men, muffled against the bitter cold,
snaked across Victoria Station. They clutched mugs or
bowls and stood patiently, eyes down or staring, as I had
been, into a world that nobody else could see but them.
I was currently helping out at the station soup kitchen. It

was a bitter and bleak January day, and I felt as cold and miserable as those poor wretches who shuffled past me.

'Oh, crikey. Sorry,' I muttered as I noticed the trail of soup splashed across the oilcloth table. 'I wasn't concentrating.'

'It's all right, love. It can't be much fun doling out soup all day, not for a young lady like you.'

'Oh, I don't mind,' I said. 'Help yourself to bread.'

'Thank you kindly, miss.' The man gave me a half nod, half bow. 'You're a real toff, you are.'

He was correct, of course. I am a real toff – Lady Victoria Georgiana Charlotte Eugenie, daughter of the second Duke of Glen Garry and Rannoch, thirty-fourth in line to the throne of England – and I was helping out at the soup kitchen for several reasons: The first reason, naturally, was that I couldn't find a proper job. I had been educated to curtsy without falling over (most of the time), to know whether a bishop takes precedence over a duke (depends if it's an archbishop or a royal duke) and which fork to eat oysters with (trick question: oysters are tipped from the shell straight into the mouth). I had never learned useful things like typing or book-keeping or even cooking. Besides, the world was in the throes of a terrible depression and even people with strings of qualifications couldn't find jobs.

My second reason for working in the soup kitchen was that Her Majesty the Queen approved of voluntary service for the good of the community at this sad time. 'It's up to us to set an example, Georgiana,' she had said to me more than once. And I have to confess that maybe this particular volunteer job was attractive because a certain Mr Darcy O'Mara had been known to help out here when he was in London. However, the most compelling reason for my selfless ladling of soup into tin mugs was that my sister-in-law, Fig, had taken up residence in our London house. Any excuse to escape from her was welcome.

After a month of soup ladling, and scrubbing out vast vats of caked-on cabbage, it had begun to lose its appeal. Especially as Darcy had done another of his disappearing acts. I should explain that while Darcy could be described as my young man, he was not in any position to make me an offer, as his family was as penniless as ours. He lived by his wits, and, I suspected, on occasion he worked as some kind of spy for His Majesty's government. He would never admit to this latter fact, however. If I had been a halfway decent temptress, like Mata Hari, I might have inveigled the truth out of him during a moment of passion. But I wasn't, and we hadn't, yet. It was a case of too much Fig and too little opportunity.

My brother, Binky, the current duke, and his wife didn't usually spend much time at our London house. Binky preferred country life on our estate in Scotland. But this winter an amazing thing had happened. Fig was about to produce a second little Rannoch. How Binky could have plucked up enough courage to have created a first child with Fig is still a matter of speculation. Why he did it a second time indicates insanity in the family.

Anyway, she was beginning to swell up like a ripe watermelon and felt in need of more pampering than could be achieved in the vast, cavernous halls of Castle Rannoch, where the wind howled down the chimneys. And so they had chosen to spend the winter at Rannoch House, our London home, where I had been camping out alone, more or less successfully, for the last year. I'm an easy-going sort of person, but it would take a saint to spend more than three days with Fig.

I sighed and ladled another spoonful into a waiting mug. Every day while I manned my post, my fingers numb with cold, that poster of the Riviera looked down from the station wall, as if mocking my currently hopeless position. And the situation was made worse because every morning travelers passed us on their way to the boat train and the Continent. Each time I looked up, porters with great mounds of luggage preceded fur-clad ladies and well-dressed men. Amazingly some people still seemed to have money in this depression.

'So you're off to the Riviera, then?' A man's voice floated across to me through the smoke from the steam engines. 'You lucky chap. It's all right for some. I have to show up at the office every day, come rain or shine, you know. Nose to the grindstone and all that. The pater demands it.'

'Well, if you will have a father who owns a private bank, what can you expect?' replied the second voice with a similar Old Etonian accent. And two young men came into view, one of them wearing a bowler hat and carrying a brolly, the other accompanied by a porter and the requisite mountain of luggage. They were a little older than I; in fact, I thought I recognized one of them as a one-time dance partner at a hunt ball. For a second we almost made eye contact, but then his gaze moved on without a flicker of recognition, as if he couldn't possibly know someone wearing a cabbage-stained apron and doling out soup.

'Not all of us are going to inherit a title and an estate, old chap,' the first man said.

'We might still have the title and the estate but we're stony broke like everyone else these days,' the other replied. 'Can't even afford to stay at the Negresco this year. If I didn't have an aunt with a villa, I don't know what I'd do. Still, a couple of visits to the casinos should make up for the meager allowance the old man gives me. With a little bit of luck, what?' And he laughed, an exaggerated haw, haw, haw sound.

They moved away, their voices lost in the puffing of a steam engine and the shouts of porters. As I watched them go, another voice rose clearly over the station hubbub. 'Do watch out with my luggage, porter, or the whole lot will come crashing down.'

I turned to see a veritable Matterhorn of trunks, valises and hatboxes heading my way on a trolley, pushed by a red-faced and struggling porter, while behind it, carrying a small crocodile train case in one hand, a cigarette holder in the other, came my dearest friend, Belinda Warburton-Stoke.

'Belinda!' I called, dropping the ladle and wiping my hands on my apron as I ran toward her.

She looked up, confused for a moment; then a big smile spread across her face as she recognized me. 'Georgie! Good God. What on earth are you doing here?'

'Obviously not on my way to the Continent like you, you lucky old thing,' I said. 'I would hug you, but I'm rather carrot encrusted at the moment.'

'Er – yes, I can see.' She took a step backward, moving her gorgeous fox fur coat out of danger. 'So you're still doing your Girl Guide good deeds at the soup kitchen. Positively destined for sainthood, darling.'

I grimaced. 'Anything's better than spending all day

at Rannoch House, with Fig telling me what a burden I am to them and how sad it is that I'm not married yet.' I studied her, wrapped in her long fox fur, with her neat little pillbox hat perched jauntily to one side. She was the height of glamor, while I was conscious of my soup-stained apron and windblown hair. 'I had no idea you were home or I would have come to visit you to cheer myself up.'

'I haven't been in London at all, darling,' Belinda said. She turned to the porter, who was hovering impatiently. 'Take my luggage to my compartment. I'll be along in a minute,' she commanded.

'As you say, miss,' he grunted and pushed the trolley into motion again. The mountain of luggage teetered dangerously as he picked up speed.

'He'll probably tip the lot onto the rails,' Belinda commented. 'I always seem to get the one clueless porter. You'd think with all this unemployment that those who got jobs would be top-notch, wouldn't you?'

'So where have you been?' I asked. 'Why haven't I seen anything of you?'

She gave a resigned shrug. 'Home in the bosom of my family, darling. I came home for Christmas, because family togetherness is expected of one, isn't it, and because Father usually gives me a generous check in my Christmas stocking, but now I'm rushing back to the Riviera as fast as my legs can carry me. Too bleak and dreary in London and nobody fun is still here. Between you and me, I'm positively sex starved. I haven't had a good roll in the hay in weeks.'

'Belinda!' I exclaimed. After having known her all this time she still managed to shock me.

She looked surprised. 'One does so enjoy it.'

I tried to imagine if it was as good as she claimed. Darcy's kisses had certainly been blissful, but I couldn't quite believe that the next part could be as great as Belinda claimed. Obviously my mother thought so. She had done it with a great many men on every continent except Antarctica.

'I don't think I could live without sex,' Belinda added. 'I could never be a nun.'

I laughed. 'They'd never have you!'

'Which is more than any man of my acquaintance could say.' She gave a wicked smile, then the smile faded. 'Crockford's was like a morgue when I popped in for a quick flutter last night. Only a few dreary businessmen. Not a wealthy playboy in sight.'

'Did you win anything?'

Belinda made a face. 'I didn't stay long. I try not to play with my own money, you know, and I couldn't find anyone *sympathique* enough to fund me. The casino at Monte Carlo will be friendlier.'

'So you're going to Monte, are you?' I tried to hide my look of envy.

Belinda hesitated. 'Ah. That part's not quite settled yet. I don't exactly have a firm invitation from anyone.'

'So what are you going to do?'

'I was planning to camp out at the Negresco in Nice and do a little scouting around, but frankly Father's check is less generous this year. I blame it on the wicked stepmother. Like your sister-in-law, she objects to family money being spent on the unmarried daughter. So I've got about enough cash to get me there, and then, who knows? I may have to have my car conveniently break down outside someone's villa, like I did in Romania.'

'Belinda. You're terrible.'

'It worked perfectly at the royal castle there, didn't it?' Belinda gave me her cat-with-the-cream smile. Suddenly she grabbed my arm. 'I've got a brilliant idea. Come with me, Georgie. We'll stage that convenient breakdown together. It would be such a lark, wouldn't it? And someone would be more likely to take us into their bosom if you were with me. Royalty does carry clout, and I gather your cousin the Prince of Wales is wintering on the Med at the moment, so you'd have a perfect excuse to be visiting him.'

'I can't,' I said, while my less sensible half whispered that it would indeed be a tremendous lark. 'Apart from the fact that I'm hardly dressed for the boat train, it's a small matter of not being able to afford the ticket for the journey. And certainly not the Negresco until we secure our invitation.'

'I'd volunteer to share a room with you,' Belinda said, 'but it might rather cramp my style.' She leaned closer to me. 'Actually, I have a particular chap in mind.'

'Another one?'

'Of course.'

'So who is this new beau? Why haven't I heard about him?'

'Not my beau yet; in fact, we only exchanged a few words and some very smoldering looks. He sat next to me at the roulette wheel at the casino before Christmas and when I was about to bet he put his hand over mine and said, "Allow me," and put a stake on for me. And it won too. He's absolutely dreamy. What's more, he's a French aristocrat of incredibly long pedigree, I gather, and frightfully rich. But we never had a chance to get to know one another properly. He regretted that he had to leave for Paris the next morning, but hoped we'd meet again in more agreeable circumstances. So I'm planning to pick up where we left off.'

'Good luck,' I said. 'Now, if you marry him, you'll have to behave yourself. The French expect their wives to be terribly chaste and demure.'

'Not their mistresses, however,' Belinda said, smiling wickedly.

'Belinda. I worry that you'll end up like my mother,' I said.

'I don't think your mother has had a bad life at all,' Belinda said thoughtfully, staring out across the smoky bleakness of the station. 'Rather fun, actually.'

'But what about when she gets old and loses her beauty and sex appeal?'

'She can make a fortune writing her memoirs. "My life – from actress to duchess to bolter." They will make Lady Chatterley look like a *Girl's Own* comic.'

'It wouldn't be the kind of life I'd want,' I said.

'Of course not. You've too much of Queen Victoria in you. You want the family seat with an adoring husband and a pack of children around you. We'll just have to find you another Prince Albert.'

'I met enough of those at the wedding in Romania,' I said. 'They were terribly stodgy and boring.'

'That's because you were comparing them to Darcy. So where is he now?'

'I've no idea. I saw him once at Christmas, then he went home to Ireland and I've heard no more. I can't blame him. Fig is so rude to him if he dares to show his face at Rannoch House. She still hasn't forgotten arriving in the middle of the night and finding us alone together, and me in my night attire.'

Belinda's face lit up. 'Georgie, you sly old thing. So you have finally done it after all.'

'Not exactly,' I said. 'I wanted to but I fell asleep.'

'You fell asleep? I don't believe it. I'm sure Darcy's love-making is not at all ho-hum.'

'No, he was wonderful. I'd drunk too much champagne, I suppose. It always goes to my head. Anyway, Fig and Binky arrived and found us and she's not allowed Darcy in the house ever since.'

'How simply maddening, darling. We'll have to whisk you away somehow. I'll try to wangle an invitation for you once I'm settled in Nice, and you try to find a way to come up with the train ticket. Perhaps someone we know is motoring down and has room in the motorcar for an extra person.'

'I hardly know anybody in London,' I said.

'You know the king and queen, which is more than most of us. Wouldn't they like to send you on a small royal tour to bring their goodwill to expatriate English people?'

'You are silly. Besides, you said the Prince of Wales is already there.'

'I don't suppose he's spreading much royal goodwill. Too interested in one particular party.'

'Oh, Lord, is she with him?'

'So one hears.'

'I bet Her Majesty's livid about that.'

From down the platform came a loud whistle and shouts of 'all aboard.'

'You'd better be off, or you'll miss your train,' I said. My face must have mirrored my own gloom.

Belinda gave me a commiserating smile. 'I wish I could spirit you with me, darling. I don't suppose you'd fit in one of my trunks?'

I laughed. The station clock began to chime ten. 'Go, Belinda, or your luggage will be on its way to France without you.'

She leaned across my dirty apron to kiss me on the cheek. 'I'll miss you, old bean. And I will try to find a way to release you from your bondage.'

'Cinderella's fairy godmother?' I asked.

'Absolutely. Glass slippers and all.'

She blew me a kiss, then hurried toward her platform. I didn't say it, but I thought that once Belinda was safely on the Riviera, surrounded by gorgeous tanned and rich men, she would forget that I even existed.

# Chapter 2

**Rannoch House**
**Belgrave Square**
**London W.1.**
**Still January 15, 1933**

It was raining as I left Victoria Station – a sleety, freezing, almost horizontal rain that stung like needles on my cold skin. By the time I reached Belgrave Square and went up the steps of Rannoch House I was feeling thoroughly dispirited. I arrived at the same time as the afternoon post and retrieved two letters for Fig from the mat. One bore a Derbyshire postmark and her mother's perfect penmanship, the other a foreign stamp. I was naturally curious about the latter. I didn't think that Fig had ever been abroad. She didn't even like abroad. She mistrusted anything foreign, to the extent that she once refused to eat chicken cordon bleu, even though we assured her the chicken had been English through and through.

But at the moment I put the letters on the salver, Fig's voice floated down from somewhere on the first floor.

'Why can't we go to the Riviera like everyone else? This climate is too depressing and it's not good for me to be depressed in my current condition.'

I couldn't hear the reply, presumably Binky's, but could hardly miss Fig's shrilly annoyed, 'But everyone else is there. London is practically empty.'

Obviously Fig's governess had not drilled into her, the way mine had, that a lady never raises her voice. Or perhaps all the rules could be broken if one was in the family way. But in any case it was a slight exaggeration that London was practically empty. Fig had obviously never traveled on the tube during the rush hour.

I fumbled with my scarf, trying to make my frozen fingers obey me. The front hall felt delightfully warm for once. Since Fig and Binky had returned to London there had been fires in all the grates and good food at every meal. A far cry from when I was trying to survive alone last year with no servants, no heating and no money to buy food. I suppose one could learn to put up with Fig for the sake of such conveniences. . . .

At that moment Hamilton, our butler, appeared with that uncanny sixth sense that butlers seem to possess that someone has arrived, however quietly one creeps.

'Welcome home, my lady. Most inclement weather, I understand.' He helped me out of my sodden overcoat. 'Shall I have your maid run you a bath? Tea will be served shortly.'

As if on cue, Fig appeared at the top of the stairs.

'I thought I heard voices in the front hall,' she said, coming down cautiously with one hand on the banister, attempting to look as frail as La Dame aux Camélias, but not quite accomplishing it with her sturdy, horsey body and her ruddy, outdoor complexion. 'I think we'll take tea in the morning room today, Hamilton. It's so much cozier in there.'

'I remember your telling our American guests once that nobody ever went into the morning room after lunch for any reason,' I couldn't resist reminding her.

'Economy, Georgiana. One uses less coal in a small room. Rules have to be bent unfortunately. I never thought it would come to this, but it has.' She scowled at me critically. 'You look like a drowned rat, Georgiana. Go and have a bath, for goodness' sake – if your maid can be trusted to run one for you without flooding the place again. Really, that girl is too hopeless for words. Tell Lady Georgiana what you found her doing this morning, Hamilton.'

Hamilton gave an embarrassed cough. It was against the servants' code to tell tales on one another. 'It really wasn't important, Your Grace, and I have spoken to the girl.'

'He asked her to help clean the silver and do you know what she did?' Fig's strident voice echoed up the stairwell to the balcony above. 'She lifted her skirt and started polishing the salt cellar with her flannel petticoat. Can you imagine?'

I thought this was rather funny, but I tried to keep a straight face. 'It saves on cleaning cloths, I suppose,' I said.

'She claimed that was the way her "old mum" always did it,' Fig continued, eyeing me triumphantly as if it was I who had been caught out. 'Hopeless, Georgiana, simply hopeless. Surely you can manage to find someone better?'

'One can't afford to pay a top-class maid from an allowance of zero,' I said sweetly. 'Which is the amount I am currently receiving from the Rannoch coffers.'

Fig flushed. 'Binky has no obligation to support female relatives past the age of twenty-one,' she said, 'even if he had the money to do so, which he hasn't. Times are very hard, Georgiana. We are having to cut back to the bone as it is, and I think Binky is being jolly generous, allowing you to stay on at Rannoch House with us.'

'I expect Cinderella felt much the same way,' I said.

Hamilton coughed again, not wishing to overhear this conversation. 'I'll instruct the girl to run your bath, then, shall I, my lady?'

'Don't bother, Hamilton. I'm going upstairs anyway. I can run it myself.'

'Yourself, my lady?' His tone implied that I was about to sell fish from a barrow in the East End.

'It's really not hard. One turns two taps and puts a stopper in,' I said. 'I've done it before.'

'As you wish, my lady.' Hamilton bowed and retreated behind the baize door.

'Really, Georgiana, you must learn to be a little more sensitive,' Fig said. 'Servants should be allowed to do their jobs. They'll become lazy if they are not constantly being given things to do. And your girl is lazier than most to begin with. You must give her a stiff talking-to, and if you don't, I will.'

I sighed and dragged my weary feet up the stairs. One doesn't realize how tiring it is to stand for several hours. Walking is no problem. I could tramp through the heather all day, but standing in one place with cold feet is dashed uncomfortable. I stopped off at the second-floor bathroom and turned on the taps full blast, then I went through to my bedroom. The curtains were drawn and the room was in half darkness. I flung down my jacket on the bed.

There was a scream. I believe I screamed at the same time as a figure reared up from my bedclothes. My heart was still beating fast when Queenie's round, vacuous moon face came into focus.

'Queenie. What are you doing lying in my bed?'

She got up in leisurely fashion, stretching like a cat. 'Sorry, miss. I must have dozed off. I always get a bit sleepy after me dinner, especially when it's stodge. You know, steak and kidney pud. And we've been getting a lot of stodge lately, let me tell you.'

'That's because Her Grace the Duchess is trying to economize,' I said.

'When it suits 'er,' Queenie replied. 'I noticed she got through half a pot of Cooper's Oxford marmalade with her breakfast toast this morning when she thought no one was looking.'

'Queenie, it's not your place to comment on your employers,' I replied, although I was secretly delighted to have this little tidbit about Fig to bring out when necessary. 'Times are hard and Her Grace economizes as she sees fit. You are lucky to be fed and clothed in this house. There are plenty of girls waiting to take your place, you know.'

'I'm sorry, miss. And I'm sorry about dozing off, I really am. I was putting your clean clothes away and I just happened to sit down for a moment and before I knew it, bob's yer uncle and my 'ead just hit that pillow.'

'You really are hopeless, Queenie.'

'Oh, I know, miss. My old dad used to say he'd pay someone a thousand quid to take me off his hands if he had the money.'

'And for the millionth time, Queenie, let us please try to

get one thing straight. I am Lady Georgiana Rannoch and so I am not a miss. I am a lady. So the way you address me is "my lady," not "miss." Can't you please try to get it right?'

'I do try, miss – Lor' love a duck, there I go again, don't I? My old dad used to say I must be twins because one person couldn't be so daft. I do try . . . me lady . . . but it just sort of slips out. I mean, you look like a miss, don't you? You don't have a crown on your head or a snooty expression or nothing. Not like her downstairs, who looks at me like I was something the cat brought in.'

'Queenie, that's enough. Go and make sure my bath isn't overflowing, then come back and lay out something suitable for dinner – a dinner dress, Queenie. Not a tweed skirt. Not my ski sweater. The green velvet will do.'

'Uh – sorry, miss, but I didn't quite manage to get the little stain out of the skirt. Remember you dropped a bit of gravy on it and you asked me to get it out?'

'That's all right. I don't suppose it matters if there's a speck or two left.'

Queenie wrinkled her little button of a nose. 'It's a little bit more than a speck, I think you'll find.'

With great foreboding I opened the wardrobe. On one side of the green velvet skirt there was a circle about six inches in diameter where the velvet had been rubbed completely clean of its nap. It looked like a Labrador we'd had once who developed a skin complaint and had to be shaved in places.

'Queenie!' I let out a sigh of exasperation. 'What have you done this time?'

'I just gave it a bit of a scrub, with your nailbrush, you know. That gravy was stuck on like cement.'

'The gravy was a speck, Queenie. You have managed to turn one speck into a major disaster. If you didn't know how to clean velvet you should have asked one of the servants.'

'They don't like me, miss. They think I'm dead common.'

'Go and attend to my bath,' I snapped. 'And I'll have to see if I have any dresses that you haven't managed to ruin yet.'

She had never heard me speak to her as severely. Her eyes opened wide and to my horror brimmed over with tears. 'I'm sorry, me lady, I really am. I know I'm clumsy. I know I'm hopeless, but I do try.'

I felt rotten as she slunk away, head down like a defeated dog. I knew I should get rid of her, but I'd grown strangely fond of her. She had come with me to the far corners of Europe. She'd been jolly brave in the face of danger and she hadn't cried or begged to be taken home from the most disagreeable of circumstances. And there was the other fact that she wasn't costing me much – apart from dressmaker bills for alterations to ruined skirts.

# *Chapter 3*

**Rannoch House**
**Still January 15, 1933**

I felt a lot more cheerful after a hot bath and went downstairs, looking forward to tea and toast – and maybe even a slice of cake if Fig had developed a sudden craving for Victoria sponge. I was about to enter the morning room when I heard Fig's voice.

'It's like a miracle, isn't it, Binky? An answer to our prayers.'

I paused outside the door wondering what this miracle could be. That Fig was expecting twins? That she'd received an unexpected inheritance?

'I suppose we can afford the fares somehow,' came Binky's hesitant reply.

'Nonsense. We'll actually be saving money. We'll be eating their food, won't we, and we won't have to heat this house. We can send the servants back to Scotland and close up the place.' I was about to enter the room when she added, 'Oh, Lord, what are we going to do with Georgiana? I hope she won't be difficult about being turned out.'

'We can't turn her out,' Binky replied. 'I do have an obligation to my sister. We'll take her with us.'

'Take her with us?' Fig's voice rose so that I would have heard it even if I hadn't been standing with my ear pressed to the door.

'It will do her good. Great opportunity to meet some suitable chaps and find herself a husband.'

I stood there with my hand on the doorknob, frozen in an agony of suspense. Where were they going and would I want to be taken with them, even if Fig agreed?

'We've given her plenty of opportunity to find herself a husband already,' Fig said icily. 'We paid for her season, didn't we? And she's just come back from hobnobbing with most of the eligible young aristocrats of Europe. She turned down poor Prince Siegfried. She's a hopeless case, Binky. She'll wind up an old maid or a kept woman, like her mother.'

'Oh, I say, that's a bit thick, old bean.'

'Well, why isn't she married yet? She's twenty-two. The bloom is already starting to fade. It's all the fault of that O'Mara person.'

'He's not a person, Fig. He is a peer's child, just like you and me.'

'An Irish peer. They have different rules of behavior over there. And the family's bankrupt. He has no inheritance and no profession. He'll never be able to support a wife, as I've told Georgiana before. I blame him entirely. He has seduced her, Binky, and now she won't think of marrying anyone suitable.'

'Maybe she'll meet someone on the Riviera,' Binky

said. My eyes shot open at this remark. 'Romantic setting and all that, what?'

'Binky, much as I would like to help your sister find a suitable husband, I must protest. Do you know how much a ticket on the Blue Train costs? And we'll have to pay for my maid and you'll need Frederick – we'll send them third class on an ordinary train, of course, but it will still be a considerable expense.'

'Then what's going to happen to Georgie? She can't go on living here with no heat and no servants in the middle of winter.'

'Of course she can't,' came Fig's impatient voice. 'The house should be closed up properly. She'll just have to go back to Scotland if she wants to continue to live at our grace and favor. We have to keep Castle Rannoch running anyway. She can take little Podge back with her when we leave, and give him some lessons. He's almost four. It's about time he learned to read and write.'

'You want to send your son back to Scotland, Fig? You don't think he should get the benefit of sun and sea with us?'

'Children flourish with a firm routine, Binky. And it would be two more tickets to France. We'd have to pay for Nanny's ticket as well.'

'Well, I think the little chap should come with us,' Binky said, more firmly than he usually spoke to Fig. 'I never had much to do with my parents. My mother died when I was a baby, as you know, and Father was always gadding about. I was left up in Scotland with Nanny and then shipped off to school at the first opportunity. I know how lonely it felt.'

'Very well, if you insist.' Fig sighed. 'I suppose we

won't have to pay a separate ticket for him if he shares our berth on the train, will we? But I really do draw the line at Georgiana. It's money we simply don't have, Binky. Simply don't have. You must be firm but tell her nicely. We'd love to have her with us but it just isn't feasible.'

I stood outside the door, my heart thumping, in an agony of indecision. Of course I was dying to go to the Riviera, but did I really want to go if the Riviera meant close proximity to Binky and Fig? One thing was certain – I didn't want to be banished to Castle Rannoch to spend the winter alone in the wilds of Scotland. Something had to be done, and fast. I took a deep breath and entered the room.

They both looked up – Binky looking guilty, Fig hostile – as I came in.

'Oh, good. Tea's ready,' I said, giving what I hoped was a bright, innocent smile. 'I'm starving after standing in that cold wind all day.'

'You're doing a sterling job, Georgie,' Binky said. 'Absolutely first rate. Isn't she, Fig?'

'She doesn't have much else to do, does she?' Fig said coldly.

'But dash it all, Fig. Not everyone would stand in the freezing cold at that bally station all day. Anyway, we're proud of you, old bean. What's more, the queen is proud of you. She told me so the other day. She said you were setting a splendid example and had more dedication to duty than her eldest son – who I gather is off on a jaunt somewhere.'

'It's good for Georgiana to keep busy,' Fig said, liberally slathering strawberry jam onto a slice of toast. 'Remember what they used to tell us in the nursery – Satan finds work for idle hands to do?'

'I'd love a real job, if there were any to be had,' I said. 'You should see some of the men I serve soup to – they look more distinguished than we do. One today was wearing his war medals. I felt so sorry for him and so angry that I could do nothing to help him.'

'It's hard times for everyone, Georgiana,' Fig said. 'Look how we've had to cut down to the bare bone.' And she popped the last of the jam-laden slice into her mouth.

'Anyway, Georgie,' Binky said, 'Fig's just had a piece of good news. You remember her sister, Ducky, who married old Foggy Farquar? Well, they've taken a place on the Riviera this winter–'

'For Foggy's health, you know,' Fig chimed in.

'–and they've invited us to stay,' Binky concluded.

'Actually, I suspect Mummy twisted their arms to make them invite us,' Fig said candidly. 'Ducky isn't the most hospitable of people usually.'

It obviously ran in the family.

'So the point is, Georgie, that we'll be taking off for the south of France as soon as we can book tickets.' There was a long pause, then he added, 'And of course we'd like you to come with us, wouldn't we, Fig?'

'Golly, I'd love to,' I said quickly.

Fig choked on her last toast crumbs. 'What Binky was trying to say is that we'd like to have invited you to come with us, but we simply can't afford another ticket. I don't know how we're going to come up with the funds for our own fares, but in my current condition – well, the doctor did say that sea air could be a wonderful tonic for me. So I hope you won't be too disappointed.'

'Oh, no, not at all,' I said, trying to sound bright.

'And if we hear of anyone who is motoring out, we'll

see if they can bring you along to join us,' Binky said. Fig coughed on a crumb again.

'But the point is, Georgiana, that we want to shut up this house completely,' she said. 'Even one person can get through an awfully large amount of coal during a winter. So I'm afraid you'll have to go back to Scotland unless you can find someone to stay with in London.'

'That's all right,' I said. 'I have a place where I'm always welcome.'

'You do?' They were both looking at me.

'Certainly. I can go and stay with my grandfather.'

This produced an impressive fit of coughing from Fig. 'Your grandfather?' she demanded when she had recovered. 'You mean the old Cockney man? The one who lives in Essex?' She spoke this last word as if it was equivalent to Outer Mongolia.

'Well, my other grandfather, the old duke, has been dead for more than twenty years,' I said. 'I don't propose to camp out at his gravesite. My living grandfather has often told me that I'm always welcome at his house, even if it is humble compared to this one.'

I saw swift looks pass between Binky and Fig.

'You can't live in Essex. The gutter press would have a field day if they found out,' Fig said.

'And the queen would be furious.' Binky was looking really worried now. 'Look here, old bean. It's just not on. A member of the royal family, even if it is a very junior branch of the family, can't just camp out in a commoner's cottage.'

'Actually, it's a semi-detached,' I said. 'Besides, I have no alternative. I don't want to be all alone in Scotland and you're closing up this house. What do you expect me to do – sleep underneath the Arches and join that soup queue?'

Binky winced. He was a kind-hearted soul, just hopelessly weak where Fig was concerned. I watched him chewing at his lip.

'I tell you what,' Binky said. 'I'll see what I can do. We'll work things out somehow, I promise.'

So did that mean they were going to find the money for my ticket after all? I didn't know whether to be excited or not.

My hopes of traveling to France with them sank a little lower the following morning. I came downstairs to hear Binky on the telephone, apparently to a travel agency.

'It costs how much?' I heard his voice rise an octave. 'For one berth? Yes, I realize that the Blue Train is special, and that it cuts out the inconvenience of changing trains in Paris. And yes, I realize that it's called the Millionaires' Train, but we're not all millionaires, y'know. And no, I would not consider taking another train, impudent pup.' He put back the mouthpiece and came toward me up the stairs. 'I had no idea it cost that much. But in her current condition I can't expect her to change trains and take a taxicab across Paris, can I?' He looked at me with despair on his face. 'Dash it all, Georgie. I wish things weren't so bally complicated. Father and Grandfather never had to count every penny. I feel like such a hopeless failure.'

'It's not your fault,' I said.

Binky nodded. 'But I can't help feeling that if I were a more enterprising sort of chap, I could make a go of things. I could grow some kind of cash crop.'

'Nothing grows in the Scottish Highlands. You know

that. And you've already sold off the best bits of land. Perhaps I'd better marry a millionaire and help us both.'

Binky put his hand on my shoulder. 'You're a good old stick, Georgie, but don't ever marry out of duty. It's an awfully long life to spend with someone you don't particularly like.' He glanced up the stairs. 'I was lucky, of course,' he added loudly. 'I was introduced to Fig and – well . . .'

I hadn't realized that he was a good liar.

Binky sighed. 'I suppose I'd better go and have a talk with the bank manager. Fig's set her heart on going, so I can't disappoint her. I really wish we could include you somehow.'

'Don't worry about it,' I said. 'Something will turn up.'

'I'll do my best for you, Georgie,' he said. 'Ah, well, better face the music, I suppose.'

And he put on his coat and stomped out into the rain. I went off to my duties at Victoria Station. There seemed to be a particularly large and jolly crowd traveling to the Continent that day. I watched them, not daring to hope that I might be following them.

I came home at four o'clock to find Binky and Fig taking tea in the morning room again, Fig with her feet up on a stool and a rug draped over her knees.

'It's all settled, Georgiana,' she said. 'We leave tomorrow. Mummy and Daddy were kind enough to wire us the money for our tickets. They are very worried about my health, you know. I'm normally such a robust person.'

'Leave tomorrow?' I asked, looking from one face to the other. 'But what about closing up the house? What about me?'

'We thought you could do that for us,' Fig said. 'Since you've now had experience with this kind of thing. We can trust you to make sure the servants pack everything up and leave the place properly cleaned, can't we? And then you can drop off the keys at Binky's club.'

'And I'm supposed to go where, exactly?'

Binky smiled. 'I told you I'd work something out for you, didn't I? Well, I had a word with Her Majesty's secretary. A good chap. His younger brother was at school with me – and the upshot is that HM wants you to call on her tomorrow morning.'

The queen? What on earth could she want with me? Certainly not to pay my fare to France. Binky would have been too proud to have mentioned his current impecunious state. And I was also sure she didn't want me to come live at the palace. I began to feel like Alice in Wonderland, falling down a rabbit hole and watching everything become curiouser and curiouser.

# Chapter 4

**January 17, 1933**
*Binky and Fig leave for Riviera. I'm due to go to
Buckingham Palace at ten. I wonder what HM has in
store for me. Wonder what I should wear. Oh, dear.*

I awoke to chaos. I had grown used to Queenie forgetting
to bring my morning tea and biscuits, either oversleep-
ing or being so engrossed in her own breakfast that she
didn't notice the time. I got up, hearing strange sounds
downstairs – raised voices, someone crying and the sound
of heavy objects crashing. If we'd been at the castle in
Scotland I might have assumed that a warring clan had
invaded or at the very least people were getting ready for
a hunt or a shoot, but one hardly hunts in London. I fumbled for my dressing gown, then I opened my door and
looked out.

A footman and maid were struggling downstairs bumping a large trunk between them.

'Careful with that.' Fig's sharp voice rose over the wail-
ing as the trunk was added to the mountain of luggage

piled in the front hall. 'Is the taxi here yet, Binky?' Then she turned to Podge. 'Nanny, for heaven's sake make him stop crying. The noise is giving me a headache. Podge, you're letting the family down by crying like that in front of the servants.'

I spotted my nephew, Podge (whose real name is Hector Hamish Robert George, Viscount Garry), clinging to Nanny and howling. He noticed me at the same moment, broke away from Nanny and started up the stairs toward me. 'Auntie Georgie, I've got to go on a train to another country and they won't let me take my soldiers with me.'

'You're going to a beach,' I said. 'You won't need toys. Will you find some shells for me?'

He looked bewildered. 'Aren't you going to come with us?'

'I'm afraid not, Podge.' I was going to say that his parents weren't prepared to pay for me, but that wasn't quite cricket. 'I'm rather busy at the moment,' I finished.

'I want you to come.' He started to cry again as Binky's voice came from the front door, announcing, 'Car's here.'

'Come along, Podge. Say good-bye to Auntie Georgie,' Fig said impatiently.

I hugged him. He clung to me.

'You see,' Fig said to Binky, who was holding the door open for the constant stream of servants and luggage, 'I told you we should have sent him home to Scotland. It's going to be unsettling for him. He's probably going to cry all night on the train and upset everyone.'

'Of course he's not. He's going to be a big boy, aren't you, Podge?'

Podge nodded tearfully and took Nanny's hand as she led him out. I watched with a lump in my throat.

'And Georgiana, we can count on you to make sure the house is properly closed up, can't we?' Fig turned to ask as she swept to the front door.

'Don't worry,' I said.

I noticed she didn't come up to hug me. Binky tried to negotiate the servants and baggage. ''Bye, old thing,' he called to me. 'So sorry you can't come with us. I hope it all works out with the queen this morning.'

And then they were gone.

'Did you want your cup of tea in bed, miss, or are you already up?' Queenie appeared, carrying the tea tray.

'You're about an hour too late and, as you can see, I'm already up,' I said. 'Tell Cook that I'll have a proper breakfast this morning.'

At least I'd make the most of my last days here by helping to use up their food. Our cook, Mrs McPherson, has always had a soft spot for me and she sent up a perfect breakfast: bacon, kidneys, tomatoes, mushrooms, fried bread and two eggs.

I finished the plate with relish then went up to select a suitable outfit for my upcoming visit to the palace. Luckily Queenie had not tried to clean my one good tweed suit yet!

I always approach Buckingham Palace with great trepidation. Who doesn't? I know they are relatives, but most relatives don't live in great gray stone palaces, surrounded by iron railings and guards in red coats. And most relatives are not queen-empresses, sovereigns over millions and millions of people across the globe. I am one of those people whose limbs won't obey them when they get nervous. I do things like trip over carpets and knock vases off tables at the best of times, so you can imagine what it's like in a palace. I'm only glad I wasn't born when my great-grandmother was still alive. I would have probably knocked her down the grand staircase and she certainly wouldn't have been amused.

Still, I tried to look jaunty and confident as I walked down Constitution Hill toward the front gate of the palace. Most people arrive at the palace in a great black motorcar, so the guards at the iron gates looked surprised and suspicious when I showed up on foot.

'Can I help you, miss?' one of them asked, barring my way, not even standing to attention or saluting. This is what happens when one doesn't own a decent fur coat.

'I'm not a miss; I'm Lady Georgiana, His Majesty's cousin, and Her Majesty is expecting me,' I said.

The guard turned as red as his jacket. 'Begging your pardon, my lady. I didn't expect someone like you to be arriving on foot.' They must have been the Welsh Guards, as he had a strong lilting accent.

'Well, I only live around the corner and the walk does me good,' I said. 'In fact, Their Majesties are very keen on walking. The king takes his constitutional around the grounds every day, rain or shine, I believe.'

'He does indeed, my lady.' The guard opened a small pedestrian gate in the bigger one and helped me to step through – which was lucky as I hadn't noticed the bar across the bottom and almost stumbled. 'Williams will escort you, my lady.' He nodded to the guard standing with him. Williams stood to attention and then marched beside me across the courtyard. I found this screamingly funny, me taking little steps in my tight skirt and Williams trying to march very slowly. We reached the entrance, and Williams saluted and marched back to his post. I went up the steps.

Inside I was greeted, welcomed and ushered not up the great stair, but up a side staircase to Her Majesty's personal sitting room in the private wing. Not nearly as intimidating as one of the official reception rooms full of priceless stuff to knock over.

'Lady Georgiana, ma'am,' the lackey said as he opened her sitting-room door.

I took a deep breath, trying to look confident while muttering to myself, 'Do not trip. Do not bump into anything.'

At the last second I saw that the lackey had stuck out his foot a little as he bowed. I managed to jump over it, with a little Highland fling type of move that made Her Majesty raise an eyebrow. But then she smiled and held out her hand to me. 'Georgiana, my dear. Come and sit down. It's bitterly cold out there, isn't it? The king has been pacing up and down like a caged bear because his doctor won't let him go out in this sort of weather with his delicate chest.'

'It is very bleak,' I agreed, 'especially at Victoria Station. The wind whips right through.'

'You've done most admirably, my dear. Setting a splendid example. That was a lovely picture of you in the *Daily Express*. I hope it inspired other young women to follow in your footsteps.'

'I'm afraid my stint may be coming to an end,' I said.

'Of course. I understand your brother wants to shut up the London house and is concerned about you.'

'Yes, ma'am. I don't know anybody else in London, and I don't have the funds to stay at a club.'

'Frightful waste of money – clubs,' the queen said.

'However, my secretary and I put our thinking caps on this morning and we have come up with what seems like a perfect solution.'

'Really, ma'am?' I think my voice trembled a little.

'The king's aunt Princess Louise, who is your great-aunt, is very much a recluse these days. She's in her late eighties, of course, and has become rather frail. I'm sure it's lonely for her, living alone in that great house. So I thought you could bring some youth and gaiety into her life.'

I gulped. All right. My worst nightmare was about to come true. The queen had made murmurings about sending me to be lady-in-waiting for an aged aunt before, and now it was actually going to happen. Binky and Fig would be sipping cool drinks and eating foie gras and I'd be walking a Pekinese and holding knitting wool. I opened my mouth but no words would come out.

'I gather you weren't keen on going back to Scotland with your brother at this time of year. I don't say I blame you. Terribly bleak and cut off in the winter.'

'Oh, no, ma'am,' I said, as her words sunk in. 'My brother is not going home to Scotland. He and my sister-in-law are going to the Riviera.'

'The Riviera? I had no idea.'

'For my sister-in-law's health. She's feeling rather frail at the moment.'

'I didn't think that "frail" would ever be a word to describe your sister-in-law,' the queen said, looking up with a half smile on her lips as a tray of coffee was wheeled into the room. 'I managed to have six children without making a fuss. One just got on with it.' The maid poured coffee and hot milk into a cup and put it down beside Her Majesty, then did the same for me. The queen then motioned her away and we were left alone. 'Did you not want to go to the Riviera with them, then? I thought it was the aim of all young people these days.'

'I wanted to go,' I said. 'It's just that—' I hesitated. It was bad form to discuss money problems. 'Well, my brother has been saddled with horrendous death duties on the estate, so . . .' I left the rest of the sentence unsaid.

'Such a silly, selfish thing to do,' the queen said, stirring her coffee fiercely. 'Your father, I mean. We were always raised to face the music, not take the easy way out. Goodness knows the king and I have been through our share of trials and tribulations.' She took a dainty sip of coffee then looked me directly in the eye. 'So you want to go to the south of France, but they haven't invited you, is that it?'

'I was told that I was welcome at the villa where they'll be staying.' I hesitated to say to Her Majesty that I wasn't sure whether that was true or not. 'They didn't feel that they could pay my travel expenses to go with them.'

The queen took a long drink of coffee, put her cup down then sat staring out the window at the clouds racing across the sky. 'This puts a different complexion on things. If I arranged for you to go to the Riviera with your family,' she said carefully, 'I wonder if you could do something for me.'

'Of course, ma'am,' I said cautiously.

'I'd like to entrust you with a rather delicate and difficult task.'

She had entrusted me with tasks before. They had usually proved difficult, dangerous or both – from entertaining foreign princesses to spying on her eldest son, the Prince of Wales. I remembered that he was currently on

the Riviera himself and wondered if I was going to be
thrust into the role of spy again.

'I am speaking to you in the uttermost confidence,
Georgiana. Not a word of this must leave this room. Do I
have your word on this?'

I nodded. 'Of course, ma'am.'

'I have great faith in you, Georgiana. You have han-
dled difficult situations before. You have proved yourself
most astute.' She moved closer to me, leaning forward
as if to whisper, although we were the only two people
in the room. 'You know how much I prize my antiques,
Georgiana.'

'Oh, yes, ma'am. I do know that.'

'They give me great solace. I am particularly fond of
my collection of snuffboxes. Such delicate little things,
aren't they? Such exquisite workmanship.'

Again I nodded.

'A valuable snuffbox is missing from my collection,
Georgiana.'

'Stolen, you mean?'

'I'm rather afraid so.'

'Isn't that a matter for the police?'

She shook her head firmly. 'I can't mention this to the
police. It's too embarrassing. You see, the snuffboxes
were on display in one of the niches in the Music Room.
Two weeks ago we held a large reception there for the
New Year Honors. Shortly afterward, I noticed one of the
boxes was missing. So the choice of culprit is either one of
the servants or one of the guests at our reception. I have
conducted a secret investigation of the servants, but those
who were in attendance that night have all been with us
for some time and have impeccable backgrounds. Which

leaves only one conclusion – a person who attended that elite gathering made off with one of my snuffboxes. It wouldn't be too hard to do. It's not like a formal dinner where everyone is seated. The crowd mills around. And especially as His Majesty and I moved through the crowd, all eyes would have been on us.'

'How terrible, ma'am. To think that one of us is a common thief.'

'I'm afraid that weakness shows up in all classes, Georgiana. Your own forebears did not always lead exemplary lives, did they? They kept mistresses and cheated at cards. But on this particular occasion the audience was not composed entirely of the aristocracy. There were entertainers and captains of industry among them. The recipients of those New Year Honors.'

I nodded. 'Do you have your suspicions?'

'It had to have been a real connoisseur who took the box. There were much flashier ones in the collection – more ornate but not nearly as valuable. The person who took this recognized the box for what it was and took it to complete his own collection, I am sure.'

'So there's no likelihood of the box being resold, then.'

'Unless it was stolen on behalf of someone else who had offered a large sum of money for it – and even then it would never appear on the open market, so I'd have no hope of retrieving it.'

'You think it has gone to the Riviera, ma'am?'

She sighed. 'It could be sitting on any mantelpiece in Birmingham, for all I know, but the only person on that guest list who truly fits the bill is Sir Toby Groper and he remarked to me that he was off back to his villa in Nice immediately after the reception.'

'Sir Toby Groper – he owns Britannia Motors, doesn't he?'

She nodded. 'One of the richest men in the country. He comes from money, of course. The Gropers acquired their wealth and status with their armament factories, and they earned themselves a peerage for their role in the Boer War. Toby was a young man, scarcely out of Oxford, when he invented a revolutionary motorcar engine. His Fearless Flyers have been wining races and rallies all over the world. So a baronet, and a rich one, but not really one of us.'

'Do you think he is the one who took your snuffbox because he's not one of us?'

She smiled. 'No, my dear. I think he took it because he has become a passionate, should one say obsessive, collector of antiques and objets d'art.'

'Why do you think he wanted that particular snuffbox? Was it because it was small enough to take?'

'Ah, you see, snuffboxes came up during a previous conversation a year or so ago, in his private box at the Brooklands Racetrack. He probably thinks I have forgotten, but I seldom forget anything. He told me then that he had been searching in vain for a snuffbox owned by Louis XVI. So much was looted from the palaces, you see, during the Revolution.'

'And the box that was taken?'

'Was given by Marie Antoinette as a present to her husband. It's a delightful little thing – enameled gold, with pictures of shepherds and shepherdesses all over it. But inside the lid is a miniature of Marie Antoinette, in a frame of perfect diamonds.'

'It sounds charming.'

'It is. I was most fond of it.' A wistful look came over her face. 'Of course I may be quite wrong. I may be maligning the poor man. But I pride myself on being an excellent judge of character and I formed the opinion that Sir Toby is the kind of man who will do what it takes to achieve any objective.'

'So what exactly do you want me to do, ma'am?'

The queen looked surprised. 'Go to his villa and retrieve the snuffbox for me.'

# Chapter 5

I think my jaw might have dropped open a little, which is not permissible for ladies of my standing. I don't think I could be blamed for being somewhat surprised, however.

'You want me to steal it?'

'Retrieve it, Georgiana. Sir Toby is the one who has stolen it.'

'And if I'm caught?'

'You will tell Sir Toby that the queen wanted her property back without causing any kind of public scandal. I don't think he'd want to make a fuss. And if he did – well, I have good documentation in my possession that the snuffbox was in the Buckingham Palace collection until recently. He'd look an awful fool, and I don't think he's the kind of man who would like to be ridiculed.'

My heart was racing. 'But I don't know Sir Toby. How am I supposed to gain access to his villa?'

You can tell how rattled I was. I had forgotten to add 'ma'am.'

'Everyone knows everyone else on the Riviera, so I'm told. You said your family is going there. Well, Sir Toby has a villa in Nice, so I'm sure you'll all attend the same parties. You're a pretty young girl and you have royal connections. You'll be invited everywhere.'

I didn't say that I thought it unlikely anyone would invite Fig and her unsociable sister, Ducky, unless they were really desperate. I felt a great weight of doom descending on me. For a moment I thought that I'd rather take up the offer of becoming Princess Louise's companion, but then my sense of adventure took over. It was exciting, after all. Better than serving soup in dreary London. Much better than sitting alone at Castle Rannoch.

I'd go to the Riviera. I'd do my best to carry out the queen's request, and if I didn't succeed, then that was too bad. At least I could ascertain whether Sir Toby had the snuffbox or not.

I could sense the queen looking at me. 'So can I count on you, Georgiana?'

'I'll do my best, ma'am.'

She smiled then. 'Splendid. You are a good girl, Georgiana. A credit to the family. I can't understand why you're not married yet. I had rather hoped that you'd find yourself a husband at Princess Maria Theresa's wedding. So many eligible young princes there.' When I said nothing she added, 'We are expected to do our duty, Georgiana. You need a place of your own in society. It's not good to be dependent on others.'

'I would like to marry, ma'am. It's just that nobody suitable has asked me.'

She patted my knee, which was an uncharacteristically familiar gesture for her. 'I'm sure it will all work out in the end. And speaking of marriage, there's one other small task you can carry out for me while you're on the Riviera. My son David is shirking his duties again and is cruising the Med on a friend's yacht. I understand that dreadful American woman was seen leaving London the other day on the boat train.'

'Mrs Simpson, you mean?'

'Mrs Simpson indeed. And one gathers that her husband was with her. She drags him around for respectability's sake. The woman has no shame.'

'I suppose we should be glad that she stays married to him. At least she can't think of marrying the Prince of Wales if she already has a husband.'

'Marrying my son? You surely don't think that David is considering – preposterous. Quite out of the question. The nation would never stand for a divorced woman as our future queen! The church would not condone it. His family would certainly never stand for it.' She paused, as if considering. 'So, Georgiana, there may be another little thing I'd like you to do for me while you're there. . . .'

'You'd like me to keep an eye on Mrs Simpson, would you, ma'am?'

She hesitated, then said firmly, 'Yes, that's it. Keep an eye on Mrs Simpson. The king has always behaved impeccably, Georgiana. We can't have the heir to the throne behaving like a common playboy and bringing disgrace to the royal family. So if you see him appearing in public with this woman, I'd like to know about it. You'll write to me immediately to let me know whether she is actually staying on the yacht with him.'

'I will, ma'am.'

She stood up. I followed suit, as one doesn't sit when royalty stands. 'Well, that's all settled then. This is most fortuitous, isn't it? You go to the Riviera with the family and I achieve my objectives as well. Very satisfactory all around. I'll instruct my secretary to make your travel arrangements.'

I was escorted from the room. As I walked through the palace I mulled over the last part of our interview. I could have sworn that she wanted to ask me to do something quite different from spying on Mrs Simpson. She had hesitated and changed her mind at the last moment. I wondered if it was another piece of cat burglary that she had wanted me to carry out. I heaved a sigh of relief. Spying on Mrs Simpson was something I knew I could do.

I left the palace feeling both excited and scared. But it was mostly excited. I was going to the Riviera after all. After that my first thought was that of every woman, when faced with a crisis – I had nothing suitable to wear on the French Riviera, especially if I was to be hobnobbing with one of the richest men in England. As soon as I got home, I opened my wardrobe door and stared in dismay at the few cotton dresses and skirts I owned. Nothing that could vaguely be called 'smart,' and no way of obtaining anything better. Belinda had already departed, taking her gorgeous gowns with her. She'd be needing them herself and I didn't think she'd be willing to lend me a few. I had nobody else I could beg, borrow or steal from. I pictured myself walking down the Promenade des Anglais in my crumpled cotton prints while silk- and linen-clad ladies stared at me with distaste. They'd think I was somebody's companion or nursemaid!

For a moment, as I went up the steps into Rannoch House, I came to the conclusion that I shouldn't go after all, then I realized that this was being ridiculous. To turn down a chance to be on the Riviera just because I didn't have smart clothes – what was I thinking? Even if Queenie was as hopeless at laundry and ironing as she was at everything else, the family we'd be staying with would have sensible and efficient French maids who would at least make me look respectable, if not fashionable.

This reminded me of the matter of Queenie. The queen hadn't said anything about paying my maid's fare, and I was pretty sure that Fig wouldn't want her at the villa, since she'd already told me to dismiss her. Poor old Queenie. The amount I was paying her wouldn't keep body and soul together if she wasn't being fed and clothed. Perhaps I should find her a temporary situation while I was away. I paused, considering this, then shook my head. I couldn't in all honesty give her a letter of recommendation. It wouldn't be fair to saddle an innocent party with her. She was, I had to confess, completely and absolutely useless.

I went into my bedroom and closed the door firmly behind me. I needed time to think this through carefully.

'Oh, botheration,' I muttered.

'Whatcher, miss,' Queenie interrupted me. 'I had a good idea about that skirt of yours what I messed up. We could get one of them silk flowers, or a bunch of them pretend grapes, and sew them over the bald spot.'

In spite of everything I had to laugh. 'Queenie, one cannot go to dinner with a bunch of grapes hanging from one's stomach. Besides, I won't be needing velvet for a while, so maybe I can send it back to Scotland with the servants. Our gamekeeper's wife is a good seamstress. I'm sure she'll be able to rescue it.'

'So where exactly are we going when they shut up the house here?' (Of course, there were no aitches in her version of the sentence.)

I took a deep breath. 'Actually, Queenie, I'm going to France with them.'

Her face lit up. 'We're going abroad again? To foreign parts? Wait till I tell my old mum, who told me I'd never amount to nothing. And look at me now, hobnobbing all over the Continent. I got quite a taste for that foreign food after I got used to it.'

Oh, golly. How was I going to put this tactfully? I had to tell her.

'You see, the thing is, Queenie–'

'Yes, my lady? See, I remembered this time – I'm improving, aren't I?' She was staring at me expectantly.

'I'll want all my summer clothes washed and pressed,' I ended lamely. 'You can do that without scorching anything, can't you?'

'I'll give it a ruddy good try, my lady,' she said.

# Chapter 6

**January 17, 1933**
*I can hardly believe it. I am going to the Riviera. Still have a few things to take care of first. Find spectacular wardrobe somehow. Sort things out for Queenie.*

I was in an agony of indecision about what to do with Queenie. I had put aside enough money to pay her for a year, but it was a pitifully small amount. Would her parents let her live with them at home? Could she find another job while I was gone? I knew I was being ridiculously soft-hearted. Anyone else would have given her the sack after a day. I had tolerated and forgiven a string of ruined clothes and other gaffes and she really hadn't shown many signs of improvement. Maybe this would be a good time to let her go and hope that she landed another job, somehow, somewhere. Since she had accidentally set her former employer's skirt on fire, I didn't think that was too likely.

Then I thought of her face when I'd announced the trip to the Continent. Most girls of her station would be terrified at the thought of going abroad. But she was excited. I sighed. What was I going to do with her? I really couldn't take her with me, but I couldn't just turn her out to fend for herself. I decided the only thing to do was to go and visit Granddad. He was wise. Besides, his neighbor Mrs Huggins would be there, and she was Queenie's great-aunt. Together they would come up with a solution for me.

The thought of visiting Granddad cheered me up instantly. He was the one person who was not fettered by all the silly rules of my class, who showed that he really cared about me. I cared about him too, but our lives were so different that it was hard for us to spend time together. I didn't belong in an Essex suburb and he didn't belong at Rannoch House. I put on my overcoat and scarf again and headed for the Underground station.

Granddad's neat little semi-detached house usually looked quite cheerful, with its gnomes in the tiny front garden. But at this time of year nothing was growing in those tiny flower beds and one of the gnomes had fallen on his face. I righted him before I knocked on the front door.

It was opened by Mrs Huggins (or should I say Mrs 'uggins, because that is what she calls herself), Granddad's next-door neighbor. She was wearing a flowered pinny over a hand-knitted jumper of orange and purple stripes. I realized that Queenie's taste in clothes obviously ran in the family.

'Well, strike me down,' she said. 'If it ain't 'er ladyship. Come on in, ducks. This won't 'alf perk up the old bloke.'

'Is he ill, then?'

She nodded as she ushered me into the narrow hallway.

'It's 'is chest again.' She leaned close to whisper the words. 'You know what it's like in the winter. He's just had a nasty cold and it don't seem to go away, so he's getting my good stew and dumplings 'til he's on the mend.'

'Who is it, Hettie?' came Granddad's voice, followed by a bout of coughing.

'It's me, Granddad.' I went through to the tiny living room. My grandfather was sitting in an armchair by the fire, a rug over his knees. His face lit up when he saw me.

'Blimey, you're a sight for sore eyes, love. Come and give your old granddad a kiss.'

I kissed the top of his bald head and pulled up a chair beside him.

'Make us a nice cup of tea, Hettie,' Granddad said. He took my hand and held it tightly. 'So how have you been, my love? Not seen you since Christmas. Been keeping all right?'

'Oh, I'm just fine, Granddad. More to the point, how are you?'

'Oh, not too bad. You know every time I get a ruddy cold it goes straight to my blooming chest. But I'm getting over it. Hettie's taking good care of me.'

'I'm going to go to the south of France,' I said. 'I wish I could take you with me. It would do you good to be in a warm climate.'

'South of France?' He gave a throaty chuckle. 'Not for me, thanks, love. They eat frogs' legs and all kinds of funny stuff, don't they? No, I never did take to France. Not after my boy Jimmy didn't come back from the Great War. So you go and have a good time, but I'm happier where I am.'

I looked at him and squeezed his hand. 'Oh, Granddad,

why do things have to be so difficult? If only I had some money I could do more for you.'

'Don't you worry about it, ducks. I've got me a nice snug little house and a garden and Hettie to take care of me. I'm happy as a sandboy.'

'I'm going to write to Mummy,' I said. 'She should be doing more for you.'

'I wouldn't take her money,' Granddad said with a brisk shake of the head. 'Not German money. Not from him. Wouldn't touch it.'

'She does have money of her own, I'm sure.'

'I told you, I'm quite happy here. So you go off to the south of France and don't give it another thought. How did you manage to wangle that, by the way? Last time I saw you, you said you were stuck for the winter with that brother of yours and his nasty wife.'

'Yes, well, they've gone to stay with Fig's sister on the Riviera, and I'm to follow them in a few days.'

'Oh, they've turned generous suddenly, have they?'

I shook my head. 'Not on your Nellie, as you would say. Actually, they don't know I'm coming. I went to see the queen today . . .' I broke off as Mrs Huggins returned, carrying a tea tray.

'Hear that, Hettie?' Granddad looked up at her. 'She went to see the queen. She hobnobs with the queen just like you and me pop down the Queen's Head Pub.'

'Fancy,' Mrs Huggins said. 'Here's your tea, then, your ladyship. Let it stew first.'

'Thank you,' I said. 'You're very good to my grandfather.'

'Ah, well, he's a lovely gentleman. He may not be a toff in your eyes, but he behaves as good as any toff.'

Granddad chuckled as she left.

'She's trying to get me to the altar, that's what,' he muttered to me. 'But I sort of like things the way they are – her in her house and me in mine. Now, what were you saying about the queen?'

'She's asked me to do a small task for her on the Riviera, so I'm going out to join the family.'

'So young Queenie will be going abroad again, then.' Mrs Huggins reappeared.

I opened my mouth but before I could reply she went on, 'Won't that make them proud of her? You should see her mum these days. She don't half give herself airs. Goes around talking about "my daughter what's employed by royalty." And lucky she got that job when she did because things ain't gone well with that family. What with her dad out of work now and her married sister's moved back to the house with her three little ones, they're in a right state there. I think it's only the thought of Queenie earning her way as a lady's maid that keeps them all going.'

'I'm not exactly sure I can take her with me,' I said slowly. 'If I didn't, then maybe she could stay with you until I came back?'

Mrs Huggins looked shocked. 'Not take her with you? Why? Ain't she turning out satisfactory after all?'

'Oh, no, nothing like that,' I lied with a bright smile.

Mrs Huggins pursed her lips. 'It wouldn't be proper for a lady like you to go traveling without a maid, would it?'

'No, I suppose it wouldn't,' I had to agree.

'Well, then,' Mrs Huggins said as if this settled everything. 'Come on, drink up that tea before it gets cold.'

The Queenie question was settled for me when the tickets were delivered to my door the next day. *Travel arrangements for Lady Georgiana Rannoch and maid* was written on the envelope. I tried not to think of the havoc she might wreak at a French villa.

The next days were chaotic as I sent off the servants and closed up the house. But then the miracle happened and I became one of those people I had so admired, following a porter to my seat on the boat train, bound for the Continent. I wished I had some way of contacting Darcy to let him know I was going abroad. As it was he might arrive at Rannoch House to find it closed up and me nowhere to be found. Really he was the most annoying man – never in one place for more than two seconds and of no fixed address. Why couldn't he have a club, like Binky, so at least I could leave messages for him? Then I realized he probably liked it that way. He didn't want to be tied down. I should accept that and try not to include him in my plans for the future. But it wasn't that easy to put him out of my mind.

I thought about him as the train steamed through grimy London backstreets. Darcy was an opportunist, like Belinda. He was good at crashing parties and securing invitations. Maybe he was already on the Riviera at this moment. My heart beat a little faster.

By the time we arrived at Dover, Queenie had obviously been enjoying herself in the third-class compartment with the other servants.

'I told them other maids that her ladyship and me goes abroad all the time and what's more we stays in blooming great royal castles. You should have seen their faces. Green with envy they was.'

I thought they were probably just sickened either by the swaying of the train or by Queenie's inappropriate boasting. 'Queenie, a real lady never boasts,' I said. 'If you want to become a lady's maid, you must learn to act with decorum.'

'Who's he when he's at home?' she asked. Actually, it was closer to "Oo's 'ee when 'ee's at 'ome?'

'Decorum. It means behave like a lady.'

'Bob's yer uncle, miss. I won't do it no more. I promise I'll act with – decoration.'

'Queenie. It might be helpful if you read some books and improved your speech. Real ladies' maids are very refined. As refined as their mistresses.'

'I can't help it if I was born dead common, miss,' she replied.

I sighed. 'Go and make sure our luggage gets on the boat and then keep an eye on it until it's safely carried ashore in France.'

We went on board. The weather had worsened and the crossing was miserable. The ship bucked and rolled and half the passengers lay green and groaning with rugs over their knees or stood vomiting over the railing. One of the few useful things I had learned from my mother at an early age was how to survive a rough sea crossing. One goes straight to the bar, when one comes on board, and orders a brandy ginger ale and a good meal. I did this. I noticed that the ship's restaurant was deserted and I was one of the few people daring to eat. The only other occupants were an elderly parson and wife and two men sitting close together at the bar. I couldn't help noticing that one of the men looked very French and was devastatingly handsome. Also that he was drinking champagne. My spirits lifted. I was on my way to the Riviera, where there would be oodles of attractive Frenchmen. I would learn to flirt like Belinda and I was going to have a good time.

As I passed the Frenchman to reach my table I heard his companion say, 'So is it *tournesols*?'

My French is pretty good but I didn't understand this last word.

Then my handsome Frenchman replied, 'No, it is only a chair. Much simpler.'

At this the first man nodded and left the bar. As the French coast came into sight the Frenchman got down from his bar stool. As he came toward me I saw a flash of recognition cross his face, followed in succession by surprise and – was it anger?

'*Que fais tu ici?*' he began, then he checked himself, frowned and nodded politely to me as he went past.

How strange. He had addressed me not only as if he knew me, but as if he knew me well. He had called me *tu*, which was the very familiar form of address. But I was sure I'd never seen him before in my life. I paid my bill and went to find Queenie and my luggage. Oh, well, one was supposed to have adventures when one went abroad and they were starting even before I reached France.

I was met by an extremely wet and windblown Queenie. 'I ain't half glad to see France, miss,' she gasped. 'All those people hanging over the side and being sick fair turned my stomach.'

'Queenie, you look like a drowned rat.'

'Well, you said to keep an eye on your luggage so I stayed with it,' she said.

I looked at her fondly. She may have been clueless in the extreme, but she certainly was loyal. She'd stayed up on deck with my luggage, even though nothing could have happened to it during the crossing.

'Well done, Queenie,' I said. 'We'll soon have you on the Blue Train, where you can dry off and have a cup of hot tea.'

We followed our porter ashore and were whisked through customs to a special platform where the Train Bleu was waiting. Even on this dark and gloomy day those Pullman coaches seemed to glow with opulence. The porter found my compartment, which had a small berth connecting for Queenie. Really, it was most civilized.

Queenie came through to join me, looking slightly less damp and wild. 'I was soaked right down to me knickers, miss. I've put them to dry on the radiator.'

It was no use admonishing her.

'And you know what I've been thinking, miss?' she went on, taking a place opposite me without being asked. 'I know I speak real common, so I've decided to better myself. When I get home I'm going to save up and take them "hellocution" lessons. People are going to think I'm a proper toff, just like you.'

Oh, golly, I'd got Eliza Doolittle on my hands now. 'Good idea, Queenie,' I said.

At that moment there was a toot and a slamming of doors, and we glided out of the station. A big grin spread across my face. I was really on my way to the south of France and adventure. About two small annoying facts I chose not to think: one, that I was to share a villa with Fig and her sister, and the other, that I was supposed to commit a robbery for the queen.

# Chapter 7

**January 21, 1933**
**On the Blue Train. Heading for the Riviera. Hooray!**

The gray, rain-splashed French countryside flashed past us, with rows of leafless poplars between brown fields of stubble. Darkness was falling as we reached the outskirts of Paris. Instead of going into the Gare du Nord, as other trains from the Channel did, this train skirted the perimeter of the city, moving through dingy suburbs and going over lots of points until at last it stopped at the Gare de Lyon on the southern side of the city. The attendant knocked on my door. 'Does your ladyship require anything while we are in the station?' he asked in French, assuming, I suppose, that anyone who traveled on this train spoke the language. 'Should I arrange for a dinner box for your maid? There is only the first-class dining car for people like yourself.'

'Thank you, that would be most kind,' I replied in the same language.

'And dinner will be served as soon as we leave the city,' he went on. 'The dining car is to your left.'

A box was delivered for Queenie, who wasted no time in tucking into it. 'Funny bread,' she said, 'and this ham tastes of garlic, but it ain't bad. My friend Nellie 'uxtable, what works down the Three Bells, said we'd have to eat frog legs and little birds. I told her not to be so ruddy daft. Just 'cos she went on the day trip to Boulogne once, she thinks she knows about France.'

'It's not polite to talk with your mouth full,' I pointed out as crumbs spattered over the seat of my compartment, 'and I think you should take your meal in your space. I am going to get ready for dinner.'

I wasn't sure whether one dressed for dinner on a train. We certainly hadn't on trains I'd traveled on before, but then they hadn't been this train. I was wearing a decent jersey dress, but I found my pearls and put on a little lipstick before I ventured to the dining car. In truth I felt a little shy about going alone to dinner. I know I'd been brought up to mix with the cream of society in theory, but in practice the cream of society rarely came to Castle Rannoch and I still felt schoolgirlish and awkward among the real social butterflies.

'*Bon appétit*, milady,' the attendant said as he held the door open for me. I passed through the connecting area and opened the door to the dining car. I looked down the rows of white-clothed tables, their silver and china gleaming in the glow of little lamps. From here I couldn't see a table that wasn't occupied and wondered what the protocol was about joining other diners and whether I could ever pluck up courage to do that.

Of course the first person I noticed was the handsome Frenchman, sitting alone with another bottle of champagne beside him. He looked up from his soup and caught my gaze. He didn't smile or nod as would have been usual. Instead he frowned at me.

'You are English?' he asked in French.

I replied that I was.

'Curious,' he replied. He was about to say something else when a voice from farther down the car called to me, 'I say. Aren't you Georgiana Rannoch?'

It was a smartly dressed English lady, probably in her late forties. She was sitting with an exquisite and obviously French woman, dressed in what looked like a man's black suit topped with a stunning necklace. I agreed that I was.

'Would you like to join us?' the first woman said. 'It's rather full at the moment but we have room, don't we, Coco?'

The Frenchwoman nodded and smiled. *'Bien sûr,'* she said, waving a cigarette holder in my direction.

The Englishwoman stuck out a hand. 'You look the spitting image of your father. I used to know him well. I'm known as Vera, by the way. Vera Bate Lombardi, and I believe we're related, at least through marriage.'

I sat down on the chair she had pulled out for me. She waved imperiously and a waiter appeared. 'My lady will be joining us, so set another place and you'd better bring us another bottle of Veuve Clicquot.'

I wasn't sure I wanted to dine with a rather bossy Englishwoman who claimed to be related to me, but it was better than standing like a wallflower.

'I actually stayed at Castle Rannoch when you were little,' she continued, 'although I don't suppose you remember me. We went out riding together once. You were a splendid little horsewoman.'

'Thank you,' I said. 'I don't often get a chance to ride anymore and I miss it.'

'So do I,' she said. 'I'm in Paris most of the year now, traipsing around behind Coco, and one can hardly get a decent gallop in the Bois de Boulogne.'

'You do not traipse behind me,' the woman she had addressed as Coco said in English. 'It makes you sound like a dog on a lead. Since you take bigger strides than I, I am usually running to keep up with you. But you must introduce us, Vera. This very English young lady will not speak to me unless properly introduced.'

I laughed, but Vera said, 'Sorry. Frightfully bad of me. Coco, this is Bertie's daughter, Georgiana Rannoch. And this is my dear friend and business partner, Coco Chanel.'

My eyes opened wider at the mention of that name. 'Chanel? The couturière?'

'The same.' She shrugged in that delightfully Gallic way. 'I do not think you wear my clothes.'

'Can't afford it,' I said. 'I would if I could.'

'So you go to stay on the Riviera?' Chanel said, eyeing me critically, almost the way the handsome Frenchman had done.

'I think that's where this train is headed,' I said and she laughed, a melodious and wonderfully sexy laugh.

'Delightful,' she said. 'I will make you model for me. I am going to unveil my new collection at a special showing for the rich English on the Riviera and you will be my perfect model.'

'Oh, not me,' I said, my face turning bright red. 'I'm frightfully clumsy, you know. I'd trip over my own feet and rip your gowns. I tried modeling once and it was a disaster. I put both legs into one half of a pair of culottes.'

This time both Vera and Chanel laughed.

'I am sure you would be splendid,' Coco said. 'Wouldn't she, Vera? Exactly the look we want to achieve – the English rose, but with naughty overtones.'

'I'm afraid I don't have many naughty overtones,' I said.

'You will, once you are mixing with that crowd on the Riviera,' Vera said. 'They are all frightfully naughty.'

'The English?'

'Oh, yes. Worst of the lot. They're so repressed at home, after all those years in boarding school, that they become positively wanton the moment they hit Calais.' She leaned closer to me. 'Your dear departed papa was no saint, I can tell you. Tell her what this collection is all about, Coco.'

'It is the mixing of masculine and feminine,' Coco said, 'of country and town, of day and night. I have borrowed some fine English tweed jackets from my friend the Duke of Westminster.'

'And some stunning pieces of jewelry from my aunt,' Vera added. 'She mentioned that I might bump into you, by the way, when I saw her yesterday.'

'Your aunt?' I was confused, not being quite sure which branch of my family she belonged to.

'Queen Mary,' Coco explained.

'Queen Mary is your aunt?'

Vera made a face. 'Not officially, of course. My mother was a Baring, of the banking firm, but I think everyone agrees that my real father was the Duke of Cambridge. Prince of Teck.'

'Oh, I see. The queen's brother.'

'She was married to someone else, of course, but I must say he treated me like a daughter and the family has always acknowledged me.'

While I was digesting this the champagne was poured. I took a sip and remembered another item in the conversation. 'You say the queen has lent you some pieces of her jewelry for your fashion show.'

Vera put her fingers to her lips. 'I'd rather that news wasn't broadcast too loudly. I promised her I'd take frightfully good care of them. You know what she's like about her things.'

'I do. That's why I'm surprised she lent you jewelry.'

'Ah, I usually get what I want out of people,' she said. 'Don't worry, we're going to watch it like hawks. Besides, it's well insured.'

'And these jewels will be worn with the gentlemen's tweed jackets?' I asked cautiously.

They both laughed. 'Of course. Isn't it divine?' Coco said. 'You know, I have always designed a masculine look for women. Like the suit I now wear. It is so freeing and very sexy too. This is the ultimate mixing of male and female. And you shall model it for me.'

'I really don't think you'd want me,' I said. 'I'd be a walking disaster. When I was presented at court I caught my heel in the train of my dress and when I stood up from my curtsy I went flying forward into Their Majesties. In the old days I'd have been hauled off to the Tower.'

They laughed again. The waiter appeared and handed me a menu. I glanced down it, reading one delicious item after another – coquilles St. Jacques, lobster bisque, duck breast, filet steak with truffles. . . . After Fig's austerity it was like stepping into a dream.

'So where shall you be staying?' Vera asked when I had ordered.

'I'm staying with people called Farquar.'

'Foggy Farquar?' She gave Coco a horrified look. 'You can't do that. You'll die of boredom.'

'My brother and sister-in-law are already staying with them. My sister-in-law is Ducky Farquar's sister.'

'God forbid. I hope it doesn't run in the family.'

'I'm sure it does,' I said gloomily, 'whatever it is.'

'I always liked your brother,' Vera said. 'Easy-going sort of chap. Good-natured.'

'And my sister-in-law is quite the opposite,' I said.

'When you get too bored, you must come and visit us,' Coco said. 'We stay at delightful Villa Marguerite.'

I duly noted the name.

'Coco has a perfectly gorgeous villa of her own but she chooses not to stay there,' Vera said.

'Too far away from Nice, where I am putting on my collection,' Coco said. 'Besides, Villa Marguerite is owned by one of my best clients. I expect her to order a lot of gowns while we are there.'

'Always the businesswoman,' Vera muttered to me.

Chanel ignored her. 'And we shall work on turning you into my model,' she added.

While we had been talking I had a strange pricking sensation between my shoulder blades. I glanced around and saw that the handsome Frenchman was watching me as he ate his dinner.

'That man,' I whispered. 'He keeps staring at me.'

Vera spun around. 'It's no good gazing at us wistfully, Jean-Paul,' she said. 'We're not going to invite you to join us. We're having girl talk.'

'This charming young lady,' the Frenchman said, in English this time, 'I do not think that she has been to the Riviera before?'

'This is Lady Georgiana Rannoch,' Vera said. 'Bertie's daughter.'

'How delightful.' He raised his glass to me. 'I shall look forward to getting to know you better.'

'Watch out for that one,' Vera muttered as we turned back. 'He eats little girls like you for breakfast and spits out the bones.'

'Who is he?'

'The Marquis de Ronchard. Old family. Loads of property in the colonies. Frightfully rich. Playboy, gambler. A little like your papa.'

It was startling to hear my father described in these terms, also to hear him called Bertie. I knew his name was Albert Henry, but I had only ever heard him called Rannoch by our equals and 'Your Grace' by subordinates. I knew he had frittered away the last of the family fortune on the Riviera. I knew he had almost gambled away Castle Rannoch, but it was still a shock to hear him described as a playboy and a gambler. To me, on the few occasions I had seen him, he had seemed rather like Binky – affable, easy-going, inoffensive. I remembered that he had got down on all fours on the carpet to play at bears with me, and I had squealed with delight and terror. It was one of the few strong memories I had of him.

'I don't think the marquis is too interested in a girl like me,' I said. 'I'm not glamorous enough.'

'He likes virgins,' Vera muttered darkly. 'Hunting runs in the blood, you know.'

'But of course he will have to settle down one day,' Coco said. 'It is required that he produce the heir on the right side of the blanket. And then he will be a good catch. For someone who doesn't mind the constant nocturnal straying.'

The meal was delicious and the conversation equally so. I felt the champagne bubbling in my head as I went back to my compartment. I found that my bed had been pulled out and made up for the night, also that the compartment now had a lingering hint of foreign cigarette smoke. Queenie, of course, was nowhere to be seen.

'Queenie?' I called.

I heard stirrings next door and she appeared. 'Sorry, miss. I must have dozed off.'

'Queenie, did you watch my bed being made up?'

'Yes, miss – I mean, meelady.'

'Was the attendant smoking when he did it?'

'Oh, no, miss. Of course he wasn't.'

'But there's a distinct smell of French cigarettes. Has anyone else been in here?'

'Of course not.'

She had admitted to dozing. My first thought was my jewel case. I don't have many jewels, but the ones I have are family heirlooms. I climbed up to get it down from the rack and was relieved to find the jewels all there. Then I opened my big suitcase and stared at it in surprise.

'Queenie, have you been in my suitcase?'

'Why would I do that?' she asked. 'I ain't touched nothing of yours. Honest.'

'Haven't touched anything,' I corrected.

'That's what I said. Ain't touched nothing.'

I stared at it again. 'That's distinctly odd. Someone has been through this suitcase. But it only contains my clothes and they're not exactly valuable or high fashion. I wonder what they could have been looking for.'

I went back out to the corridor and located the Pullman attendant.

'Did you see anyone going into my compartment?' I asked him.

He shook his head vehemently, but then added, 'But I have been making up all the beds. Someone could have come past while I was occupied, my lady. But your maid is present, no? She guards your possessions.'

He obviously didn't know Queenie. I walked back, perplexed and feeling rather unsafe. Had Queenie surprised someone just when he'd started going through my things, before he'd located my jewel case? I put it behind my pillow before I fell asleep.

# *Chapter 8*

*January 22, 1933*
*Lovely fine day. On the Blue Train going through France.*
*Things are looking up!*

I woke to brilliant sunlight seeping in past the blinds and lay feeling the gentle swaying of the carriage for a while before I remembered where I was. I had slept brilliantly, thanks to the comfortable berth and the generous amount of champagne I had drunk the night before. I looked at my watch. Eight fifteen. No sign of Queenie. I supposed that I couldn't expect her to find her way to a dining car on a foreign train and come back with a tea tray. I sat up and leaned across to open the blind. It shot upward and there was sparkling blue sea beside us. Umbrella pines clung to rocky headlands. We passed small clusters of houses, pastel painted with dark green shutters and dusty courtyards. It was all so foreign and terribly exciting.

I got up and washed at the pint-sized basin in my compartment, then when I went to find a summer dress, I remembered my strange suspicion of the night before. By daylight it seemed silly to think that someone had rummaged through my suitcase and left my jewels untouched. Now I'd never know. I took out one of my summer dresses. By the time I was dressed, there was still no sign of Queenie. I slid open the connecting door and saw she was still lying there, snoring and mouth open. Not a pretty sight.

'Queenie, wake up. We'll be arriving soon,' I called, then shut the door and went in search of breakfast. The dining car was empty apart from two women, with similar sleek caps of black hair. They were a little older than I and certainly more smartly dressed. I was seated at a table across from them. When I asked for croissants the waiter shook his head. 'On this train they always demand the breakfast Anglais,' he said. 'They are wishing the bacon and the eggs.'

I settled for a poached egg. I was just pouring myself a second cup of coffee when I heard one of them say, 'Shall we be seeing anything of Darcy, do you think?'

I paused, the coffeepot frozen in my hand. I tried not to listen, but one can't help oneself in such circumstances.

'I expect so,' the other woman said, pausing to light up a cigarette. 'We know she's going to be there and he's so good about visiting the child.'

'I suppose he feels responsible.'

'More than that. He adores that child. Absolutely dotes on the little chap.'

'Well, he's the only heir at the moment, isn't he?'

'Hardly the heir, darling.' The woman took a long drag on her cigarette, then smiled.

'Well, you know what I mean. Anyway, it will be fun to catch up with old Darcy again. I've hardly seen anything of him for months. I don't know what he's been doing with himself.'

'I heard there was a new love in his life.'

'Another one? I can't keep up.' And she laughed.

I managed to put down the coffeepot without spilling the contents and got to my feet.

'You are finished, my lady?' The waiter appeared at my side. 'I cannot bring you some fresh fruit? Some more toast?'

'No, thank you.' I hurried out of the dining car, wrenched open my compartment door and stumbled in, nearly falling over Queenie, who was cramming items into one of my suitcases.

'Careful with that,' I snapped. 'You'll crease everything.'

She looked up, surprised and hurt. 'Don't vex yourself, my lady. It shall be done according to your wishes,' she said.

'What did you say?'

'I read one of them magazines last night – *The Lady*, it's called. Ever so posh, and a servant said that in one of the stories. "It shall be done according to your wishes." That's what she said. I was thinking about what you said, see. About me sounding dead common and that I should learn to speak proper like what you do. So I thought I'd start improving meself right away.' She grinned, then peered at me. 'Are you all right, miss? You look as white as a sheet. It's all this swaying around. You'd better sit down.'

I noticed for the first time that the attendant had been in and turned the beds back into seats. I sat. Queenie went on with her packing, chatting as she did so. 'They had lots of pictures of posh folks in that there magazine, but I didn't see yours. You should get out more, miss. Mingle in society – that's what they call it, don't they?'

I wanted to shout at her to shut up. Instead I turned and stared out the window. It didn't have to be the same Darcy, did it? There was more than one Darcy in the world, although it wasn't a common name. And how many Darcys were heir to a title? I knew in my heart that it was he and a great weight of doom came over me. He had a child he'd been hiding from me. He had another woman in his life. I was just one of a string of girlfriends. I didn't matter at all.

'It's time to stop this stupid nonsense,' I said to myself. 'Clinging to a false hope that one day we can marry. Well, I can't afford to wind up an old maid. I'm going to do what I was supposed to and find myself a suitable husband and forget that Darcy O'Mara ever existed.'

I pressed my lips together hard, worried for an awful moment that I might cry. The attendant tapped on my door. 'We shall be arriving in Nice shortly, my lady.'

The train began to slow. Then it glided to a halt at Nice Station. Porters swarmed on board. Two of them grabbed my bags. I commanded Queenie to follow them and not let them out of her sight. I descended to find the bags already on a trolley and off we went at a great rate to find a taxi.

'The Villa Gloriosa,' I said to the taxicab driver.

'*Comment?*' he asked, meaning 'What was that?'

I repeated the name. 'You know your way around Nice, do you?'

'*Oui, Madame.* But I am not sure of the location of Villa Gloriosa. On what street is it to be found?'

I fished for the address and gave it to him. He pursed his lips as if he was not impressed.

'Is it far from here?' I asked.

'Not far.'

We set off – through small backstreets with balconies and peeling shutters and then out to that magnificent thoroughfare, the Promenade des Anglais. It was just as fine as it had looked in the poster – lined with palm trees, with elegant couples strolling and the sea beyond – sparkling in unbelievable shades of turquoise and azure. In spite of everything my spirits rose. Soon I'd be sitting on a terrace above that glittering sea, or strolling like those people on the Promenade, and I'd meet fascinating, witty new men, and I wouldn't have to be with Fig every minute of every day. . . .

After a little way we turned off the boulevard and went inland again, and the atmosphere quickly deteriorated. We turned up a small street with a repair shop on the corner. *Get your punctures repaired here*, was the slogan painted on a white wall. The road began to climb a little, with nondescript buildings on either side, then it turned into a lane.

'Are you sure this is right?' I asked.

'*Oui, Madame.* This is undoubtedly the address you have given me.'

'Then it's nowhere near the sea?'

'Apparently no, *Madame.*'

The lane narrowed until it was just wide enough for the taxi, with a high rough stone wall on either side. Then it stopped at high wrought-iron gates. The driver got out and opened the gates with difficulty. I found myself looking at a wild garden of dark, overgrown shrubs and beyond that a tall, plain house, its green shutters closed so that it gave a hostile, unfriendly impression.

'This is Villa Gloriosa?' I repeated to the taxi driver.

'*Oui, Madame.* See, it says so, on the plaque on the wall.'

Whoever had named it had strange delusions of grandeur, or was near-sighted. I got out and walked down a narrow path between overgrown Italian cypresses, which reached out to scratch me in unfriendly fashion as I passed, then knocked at the front door. The paint was peeling and the big oak door did not have an air of being opened frequently. I heard footsteps and then the door creaked open.

A large woman stood there, dressed head to toe in black. She stared at me.

'*Bonjour,*' I said, giving her a pleasant smile. 'I am Lady Georgiana Rannoch. I am expected.'

'No, you are not,' she said, eyeing me coldly.

'But yes,' I insisted. 'I have come to stay. I sent a telegram.'

'I know of no telegram.'

'I am the sister of the duke.'

'I know of no duke,' she replied, and as if to emphasize this she folded her arms across her enormous chest.

Light was beginning to dawn. Obviously the fool of a taxi driver had got the wrong address. 'This is the Villa Gloriosa?' I asked.

It was.

'And it is currently rented by a Monsieur and Madame Farquar?'

'Farquar? *Oui,*' she said.

'Then I am in the right place. My brother and sister-in-law are staying with Monsieur and Madame Farquar and I am to join them.'

'I was given no instruction that another guest was expected.'

'Then please go and fetch your master or mistress and they will explain to you.'

The arms remained folded. 'They are out,' she said.

'When will they return?'

'I don't know. They took a picnic.'

'What happens here?' I heard the cab-driver asking behind me as he arrived with Queenie and the baggage.

'This person doesn't want to admit me,' I told him.

'Who gives you authority not to admit the English milady?' the cab-driver demanded. 'This is an English milady.'

'This house is rented to Mr Farquar. Until he says yes, I do not admit strangers.'

'Well, I'm not going to sit on the doorstep,' I said. My temper was wearing thin and I decided that I had been polite long enough. 'Do you think I would come all this way, with my maid and my bags, if I was not invited to stay here? This is no way to behave to an English milady.' I turned to the taxi driver. 'Bring the bags inside.'

The woman in black looked as if she was considering whether to stand in his way or not. He was a burly man and in the end she sniffed and stood aside. 'There is nowhere for her to sleep. She can wait in the salon, until Monsieur and Madame Farquar return,' she said, moving ahead to block the staircase as if I might decide to sprint up it any second.

The salon was gloomy in the extreme. It smelled musty, almost damp, as if it had been neglected for a long time. In fact, I suspected that mushrooms were growing in the darker corners. It was cold but there was no fire in a tall marble fireplace. The shutters were closed and the furniture was dark and heavy – and uncomfortable too. I sat on a sofa that had the most surprising lumps and bumps and waited. Queenie perched on my trunk in the foyer. To begin with I had been angry. Now I began to feel more and more uneasy. I had sent a telegram. They knew I was coming. So perhaps I wasn't welcome after all.

# Chapter 9

*January 22, 1933*
*Villa Gloriosa. Talk about misnamed! Nothing in the*
*least glorious about it. Furthermore was not made*
*welcome. Did I do the right thing, coming here?*

The day wore on. I began to feel hungry, but I thought my
chances of getting something to eat from the harridan were
not good. Surely Podge would have to come home to take
his afternoon nap, wouldn't he? I wouldn't have minded
exploring the garden, but I was sure that, once I was outside, the dragon woman would not allow me in again. I
heard a clock in another room strike one, then two.

Queenie poked her head around the door. I had left her
guarding the luggage in the front hall. 'I ain't half hungry,
miss,' she said. 'Don't they have no dinner in this house?'

'Dinner is in the evening, Queenie,' I said. 'Remember
what I told you. Only the lower classes call their midday
meal dinner. To us it is lunch. But the answer is that I
think it unlikely that we'll get anything to eat until the
family returns.'

'We could go and stay in one of them hotels. A darned sight friendlier than that old woman.'

'I agree,' I said, 'but I don't have the money for hotels. We'll just have to wait.'

'I got a bar of chocolate we can share,' she said generously and broke a Cadbury's in half for us.

At about three o'clock there were voices and footsteps on the gravel. I went to the door of the salon just as the front door burst open and Podge rushed in ahead of the grown-ups. He jumped in surprise when he saw me then his face lit up with recognition.

'Auntie Georgie! You came after all.' He turned back. 'Mama. Papa. Auntie Georgie came.'

I looked up to see four adults looking at me with a mixture of surprise and horror.

'What on earth are you doing here?' Fig demanded.

'Good to see you, old bean,' Binky said. 'So glad you could make it, but you might have warned us.'

'I sent a telegram, two days ago,' I said.

'We received no telegram.' The woman who spoke looked like an older, haughtier and grumpier version of Fig. 'To what address did you send it?'

'The Villa Gloriosa,' I said.

The large red-faced man with an impressive handlebar mustache sniffed. 'Damned Frenchies got it wrong again, I suppose. Hopeless – foreigners don't have a clue, do they? There's a Villa Glorieux as well and they've mixed us up before.' He came toward me, hand extended. 'I'm Foggy Farquar. So you're Georgiana. Good to meet you at last. Welcome to the humble abode.'

At least the males in the party were pleased to see me. 'Thank you.'

'And this is my wife, Ducky.'

'My sister, Matilda,' Fig corrected. 'Matilda, this is Binky's sister, Georgiana.'

Matilda? I tried not to grin. A Hilda and Matilda in one family. I could see that nicknames like Ducky and Fig were preferable. We shook hands. Hers was bony, like clutching a claw.

'I'm sorry I gave you a shock,' I said, 'but I really did send the telegram.'

'How did you get here?' Fig asked. 'I didn't think you had money for the fare. Did you come second class on ordinary trains?'

'No. The Blue Train like you.' It gave me great satisfaction to say the words. 'The queen paid for my ticket. She thought I looked too pale and needed sunshine.'

'The queen?' Ducky Farquar said. 'She paid for your ticket?' She glanced at Fig.

'The queen seems to have a soft spot for Georgiana,' Fig said icily.

'She's very kind to her relatives,' I added, just to remind them that I was related to royalty and they weren't. 'And since Binky and Fig had said I was welcome anytime at the villa . . .' I left the rest of that sentence hanging.

Ducky shot Fig a look of pure venom. 'Of course you are welcome,' she said, 'but the question is – where are we going to put you? The house is not at all large. Much smaller than described in the advertisement. Quite poky, in fact.'

'You don't have any spare bedrooms?'

'Not on the main floor. There may be rooms up in the servants' quarter in the attic. But we couldn't put you up there with the maids. It wouldn't be the done thing, would it?'

'She could bunk in with Maude, couldn't she?' Foggy suggested.

'Maude?' I asked.

'Our daughter. Yes, I suppose Maude does have a large room. But it would be up to her. You know how sensitive she is, and how particular.'

'Well, ask her, Ducky,' Foggy said impatiently. 'Where has the child got to now? Maude?' he called.

A face poked around the front door. A sullen face, a plain face with pigtails. She was a girl of about ten and she stood eyeing her parents defiantly.

'Maude, this is Georgiana, Binky's sister. Is it all right if she bunks in with you?'

Maude looked at me with pure distaste. 'I need space for my dolls,' she said.

'There are no other rooms, dearest,' Ducky said. 'And she is your aunt, sort of. And she has come a long way. And it might be nice for you to have a chum to talk to.'

'I don't like talking,' Maude said. If ever a child had been well named, it was this one. She looked just like a Maude.

'She's very sensitive,' Ducky repeated. 'She'll need time to come around.'

'If there's nowhere for me here, I shall have to go home, I suppose,' I said. 'The queen will be disappointed.'

That was my trump card, as I knew it would be.

'We can't let the queen think that we gave Georgiana the cold shoulder,' Fig said. 'We'll have to make room for her somehow.'

'I suppose we could put a camp bed for her in the

library,' Foggy suggested. 'Nobody ever goes in there, do they?'

'It's a rum do, Georgie,' Binky said. 'This house has a library, a smoking room, a music room, a billiard room, but a distinct lack of bedrooms and bathrooms.'

'Auntie Georgie can sleep with me and Nanny,' Podge said, moving to my side in a display of solidarity.

I thought that would be an admirable solution.

'Nanny and me,' Fig corrected. 'Please make sure you get your grammar correct, Podge. And it wouldn't be healthy to have three people in one bedroom. Not enough fresh air.'

'And my maid?' I asked.

Fig noticed Queenie for the first time. 'You brought that person with you? What on earth possessed you, Georgiana?'

'One does need a maid, and she's the only one I have.'

Fig turned to Ducky. 'She is the dreadful girl I told you about. Absolutely from the gutter. Hasn't the slightest idea how to behave in polite society.'

'Nevertheless, she needs somewhere to sleep,' I insisted.

'She'll have to share with your girl, Fig,' Ducky said with a sigh. She turned to Queenie. 'Take your mistress's things upstairs, girl.'

'It shall be done as you desire, madam,' Queenie said with her mock posh accent.

'How dare you try to imitate your betters,' Fig snapped. 'Honestly, Georgiana, she'll have to go. Start looking for a French maid immediately.'

At that moment the gargoyle in black stepped from the shadows and rattled off a string of French at us. I think I was the only one who understood. 'She says she had no idea that I was coming because nobody told her and where do they think I am going to sleep?' I translated. It was clear they were all terrified of her. 'Who is she, anyway?'

'Madame Lapiss. She's the housekeeper. She's frightful,' Foggy said.

'She's going to sleep in the library,' Fig said in very bad French.

'Impossible! Valuable books will be ruined!' The gargoyle waved her arms and flashed her eyes, glaring at me as if I might be capable of any kind of vandalism.

'Only temporarily,' Fig explained.

The gargoyle gave a large and dramatic sigh, grabbed my heaviest suitcase and stomped upstairs with it to a large gloomy library. The walls were lined, floor to ceiling, with old musty books. Most of the floor space was taken up with a mahogany map table. We managed to push this against a wall and there was just room for a camp bed. Nowhere to hang my clothes. No mirror. Clearly they didn't want me to stay long.

I felt tears of anger and frustration as I unpacked some of my toiletries and put them on the table. I should never have come. If the queen had wanted me here, she should have given me money for a hotel. She should have known that any relative of Fig's would be stingy in the extreme.

I freshened up and came downstairs to see if tea might be imminent. Through an open door I heard Fig's voice, or was it Ducky's? 'At least she can keep an eye on the children, can't she? And she could give Maude some lessons; then you wouldn't have to look for a tutor.'

'Maude's a particularly bright child. I'm not sure your

sister-in-law would be up to the task. But I suppose we could try. It would save considerable expense.'

I coughed as I entered the room. 'Is it teatime?' I asked.

'We're not having tea while we're here,' Ducky said. 'We're dining early so that Maude can join us, as we are on holiday. It's good for her to learn to participate in adult conversation.'

'We've had nothing to eat all day,' I pointed out. 'You don't mind if I ask your cook to make us sandwiches, do you?'

'I suppose not,' Ducky said grudgingly.

'And Georgiana,' Fig added, 'we thought you might help out with the children. Give them some lessons, you know. Otherwise they'll just run wild.'

I managed to obtain a cheese sandwich for Queenie and myself, but my stomach was growling by the time the dinner gong went and I went down in anticipation to find that dinner was cold ham and a couple of lettuce leaves with boiled potatoes. It was served by the gargoyle, with the occasional sigh and groan as she walked behind us.

'Cold ham, old thing?' Foggy asked. 'Didn't we just have ham sandwiches for lunch?'

'Last-minute substitution, I'm afraid,' Ducky said. 'I told her to make beef casserole and I discovered it was swimming with garlic and onions. I couldn't serve that to Maude. Really, these people have no idea.' She turned to me. 'Couldn't even make a steak and kidney pudding, can you believe? And breakfast – had never heard of kidneys for breakfast.'

'And eggplant,' Foggy added. 'Will keep trying to serve us something called eggplant. Doesn't taste anything like an egg.'

'And she can't make proper puddings, can she, Mummy?' Maude chimed in. 'I wanted rice pudding but all I got was silly fruit.'

I finished my one slice of ham in silence. Then I remembered why I was here.

'Tell me,' I said, 'do you know Sir Toby Groper?'

'Know of the bounder, but don't know the man personally,' Foggy said. 'Not really one of us, you know.'

'N.O.C.D. Made his money in trade,' Ducky added. The former meaning 'not our class, dear.'

Everyone at the table shuddered.

'And not just trade,' Foggy went on, warming to his subject. 'Armaments. I mean, our ancestors were involved in the East India Company, but that was decent trade. Respectable. Bringing civilization to the natives at the same time. His family supplied guns to both sides in every damned war.'

'Really? I thought he made his money from motorcars,' Ducky said.

'Since the war, yes,' Foggy said.

'I heard there was some scandal about that too,' Binky chimed in. 'Didn't he swindle his partner or something?'

'Did he?' Fig asked.

'Maybe not swindle, but there was some question about who actually invented that bally motor of his. Some kind of lawsuit. Didn't the other chap kill himself?'

'Horrible little man,' Ducky said. 'I understand he swans it down here on the Riviera. Ostentatious great yacht and a villa full of artworks. No taste at all, of course.'

'Where is his villa?' I asked.

'No idea.'

'So you don't ever meet him at parties?'

'We don't go in for parties,' Ducky said. 'All that loud music and people getting drunk. We don't drink.'

Of course I realized then that there was no wine on the table.

'A quiet game of bridge or whist is more our style,' Foggy added. 'And Ducky does jigsaw puzzles.'

Oh, Lord, how was I ever going to meet Sir Toby if I was stuck at Villa Gloriosa drinking water, tutoring children and doing jigsaw puzzles?

Dinner ended and we went through to the gloomy salon where the others played whist. It was played in silence apart from Ducky occasionally accusing her husband of cheating. They went to bed before ten, so I made my way to the library and changed into my nightclothes. I was just coming back from the bathroom, which was up another flight of stairs, when a figure loomed out in front of me. It was Foggy, in an awful red-and-white-striped dressing gown looking like a human barber's pole.

'Awfully glad you're here, young lady,' he said. His face looked particularly red in the dim light, and his eyes a little bleary. 'Liven things up a little, what?' He moved out to block the way in front of me. 'I must say, I'm looking forward to getting to know you better.' He was looking down at me with what can only be described as a lecherous leer. I, with my limited experience of Life and Men, nevertheless knew lechery when I saw it. I also realized something else. He was blowing alcohol-laden breath at me. Ducky might not approve of drink, but Foggy had certainly been knocking it back in private.

'It must be frightfully lonely down in that library,' he went on, while I stared at him in horror. 'So completely cut off from the rest of us. I'd better check on you from time to time to see that you're all right.'

'Don't worry about me,' I said. 'I shall be perfectly safe. I'll lock my door.'

'Foggy? Who are you talking to?' came Ducky's strident voice from the end of the hall.

'Just coming, old thing. Wanted to make sure our new arrival had everything she needed.' He loaded those last words with double meaning. And to my horror, he reached out to touch me. I wasn't sure which part of me he was aiming for, but I didn't wait to find out. I pushed past him and fled down the stairs. Then I locked the library door. 'Oh, golly,' I muttered. This was an added complication I didn't need. If Ducky found out that Foggy was chasing me, she'd probably think I was encouraging him. Why did men have to be so bloody stupid? (I know a lady never says 'bloody.')

The thought of men and their stupidity brought something rushing back that I had kept firmly from my conscious mind all day. There are other men called Darcy, I told myself over and over again. I was probably worrying over nothing.

# Chapter 10

*Villa Not Very Gloriosa, Nice*
*January 23, 1933*
**Help. Must escape immediately. Choice between dusty
musty library and sharing with the most unpleasant
child I've ever met. And nocturnal visits from the
lecherous Foggy. Not to mention serious lack of food and
entertainment and no chance to meet Sir Toby.**

I rose early with one thought in mind. I had to find Belinda
and somewhere else to stay.

I dressed and went down to breakfast. Queenie
appeared from the kitchen, brushing crumbs from her
front. 'I was going to bring you tea, miss, but they didn't
have no tea, only coffee, and besides, your door was
locked.'

'It's all right. I'm up now and I don't think I'd have
dared to eat or drink anything in that library,' I said.

The gargoyle appeared, hands on hips. 'Breakfast?
They do not want breakfast until nine. They are very late
risers.'

'How about some coffee and croissants now, to keep me going?' I asked.

'Maybe possible.' She shrugged and sniffed, went away and came back with a cup of strong black coffee and some of the previous day's stale bread, sliced with a small dish of apricot jam.

I ate a couple of mouthfuls and had a swig of coffee, which was disgusting and tasted like liquid tar, then I left a note saying that I had gone out for a walk. A long walk, preferably.

I stepped outside to a delightful day. The sun was shining. The sky was blue and the air was perfumed, just as I had imagined it when I stood in Victoria Station. All things considered, it was better being here than serving soup. I followed the lane down into town and eventually came to the seafront, where I stood leaning against the railing, watching early risers take their morning constitutional. The sea sparkled in the morning sunshine. Farther down the Promenade there was an impressive-looking pier and behind the town green hills rose, dotted with villas – like the one in which I had expected to stay, no doubt.

I stood for a while, just drinking in the scene, breathing the fresh salty air. It would be no good looking for Belinda too early. She rarely rose before ten – and she probably wouldn't be in her own bed anyway. But at least if she was staying at the Hotel Negresco, as she had mentioned, I could leave a note for her and meet her later.

The enticing smell of freshly baked bread reminded me that I needed breakfast. There were several little open-air cafés along the boulevard. I stopped at one and indulged in good coffee and a basket of croissants. Much later, feeling full and content, I followed the boulevard until I came to the Hotel Negresco, a glittering white building topped with pink Eastern-style domes. I went up the steps and into the marble foyer. A young man in blue and gold uniform leaped up immediately to ask how he could assist me. I asked for Miss Warburton-Stoke. The young man went to have a conversation with another man in a smart suit. The latter checked a ledger then came over to me. The young lady was not registered at the hotel. Had she not been there at all during the past week? I asked. Again he shook his head. He was not aware of a young lady of that name.

Now what on earth was I going to do? It looked as if I might be trapped sharing a room with an obnoxious child at the Villa Gloriosa, dying slowly of starvation while I dodged the attentions of Foggy and the awful Madame Lapiss. Not an enticing prospect. I supposed I could find the casino and camp out there later in the day in the hope that Belinda would show up. I was about to walk away when another thought occurred to me.

'Sir Toby Groper,' I said. 'Does he come into the hotel much?'

'Sir Toby? Sometimes. But not at this time of day. A drink with friends late in the evening maybe.' And he shrugged in that particularly unhelpful Gallic way.

'Do you know where his villa is?'

'Of course. It is on the Petit Corniche in the direction of Monte Carlo. About one, two kilometers beyond the town. But you cannot see it from the road. It is hidden away in a little cove.'

At least I knew where to look now. And maybe I could enact the sort of drama Belinda was so good at – twisting my ankle outside the gate, or being almost knocked over by a speeding car – yes, that was a good one. I wasn't sure I could carry it off as well as Belinda, but it was worth a try.

I came out of the hotel and stood on the steps, wondering what to do next. Certainly not go back to the house of horror. I decided to take a look at the town and turned inland past the grounds of an elegant villa until I came to an area of commerce. Shops were just opening up their shutters and shopkeepers were putting out their wares. They called across to each other, good-natured insults and salutations in the strong southern dialect. I reached a little cobbled square, lined with more outdoor cafés, and suddenly there, drinking coffee, were my two new acquaintances from the train. I went over to them, delighted to see friendly faces.

'How good to see you,' I said. 'I thought you were staying at a villa.'

'Oh, we are,' Vera replied. 'But Coco has to meet a man from Grasse to discuss her new perfume, so we had the chauffeur drive us into town. But I'm surprised you're so pleased to see us. We thought we'd been given the cold shoulder, didn't we, Coco?'

'We were mortified. We did not know what we had done to offend you,' Coco Chanel agreed.

'What do you mean?'

'We spotted you yesterday evening, going into the casino. We called out to you but you passed us without saying a word.'

'The casino? I wasn't at the casino. I was at the villa all evening.'

'Strange.' Vera looked at Coco. 'I could have sworn it was you.'

'Absolutely. You must have a twin.'

'How fascinating,' I said. 'I wish I had been at the casino. I spent a dreadfully dull evening with my family.'

'You must come and dine with us sometime,' Vera said. 'Our hostess has an excellent chef.'

'What do you mean, *dine*?' Chanel demanded. 'You must come to the villa this afternoon so that I can fit you for the clothes you will wear when you model for me at the unveiling of my collection.' She held up a warning hand as I was about to speak. 'Do not say no. I will not hear of it. I absolutely insist. You are the look that I want – the true British aristocrat, isn't she, Vera?'

'Oh, rather,' Vera agreed.

I felt my face going red. 'No, really, you don't want me. I'll do something terrible and embarrass you, I know I will.'

'Nonsense.' Coco laughed. 'As Vera will tell you, it is quite impossible to embarrass me. I have survived all kinds of scandal in my life. I have developed a very thick skin. So come to the villa. Try on the clothes. You will see that what I ask you to do is not so terrible. Shall we say three o'clock?'

It certainly was tempting. I might be invited to stay for dinner and have something decent to eat. And I'd be away from my relatives.

'All right,' I said. 'I will come.'

'It is called Villa Marguerite,' Vera said. 'Out on the Petit Corniche – that's the headland you see if you face to the east. You'll need to take a taxicab. It's too far to walk.'

'The Petit Corniche? Is it anywhere near Sir Toby Groper's place?'

'My dear, positively on top of him.' Vera laughed. 'We

look down on his gardens and his swimming pool. Lovely place it is too – private beach and dock. And you should see the size of his yacht. I believe it's bigger than the Duke of Westminster's, isn't it, Coco – and that's saying something.'

That settled it. If becoming a fashion model was the only way to have a chance to meet Sir Toby, then I'd have to do it, and pray that I didn't make too big a fool of myself.

I arrived home to find the relatives sitting on deckchairs on the lawn. They looked quite peeved as I approached.

'Where have you been all this time?' Fig demanded.

'I went to have coffee with friends in town,' I said.

'Friends?' Fig demanded. 'I didn't know you had friends here. Did you know she had friends here, Binky?'

I could see her brain working. *If she has friends, she can stay with them.* That was what she was thinking.

'Actually, people I met on the train,' I said. 'One of them is a relative of sorts. Vera Bate Lombardi. Do you know her?'

A look passed between them. 'Know *of* her . . .' Ducky said.

'Isn't she the Duke of Cambridge's . . .'

'Yes,' Ducky said firmly.

'And Coco Chanel, the dress designer,' I added.

'Chanel? You know Chanel?' The two women's faces immediately lit up.

'Yes. I'm going to be modeling for her new collection,' I said breezily. 'She's unveiling it at a big party in a few days' time.'

'And she wants you to be a model? You, of all people?' Fig looked at me as if she couldn't believe Chanel could be that desperate.

'I'm exactly the type she wants for her new collection,' I said. 'I'm going to her villa this afternoon to try on clothes. I probably won't be back for dinner, so don't wait for me.'

Frosty silence.

'We rather hoped you'd be a help with the children, not rushing off every second,' Fig said. Ducky nodded.

'I thought you brought Podge's nanny with you,' I couldn't resist saying. 'You don't exactly check up on him too often at home.'

'He comes down to us every teatime, doesn't he, Binky?' Fig sounded affronted. 'Every teatime regularly. And of course we brought Nanny. What we were hoping for was some schooling from you. He needs to learn to read and write.'

'And Maude shouldn't fall behind in her lessons either,' Ducky said. 'Not if she's to get into a top school. We have her down for Roedean, you know.'

'Then I'm afraid I'd be hopeless,' I said. 'I only know how to walk around with a book on my head.'

'You speak French,' Fig said. 'You could teach the children that.'

She was determined that somehow I was going to earn my keep. I glanced down at her, thinking what an unpleasant person she was. I had observed several murders in my life. Hers, I believe, would be justified.

To show willingness to a point I gave both children a half hour's drilling in French. I rather wished I knew more naughty words. I'd have taught them those – especially Maude. Lunch was even grimmer than dinner and breakfast had been. A small square of cheese was placed in the middle of the table with more bread, some tomatoes and olives.

'We like to eat lightly at lunchtime,' Ducky said. 'Healthy for the digestion.'

After lunch they went for a siesta. I put on my least unfashionable frock, applied a touch of rouge and lipstick and set off for the Villa Marguerite. I had been told it was too far to walk, but there was no hope of finding a taxi-cab closer than the seafront. It was a delightfully warm afternoon, and the beach looked so inviting – with its gay changing cubicles, lines of wicker chaises, topped with bright blue cushions, and bright blue umbrellas. I was a little disappointed to find that the beach was made of stones, not sand, but nobody else seemed to mind. People in bathing suits were sunning themselves. I observed them, amazed at the daring nature of the bathing suits. Many of the women's suits were absolutely backless and the men wore what could only be described as black underpants. Nanny would have swooned on the spot.

Not too many of the bathers dared to put more than a toe in the ocean, I noticed. The brave ones were nearly all children. There was one particular little boy with a mop of dark curls who ran fearlessly into the waves, then ran out again, screaming, as a bigger wave approached.

A man got up from a deckchair and took his hand, leading him to the water this time and helping him to jump over the waves. He had similar dark curls and there was something familiar about the way his hair curled at the nape of his neck. Then he turned around and my heart did a flip. It was Darcy. As I watched he looked back at a slim, dark-haired woman lounging on a wicker beach chair in a strapless bathing top, her long black hair curling seductively over one shoulder. She must have said something because he burst out laughing and ruffled the child's hair. So it was true. He had a mistress in France and a child that he had never told me about.

I felt as if a knife was ripping my insides in half. I just wanted to get away. I stumbled onward, colliding with an old colonel, who barked at me, 'I say, watch it!'

I muttered an apology and kept on walking, faster and faster, as if walking fast enough could take away my pain. At last I reached the old port and had to stop. I was out of breath and had a stitch in my side. I was also leaving the desirable part of town. There didn't appear to be any taxicabs around here. I had to retrace my steps to the boulevard before I found one. The road started to climb, giving me a view down at the port with its collection of expensive yachts mingling with simpler fishing boats, and then the town was left behind and the road hugged a rocky headland, with the sparkling sea on one side and elegant villas clinging to steep cliffs. They ranged from the traditional Mediterranean villa, pastel colored with gay shutters, to neoclassical or horribly spare and modern. Before us was now a new bay, dotted with lovely white yachts. The cab turned off the main road and dropped to a small, secluded cove.

'Villa Marguerite,' the cabby said. It was set behind a high stone wall, but through the wrought-iron gates I glimpsed a charming square traditional villa, a sort of warm pink with dark green shutters and a red-tiled roof, set amid manicured lawns. I opened the gate cautiously and went up the raked gravel drive to the front door.

It was opened by a white-capped maid. I told her I had come to see Madame Chanel and she was expecting me. She bobbed a curtsy and invited me into a cool marble foyer.

'Please wait here,' she said in French.

'Who is it, Claudette?' a rich voice echoed down the stairs.

'A visitor for Madame Chanel, *Madame*,' the maid said.

'Madame Chanel is out on the terrace. I'm just going out. I'll escort her myself.'

The speaker came down the stairs, elegant in scarlet wide-legged pajamas and a little Japanese jacket. Her blonde bobbed hair was a perfect shining cap, and her eyes still as wide and blue as any schoolgirl's. They opened even wider when she saw me.

'Good God, Georgie, what are you doing here?'

'Hello, Mummy,' I said.

# Chapter 11

**January 23, 1933**
*At the Villa Marguerite. Delightful day.*

She tapped down the marble staircase in high-heeled backless shoes to embrace me. We kissed, half an inch from each other's cheeks as usual.

'But nobody told me you were coming to the Riviera,' Mummy said, pouting as if I'd been keeping secrets from her.

'You didn't exactly let me know you were going to be here,' I pointed out. 'Or invite me to stay.'

'Darling, I thought you'd be busy in London, romping around with the delicious Darcy.'

'Well, the delicious Darcy is no longer in London and no longer delicious,' I said.

'Oh, dear. What happened?'

'He has another woman,' I said.

Mummy shrugged. 'He wasn't the type to stay around for long, was he? Never mind. Plenty of other fish in the sea.'

'For you, maybe. Not for me. Where's Max?'

'At home in Germany.' She made a face. 'Suddenly it's all work, work, work. You know what Germans are like. I told him I needed sunshine and gaiety but he wouldn't budge from his silly old factories. They are making new and clever tanks that can fire on people miles away and go over buildings, I gather. So militaristic, the Germans. It's all to do with that silly little man Hitler. Everyone is saying he's going to get into power. How can anyone take him seriously with that mustache? He looks like a hedgehog.' And she laughed gaily.

'It is good to see you,' I said, smiling because one had to smile when my mother was around. 'So you fled to the Riviera alone, then?'

'Had to, darling. Couldn't stand that dreary winter another second. So who are you staying with?'

'With Fig and Fig's sister.'

'Oh, God. You're not!'

'I am and it's beyond awful. I have to sleep on a camp bed in the library, Mummy, and they hardly eat any food and Foggy Farquar tried to fondle me.'

'Well, you must come and stay here, of course,' Mummy said. 'We'll send someone for your things right away.'

'Do you think the owner of the villa would mind?'

She laughed again. 'Silly child. I'm the owner.'

'You?'

'Don't you remember I told you that the divine Marc-Antoine had given me a little villa on the Riviera?'

'Marc-Antoine – was he the racing driver?'

'Killed so tragically and so young. I adored him, you know. I really believe he was my one true love.'

'Mummy, you've had so many one true loves.'

'But not like Marc-Antoine. And he gave me this little villa just before he was killed. He must have had a premonition, I believe. "I want you to think of me and be happy, *chérie*," he said.' And she gave a shuddering and dramatic sigh that would have had the audience weeping in every West End theater.

'This is supposed to be a "nice little villa"?' I looked around the spacious foyer, up the wide sweep of marble stairs to the gallery with rooms going off it in all directions. 'It looks rather grand to me.'

'Not by Riviera standards. Anyway, it suits me very well. My little bolt hole, I call it. Whenever the world is unkind, I rush straight here.' She took my hands. 'Let me take a look at you. Rather pale and pasty faced. You need sun and fresh air and feeding up. Come on out to the terrace.' She took my hand. 'How funny that you didn't know this was my villa. So you came to see Coco – I can't think why. You certainly can't afford her clothes.'

'She wants me to model for her new collection.'

Mummy burst out laughing again. 'You, a model? Don't be silly, darling, you'd be hopeless. Remember how you tripped over your train when you were presented?'

'She says I have the look she wants,' I replied haughtily. It was all right for me to claim I was hopeless, but not other people, least of all my mother.

'If you stood still like a statue, maybe. Not if you moved.'

We emerged to a sun-splashed terrace, built out over the water. Vera and Coco Chanel were sitting at a wicker table, heads together over a sheet of paper. 'More like this, I think,' Coco was saying, waving a cigarette in her left hand.

'Look who I have found,' Mummy announced. They looked up.

'Ah, my little model,' Coco said, holding out the hand without the cigarette to me. 'So you have met our charming hostess, have you, *ma petite*?'

'Many times,' I replied. 'She's my mother.'

'But of course. How silly of me. I should have remembered. It's just that . . .'

'I know, we look nothing alike,' Mummy said. 'Poor child inherited her looks from Bertie.'

'And Mummy doesn't like to admit to me,' I added. 'I remind people that she's old enough to have a grown-up daughter.'

'Silly child. You know I adore you,' my mother said.

'Come and sit beside us, *ma petite*,' Coco said. 'I will show you the outfit we have planned for you.'

'You're not really serious about using Georgie as a model, are you?' Mummy said. 'Coco, darling, the girl was born clumsy. She can't walk two steps without tripping over her own feet – which are exceptionally large, by the way.'

'Nonsense, she will be splendid when I have worked with her,' Coco said. 'See, *ma petite* – is this not a fabulous outfit that I have created for you?'

I looked at the drawing. It was as she had described it – a man's tweed sports jacket, open to reveal a frilly blouse of ecru lace, black silk pajamas and what looked like an extravagant necklace of pearls and precious stones at the throat.

'Astonishing,' my mother exclaimed, peering over Coco Chanel's shoulder. 'I don't think I shall ever want to look as masculine as that, darling.'

'Ah, but it is so sexy. You will see the eyes of the men at my collection.' Coco looked up at Vera and smiled. 'They will want to rip that jacket off her – and those pajamas too.'

'This is my daughter we're talking about,' my mother said. 'She's led a very sheltered life.'

'Then it's about time she learned what the world is all about.' She stood up. 'Come. We go to my room and we will try on the clothes.'

She was about to lead me from the terrace when a scream came up from down below, followed by a large splash. I ran over to the railing and looked down.

'It's only that silly woman,' Coco said scornfully. 'No class at all. I grew up poor but I learned to acquire class. She has not.'

I realized that I was looking down onto another property below. There were lovely terraces, full of great terracotta urns of spring flowers, and a huge swimming pool above a little cove with private beach. A sleek teak motorboat was moored at a dock and out in the ocean beyond was a vast white and blue yacht. A young woman with brassy blonde hair was splashing and wallowing in the pool while a portly older man in a bright red bathing costume stood on the side, laughing at her.

'You beast. You cruel beast,' she was shouting. 'Now you have ruined my hair.'

'Is that Sir Toby Groper?' I asked.

'It is. Odious little man,' Mummy said.

'And that's his wife?'

My mother chuckled. 'Darling, you are so delightfully naïve. His wife is somewhere else. That is Olga, his mistress. She's a Russian émigré, claims to be royal but nobody believes her. She probably comes from the gutters of St. Petersburg.'

'Or she isn't even Russian, and she comes from the gutters of Paris,' Coco added.

'Why did you call him an odious little man?' I asked.

'Because he wanted Max to go into a joint venture with him building racing cars. Max said he wouldn't trust him an inch. All he wanted to do was to look at Max's designs and then steal them for his own cars.'

'So you don't mix with him socially?'

Mummy sighed. 'Darling, this is the Riviera. Sooner or later you wind up at the same party as everyone else. And one always bumps into everyone one knows at the casino. Speaking of which, we have to send someone for your things and we'll take you with us to the casino tonight.'

'No, you will not,' Coco said firmly. 'She is not to appear in public before she has modeled my creation at my soirée. I want to create a stunning surprise with her.'

'You might well do that, when she falls off the catwalk and lands in the lap of the nearest dowager duchess,' Mummy said.

'Do not pay attention to your mother,' Coco said. 'I have faith in you. When I have finished training you, nobody will know you are not a professional. Come, we go to work now.'

'Where should I send Franz to pick up your clothes, darling?' Mummy asked.

'I'd better go in person,' I said. 'It wouldn't be polite just to have someone grab my clothes and vanish with them.'

'It didn't sound to me as if they'd been ultrapolite to you.'

'No, but as Nanny always said, a mark of true breeding is treating everyone with respect. Besides, I shall enjoy seeing their faces when they find out I'm going to be staying with Coco Chanel.'

Mummy laughed melodiously. 'See? I knew there was something of me in you after all.'

The outfit Chanel expected me to wear was hanging from a rail. It looked very strange to my eyes – the tweed so tweedy, the blouse so lacy and the pants so chic and elegant. I put it on and stared at myself in the mirror.

'Formidable,' Coco said, nodding as if very pleased with what she saw. 'What did I tell you, Vera?'

'You're going to wow them, old thing,' Vera agreed.

'Is there supposed to be a necklace?' I put my hand up to my bare neck.

'There is. One of the queen's, which at this moment is residing safely in the bank vault,' Vera said. 'I'll collect it right before the event and have two stout gendarmes to accompany me and keep an eye on it. I promised Her Majesty that I wouldn't take any chances.'

'But it will be the crowning touch. You will see,' Coco added. 'But we need shoes. They must be very high. Do you have any high-heeled wedges?'

'I don't really wear high heels. I'm so tall.'

'Definitely high heels,' Coco said. 'Vera, you must go and buy her a pair this instant. What size?'

'English size seven,' I said, wincing, because I do have big feet.

Vera departed. Coco clapped her hands. 'Now off with the clothes and we get to work.'

The shoes arrived – the heels very high. I staggered around like a person on stilts. 'No, like this!' Coco commanded. 'Again. Glide, not stomp.'

After a grueling two hours of working with Chanel, practicing my walking and turns, I finally headed back to the Villa Gloriosa in a taxicab. I thought they would be glad to see the back of me, but both Fig and Ducky seemed seriously put out. 'Well, that's gratitude for you,' Fig said, glancing at her sister.

'But there wasn't room for me here,' I said. 'I couldn't go on camping out in the library.'

'But Maude was so looking forward to your sharing her room. She actually moved her dolls, all by herself. And she was looking forward to your French lessons too.'

I suspected that Maude was only looking forward to sharing her room with me so that she could boss me around. 'I'm sure I can come to visit and give the children an occasional French lesson,' I said, 'but I might suggest that Nice is full of French people who would be more useful at teaching French than I. Besides, my mother looks forward to spending time with me.'

'Is it wise to stay with your mother?' Fig asked. 'I mean, she does have a reputation.'

'Well earned,' I replied with a smile. 'And anyway, I need to be on hand to work with Coco Chanel.'

'Chanel is staying with your mother?' The two women exchanged looks of pure venom.

'One of her best clients, I understand,' I said. I was actually enjoying myself for the first time in ages.

'It just shows you that virtue doesn't pay,' Ducky said. 'You and I have been faithful wives and mothers while Georgie's mother has had a string of men – usually someone else's husband – and she winds up with her own villa and the money to afford Chanel, while we have ten-year-old tweeds.'

'Ah, but she's stunningly good-looking,' I said. 'And she was a great actress too.'

They had no answer to this one, so I bundled Queenie and my clothes into a taxi and left the Villa Gloriosa, for good, I sincerely hoped.

# Chapter 12

*January 25, 1933*
*At Villa Marguerite. Much more glorious than the*
*Gloriosa. Divine, in fact. Good food, sun – at least there*
*would be sun if Madame Chanel were not working me*
*every second.*

The next two days I was drilled by Coco Chanel over and
over again and eventually I began to believe that I could
actually do this.

'You see,' she said. 'You are turning into an elegant
woman before my eyes. All it took was a little molding.
You will dazzle them tonight. Now go and rest.'

'I was thinking of going down to the beach for a swim,'
I said. 'How do I get down from here?'

'I understand that is Sir Toby's private beach,' Coco
said, 'so you should not go there. If we wish to swim we
must do so from the rocks. And I do not wish you to risk
injuring yourself before my soirée. Besides, the ocean is
too cold.'

As soon as she had gone I went into the grounds. I was

not about to obey her; I was dying for a swim. It had also occurred to me that meeting Sir Toby by accident on my way down to the beach – which of course I didn't realize was private – would be my only chance to get into that villa. I put on my bathing suit – a hopelessly girlish and unflattering garment of sagging black wool – then my stoutest sandals and made my way to the back of the property where the tamed gardens gave way to rocky cliffs. I'd spent my life climbing and clambering over rocks in Scotland so I was able to pick an easy route downward. Of course the mountains in Scotland are granite, which doesn't crumble. Here the cliffs were sandstone, which does. I put my foot on a rocky outcrop, which promptly gave way, and I found myself slithering down ungracefully. I came to a halt in the bushes by Sir Toby's pool. The villa stood right behind it, French doors open. This wasn't a good idea – it smacked of trespassing and would not put me in Sir Toby's good books. I might even find myself shot at or attacked by guard dogs.

I was looking for a way to climb back up to safety when I heard voices – raised voices. At first I couldn't make out words but they were having a good old fight. Then they came closer.

'You bastard!' a woman's voice screamed.

'Do you think I'm stupid, you little tramp?' a man's deep voice responded.

Then the woman stepped out onto the terrace and turned to glare into the house. 'You will regret this, I promise you. Olga does not forgive or forget.' She waved a fist, as if in a curse. Then she snatched up a bag she had left lying on a table and stalked away. This was no time to meet Sir Toby. I made my way back up the cliff.

When I got to my room I was met by an excited Queenie.

'Cor, miss. Did you hear that? A right going-on down there, weren't it? Going at it hammer and tongs. They was using words no lady or gentleman ought to use. It was just like the pictures – or outside the Three Bells on a Saturday night.'

'That just shows you that money does not make breeding, Queenie,' I said.

I tried to rest, but I was too keyed up. Now that I had time to worry, I was picturing all the things that could go wrong at tonight's affair. I didn't want to make a spectacle of myself. I must have been insane to have agreed to parade up and down in front of a crowd of rich and famous people. Why on earth had I agreed? Wanting to meet Sir Toby was only half of the explanation. Coco Chanel had such a forceful personality that it was hard to say no to her.

Late that afternoon we took a taxi into town. I found that the event was to take place at the casino on the pier.

'We'll drop you off at the Negresco while Vera and I go to check that my models have arrived safely from Paris,' Coco said. 'Have some tea. We will come for you to rehearse when we are ready.'

I was glad to know that the rest of the collection would be modeled by girls who knew what they were doing, even if they would show me up as a hopeless amateur. As we came into the hotel foyer an elegant, gaunt and obviously well-bred woman was standing at the reception desk, hands on hips.

'That's the best room you have?' she was asking in strident English.

'*Oui*, my lady. The hotel is full because of the fashion show tonight. People have come from all over the Riviera.'

'Well, I suppose it will have to do for now,' she said, flinging the end of a mink stole angrily over her shoulder. 'And I don't want my husband to know that I am here, is that clear? He is not to be told.'

'Of course, Lady Groper.'

I observed her with interest. So that was the absent wife. I wondered if Sir Toby had been tipped off to her arrival and thus had thrown out his mistress. If she was staying here, and she came in to take tea, maybe I would have a chance to strike up an acquaintanceship with her and thus gain access to the villa. But I had no time for scheming now. My heart was already thumping with anticipation.

Tea was brought to me in the paneled bar just off the foyer. I sat and sipped, trying to stay calm and observing the elegant people who passed. So many people with so much money. Were we really in a depression? When Vera arrived to collect me, we passed another woman standing at the reception counter, also speaking English but with an American drawl this time.

'Yes, I know I told you we wanted the room for a month,' she snapped, 'but I've changed my mind. We've been invited to go cruising on a friend's yacht and we'll be leaving in the morning.' I recognized her instantly, even with her back to me. It was Mrs Simpson.

'What?' she asked, as the reception clerk must have murmured something. 'No, I do not intend to pay for a room I won't be using. Ridiculous. You're lucky that I put this place on the map by staying here in the first place.'

With that she turned to sweep away and saw me. 'Good

God, it's the actress's daughter,' she said. 'I shouldn't have thought the Negresco was your style, honey. What are you doing here?'

'Actually, I'm staying with my mother at her villa,' I said evenly, not prepared to let her rile me this time.

'Ah, so that's it. Mummy's finally bringing you out into society, is she? About time. But she'd better keep a close eye on you here. There's no stiff upper lip when the British are abroad.' She gave a dry chuckle. 'Incidentally, I saw your mother at the casino last night, but minus the German beau. Is that affair finally passé?'

'Not at all. He's busy working in Germany and my mother needed sunshine, as simple as that.'

Mrs Simpson was still giving me that patronizing smile I found so annoying. 'It's never as simple as that, honey. I'd like to bet she has her eye on another man.'

'You would know about those things more than I,' I said. 'Will your husband be going on your cruise with your friend?'

'Of course. I like to keep my men where I can see them.' She laughed as she walked past me and up the staircase, trailing her fur coat behind her. I turned away to join Vera, who was waiting for me at the doorway.

'So you've met our famous American, I see. She's quite a character, isn't she?' She waved to Mrs Simpson and smiled.

'You like her?'

'I find her amusing. She's part of my set, and she wears Chanel suits. I don't think "like" comes into it,' Vera said. 'Come on. Coco's ready for us.'

I made a mental note to find out if that friend Mrs Simpson had mentioned really was the Prince of Wales, and whether her husband was going to accompany her on the yacht. Then I had no time for any thoughts.

I was led across the boulevard and onto the pier. It was designed very much in the style of piers at home – an ornate domed iron-framed building in the Middle Eastern style with lots of minarets. As we stepped inside the foyer the last rays of evening sun were shining through the glass dome above our heads, bathing the scene with an unreal pink glow. Vera walked briskly ahead across the foyer and through an arched doorway. One of the two long casino rooms had been cleared of gaming tables and a catwalk had been erected down its center. Around it were rows of gilt chairs. This room had a normal ceiling from which several impressive chandeliers hung. At one end curtains were draped around a doorway. We passed through these to find ourselves in a dressing room. The real models had arrived from Paris and were already occupying the room – tall thin girls with pouty red lips and black Marcel waved hair, with names like Chou-Chou and Frou-Frou and Zou-Zou. They eyed me with amusement and talked about me behind their hands, never once thinking that I understood French rather well.

One look at them and it was obvious that I'd stick out like a sore thumb. But I couldn't back out now. Chanel put us through a final rehearsal. The other girls strutted out, hips thrust forward and shoulders swinging, managing to look sexy and glamorous in whatever Chanel made them wear. My turn came and I managed to walk up and down the catwalk. But my feet felt like lead and I was sure I looked like an unsteady, ungraceful schoolgirl. The behind-the-hand giggles from the other models seemed to indicate that my suspicion was right.

A light meal was served to us in a gloomy back room, but I was too nervous to eat. Then it was time to go back to the dressing room, where an elderly Frenchwoman waited to boss us around. Make-up was applied to my face – unfamiliar red lips and kohl-outlined eyes. My hair was styled with a curling iron. I was helped into my outfit. From beyond the door I could hear the buzz of conversation, the chink of glasses and in the background a piano playing. Vera came in carrying a leather jewelry case. We caught a glimpse of a large gendarme, whom Vera motioned to stay at the door.

'Here we are. The famous necklace,' she said. She opened the case. It was stunning. Several rows of perfect pearls, interspersed with clusters of diamonds and teardrop diamonds hanging down at intervals. She made me turn around so that she could put it on me. It felt cold and heavy on my neck. I glanced in the mirror and reacted with surprise. The choker made me look haughty and – well – regal. I noticed the other models staring at me, as if they'd noticed who I really was for the first time. Now I knew exactly how Cinderella felt when she put on that glass slipper and it fit!

Coco went past the curtains that had been rigged at the doorway and we heard thunderous applause. We couldn't hear the words of her speech but then someone hissed in French, 'Zou-Zou, ready, go.' And the first model strutted out of the room to be met with a burst of applause. She was followed by Frou-Frou and Nou-Nou and the others. They reappeared and changed with lightning speed before going out again. My turn was coming closer and closer. I found that I couldn't breathe.

*'Allez, allez,'* an elderly Frenchwoman hissed in my ear

and pushed me toward the doorway. I stepped out and was blinded by spotlights shining on me and the crackling of flashbulbs from press cameras.

'And for my pièce de résistance I give you the royal look, as modeled by a member of England's ruling family, Lady Georgiana Rannoch,' Chanel announced.

There was a gasp, and then applause. The catwalk stretched into darkness, looking about a mile long. I was conscious of upturned faces, sparkling jewels, champagne glasses. I forced one foot in front of the other, trying to walk as I had been taught. I was going to do this. I had done harder things in my life. I was not going to stumble. Step followed step. I was going to get through it.

Then, suddenly, my foot wouldn't move, as if something was holding it fast to the floor. I felt myself pitching forward, stumbling, trying to right myself. I might have done so, but I had reached the end of the runway. Flashbulbs went off in my face, blinding me. I vaguely heard gasps of horror as I staggered, then pitched forward into blackness. There were screams and shouts of alarm. I braced myself for the moment when I hit the ground. Instead I landed on something soft. There was a grunt, then an exclamation in what sounded like Russian. I opened my eyes and looked up to find that I really had done what my mother had predicted. I had landed in the lap of a large dowager.

Hands grabbed at me.

'Easy on. You'll be all right.' A young man took hold of me and yanked me off the poor woman's lap. She was now protesting loudly in Russian and fanning herself.

Faces came into focus in the darkness.

'I say, Georgie, are you hurt?' I was mortified to see it

was the Prince of Wales. He took my hand, helping me to right myself.

More flashbulbs popped and the smell of sulfur hung in the air.

'She is in shock, the little one,' said another male voice, and again I was more than mortified to see it was the handsome Marquis de Ronchard, pushing past other people to be at my side. 'A chair and some brandy. Quickly.'

'Lights. Lights!' someone else shouted and the big chandeliers thrust the room into brightness. I was led away from the catwalk, mumbling apologies to the fat dowager and the world in general.

'Whoever thought that kid could be a model needs their head examined,' I heard Mrs Simpson's voice say from close by. 'She's about as graceful as a drunken giraffe.' And she gave that brittle laugh.

'Pay no attention to that awful woman,' my mother said as she pushed past to reach me. 'She's just jealous because you're young and nubile and she's old and dried up.' She made sure that lovely voice projected so that Mrs Simpson would hear. 'Darling – are you all right?' Then she leaned closer to me. 'Don't say I didn't warn you.'

'I don't know what happened,' I said as Chanel hurried over to us. 'It was as if my foot caught on something. One moment I was going forward, the next I couldn't move.'

'But the runway is smooth, you see.' Chanel turned back to examine it.

'Maybe she caught her trouser leg in her shoes,' Mummy suggested. 'She did say she wasn't used to wearing high heels.'

'Not possible,' Chanel said. 'The trousers are not wide enough.'

'You don't know Georgie,' my mother said. 'Many things are possible for her. Here, darling. The kind gentleman has brought you a chair. Sit down.'

I sat. Someone thrust a glass of brandy into my hands. I sipped, coughed and sipped again.

'Are you unhurt?' Coco asked.

'I think so. I may have scratched my cheek on that lady's jewelry.' I put my hand up to my face then ran it down to my neck. 'The necklace!' I cried. 'It's gone.'

# Chapter 13

*The casino on the pier, Nice*
*January 25, 1933*
*Dying of embarrassment. Why did I agree to do this? I knew it would go wrong.*

'Shut the doors,' Vera's voice rang out. 'Nobody is to leave the room. A valuable necklace Lady Georgiana was wearing is missing.'

A horrified whisper went through the crowd, which was the biggest display of alarm one would expect from an aristocratic gathering.

'You're not suggesting one of us might have stolen it,' a woman's voice demanded from the back of the room.

'It must have come off when she fell,' someone else said. 'Come on, chaps. Let's get down and search the floor.'

Tuxedo-clad men got down on their hands and knees and were soon searching diligently. The poor dowager on whom I had landed was assisted to her feet and led to a safer location, still fanning herself. Soon everyone around was involved in the search. Even women in their evening finery were crawling around on all fours between the rows of chairs. If it hadn't been so horribly serious, it would have been funny. But the necklace was not found.

'Did it fall somewhere inside her clothing?' someone else suggested.

I felt my pockets and inside my blouse, then shook my head.

'I'm sorry to say this,' Vera announced, 'but I have sent one of the gendarmes to summon his superior. Everyone will have to be searched.'

'This is an outrage!' Mrs Simpson said. 'There are some very important people in this room. Obviously they haven't taken a stupid necklace. Try searching the hired help.'

'There were no waiters near the stage when she fell,' someone else pointed out.

'My wife is feeling faint. She needs fresh air,' a distinguished, military-looking man complained.

'I'm sorry, but nobody is to leave,' Vera said firmly.

She had now brought in one of the gendarmes to help her guard the door. 'I ask for a little patience,' she said. 'This necklace must be found. It is extremely valuable.'

Again a whisper went through the crowd. I was sitting on the chair, sipping my brandy, trying to recollect exactly what had happened. Had I felt anyone touching the necklace? I was fairly sure I hadn't. Surely I would have noticed hands at the back of my neck. But then, I was rather shocked at the time. It was suggested that the necklace could have somehow rolled under the catwalk, in spite of the heavy velvet drapes around it. A couple of young men obligingly held up the drape while the waiters were instructed to crawl beneath it. But they came out empty-handed.

'The necklace must be somewhere in this room,' Chanel said, pacing up and down past me. 'We would have noticed if anyone had opened a door after you fell. We would have seen the light coming from outside.'

'I don't know how I fell,' I said. I got up and made my way back to the catwalk. The surface was smooth wood. I couldn't see any bumps or nails sticking up or any kind of projection. I was forced to admit that my well-known clumsiness had caused this. I should never have agreed to model the clothes. I had only myself to blame. People in the salon were getting progressively more annoyed. Mutterings turned to mumblings to raised voices. Just when it looked as if there might be a mutiny and they might force their way out, the doors were flung open and a little man stood there. He had an impressive black mustache out of all proportion to his size and he stood surveying the crowd with an air of distaste.

'Nobody is to move,' he said in heavily accented English. 'I am Inspector Lafite of the Nice Police. I understand that a robbery has happened here.' (Actually he said 'a rubbery 'as 'appened 'ere.') 'But 'ave no fear. I shall find the culprit and bring 'im to justice.'

'This is ridiculous,' one of the bejeweled ladies said, fanning herself with her program. 'We're English aristocracy, not Continentals. We don't go around stealing things.'

The crowd parted as Inspector Lafite strode through the crowd until he reached the catwalk. 'You Engleesh,' he said, looking around us with scorn, 'you think you can come here to France and behave badly. You think we French have no laws, do you not? You mistake yourselves. But I tell you, the police in France are not easily outfoxed. Now, please describe the missing item to me.'

'It was a choker,' Vera said.

'A joker? The joker stole this item as a joke?'

'No, the item was a choker.'

'You think you can mock Inspector Lafite?' he demanded.

'I'm not mocking, you silly man,' Vera said in an exasperated voice. 'I'm describing the stolen piece of jewelry.'

'Ah, so you admit it was jewelry.'

'A choker. A necklace that is worn up around the neck.'

'A necklace. Why didn't you say so? From whom was the necklace stolen?'

'I was wearing it,' I said, 'but it didn't belong to me.'

He walked up to me until he was standing a few inches away. He was about four inches shorter than I so he had to stare up into my face. 'And your name is?'

'Lady Georgiana Rannoch,' I said.

'Ah. An English lady. But you wear jewels that do not belong to you?'

'I was a model in Madame Chanel's fashion show,' I said. 'The necklace was part of my outfit.'

'A valuable necklace?'

'Very valuable,' Vera said.

'It belongs to you, *Madame*?'

'No, to a very important English royal person. I am not at liberty to divulge her name, but the piece is priceless. I was taking every possible precaution with it – it was locked in the bank until it was needed for tonight's show. Two of your gendarmes escorted me to the hotel and stood guard outside the doors. Nobody could have come in or out without their noticing.'

'Then–' Inspector Lafite paused dramatically. 'It must still be in this room. Have you searched the room?'

'Of course.'

The inspector turned back to me. 'Did you feel a thief removing this necklace from your person?'

'No,' I said. 'I tripped and fell and when I got up, the necklace was missing.'

'Ah. You fell to the floor?'

'No, I landed on that lady over there.' I pointed to the large Russian.

'Then it is possible that the necklace came off and is concealed somewhere about the person of *Madame*,' he said, regarding the lady's large bosom.

A slim older woman with aristocratically high cheekbones and iron gray hair stepped between the inspector and the Russian lady. 'This is the Princess Theodora Fedorova,' she said in such a commanding voice that the inspector was stopped in his tracks. 'Related to the late czar. You are not about to search her. She would have noticed if the necklace had lodged somewhere on her body.' And she directed her gaze at the princess's impressive cleavage. Her accent was charmingly French but she spoke in English.

'You witnessed this fall, *Madame*?' the inspector asked in his own language.

'Of course. I was seated beside Her Highness.'

'And may one ask your name?'

'You may. I am the Princess Marie Bourbon de la Fountaine-O'Day, related to the kings of France. Princess Theodora stays at my residence in Paris. We have just arrived here in Nice for our health. The princess has been stricken with rheumatics recently and the physician prescribed a climate that was less damp. Paris can be rather damp in winter, as I'm sure you know.'

The inspector wanted to interrupt before she told their entire life stories, but her demeanor was so regal that he waited, shifting uncomfortably, until she took a breath.

'Highness, would you be gracious enough to tell me what you saw?' he asked finally in French.

'I saw the young lady stumble. She tried to right herself but flashbulbs went off and must have blinded her. She was not able to save herself before she tumbled off the end of the runway. The Princess Theodora was sitting immediately below the runway and the young lady landed on top of her. I stood up to help but a young man came to her aid.'

'Where is this young man who came to the assistance of Lady Rannoch?' the inspector asked in English, turning to the assembled crowd.

Nobody came forward.

'Do you see this man in the room?' the inspector asked.

The princess looked around. 'I don't think so, but in truth I was concentrating more on my poor friend who was suffering from the arrival of Lady Georgiana on top of her.'

The inspector turned to me. 'Can you describe the young man for us?'

'I don't think I really saw him,' I said. 'He was helping me up from behind when other men came to assist him.'

'Ah, a gang at work. I knew it,' the inspector said.

'On the contrary,' I replied. 'One of the men was my cousin, the Prince of Wales, and the other was the Marquis de Ronchard.'

'My apologies. Your Royal Highness. Marquis.' The inspector gave a groveling bow to each in turn. 'How good of you to come to this young lady's assistance.'

The two men mumbled, 'Not at all,' almost in unison. I was still in such a state of shock that I found this funny and had to stifle a giggle. This did not go unnoticed by the inspector. He stared at me, frowning. 'I am wondering if this was not some kind of clever scheme among you Engleesh, maybe to collect the insurance on this piece. A mysterious young man who is no longer in the room – I ask myself, does he really exist? Where do you think he could have gone?'

'He can't have left the room,' Vera said. 'The doors were closed and the only way out was past that curtain into the models' dressing room. They would have seen if anybody tried to escape that way.'

'This young man – he was English?'

'Oh, yes,' I said. 'His voice sounded very English.'

'You hear that, LeClerc?' the inspector barked to one of his men. 'You are to search for a young Englishman. Go through those curtains to the models' dressing room. See if a young Englishman escaped that way.'

The young gendarme went through the curtains, only to be greeted by screams. Obviously the models were still changing. He returned, red-faced, a few seconds later.

'They have seen nobody, Inspector.'

The inspector sighed. 'Then I have the unpleasant task of asking my men to search each person in this room before you are permitted to leave.'

This created an uproar.

'Absolute outrage,' a man spluttered. 'You're not putting your hands on my wife.'

'Besides, we were nowhere near the place where this theft took place,' another man complained.

'This young man could have passed the stolen jewelry

to an accomplice,' Inspector Lafite said. 'Everyone in this room is a suspect until proven innocent. You will please line up.'

'Only the men, surely,' someone said. 'The ladies are wearing evening gowns. They hardly have anywhere to conceal a stolen necklace.'

'I presume they bring evening purses with them. Ladies go nowhere without the comb and the powder compact, do they not? And they could even hide it up their skirts.'

'Nobody is going to look up my skirt,' a large woman said fiercely.

'Really, this is all too silly,' Mrs Simpson said, moving closer to the prince and slipping her arm through his. 'Why don't we go to the bar for a drink until this is all over.'

'No, Wallis, we have to set an example,' the Prince of Wales said. 'We should do all we can to help. Here, Inspector, you can search us first, if you like.'

Reluctantly the other people in the room lined up to be searched. One thing we British do well is to join a queue. I allowed myself to be inspected, then I went over to the two elderly princesses. 'I'm so sorry, Your Highness,' I said in French. 'I do hope I did not hurt you.'

'Fortunately you do not weigh much,' the Russian princess said in slow, even French. 'It was more shock than harm.'

Princess Marie took my hand and patted it. 'What a distressing thing to have happened, *ma petite.* I knew your dear grandmother well. We were childhood playmates. And your dear great-grandmother – *mon Dieu*, but she was a terrifying woman. So small but so powerful. I was always struck dumb in her presence.'

'I never met either of them,' I said. 'My only grandparent still alive is my mother's father.'

'He was an English nobleman, I presume, because I believe I am acquainted with all those in the *Almanach de Gotha*.'

'He's a former London policeman.'

'A policeman? You mean a commoner?' If she had been wearing a lorgnette she would have raised it and peered at me.

I nodded. 'My father married an actress.'

'Your father always was such a silly boy.' She shook her head. 'But who am I to criticize – I who married an Irishman.'

Even in my current state of shock this comment registered. 'You did?'

'A big mistake, as my family told me. But I was twenty-one. I had my own fortune. My husband was of noble family – so charming and handsome, but an absolute scoundrel. He went through my money then ran off with an American heiress. So let that be a lesson to you, my dear. Stay away from Irishmen.'

After everything else that had just happened, I felt as if I might disgrace myself and cry. I fought to keep my face calm and I smiled. 'I'll remember,' I said.

The line of those to be searched had dwindled and the room emptied. Coco Chanel came up to me. 'Come, *ma petite*. Let us go.'

'Go where?'

'Across the hall to the casino where I hold a party to celebrate.'

'Celebrate?' I said. 'I ruined your lovely collection. I allowed the necklace to be stolen.'

'Nonsense,' she said, waving her cigarette at me. 'I love sensations. Now everyone will remember this forever. We will make the front page of tomorrow's newspapers. The whole world will see my new design.'

I glanced across at her. I had heard that she was an ambitious and ruthless woman. Was it possible that she arranged for my accident? Or at least that she took me as a model because there was a good chance I would fail and thus give her publicity?

'But what about the queen's choker?' I asked. 'I feel terrible about it.'

Coco shrugged. 'What can we do? It is now in the hands of the police, although judging from that sad little man, I do not have much hope. So we have no choice but to forget about it for the present and go to the casino.'

I winced. I felt I should be doing something personally to recover the necklace, but I had no idea what that might be. Then I decided that most of the guests from this event would be at the party at the casino and it would be a good opportunity to observe them and thus rule out those who could not be suspects.

'I'll go and change,' I said.

Coco put her hand on my arm to stop me. 'But no. Continue to wear the ensemble, I beg you – you will cause heads to turn at the casino and everyone will know you as chic.'

I wasn't so sure that a man's tweed jacket and lace blouse really made me look elegant, but I supposed that anything Coco did would be counted as chic. 'I must take these shoes off, though,' I said. 'They are hurting me. I think Vera bought them one size too small.'

'If you must, you must.' Coco shrugged.

We went through to the changing room. For some reason I found it hard to walk and almost stumbled again. When I took off my shoes, I noticed something. One of the soles looked as if it had a darker patch on it – as if I had stepped in something. I touched it dubiously. The outer layer was smooth but there were places where that outer layer had worn away, exposing an inner layer of substance that was tacky. Incredibly tacky. I had been set up to stumble and trip. And cleverly too. Someone had painted a substance on the sole of my shoe – some kind of glue, and maybe a varnish over it. The first few steps would have been fine but as the outer hard layer was breached, then the tacky substance would have rooted me to the floor. It seemed more and more likely that someone knew I'd be wearing the queen's necklace tonight and had planned a very clever robbery.

# Chapter 14

***Still January 25 and still at the casino***
***Wishing I could be somewhere else.***

I really didn't want to go to the casino. Frankly I wanted
to go home and straight to bed. I never wanted to face any
of these people again. But Coco was insistent. 'You think
this is a big thing, but I say it is a trifle. If this is the worst
thing that happens to you in your life, then you are lucky.
I had to suffer the death of the man I loved. That was so
painful that anything else since means nothing.'

Of course my thoughts went instantly to that image of
Darcy on the beach holding hands with a child and smiling down at the woman with long dark hair. Chanel was
right. Nothing could be as painful as that. I put on more
comfortable shoes, wrapping the high-heeled wedges with
the tacky sole carefully in the suitcase I had brought with
me. Then I toned down my stage make-up and we joined
Vera, who was waiting for us at the doorway.

'Your mother went on ahead. She said she'd open the
champagne.'

'I really don't see how we can drink champagne when we have lost the queen's necklace,' I said. 'She will be furious. You know how she prizes her possessions.'

Vera nodded. 'I know. I feel rotten, knowing I've let her down when I promised her so faithfully that I'd take care of her jewels. I still don't see how anyone can have taken the damned thing. It must have been someone supernatural who vanished into thin air.'

'Or a very clever professional thief,' Coco said.

'I feel I should be doing something, but I have no idea what,' Vera said. 'I have no confidence in that inspector. The man appears to be a bumbling fool. Do you not know anyone in the Sûreté in Paris, Coco? Someone we could ask to come down and take over this delicate matter with as little scandal as possible?'

Coco shrugged. 'Yes, I have friends at the Sûreté, but they can't just come and take over,' she said. 'It is like your Scotland Yard. They have to be invited by the local police and I do not think this little man would welcome outside interference, do you?'

'Then we must try to recover the necklace ourselves,' Vera said. 'Keep your eyes and ears open, Georgiana. Someone must have seen something pertinent when you fell.'

'I'm afraid they were looking more at the spectacle of me sprawled over the poor Russian princess and then the Prince of Wales helping me to my feet. But I will keep my ears open for the young man who disappeared. I know what he sounded like even though I only have the vaguest impression of what he looked like.'

Coco went ahead across the hall and into the casino. Chandeliers sparkled in the glass dome above. The place was already packed and the panic I always feel in crowds rose up in my throat. It was so elegant and so glittering – quite unlike the dreary world I usually lived in. Coco pushed us through the crowd to find my mother and the champagne. As soon as I spotted her, I saw the reason for her early departure. She was standing with the Marquis de Ronchard, looking up at him with an entranced expression on her face. I had seen that expression before. It might have seemed soft and feminine, but it was really the expression of a tigress on the prowl. Few men could resist my mother.

I felt a stab of annoyance. I didn't really want the marquis to like me, did I? But it was galling to know that Mummy had instant sex appeal that always seemed to work, while I had inherited none of it. At that moment the marquis turned and saw me. His eyes lit up. 'Ah, *ma chérie*. You have come. I hoped you would. You are putting on the brave face. So English.' He came over to me and took my arm. 'Have you recovered from your ordeal? Come, let us find the champagne.' He led me up to the bar and snapped his fingers. Champagne was produced and poured.

'I know we have not been formally introduced and as a British noble lady you obviously find this reprehensible,' he said, not taking his eyes off me, 'but we have been thrown together in so many different situations that I feel we already know each other. My first name is Jean-Paul, and yours, I gather, is Georgiana. I hope you will treat me as an old chum.'

I looked up at him and laughed. 'I don't see you as the type of man who would be a chum to anyone, especially not to a woman.'

'Ah, very astute of you. Wise as well as charming,' he said. 'You and I will get along famously.'

At this point my mother coughed and held out her empty champagne glass to be refilled.

'And do you know this delightful lady?' Jean-Paul asked me, indicating my mother.

Mummy shot me a look that said quite clearly *Do not tell him that I'm your mother.* I weighed up whether to ignore the look, then decided she might throw me out of her villa. I certainly didn't want to return to the Villa Gloriosa.

'Yes, I know her well,' I said.

'She is delightful, is she not? So ravishing. So witty.'

'Isn't she,' I replied, 'and so generous too. She's treating me to a lovely time at her villa and she's promised to buy me a Chanel dinner gown.'

'But of course. Your figure is made for Chanel. The boyish look. No curves at all. I find it delightfully fresh.' And he looked at me in a way that made me feel quite strange. It was almost as if he were making love to me with his eyes. 'When you have decided on the gown, I will take you out to dine and dance in it. It will be a christening ceremony, no?'

'We probably won't choose a gown for her until we get back to Paris,' Mummy said in a clipped voice. 'Chanel does not carry around suitcases of her clothes, you know.'

'She can design a dress for you right here, I am sure, if you ask her nicely,' the marquis said. 'I know of a good little seamstress who can run it up for her in an instant. Where is Coco? Ah, over there. I shall go and arrange the whole thing for you.'

And he went. Mummy looked at me half angrily, half

admiringly. 'I must say, you pulled off that little stunt rather well, didn't you?'

'I didn't tell him you were my mother,' I reminded her. 'My silence can be bought.'

'You've grown up,' she said. 'That Darcy O'Mara obviously taught you a thing or two.' Then she laughed. 'Still, you are more fun this way. I was worried for a while that you'd turn out to be boring. And I rather believe the gentleman is interested in you.'

'Do you think so?'

'Darling, he was positively undressing you with his eyes. But beware. He's not an Englishman. He'll have you into bed before you know what's happening to you.'

'Is that what you hoped would happen to you?' I asked.

'You are becoming very cheeky,' she said, but she laughed again. Then she sighed. 'I must admit that a little fling might add some spice to my dreary little life. I do sometimes long for someone with a little more joie de vivre than Max. He can be so boring out of the bedroom.'

'The fact that you don't speak German and he doesn't speak much English hardly makes for witty conversation.'

The casino was becoming more and more crowded. People came up to me to inquire about my health, to offer commiserations on my accident and to speculate about the missing necklace. I began to feel uncomfortable, almost claustrophobic, so I eased myself through the crowd until I was standing among the potted palms by the wall. The room was packed with elegant and rich people, all of whom appeared to know each other and were chatting away merrily. I looked longingly at the entrance and wondered if I could slip away. What was I doing here? I didn't belong among these people. The problem was that I didn't know where I wanted to be. Certainly not at home in Scotland, and not trying to fend for myself in London either. It struck me that I hadn't yet found my niche in life.

At that moment a couple approached me. At first I thought they were a romantic couple, moving into the shadows among the palms to be alone. But then the woman turned to the man and said, 'How dare you.' She almost hissed the words. 'You're a swine, Toby.'

And I saw that it was indeed Sir Toby Groper, and Lady Groper with him. Had she discovered the mistress, I wondered. I hastily ducked back into the alcove, shielded by a potted palm tree.

Sir Toby turned back to her and I saw that he was grinning. 'Haven't you heard the old saying, what's good for the goose is good for the gander?' he said. 'If you want a divorce, my dear, and you're trying to cite my bad behavior, did you not think I'd send out feelers to uncover yours? And yours is so much more delicious. Everyone expects a man to have a showgirl mistress – but a cabinet member? I could bring down the government if I wanted to.'

'You wouldn't dare.'

'Oh, I dare most things,' he said. 'I've dared all my life, which is why I'm where I am today. So do your worst, Margaret, my dear. I love a good scrap.'

'One day you'll go too far, Toby,' Lady Groper snapped. And she pushed her way through the crowd to the exit. Sir Toby watched her go with that same amused expression on his face. Then he forced his way up to the bar. 'Whiskey,' he barked, 'and make it a double.'

I was about to move out of my hiding place when I touched something warm. I gasped and looked around. It appeared I was not alone. A tall, rangy young man with hair flopping boyishly over his forehead was flattened against the wall behind the potted palm. He put his fingers to his lips as Sir Toby walked away, then heaved a sigh of relief.

'Phew, that was close,' he said. 'I didn't want them to see me. There would have been the most frightful stink.'

I recognized his voice. 'You were the one who helped me up when I fell,' I said. 'And then you vanished.'

He nodded. 'When they announced that a necklace had been stolen and the burly policeman made his entrance. I thought it was about time I did a bunk, rather than answer annoying questions.'

'But how did you get out of the room?'

'Easy enough. Everyone was watching you. As that large gendarme stepped through the door, I slipped out behind him. I'm rather good at doing that sort of thing.'

I eyed him suspiciously. 'Then you took the necklace.'

He grinned. 'I'd hardly be likely to confess if I did, would I?'

'Then why did you try to escape, if you didn't?'

'The answer to that is simple, old bean. Didn't want the dear old mater and pater to know I'm here.' He held out his hand. 'I'm Bobby, by the way. Bobby Groper.'

'Then Sir Toby is your father?'

'Precisely. And that fierce dragon of a woman is the mater, Lady Margaret. I'm supposed to be up at Oxford, you see.'

'So what are you doing here?'

'What everyone else does on the Riviera. Enjoying some fun and sun.' His expression grew somber. 'Actually, I got sent down, but the old boy won't have heard about it yet. So I thought I'd come in person to soften the blow. Do some explaining, y'know. But then the mater showed up and all hell broke loose and I realized that this was not the right time to announce that his son and heir was in disgrace.' He paused, chewing his lip like a little boy. 'The old boy's rather hot on education and all that bosh. I say what's the point when one is going to inherit rather a lot of money one day, but that's not how he thinks. He still has the spirit of those dreadful factory-owning ancestors. You know – hard work, elbows to the grindstone, or whatever the saying is.'

'So you failed your exams, did you?'

'Not exactly.' He made a face again. 'Little matter of a forged check. It's all the pater's fault, you know. He keeps me so dashed short of ready cash that I was a bit strapped, and a fellow was rather twisting my arm to pay up some gambling debts – so, well, I only intended to borrow the money until I could cadge some more out of the old man, but the rotter reported me to the master.' He paused, looking at me thoughtfully. 'I say, you don't like roulette, do you?'

'I've never really tried.'

'It's frightfully fun. I could teach you.' He looked hopeful.

'I'm sure you could, but I have no cash to play with. I'm as broke as you are.'

'I say, that's damned bad luck. It's no joke being broke, is it? Especially when the old man is rolling in dough.' He sighed. 'Oh, well, it doesn't matter. I couldn't very well play tonight. Not with my father mooching around the place. I'll have to lie low until things calm down and Mama goes home in a huff. I expect someone will offer me a sofa to sleep on.' He gave a cheerful smile. 'Well, toodle pip. Good to meet you. Georgiana, isn't it?'

'Most people call me Georgie,' I said.

'Splendid. So if I manage to soften up the old man and he says all is forgiven and invites me to stay at the villa, then maybe you and I can go out for a night on the town, and I'll teach you to play roulette with his money.'

'We'll see,' I said, half laughing. There was something rather appealing about him. We moved out of the alcove. Bobby glanced around him before walking purposefully to the door. I watched him go, not quite sure about him. He seemed a typical likeable young Englishman, but the ease with which he had left that salon undetected indicated that he had done that sort of thing before. And also the forged check. . . . Then I realized that he had never tried to say that he didn't steal the necklace. Somebody took it, and he was the only one who successfully left the room before he could be searched.

# Chapter 15

## Still at the casino

I wondered if I could ask my mother to have her chauffeur take me home. I started to move back into the crush around the bar, looking for her, or Coco and Vera.

'I say, it's you. Are you all right?' Another young man stepped out to block my path. He looked familiar somehow and I realized I had seen him at Victoria Station when I was serving soup. 'You took a nasty tumble back there,' he said. 'No bones broken?'

'Only my pride,' I said. 'I felt like a complete fool.'

'Damned Frenchies,' he said. 'What's the betting there was a nail or something sticking out of that stage thing that made you trip. Can't build anything properly to save their lives, these foreigners. You should see the botched job they did on our villa roof. Least little wind and tiles rain down like confetti. Give me good old English workmanship any day.'

'And yet you come here for the winter,' I pointed out.

'Ah, well. They do know how to cook divinely,' he said.

*Rhys Bowen*

'And the wines . . . and the weather is decidedly better. I'm Neville, by the way.'

'Georgiana.'

We shook hands. I decided how pleasant it was not to have to go through the formalities of home. In England we would have had to wait to be introduced properly by a third party. Here we could be on a first-name basis.

'I thought you looked jolly pretty when I saw you before,' he went on.

'Really?' Was it possible he'd actually noticed me doling out soup? 'At Victoria Station, you mean?'

'No, here in Nice the other day,' he said. 'Remember you passed me on your bicycle and I called out to you and you smiled?'

'That wasn't me,' I said.

'Must have been. Looked the spitting image of you. Even the smile was the same.'

'But I don't own a bicycle.'

'Are you sure? It was on the road from our villa. I was walking my aunt's dog, remember.'

'No, it really wasn't me,' I said. 'I've only been here a couple of days. I walked along the seafront once, but that was it.'

'Well, I'm dashed,' he said. 'I could have sworn it was you. I don't usually forget pretty girls, you know. Well, no matter. We've met now. Come and have a drink.'

I allowed him to steer me back toward the bar. Two young men had shown interest in me in the space of a few minutes. Perhaps things were looking up after all. As I looked around while Neville ordered drinks, I saw a face I knew well. Belinda had just come into the room, wearing emerald silk pajamas with a halter top that only just managed to cover the important parts. Her face broke into a smile, she gave a delighted scream and she rushed toward me, arms open.

'Darling, it is you! You came after all. I thought I saw you yesterday and I called out your name but you couldn't have heard me because you didn't stop. But now you're here. How splendid. Where are you staying?'

'At my mother's villa. It's lovely – right on the cliffs overlooking the Med. And where are you? I asked at the Negresco but they said you hadn't been there.'

Belinda made a face. 'No, it was a little too pricey for me, given my current situation, so I had to opt for somewhere more humble. I'm at a little pension a couple of streets back from the Promenade.'

'So nobody's invited you to stay yet? You haven't tried the famous breaking-down routine?'

She frowned. 'I tried it once and the gentleman in question was kind enough to send his man out to fix my car. It only worked in Transylvania because we were miles from the nearest habitation.'

'I'd invite you to stay with me, but Mummy has other guests.'

'It's all right. I have my eye on a certain man. So far it's been slow going but I'm quite determined he's going to notice me.'

I moved closer to her. 'Who is he? Do tell.'

'Well, he's a Frenchman, darling, and absolutely gorgeous. And a marquis to boot.' She grabbed my arm. 'Ooh, there he is now. Look, over there. Coming toward us. Finally he remembers who I am.'

And there was the Marquis de Ronchard, coming toward us with an expectant smile on his face. Of course,

I thought. He's seen Belinda. And I felt a small stab of disappointment.

'Ah, there you are, you little minx,' he said to me. 'I have good news to report. Madame Chanel will be more than delighted to design a gown especially for you. What is more, it will be a present to thank you for participating in her fashion show.' He appeared to notice Belinda for the first time. 'And who is your charming friend? Please introduce us.'

'My best friend from school days, Belinda Warburton-Stoke,' I said. 'Belinda, may I present the Marquis de Ronchard.'

'*Enchanté*, mademoiselle,' he said as he took her hand and kissed it. 'Any friend of Lady Georgiana's is a friend of mine.'

I then expected that he would whisk Belinda away to a tête-à-tête. Instead he put his arm around me. 'What do you say – shall we go and play the tables now?'

'Oh, someone was actually getting me a drink,' I said. 'That young man over there.'

Jean-Paul waved this away. 'He can give the drink to your delightful friend instead. I intend to keep you for myself. Come, roulette is calling. I have a feeling that you will bring me good luck tonight.' He bowed to Belinda. 'Mademoiselle, I hope you will excuse us, but I have been trying to lure this enchanting young lady away all evening and now I seize my chance. The young man who now approaches will be delighted to keep you entertained, I'm sure.'

And he whisked me away past an astonished Belinda. I tried not to grin like a schoolgirl. For once in my life the attractive man had chosen me over Belinda and over my mother. Maybe it was because of the Chanel outfit. Maybe clothes did make the woman after all!

Jean-Paul de Ronchard steered me through the crowd to a large gaming room. As we progressed he nodded and exchanged greetings with almost everyone we passed. I was still in a state of shock that I had beaten out Belinda and my mother. A small warning voice at the back of my brain whispered that this was a dangerous Frenchman, but at the moment I didn't care. As we arrived at the roulette table a place was vacated and Jean-Paul steered me toward it. The man who was leaving, with a sizeable stack of chips, turned toward us and I saw it was Darcy.

He recognized me at the same moment and his eyes lit up. 'Georgie – well, I'm damned. What are you doing here?'

'Good evening, Mr O'Mara,' I said, fighting to keep my voice even.

He laughed, a trifle uneasily. 'Why the sudden formality?'

'I believe it's simpler if one keeps things formal. And since you ask, I'm wintering on the Riviera like you,' I said.

'Actually, I'm only here for a brief stay – on a spot of business,' he said.

'Oh, really. Business.' I stared at him coldly.

'Yes. Business.' He was frowning now. 'Is something wrong?'

'With me? No, everything is perfect,' I said. 'I'm having the time of my life.' I took Jean-Paul's arm. 'The marquis is going to teach me how to win at roulette,' I said. My gaze dropped to the stack of chips Darcy was holding. 'I see you already know how. Congratulations. I hope you enjoy your winnings. Now if you'll excuse us. I'm sure you have someone waiting for you – more than one person, actually.'

I eased into the seat at the table and Jean-Paul perched on the arm beside me. 'Two hundred to start with,' he said to the croupier, throwing some notes across the table.

I could sense Darcy still hovering behind me.

'Georgiana – what's the matter with you?' he asked. 'Why are you acting like this?'

I looked back at him. 'Maybe I've seen that there is no sense in pursuing a romance that can't go anywhere,' I said. 'Maybe I want a man who can devote himself to me and take care of me – and only me.'

Jean-Paul put a hand on my shoulder, then looked back at Darcy. 'I think the young lady wishes you to leave now. You are distressing her.'

'Very well,' Darcy said. 'If that's what the young lady wants.' He held my gaze for a long moment, then pushed his way angrily through the crowd.

'You seem to be a very popular young woman,' Jean-Paul said. 'So many suitors. I see that I shall have to fight a duel for you before long. I had better brush up on my fencing skills.'

I tried to force a bright smile, but inside I felt as if that knife was cutting me in pieces again. If he has another woman and a child, I told myself, he can never love you wholly. And I tried to shut out the image of those dark eyes filled with bewilderment and hurt.

'Now concentrate,' Jean-Paul said, 'and I will show you how to become a rich woman. It is all a question of playing the transversal plain.' And he started to explain the odds of playing each line of three and his way of shortening those odds. He put a pile of chips down on the side of the board. The wheel spun and stopped. A number was called. More chips were pushed in Jean-Paul's direction. The process was repeated. The pile of chips grew bigger.

'How old are you?' he asked.

'Twenty-two.'

'Such a lucky number,' he said and pushed a stack of chips onto that number.

The wheel spun, slowed and landed on twenty-two. This time the amount of chips was impressive. Jean-Paul pushed them over to me.

'What is your system for doing that?' I asked.

He laughed. 'Sometimes a little luck doesn't hurt either. Now I leave it to you.'

I started to play as he had instructed. And kept winning steadily. Not every time, but enough to make that pile of chips grow. Each time I won, I looked up at Jean-Paul and he smiled at me. He really had a wonderful smile. Now I found myself wondering how the evening might end. If Jean-Paul offered to drive me home and took me to his villa instead – well, that could only mean one thing. And was that what I really wanted?

'He has to settle down sometime,' Coco had said. He was rich and attractive and a marquis. What more did I want?

The question was settled for me by the arrival of my mother, followed by Coco and Vera. 'There she is.' I heard my mother's voice behind me. 'And look how well she's been doing too. You must have been coaching her, Jean-Paul.'

'On the contrary, she has a natural feel for the game,'

Jean-Paul said. 'A very talented young woman. I must thank you ladies for introducing us. Now I think my time in Nice will be most pleasant.'

'Well, we've come to take her away from your clutches,' Vera said. 'Claire has sent for her car, so it's time to say adieu.'

Jean-Paul took my hand. 'I would be happy to drive her home later.'

'She's had a very long and tiring day, haven't you, my sweet?' my mother said, her eyebrows raised in warning.

Much as I was tempted to show my mother that I was no longer a little girl who needed to be protected, I realized this was true. I had had a long and tiring day. I was exhausted. I had once fallen asleep when Darcy tried to make love to me. I rather feared the same thing would happen if Jean-Paul tried to seduce me tonight. Not an auspicious start to a relationship.

I got to my feet. 'I really must go home now, Jean-Paul. Thank you for a lovely evening.'

He kissed my hand. 'Until we meet again, *ma chérie*,' he said. 'And don't forget to cash in those chips.'

'Oh, no, it was your money.'

He stacked the chips into a rack. 'No, no. They are your winnings. Now, no arguing and off you go.'

As I headed for the cashier's booth, while the other women went outside to meet the car, I found that I was standing next to Sir Toby Groper. The chips in his pile were of a much higher denomination than mine.

'A good evening, Sir Toby?' the cashier asked.

'Not bad. Made up a little for a damned run of bad luck,' he said. He turned and looked at me. 'And I see the young lady hasn't done badly for herself either.'

I realized I had to seize this moment. What I had seen of Sir Toby did not make getting to know him an attractive proposition. He had shown himself to be dangerous as well as aggressive. And I could well believe that he had walked out of Buckingham Palace with the queen's snuffbox in his pocket. But I had already lost one of the queen's prized possessions tonight. I owed it to her to fulfill my promise and recover another one. I plucked up courage. It was now or never. 'Oh, just call it beginner's luck,' I said, trying to sound keen and girlish. 'It was my first time playing roulette. But you're Sir Toby Groper, aren't you? I'm staying at the villa next to yours. I look down with envy on your lovely swimming pool.'

'I keep it at eighty-four degrees,' he said. 'Like a bath. You must come and swim in it sometime.'

'Really? Do you mean that? I say, thanks awfully,' I replied. 'It's very kind of you.'

'Not at all. A young lady like yourself will enhance the scene for me.' He paused, regarding me rather unpleasantly. 'So you're staying with the famous Claire Daniels, are you? What do you think of her? Everyone talks about her great sex appeal but I don't see it myself. Looking her age, I'd say.' He leaned closer to me. 'So tell me, is there still a man in the picture? That German fellow? Haven't seen him around.'

'He's at home in Germany, working,' I said, 'but she remains devoted to him.'

'Can't see why, myself,' he said. 'The man is a boor, a bloody great boor. But I must say she has good taste in guests. What is your name, little lady?'

'My friends call me Georgie,' I replied coyly, I hoped. I didn't think it was the occasion to reveal my full identity, since he'd just trashed my mother and stolen from my royal kin.

'Well, then, Miss Georgie, I hope you'll come down and swim in my pool one day soon. And maybe we could go for a spin on my yacht.'

'Could we really? I adore yachts.' I wasn't sure if I was overdoing it.

'Then it's settled,' he said. 'Come over and I'll take you out on the yacht tomorrow. Come anytime you like. I'll have the crew standing by.'

'That's so kind of you, Sir Toby,' I said. 'I'm really looking forward to it.'

'Not at all. Delighted to help out. See you tomorrow then.'

I gave myself a pat on the back as I left. I had positively had him eating out of my hand. Now if I could just find out if he had the queen's snuffbox at the villa, it should be an easy enough matter to slip inside and pinch it when I went down for a swim. Suddenly I felt very daring and worldly. I had flirted with a dashing marquis. I had been invited out by two English boys and wangled an invitation from Sir Toby. All in all a good evening – apart from falling off a runway, losing the queen's necklace and seeing Darcy.

I came home to find Queenie waiting up loyally for once.

'My feet are killing me,' I sighed as I flopped onto the bed.

'You can soak them in that little footbath as soon as I remove your smalls. I have been washing them out in it,' Queenie said.

'Footbath?'

'In the bathroom. Ever so handy it is. I was thinking

of going down to the seashore tomorrow to see if I could catch some crabs. We could keep 'em in there until they're wanted.'

With curiosity I followed her into the bathroom. There were my underclothes soaking in the bidet!

'Queenie, that's not exactly a footbath,' I said.

She looked puzzled. 'Then what is it for? It's not a toilet. It's too low for a basin.'

'It's–' I said. 'This is France. You figure it out.'

# Chapter 16

*Villa Marguerite*
*January 26, 1933*
**Today I go for a sail on Sir Toby's yacht and with any luck I return with the queen's snuffbox.**

I woke to find Queenie bending over me, a tea tray in her hands.

'I figured it out, miss. It's for yer bum, ain't it?'

'Absolutely right, Queenie.' I got up laughing. It was still early and the sea looked like polished pearl with wisps of haze hanging over it. I dressed and went out to walk in the gardens. The air was crisp but not cold. I came out onto a lower lawn area and found I could look down at Sir Toby's swimming pool. The French doors of his villa were still firmly shut. But even as I watched, one of the doors opened. A young man came out and stood on the terrace. For a moment I thought it was Bobby and he had placated his father after all. But then I saw that this young man was less boyish-looking, less English-looking, with slicked-back hair and the face of a Romantic poet – a

Roman nose and a sallow complexion. He stood outside the French doors, staring out at the swimming pool. For a long while he didn't move, just standing and staring, then he untied the terry robe he was wearing and let it fall to his feet. I was shocked to see that he had nothing on under that robe. I knew I shouldn't look, but frankly I was fascinated. I'd never had a chance to observe a naked man at my leisure before. Actually, I'd never had a chance to observe a naked man at all. And this one was rather well built too, like the statue of Michelangelo's *David*, which I had studied earnestly with my friends on a school trip to Florence.

Then my chance for observation was cut short. There were broad steps at that end of the pool. He stepped onto the top one and stood, ankle-deep in water, looking around for a moment before he dove gracefully into the pool, cutting through the water with strong, effortless strokes. The visit to Sir Toby took on a more appealing aspect – I would be introduced to his guest and express delight that we were next-door neighbors. Maybe he was an Italian count, or another French marquis. Suddenly it seemed I was turning into a man-chasing flirt – quite unlike me. Well, why not? I asked myself. Now that there wasn't one particular chap in my life, then the more the merrier. And who knows, maybe I'd finally do what was expected of me and marry well.

I made my way back up through the gardens and arrived on the terrace to find a council of war going on at the breakfast table.

'We'll have to do something,' Vera was saying. 'We can't sit back and leave it to that pompous little twit. He'll be worse than useless. You'll have to call your friend in the Sûreté, Coco. Persuade him to come down and take over the case.'

'He can't just come down and take over, my dear,' Coco said. 'I explained that to you last night. He would have to be invited by the police of the region, and that inspector certainly will never allow anyone to step on his extra-large toes.'

'You noticed that too, did you?' Mummy said. 'He did have big feet for his size. That's why I thought it was so funny his name was Lafite.'

They laughed at this. Then Vera grew somber again.

'We will have to start investigating ourselves,' Vera said. 'There is no other option. I must recover that necklace or Her Majesty will never forgive me. I'd never forgive myself.'

'It wasn't your fault,' Mummy said. 'You kept the wretched jewels in the bank. You brought them to the room under police guard. Who was to know that Georgie was going to tumble off the stage and that someone would be quick-thinking enough to snatch them in an instant?'

I started to mention the tacky substance on the sole of my shoe, then shut my mouth again. I wasn't wholly convinced that Madame Chanel herself had not caused the accident to create a sensation, as she put it.

'It's a pity my grandfather isn't closer,' I said. 'He'd know what to do.'

'Your grandfather? That fearsome Scottish man with the big beard? I thought he'd been dead for years,' Vera said.

'No, I mean my other grandfather.' Mummy shot me a warning look. She didn't like revealing her lowly ancestry any more than she liked disclosing that she was old enough to have a grown-up daughter.

I ignored her. 'He was a London policeman until he retired. He's very good at this sort of thing.'

'Well, then' – Vera brightened up – 'let's ask him to come out and help us, shall we?'

'I don't think he'd come,' I said. 'He couldn't afford the ticket, for one thing.'

'We'd pay for his ticket, of course,' Vera said.

'I still don't think he'd come. He's never been abroad. He has a distrust for anything farther away than Southend.'

Vera turned to Mummy. 'He's your father, Claire. You invite him. Tell him how much we need him.'

'And he has had such bad bronchitis, Mummy,' I said, warming to this now. 'The climate would be wonderful for him if we can persuade him to come.'

'He wouldn't come if I asked him,' Mummy said. 'You are the apple of his eye. You invite him.'

'And he can stay here?' I said.

'Of course. If he doesn't mind roughing it. I don't think he'd want to stay in the house, would he? Not his thing at all. There's a gardener's cottage that's unoccupied at the moment. It never seemed worth having a live-in gardener since I only come here once in a blue moon, and one can always find handy little men when one wants them.'

'A cottage? That's wonderful.' I found there was a big bubble of happiness inside me at the thought of having Granddad close by. 'I'll send him a telegram, shall I? I'll tell him we're in trouble and desperately need him. And we've taken care of his journey for him. And it will be so good for his chest to be in this climate.'

'That's turning into an expensive telegram,' Mummy pointed out.

'I'll shorten it a bit, then. But I did win money at roulette last night, so I can afford it. Also Jean-Paul taught me a method of winning.'

'This child will have to be watched,' Mummy said. 'I have a feeling that once she's started down the road to ruin, there will be no stopping her.'

'Just like you,' Vera said.

Mummy laughed. 'Exactly.'

'If we send him a ticket, all arranged, he'll feel obliged to come, won't he?' Vera said. 'I'll see to it when we go into town today.'

'I don't suppose Granddad will be able to come for a few days, even if he agrees to come at all,' I said. 'We should get working on this straight away.'

'What do you suggest we do?' Vera asked.

'Granddad always says "start with what you know." Somebody knew the jewels were real. Usually at a fashion show one would expect the accessories to be paste, wouldn't one? So who would have heard that you were borrowing the queen's jewels?'

'Servants at the palace, but they are all devotedly loyal. And besides, they'd have opportunities to steal a piece anytime they felt like it. So apart from them . . .'

'An employee at the bank,' Mummy suggested. 'I presume you told them what you were locking in their vault.'

'I did not,' Vera said. 'One does not tell bank employees what one is putting in a vault. Of course I had to tell the local gendarmerie that the jewels were valuable. But the police don't normally go around stealing things. So apart from them, I really can't think.'

'Surely Coco publicized the fact that you were going to use the queen's jewels,' Mummy said. 'Wasn't that part of the appeal of the collection – royal and simple, masculine and feminine?'

'Well, yes,' Coco admitted, looking a trifle uncomfortable. 'I may well have spoken about this.' She gave a delightfully Gallic shrug.

'So actually, anyone in that room would have known that royal jewels were going to be worn with the outfits?' Mummy insisted.

'If you put it like that, yes,' Coco agreed.

'So we're back to square one.' Vera sighed.

'Do you have a guest list of everybody who attended?' I asked.

'We have a list of people to whom invitations were sent,' Coco said.

'And there was a guest book at the door,' Vera added. 'But how does that help? I don't suppose anyone signed in with "jewel thief" next to his name.'

'No, but we can eliminate quite a few people right away. Elderly colonels and their wives. Those old princesses. None of them are likely to have taken a necklace,' I said.

'I don't know,' Mummy said thoughtfully. 'Some of those old Russian princesses are frightfully hard up these days. Perhaps the necklace did fall into that old woman's cleavage and she decided to say nothing about it.'

'Oh, surely not,' I said. 'Princesses have honor drummed down their throats from the day they are born. They'd rather starve than do anything to let the side down.'

'Try starving one day,' Mummy said. 'I noticed that the old French princess was rather taken with you, Georgie. You could pay them a visit.'

'What, and search their house while I'm there?'

'No, but you could let them know how terrible Vera and

Coco feel about letting the Queen of England down. Play the old honor card. You'll notice their reactions.'

'I could do that, I suppose,' I said. I paused before saying my thoughts out loud. 'The one we should really look into is Bobby Groper.'

'Who is that? A relation of Sir Toby?' Vera asked sharply.

'His son. He was the young man who helped me to my feet and then disappeared.'

'And you found him again? How clever,' Coco said.

'It wasn't particularly clever,' I said. 'We were hiding out in the same alcove.'

'I didn't know his son was staying at the villa,' Mummy said.

'He's not. He's supposed to be up at Oxford, but he's been sent down in disgrace. He's sleeping on a friend's couch and hiding out until he thinks the time is right to tell his father.'

'And just how did he manage to disappear from the room?' Coco asked.

'He claims he was standing next to the door and slipped out behind the gendarme when the latter came in. He says he's quite good at doing things like that.'

'A slippery young man, then?' Mummy suggested. 'And certainly the one with the best opportunity apart from the princess's cleavage. Again, you'd be the person to deal with him, Georgie. Try out your feminine charms on him and get him to confess all.'

'Golly, you make me sound like Mata Hari,' I said with an embarrassed laugh. 'I did half suggest that he took the necklace and he just laughed it off. Never exactly said that he didn't. And he does have a good motive – his father keeps him short of cash. He has gambling debts, and he's opportunistic.'

'And he was the only one who actually had his hands on you when he pulled you up,' Coco said.

'Well, the Prince of Wales helped me up too, but he wouldn't steal his mother's necklace.'

'Ah, but what about that Mrs Simpson?' Mummy said venomously. 'I wouldn't put it past her.' Mummy and Mrs Simpson had developed an instant loathing for each other, which I found amusing.

'Mummy, he has enough money to have an identical piece made for her if she wants it,' I said.

'And the same goes for Jean-Paul,' Coco said. 'He was also one of the first on the scene, wasn't he? But I don't believe he actually touched you, did he, *ma petite*?'

'No, I think he went ahead to find me a chair and a glass of brandy. Besides, he's rich too, isn't he?'

'One of the richest men in France, so we hear,' Coco said. 'And he has his eye on our little Georgiana, I think. Not a bad match, *ma petite*. Wealth and a title. And what is more, he will keep you happy in bed.'

I tried not to blush.

'He's too old for her,' my mother said. 'I believe he'll settle down with a more mature woman. That type always does.'

'Are you putting yourself forward as a candidate?' Vera asked.

'Of course not.' She paused, considering. 'But he does have the most wonderful come-to-bed eyes, doesn't he? Should we invite him round for dinner, do you think?'

'Enough of this idle chatter. I think we should concentrate on recovering the queen's choker,' Vera said. 'We will go into town this morning. I will go to the station and see if anyone who was at the party left Nice in a hurry. I will also give a description of the stones to the local jewelers, just in case someone dares to break up the necklace and tries to sell the stones separately. And Georgiana must send her telegram to her grandfather immediately, and then visit the princesses and try to find the young master Groper.'

'We have a busy morning ahead of us, it would seem,' Coco said. 'I shall go into town as well, to see if the Paris newspapers have arrived. I want to know if we made the front page.'

'My dear, you live for notoriety. It's not healthy,' Vera said.

'Nonsense. It is very healthy. We all seek fame. I'm just honest about it.' Coco stood up and went over to the railing, looking out over the ocean. 'It looks as if the weather will break later,' she said. 'We should get busy right away.'

I took a deep breath, not at all comfortable about confronting three such formidable women. 'I don't know if I'll be able to do all those things today,' I said. 'I have a date with Sir Toby Groper.'

# Chapter 17

*Villa Marguerite*
*January 26, 1933*
*Weather not too promising. If I'm to go sailing it should be soon, but Mummy has other plans.*

'Sir Toby?' My mother wrinkled her nose. 'What on earth for?'

'He invited me to swim in his pool and take a jaunt on his yacht,' I said. 'I felt I should take him up on it before he forgets.'

'I can't think of anything worse than swimming in a pool with something resembling a pink walrus,' Mummy said. 'Besides, I don't think Olga is going to welcome the presence of a younger woman. She'll probably push you off the cliff when nobody's looking.'

'I believe Olga has departed, judging from the scene I witnessed yesterday,' I said.

'Dear me, I wonder what brought that on?' Mummy said.

'Something he'd found out about her, I gather. She was livid and stormed out uttering curses.'

'Fascinating. In that case I insist that you go and visit him immediately and get all the juicy details. I adore scandals, don't you, Coco?'

'You know I do,' Coco said.

'I say, you two,' Vera said peevishly, 'surely the queen's necklace is more important than gossip with Sir Toby. We must forge ahead with our investigation. The telegram and the princesses . . .'

'I simply couldn't call on the princesses at this hour of the morning. It isn't done, is it?' I said. 'And as for Bobby Groper – you know very well that young Englishmen only rise before noon to hunt. So I think I can safely leave them until this afternoon. And you could send the telegram for me when you go into town, couldn't you, Mummy?'

'I suppose I could,' my mother said with a sigh as if this was a huge imposition, 'but I can't understand this fascination with Toby Groper. Why is it so important you go to visit him? He's not attractive, he's only just about socially acceptable and he's not even pleasant.'

Oh, dear, what could I say? 'I know all of those things. But – well, you have to understand, after the austere life I've led, an invitation on a yacht as well as a swim in a heated swimming pool does sound frightfully exciting. Who knows when I'll ever be invited on a yacht again?' I realized even as I was saying these things that they made me sound horribly shallow.

Coco came and put an arm around me. 'She's young; she's excited about being on the Riviera for the first time. Who can blame her?'

'If she wants fun and romance, she should not be looking in the direction of Toby Groper, that's what I'm 'saying,' Mummy said. 'Old enough to be her father and with terrible taste in women.'

'Besides, one hears that Lady Groper has arrived on the scene,' Vera added. 'She's a fearsome woman if ever there was one. I remember her from my coming-out days – Lady Margaret Huntingdon-Blague, daughter of the Earl of Romney. Even then she was what one might call strong-willed – bloody-minded would be more like it.'

'I have no intention of showing any romantic interest in Sir Toby,' I said.

'Then it must be his son,' Coco exclaimed. 'Nobody goes to all this trouble for a swim in a pool.'

'Do you tie everything in to sex?' I asked.

'But of course. Doesn't everyone?' Coco laughed.

'Anyway, the same goes for Sir Toby as those other people,' Mummy said. 'He won't be up and ready to receive guests for hours.'

'One of his guests was up and swimming in the pool really early.' I tried to toss off the words, but instead I felt myself blushing at the memory of that beautiful naked body.

'Even so, I don't think you would endear yourself to Sir Toby if you arrived on his doorstep too early,' Mummy said. 'As you said, it simply isn't done. Not that he would know – nasty little upstart.'

I thought that was rather amusing, coming from the daughter of a London policeman, but Mummy still acted the role of Duchess of Rannoch, even if she no longer officially held the position. Breakfast arrived and we worked our way through coffee and croissants while my table companions argued about what they should be doing to recover the necklace and how they could prevent the news from coming to the queen's ears. As they talked, I was planning out exactly what I'd say to Sir Toby Groper. He didn't know who I was last night. At some time I'd either have to lie to him about my name or tell the truth. Either was fraught with difficulty: If I told him I was one of Coco's models, he could have me arrested for stealing the snuffbox – provided I managed to get my hands on it. However, if I told him my true identity, he would realize that he had insulted my mother and that I came with strong royal ties – so he might well hide the snuffbox away.

No, I had to play the ingénue, the young, carefree girl-about-town – which wasn't going to be easy. I was young, and reasonably carefree, but I had never been the girl about any kind of town in my life! I considered going to find Belinda and bringing her along for authenticity, but I didn't want to involve her in any kind of potential scandal. To tell the truth, I felt a little guilty about Belinda. She had been an absolute brick for me in the past, and now she was stuck in a miserable pension while I was enjoying this delightful villa.

'Mummy,' I interrupted their discussion. 'You remember Belinda, don't you? My friend from school?'

'The naughty one? The one you said was turning out like me?' She smiled.

'She's here in Nice and she doesn't have much money at the moment so I wondered if we could squeeze her in here, at the villa.'

'She wouldn't want to be this far out of town, darling,' Mummy said dismissively. 'Too cut off from all the exciting goings-on. It does rather put a damper on nightlife, unless she wants to pay for taxis.'

'But if she wanted to come – is there a spare bedroom she could have?'

My mother shrugged charmingly. 'Darling, I'd love to help but one does like to keep a couple of good bedrooms available just in case someone interesting turns up out of the blue – like my darling Noël, for example. Noël Coward, I mean. He promised he'd come to visit.'

'I heard he had a young lover – of the male persuasion,' Vera said bluntly.

'As Georgie said so wisely, does one really need to tie everything in to sex?' Mummy laughed and tossed back that gorgeous blonde hair. 'He is the most amusing man I have ever met and he makes me laugh. Max never makes me laugh. Max never makes anyone laugh.'

'I think it's time you said bye-bye to Max,' Coco commented, stubbing out her cigarette in the butter on her plate.

'I suppose you're right. But he is so frightfully rich and generous, and the sex is quite divine,' Mummy said, 'although I really don't think Germany will be the place for me soon – not with that silly little man Hitler shouting at everyone.'

'He can't possibly last,' Vera said. 'He is too ridiculous for words. Surely they must see through him soon.'

'One hopes,' Mummy said. She got up. 'Well, to work, my darlings. Georgie, go and compose your telegram. Vera and Coco can start going through their guest list. I think I'll go and turn my considerable charms on the inspector with the big feet. He had his men take names and addresses, didn't he? Then we can see who gate-crashed.'

I looked at her with surprise. She was so beautiful that there were times when I forgot how sharp she was. I went upstairs and worked hard on my telegram to Granddad. It had to be perfect to lure him out of England when he had avowed never to set foot abroad.

*GRANDDAD. I'M IN A SPOT OF TROUBLE. REALLY NEED YOUR HELP. COULD YOU POSSIBLY COME? LADIES HERE WILL ARRANGE FOR YOUR FARE AND TICKETS. BESIDES THE CLIMATE WOULD BE WONDERFUL FOR YOUR CHEST.*

When I took it downstairs it produced peals of laughter from the others.

'One can see the child has never sent a telegram in her life,' Coco said. 'The secret, *ma chère*, is to take out all unnecessary words or it costs a fortune. *Voilà.*'

She went through, striking out most of what I had said.

*IN TROUBLE. NEED YOUR HELP. FARE PAID. ALL ARRANGED. ALSO CLIMATE BENEFICIAL. RSVP IMMEDIATELY.*

'It sounds so impersonal,' I said. 'I don't know if he'll come if he gets that.'

'Let the child say what she wants.' Mummy took the paper from Coco. 'We don't exactly need to economize, do we?' And she walked off with my original telegram.

Meanwhile I went upstairs to dress for my encounter with Sir Toby. I put on my cleanest, least crinkled cotton frock and dared to add a touch of rouge and lipstick. When I came down again I was met by two critical stares.

'This is what you wear to visit Sir Toby?' Chanel asked.

I nodded.

'*Ma petite*, you will not get any gossip out of him dressed like that. You are supposed to enchant him. Instead you look like a schoolgirl collecting donations for the starving children in China.'

'I say, that's a bit harsh,' Vera interjected, but added, 'I do see her point. It's not the most alluring of dresses.'

'I don't think I mean to allure him,' I said.

'But at least you should charm him,' Coco said. 'Show us your wardrobe. What else do you have?'

Reluctantly I led them upstairs. Even more reluctantly I opened the wardrobe. Even to my eyes at home my wardrobe was not what you would call chic. To the most fashionable woman in the world it would obviously appear as—

'*Mon Dieu*,' Coco exclaimed. 'Where do you find your clothes? At the convent? These are the clothes of a young woman who wishes to become a nun.'

'I haven't had the money to buy anything recently,' I said, my cheeks flaming. 'My brother cut me off and it's not easy trying to survive alone.'

She looked at me with sympathy. 'This I know. I have survived alone all these years. But then I had a talent. You must find your talent, my child. And in the meantime, we must help her, Vera. What do we have that she can wear today?'

'It is too bad that her mother is so petite,' Vera said. 'She would not fit into any of Claire's clothes.'

'We must take her on a shopping expedition,' Coco said. 'This very morning. It will be fun. Come on. Let's find Claire and go into town.'

'But what about my visit to Sir Toby?' I asked, torn

between wanting to do my duty and the thought of Coco Chanel buying me clothes.

'I think we all agree that you cannot visit him dressed in such unsuitable clothing. Besides, he is probably still snoring, like all good Englishmen.' Coco dismissed this with a wave of her hand. 'Just a quick jaunt to Galeries Lafayette for the basics of survival. Later I can take you under my wing properly and get you set up for society.'

Galeries Lafayette turned out to be a department store in Massena Square – a huge area of red colonnaded buildings with fountains and statues. It was peopled with the most incredibly elegant women and I was horribly conscious of that cotton frock. The assistants almost fell over each other in their haste to reach Chanel. The basics of survival turned out to be a pair of wide-legged white linen trousers, a little navy linen jacket and a striped matelot shirt. 'When on the French coast, what else but the look of a French sailor,' Chanel said. 'Chic and fun.' She even managed to find me a jaunty French sailor's hat. When I put them on I had to agree that I did look amazingly chic. Maybe there was hope for me after all.

As I stepped from the store into the blinding sunlight I almost collided with two women looking at the window display. I went to apologize but before I could utter a word Fig's sharp voice said, 'Georgie, it's you. What are you wearing? I hardly recognized you.'

'Thanks,' I said with a satisfied smile. 'Coco Chanel just bought the outfit for me at this store.'

I could positively see their jaws drop. 'Coco Chanel? At Galeries Lafayette? What on earth for?' Fig demanded.

'She's taken me under her wing.' I tried the Gallic

shrug. 'It's good to see you, Fig. I hope all is well at the Villa Gloriosa.'

Fig frowned. 'We've been so worried about you. We've just heard that you were involved in some kind of scandal last night – a stolen necklace? I did warn you about staying with your mother, didn't I, Ducky?' Her sister nodded, both of them staring at me as if I was a fallen woman now. 'Binky's quite upset. He thinks you should come back and stay with us immediately.'

'Thank you for the kind offer, but I prefer a lovely bedroom overlooking the ocean to a camp bed in a library,' I said. At that moment Coco and Vera arrived to join me. 'Sorry, I have to run. Madame Chanel doesn't like to be kept waiting.' I flashed them a brilliant smile. 'Isn't shopping at Galeries Lafayette fun?'

# Chapter 18

*About to visit Sir Toby Groper. Will I have the nerve to swipe the snuffbox?*

I left Mummy, Vera and Coco in town, ready to do battle with the obnoxious Inspector Lafite again, visit jewelers, and snoop around at the casino and station, while Franz, Mummy's chauffeur, ran me back to the villa.

I felt a little trepidation as I made my way to Sir Toby's place, attired in my new ensemble. I had never been a thief before. If I found the snuffbox, would I dare to take it? Another thought crossed my mind as I approached the tall wrought-iron gates. I had heard and seen enough to know about Sir Toby's ruthlessness and recklessness. If he had dared to pocket a snuffbox from Buckingham Palace, was it possible that he had known the necklace I would be wearing belonged to the queen? Was it also possible that his son was in league with him and together they had managed to steal it? I would have to tread very carefully. Frankly, I almost lost my nerve when I spotted the villa, nestled among umbrella pines.

It was a low, dazzling white building with an impressive portico of Roman columns. The thought of a vestal virgin going to the sacrifice did cross my mind. I knocked and the door was opened by the young man I had seen that morning. He was now fully clothed – remarkably formally for the Riviera in a dark jacket and striped pants. I tried to put the image of his naked body from my mind.

'Hello,' I said, trying to sound bright and jaunty. 'I've come to see Sir Toby.'

'Who may I say is calling, miss?' he asked.

'La–' I started to give my full name, then swallowed it back. 'My name's Georgie. I'm staying at the villa next door and Sir Toby invited me for a swim in his pool or maybe a sail on his yacht.'

'Please come in and wait while I inform Sir Toby of your arrival,' the young man said formally, giving a little bow.

It suddenly dawned on me that he was not a guest, but one of Sir Toby's servants. I wondered if his master had given him permission to swim in the pool. I tried to imagine one of our servants daring to swim nude – not that we had a pool, and the loch was too cold for nude bathing – but I'm sure they would never have considered such unseemly behavior. The words 'Not quite one of us,' a sentiment expressed one way or another several times to describe Sir Toby, passed through my head. Perhaps servants of the old school didn't want to work for him, in spite of his money.

I waited in a circular entrance hall with a white marble floor. Around the walls were Roman or Greek busts – and

I was pretty sure they were not copies. From a room beyond a voice boomed, echoing unnaturally loudly, 'Yes, Johnson, what is it now? A visitor? Well, you can see I'm in the bath, damn it. If it's that slimy little toad Schumann again, tell him he's wasting his time. He'll get nothing out of me and if he tries to pursue this, he'll be sorry.'

There was a pause. Then I heard him say, 'What? Who? Well, that's different. Show her into the drawing room, get her something to drink. I'll be along in a jiffy.'

Johnson appeared, looking a trifle embarrassed. 'Sir Toby suggests you wait for him in the drawing room, miss,' he said.

'I heard.' I shared a grin with him.

'This way.' He led me through the entrance hall into a sumptuous room. The walls were lined with what even I, with my lack of knowledge, recognized as paintings of masters old and new. Wasn't that a Renoir, and that a Van Gogh? And on various shelves and tables there were beautiful objects – cabinets of fine porcelain, silver bowls and, in a glass-topped table, I thought I recognized his collection of snuffboxes. I inched closer.

'What may I bring you to drink?' Johnson asked.

'What? Oh, a citron presse would be very nice,' I replied.

'A what, miss?'

'Fresh lemonade, you know.'

I moved toward the table. What a lot of snuffboxes there were – silver ones, gold ones, boxes carved out of jade . . . and surely that was the queen's box in the middle? I tried to remember the exact description. I'd only know the truth if I could open the lid and see the picture of Marie Antoinette in a frame of diamonds. I wondered how easily the lid of the table would lift up – oh so casually I put my hand on it and started to raise it gently until –

'Ah, there you are,' boomed the voice behind me. 'Delighted you came, my dear.'

I let the lid fall and spun around, red-faced. Sir Toby was wearing white trousers and a striped fisherman's jersey, rather like mine. Only his was a little tight and stretched over a large paunch. He bore down on me, holding out his hand. 'Absolutely delighted. Nothing like a bright young face around the place to cheer me up. Has that man of mine brought you a drink yet? No? The boy is hopeless. Came with good references but he'll have to go. My last manservant could read my mind, you know. I never had to ask for a thing.'

'What happened to him?' I asked.

'Had to let him go. Found he'd been helping himself to my good Scotch. The really good stuff. Couldn't tolerate that. This young chap doesn't drink.' We looked up at the light tap of feet on the marble. 'Ah, there you are, Johnson. Oh, and you've brought my whiskey. You may just be all right after all.'

Johnson placed my drink on a low table, bowed then retreated.

Sir Toby poured himself a generous amount of Scotch and raised his glass to me. 'Down the hatch.' He drained the glass. 'So why on earth are you staying with the old hens next door? I'd have thought a bright young thing like you would have more fun somewhere in town.'

I thought carefully before I answered. 'I've been doing a spot of modeling for Chanel. She wanted me to stay with her so that she could work with me.' Which was the truth. I've always found it easier not to lie whenever possible.

'Ah, so you're a model. That explains it. Do you do your modeling in London or Paris?'

'I don't really model professionally,' I said. 'I just do it occasionally to help out friends.'

'Of course. Of course. Well-brought-up girl like you – it wouldn't be seemly to work for your living, would it?' He laughed heartily. 'So how do you like my humble abode?'

'It's magnificent,' I said. 'You have so many lovely things.'

'I'm a bit of a collector,' Sir Toby said smugly. 'I like to have beautiful things around me. You see that painting? It's a Turner – one of my favorites. And the sunflowers? Van Gogh. And that picture of a chair beside it. Another Van Gogh, painted in Arles. He's going to be worth a mint one day, take my word for it.'

'So you prefer recent masterpieces, do you?' I asked innocently.

'I collect the best of every century,' he said. 'Those busts in the hall – from ancient Rome. That silver? Georgian. And that little table in the corner – Louis XIV. I don't specialize in any particular country or period – anything rare and valuable. That's what I collect. The art in this villa alone is worth a mint. And I've even more in my country house in England.'

Before I could come up with any kind of sensible question to bring the subject to snuffboxes, he clapped his hands. 'So what are we waiting for? I promised you a sail, didn't I? The yacht's out there and ready to go, so let's go down to the dock. Johnson!' he yelled.

Johnson appeared.

'You've got the list of things I want done in town, haven't you? You can take the car. And take the rest of the afternoon off if you like. I'll be dining out.'

With that he ushered me out through some French doors, then down a flight of steps cut into the cliff, to a jetty at which the sleek teak launch I'd seen before was tied. He jumped down into it with surprising agility for a man of his age and build, then held out his hand to me. I thought he held it rather overlong and squeezed it a little hard. Then he was all business, starting the motor, untying the ropes and steering us out into the blue water. When he was clear of the dock he opened the throttle and the boat shot forward, heading to the great blue and white yacht anchored a few hundred yards offshore. Uniformed crew lowered a ladder and came down to assist us. I was helped on board and heard the sound of the anchor being raised.

'I thought we'd go down the coast to Monte.' Sir Toby took my elbow and propelled me forward to a canopied area at the bow as the yacht began to move. 'Lovely stretch of coast all the way. Splendid place, Monte. Ever been there?'

'Never,' I said, my eyes feasting on that magnificent coastline – the steep cliffs plunging into the ocean with villas perched on apparently sheer slopes. It was breathtaking. I also noticed clouds building over the mountains and felt the stiff wind in my face as the yacht came out of the bay.

Sir Toby pointed out another, even bigger, white yacht that was steaming further out to sea. 'See that? Duke of Westminster's bloody great monstrosity. Pretentious, wouldn't you say? He has the casino at Cannes fire a twenty-one-gun salute to him when he comes into the harbor. He's got the Prince of Wales on board at the moment, did you know? And I rather fancy a certain American woman may have joined the party by now.' He gave me a nudge. 'Let's see if we can race them to Monte, shall we?' He turned to one of the young men standing at attention behind us. 'Full steam ahead, Roberts.' Then he took my arm again. 'Come and make yourself comfortable, my dear.'

'Oh, can't we stay here and look at the view? It's simply lovely.'

'Plenty of time for the view later. I've got a bottle of champagne on ice inside.'

He opened a door into a saloon as large and impressive as most drawing rooms, with windows almost all around. There were leather sofas and great bowls of flowers on the tables and a well-stocked bar in one corner. He motioned me to sit, then barked out orders to a crew member who hovered behind us. 'You can open the champagne now and tell the chef we'll be wanting something to eat soon. And none of that mamby-pamby French stuff either. Good hearty English food, tell him.'

I could hear the deep throb of the engine and the boat started to rise and fall as it cut through waves. Champagne was opened and a glass handed to me.

'Drink up,' Sir Toby said, draining his own glass. 'Plenty more bottles where that came from.'

'It's rather early yet,' I said cautiously.

'Nonsense. I know you bright young things – knocking back the booze at nightclubs, and a spot of snorting as well, what?'

'Not me,' I said. 'I rarely drink or go to nightclubs. Too expensive and money's tight these days.'

'Ah, so that's the attraction, is it?' Sir Toby laughed. 'I thought it had to be. I didn't think you fancied me for my looks.'

Fancied him? Perhaps I had gushed a little too much the night before. 'I really just admired your swimming pool and your yacht.'

He patted my knee. 'That's all right. I understand. It's not easy trying to survive in the big world these days. You young models need what the Yanks call a sugar daddy. Well, I'm as sugary as they come.'

I stood up. 'Oh, no, I really didn't mean . . .'

'What's the matter? Getting cold feet now we're alone?' He laughed. 'Too late for that, my dear. We're out at sea and the only people within shouting distance are crew members trained by me to look the other way, no matter what.' And he grabbed my arm, pulling me down onto him. Then he tried to kiss me with big wet lips. I squirmed and wriggled. 'Let go of me. You've got the wrong idea.' (Yes, I know a lady never says 'got', but this was a stressful moment.)

'But I have a very good idea,' Sir Toby said. 'I like 'em young and virginal and believe me, my dear, you'll like what I can offer.' And his large, meaty hands were fumbling to remove my fisherman's shirt.

'Stop it, please,' I said, grabbing one of his hands.

'A touch of modesty. I can understand that,' he said. 'Well, we've a good selection of bedrooms. Young ladies often like the pink one. Lovely bouncy bed in there. Come on.' He grabbed my wrist and started to drag me across the saloon, then down a long wood-paneled corridor. My heart was beating so loudly that I was sure it must have echoed back from those walls.

'Let go of me,' I shouted, as anger overtook fear. 'I am not going to bed with you and that is that.'

'Frankly, you don't have much choice, my dear.' He continued to propel me forward.

'When we get back I'll go to the police and report you for rape.'

He gave a great guffaw of laughter at this. 'To the police? For rape? A young girl who begs Sir Toby to take her out on his lovely yacht? Flutters her eyes at him? The police would understand that you got what you were asking for. They are men of the world. Now, shut up and be a good girl.'

'I want to be a good girl,' I said, 'and that doesn't include making love to a complete stranger.'

'Oh, come on. You bright young things . . .'

'And another thing – I'm not a bright young thing. I'm a' – I was about to say 'member of the royal family'; I only swallowed it down at the last second – 'respectable girl from a good family,' I finished lamely. It only made him laugh all the more as he tried to shove me down a steep staircase ahead of him. I turned and kicked him hard on the shin, then pushed past him back onto the deck. Then I ran. I don't know where I thought I was running to. It was a big yacht, but I couldn't play catch-me-if-you-can forever, could I?

The breeze had turned into a strong wind and met me full in the face as I came out onto the deck. Also there was now a big swell. I thought about diving off and swimming but the land looked awfully far away. Good swimmer that I was, I didn't think I could make it. Besides, great storm clouds were now moving in closer. I wondered hopefully if this would make us return to port.

'You can't escape, you know, you silly girl,' came Sir Toby's voice after me.

I ran to the other end of the deck and ducked behind a life raft. Then, over the throb of our engine I heard the higher whine of a speedboat. I stepped out and waved desperately as the boat came racing toward us, sending up a sheet of spray. The speedboat driver waved back and approached the yacht. When he was close enough I saw that it was Jean-Paul de Ronchard.

'Jean-Paul!' I shouted.

He slowed the speedboat to a crawl.

'Help me. I want to get off!' I shouted.

'Come on then. Jump!' he shouted back.

It was a long way down to the water and the boat was rising and falling with the swell of the waves. I hesitated.

'You do know how to swim, don't you?' Jean-Paul shouted.

'Of course, but . . .'

'Then jump. I won't let you drown.' He had cut the motor and bobbed alongside.

'Ah, there you are, you minx,' Sir Toby boomed, coming around the corner toward me.

I took a deep breath, climbed over the railing and jumped. I hit cold water, went under, then came up to see the speedboat a few yards away.

'Here.' Jean-Paul threw me a life belt. I grabbed it. He reeled me in and hoisted me on board.

'Thank you. You don't know how glad I am to see you,' I gasped as he revved up the motor and we sped away. 'How lucky that you happened to come this way.'

'Nothing to do with luck, *ma chérie*,' Jean-Paul said, reaching for a large fluffy towel and handing it to me. 'I was sitting on my own terrace, just across the cove, reading the morning newspapers – where you and I both feature nicely, I might add – when I heard a boat's motor start up. I looked up and saw you going out to Sir Toby's yacht. Knowing his less-than-honorable reputation with young women, I decided to give chase. I jumped into my speedboat and came to the rescue.'

'I'm so glad you did. He was trying to – you know.'

'Get you into his bed. Naturally. He has that reputation.' He slipped an arm around my shoulder. 'But you are safe now. I will take you home and dry you off and all will be well.'

His arm was warm and comforting around my shoulder as we made for the shore.

It did cross my mind that I might have leaped from the proverbial frying pan into the fire. Jean-Paul also had a reputation, didn't he? But I didn't exactly find him repugnant. Besides, he was a true gentleman – a marquis, not a trumped-up arms dealer from the lower classes. Somehow I felt safe with him. He confirmed this by saying, 'The English – I will never understand. They think it is manly and bold to force a woman into bed. The Frenchman, he would never do that. If a woman says no to him, he sees this as a challenge. He tries to seduce her little by little, with charming gestures, presents, flowers, plenty of attention, until one day, she comes to his bed willingly and with anticipation. And if she still says no, then there are plenty more fish in the sea, as you say.'

And he laughed.

# Chapter 19

**January 26, 1933**
***At the villa of Jean-Paul de Ronchard – imagine! If only
Belinda could see me now – oh, and Darcy.***

The coastline neared with its fabulous villas dotting
the rugged shoreline. Jean-Paul slowed the motor as he
steered his boat into a little cove. I could see the gleaming
white of Sir Toby's villa just across the cove. Ahead of us
was a jetty, to one side of it a small crescent of beach and,
above it, a lovely Tuscan-style villa with red-tiled roof and
green-painted shutters.

'Welcome to my humble abode,' Jean-Paul said. Before
we reached the dock, a manservant in a white jacket
appeared and made fast our boat. Jean-Paul jumped out
and helped me ashore.

'A slight calamity, Pierre,' he said. 'Run and fetch a
towel and one of my dressing gowns for milady. The light
blue to go with her eyes, I think.' He took my hand and
led me toward the house. 'Go to the bathroom. Take off
your things and Pierre will make them as good as new in
an instant,' he said.

'Oh, no, really, that's not necessary,' I protested. 'I'll drip all over your lovely floor. I'm really not far to the villa where I'm staying. I could just walk home.'

'Absolutely not,' Jean-Paul said firmly. 'You cannot return home in that state. If you do, there will be questions asked. You will tell them the truth and instantly there will be three tigresses trying to get at Sir Toby's throat. This is not wise. Sir Toby is not a nice person. You do not wish to make an enemy of him. My advice is to let Pierre repair your clothing and pretend that nothing has happened. And as for my floor – marble can withstand any number of drips. So this way to the nearest bathroom.'

He led me across the floor of a large sunroom with a bright tiled floor, wicker chairs and striped cushions. Beyond I could see more ornate rooms with paintings and objets d'art to rival Sir Toby's. A door was opened for me to a bathroom large enough to hold an orchestra. Pierre reappeared with the dressing gown and a huge fluffy towel with a crest embroidered on it. Jean-Paul closed the door for me. 'Take your time,' he said. 'Put your wet clothes outside the door, then enjoy a bath or a shower.'

I did as he suggested, pouring a bath almost large enough to swim in and indulging in some heavenly scented bath salts. As I lay there I considered the fact that Jean-Paul might settle down one day and what it would be like to be the Marquise de Ronchard. The thought didn't entirely displease me. Then I dried with the fluffy towel and put on the blue silk dressing gown. He was right. It did match my eyes. Cautiously I opened the bathroom door and ventured out. Jean-Paul had been sitting waiting for me and sprang up.

'*Voilà*. You look *magnifique*. Come – Pierre has been working a miracle as usual. I have told him to prepare lunch. You must be starving after such drama and your courageous dive to safety.'

He led me out of the house and down the steps to the small crescent of beach. There a table had been set up at the water's edge with a white starched tablecloth, gleaming silverware and two wicker chairs. A bottle of champagne sat in a silver bucket with two glasses beside it.

'I always eat in the open air when I can. Besides, you should return to the sea so that it no longer represents a negative experience to you. It's like falling off a horse. You must get straight back on.' And he laughed. He had a truly wonderful laugh. His eyes absolutely sparkled.

'You have sand on your beach,' I exclaimed, feeling the softness under my feet.

'Of course. I had it brought in. One does not like to walk on stones. Most disagreeable for bare feet. And even worse to lie on.' And he looked at me in that special way again, as if lying on the beach was something that might happen later.

Pierre pulled out a chair for me and put a white linen napkin in my lap. As if in a dream, I sat. Champagne was poured. Jean-Paul held up his glass to me. 'To an interesting woman, whom I look forward to getting to know better,' he said, clinking glasses with me. His eyes held mine for a long time and I felt a shiver of excitement. Had anyone ever looked at me like that before? Maybe Darcy, but I was trying hard to put him from my mind.

Plates of hors d'oeuvres appeared: caviar, smoked salmon, oysters, stuffed mussels, pâté de foie gras, olives, tomatoes, an impressive cheese board and crusty bread to go with them. I looked at them with anticipation, waiting to take my cue from him.

'Well, eat up,' he said. 'I prefer little dainties like this to a heavy meal during the day, don't you? Here, try the oysters. I have them flown in from Brittany.' He stabbed one with his fork then leaned forward and fed it to me. It was an incredibly intimate gesture and I shivered as the cold fork touched my lip.

'You do not like oysters?' he asked.

'I adore them.'

'And caviar? You like caviar?' He spread a generous dollop onto melba toast and popped that into my mouth.

'One moment,' he said. He picked up his napkin and touched my bottom lip, ever so gently. 'One morsel of caviar was left behind,' he said.

We continued to eat, with Jean-Paul feeding me every time I stopped and Pierre refilling that champagne glass.

'Something is missing,' Jean-Paul said suddenly. He tapped his head as if an idea had just come to him. 'Music. Pierre, where is the music?'

A gramophone was produced and soon French café songs, sung in a throaty female voice, were echoing back from the cliffs.

Jean-Paul got to his feet. 'Come, *ma petite*. We should dance – no?'

'Here?' I giggled nervously, conscious that I was wearing nothing under his silk dressing gown and that we were standing on a sandy beach.

'Where else?' he asked, holding out his hand to me. He took me into his arms. I was horribly aware of his body pressing against mine. But our dance had scarcely begun when the first drops of rain fell. 'Umbrella, Pierre!' he commanded.

And miraculously a large umbrella was opened and held over us as we danced. It was romantic but at the same time bizarre to be dancing on sand with the lapping waves to one side and the raindrops pattering on the umbrella over us.

It was a French café song, sung throatily and with great passion. I was feeling rather confused myself. Did I feel passion for this man? What would happen when the dance was over? He was smiling down at me, his eyes holding mine. Then slowly he leaned to me and his lips brushed mine. The effect was electrifying. Then he kissed me again, his lips playing with mine now, making me want to respond to him. And I knew I was responding. I could feel myself pressing my body against his . . .

Without warning the heavens opened. Thunder grumbled nearby and lightning flashed.

'I think we have to concede that the gods are not being kind,' Jean-Paul said. 'A little rain is good, but this – to stay out in this is madness. We do not wish to be struck by lightning, and you have already had one soaking today. Come.' He took my hand and led me back up the steps into the house, while the faithful Pierre kept the umbrella over us so that we remained dry all the way. Once inside, I found that my white linen trousers and sailor top had been cleaned and pressed for me. I went into the bathroom and changed into them.

'I regret that the weather has been unkind enough to cut short what could have been a delightfully romantic afternoon.' Jean-Paul was waiting for me as I came out of the bathroom. 'But no matter. I will drive you home now and you will rest and change into something ravishing. I will call for you at eight o'clock and we shall go for a delightful dinner and then we shall dance with no rain falling on us. Does that idea please you?'

'Yes, it does,' I said.

'Excellent. I look forward to it with great anticipation.'

I floated out of there, my head full of champagne and romance. The whole afternoon was so improbable it was quite outside my sphere of experience. Things like this happened to my mother and Belinda. They didn't happen to me. But it was happening. I was the one whom Jean-Paul was pursuing – a rich, powerful man wanted me. I hoped Darcy had noticed last night whom I was with. I hoped he couldn't sleep, thinking about the mistake he had made in losing me!

There was a most sleek and impressive car waiting outside. It was a sports car but the top was up because of the rain.

'Your car is lovely,' I said, sounding hopelessly girlish and unsophisticated, I'm sure.

'Yes, it is, rather,' Jean-Paul replied. 'It's a Voisin, the most desirable of French automobiles.' He helped me in and off we went. He drove rather fast but well around those hairpin curves and pulled up outside our front door.

He took my hand and kissed it. *'À bientôt, ma petite,'* he said. The rain had abated to a drizzle as Jean-Paul drove away, spraying gravel. I opened the front door to find the villa deserted. Claudette told me that the ladies had not returned from town and she didn't know when they would come back. Her shrug indicated that she didn't much care. I went up to my room and found Queenie sitting on my bed, shoveling the remains of a croissant into her mouth. Crumbs were everywhere. Before I could admonish her she jumped up, brushing crumbs wildly all over my eiderdown.

'I ain't half glad you're here, miss,' she said, her mouth still full. 'I had to come up here to get away. They are all foreign in this place.'

'Yes, well, they would be. We're in France,' I pointed out.

'But they don't like me. Down in the kitchen they speak Froggy to each other and look at me and laugh. One of them told me I was not a proper lady's maid just 'cos I said I didn't like their Froggy food and I'd take a plate of bangers and mash or bubble and squeak any day.'

'Well, that's true as well,' I agreed. 'You still have a lot to learn, Queenie. Among other things, you still call me "miss."'

'Well, blow me – I still do, don't I?' she said. 'I don't seem to be able to get it into my thick head that I'm supposed to say "my lady." It seems so queer, I suppose.'

I suppose I'd had an emotionally fraught day. Usually I'd have laughed off her last words but I found myself saying, in my most autocratic voice, 'Nevertheless, I am a lady and that is my title. You'll have to get used to it sometime if you want to stay in my service.'

'I'll try harder, I promise.' She looked quite shaken and I felt bad immediately.

'We'll hope for a miracle, shall we?' I relented and smiled at her. 'And you can start by laying out my clothes for this evening. I want my nicest evening dress – the nicest one that you haven't ruined with ironing it wrongly, that is. And the right stockings and shoes and underwear and jewelry. Can I leave those to you? I'm going out on a very important date.'

'Are you, miss? What, with a foreign gentleman?'

'With a foreign gentleman – actually, a foreign marquis. And a very handsome and rich one. So I want to look as good as I can.'

'Bob's yer uncle, miss. Don't you worry. I'll help you tart yerself up.'

'Queenie,' I said, shaking my head, 'I don't think you'll ever make a proper lady's maid.'

I went downstairs and lay on a sofa in the pretty little writing room that looked out over the sea. The rain squall had passed and already there were patches of blue sky between clouds. I tried to rest but I was too keyed up. One way or another tonight was going to be a life-changing experience for me. I had no idea whether Jean-Paul would drive me home after dinner and dancing or take me back to his villa, where Pierre, like Sir Toby's men, had been trained to turn a blind eye to all kinds of goings-on. Was that what I wanted? Wasn't I merely flattered that someone as desirable as Jean-Paul was paying attention to me? Wasn't part of my motivation that I wanted to punish Darcy? And did I really want to give up my virginity to someone like Jean-Paul, who would probably lose interest in me tomorrow? But then, I was twenty-two and a half and it was about time . . . besides, Jean-Paul had made it perfectly clear that he would never force a woman if she didn't want to. Unlike that brute Sir Toby–

I sat upright again. After today I could never go back to his villa. I had failed the queen in my task. Well, maybe not quite. I looked out the window. There was no sign of his yacht yet, which must mean he was still out at sea – and that the villa was temptingly vacant – except for

Johnson. I knew he had been sent into town on an errand so he might well not have returned either. If there had been other servants they were not in evidence while I was there. Might it be possible to climb down the cliff and enter the house by the French doors by the pool and then take the queen's snuffbox?

The thought of it made my heart lurch. Then I decided that if I bumped into a servant, all I needed was a good excuse for having come back. I had left my – what? I hadn't come with the proverbial gloves or purse. I had come with nothing. An earring – that was it. Small enough to have rolled under something. I had lost a valuable pearl earring and I wanted to see if it fell out while I was at Sir Toby's. Yes. That was satisfactory and should appease Johnson or anyone else I met. I went upstairs and took out one of my pearl earrings to use as evidence.

'Oh, I didn't know you wanted yer pearls tonight, me-lady,' Queenie said, looking up from laying things out on my bed. I noticed she had put out my daytime lisle stockings to go with my evening wear. 'I thought you said pearls were for daytime.'

'They are. I just needed this earring. Maybe the amethysts for tonight?'

I changed out of my white linen trousers and put on an ordinary skirt and blouse and sandals. Then I ran back downstairs, my heart still racing. It was a perfect time – the others weren't home yet. Neither was Sir Toby. Nobody to see me climb down the cliff and sneak past his swimming pool. Out of the back of the house, across the terrace and down through the bushes to one side of the stone balustrade I went. It was no longer raining but the hillside was slick with reddish mud. I slithered and slipped my way down, clinging to pine trees and shrubs as I descended not at all gracefully.

At last I reached the oleanders around Sir Toby's pool without sitting on my bottom once – quite an achievement. I peered through the leaves at the house. No sign of movement. One of the French doors appeared to be still slightly open. Perfect. All I had to do was tiptoe around the pool . . . I emerged from the shrubs, holding my breath, and moved forward cautiously. The pool deck was slippery with rain. I should take care not to lose my footing and fall in, because a big splash would certainly . . . I glanced into the pool and let out an involuntary yelp of horror.

Sir Toby was in his pool. I leaped back behind the nearest bush. How could he be home already when his yacht was not there? I peeked through the branches. He didn't appear to have seen me. That's when I noticed that he was lying face down, sprawled across the top step, half submerged in water, and across the back of his head was a red stain that was turning the water around him pink.

# Chapter 20

**January 26, 1933**
**Villa Marguerite. Sir Toby is dead in his swimming pool.**
**Oh, crikey.**

I didn't know what to do. If I shouted for help, I'd have to explain my presence trespassing in his back garden. I started to inch away until I reached the shrubs around the perimeter, then I slithered and clawed my way back up the hill until I was standing safely on my mother's terrace. I felt as if I was about to be sick. He had to be dead, didn't he? He hadn't moved, and his head – my stomach heaved. The back of his head had been smashed in. I leaned over the railing and noticed that I could see him from there, sprawled on that broad top step, half submerged in water.

I should call the police but had no idea how to do this in France. So I should alert the servants and have them do the calling.

As I walked toward the house I heard voices echoing in the marble hallway.

'And that funny little man's face – wasn't it a picture,

after I said we were bringing in a top English policeman!'
My mother's voice, carrying clearly.

'And he said, "But this is France, *Madame*. An English
policeman has no power to investigate a crime committed
in France. It is an outrage. It will not be permitted."'

Then they went into peals of laugher. I hurried inside
to join them.

'Oh, there you are, darling. How was the visit to Sir
Toby? Did you get the scoop on what happened to Olga?
We've been laying bets on why she left. Such fun. And
we–' She broke off. 'Are you all right? You look as if
you've seen a ghost.'

'It's Sir Toby,' I said. 'Come and look.'

I led them outside and made them lean over the railing
to look down at Sir Toby's pool.

*'Mon Dieu,'* Coco said. 'Is he drowned? Call for help. He
may still be saved, perhaps.'

'No, I'm sure he's dead,' I said. 'I saw him in the pool
and thought he was just swimming, you know – then I saw
the back of his head was all horribly bloody.'

'How awful,' Mummy said. 'He must have fallen and
hit his head, then collapsed into the pool.'

'We should call the police,' Vera said.

'Why should we notify the police?' Coco asked. 'Let
his servants do this if they wish. It is strange that none of
them has noticed the plight of their master. We can alert
them to this matter, if you wish.'

'No, don't,' I said sharply, causing all three women to
look at me. 'They might touch something and disturb
evidence.'

'Evidence?' my mother asked.

'We have to view it as a crime scene,' I said. 'He can't

have hit the back of his head and then fallen forward
into the pool. That just isn't possible. Someone must have
come up on him from behind and hit him over the head
so that he fell into the water.'

'Good God,' Vera said. 'Are you suggesting that somebody killed him deliberately? Murdered him?'

'Well, it does seem that way,' I said. 'That's why I think
we should call the police – and just pray they don't send
out the same awful inspector.'

'You'd better do it, Coco,' Mummy said carelessly. 'You
know how bad my French is.'

Coco went into the hall and we heard her rattling away
on the telephone in French, 'Yes – a man floating in his
pool. Of course he appears to be dead. Nobody lies in
a pool without moving unless he is dead. And yes, you
should send someone out immediately.' She replaced the
receiver. 'Idiots, all of them.'

About fifteen minutes later a police motorcar drew
up outside and we were relieved to see that it contained
two smart young gendarmes. They were most polite and
almost in awe of Coco as she ushered them through to the
terrace and then pointed down at the body.

'Do you happen to know who this man is?' one of the
policemen asked.

'Yes. Sir Toby Groper. He owns the villa,' Mummy said.
'At least I presume it is he. We can't see his face, but the
body looks like him. Disgustingly fat around the middle.'

'How long ago did you discover this shocking scene?'
the young man asked.

'We only just arrived home to be greeted by Lady
Georgiana with the news,' Vera said.

'And I had only just made the discovery myself,' I said

quickly. 'I was on my way into the house to call the police when my' – I was going to say 'my mother' but I changed it rapidly – 'when these ladies came home. I had just got back myself from an afternoon at a friend's house.'

I saw Coco and Vera give each other a glance. I saw them comprehend what I had realized a few minutes earlier – that I had been on Sir Toby's yacht and was probably one of the last people to see him alive. For all they knew, I only just left him a minute or two before the murder. This put me in a difficult position. I was glad that I had been with Jean-Paul. At least the police would believe him if he told them that Sir Toby was alive and well when I leaped off his boat. Oh, dear – that wouldn't look good either, would it? I decided that, for once, silence would be golden.

The young gendarme began to cross the terrace on his way back to the front door. Then he turned back to us. 'Does this Sir Toby live alone at his villa?'

'His wife was in town yesterday,' I said. 'I saw her checking into the Negresco, so I don't believe she was staying at the villa.'

'Why was that, do you think?' the policeman asked.

'I'm afraid I can't tell you. I don't know Lady Groper,' I said. 'And I also met his son at the casino, but I couldn't tell you where he was staying – with friends, I gather.'

'So none of them was staying with the poor papa?' he asked. 'Does this not seem strange?'

'As I said, we don't know the family,' Vera said firmly.

'So he would have been in the house alone, apart from the servants?'

'We don't know,' Coco said, sounding rather irritated now. 'Madame Daniels, who owns this villa, has no social contact with her neighbor.'

'Then we will trouble you no more.' The young gendarmes bowed and left us. The moment they had gone the three women turned on me. 'You said you spent the afternoon with a friend. So you didn't go to Sir Toby after all?' Coco asked.

'I did go,' I said. 'I went out on his yacht. But then Jean-Paul came by in his speedboat and I went off with him to his villa.'

I saw Mummy's eyebrows rise.

'Where he treated me like a perfect gentleman,' I said. 'Unlike Sir Toby, who tried to make a horrible pass at me. Groper was a good name for him. He was all hands.'

'The nasty little swine,' Mummy said. 'It's too bad he's dead. I'd have liked to deliver a knee where it could have done some damage.' (You can tell at times that she wasn't born a lady, can't you? But I have to say I didn't disagree with her.)

'I think it might be best, given the circumstances, if you don't reveal the full details of what happened on Sir Toby's yacht,' Coco said carefully. 'Seeing that someone may have hit him over the head.'

'You don't think anyone could imagine that Georgiana was somehow involved in his death!' Mummy said indignantly. 'That's absurd.'

'To us, yes. But to an annoying little *inspecteur* who can't see past the end of his nose, he might jump at such an available suspect.'

'I can't lie to the police,' I said.

'No, but you can truthfully say that you went for a sail with Sir Toby earlier in the day and later were with the marquis. Thank God he's a respected alibi!'

As she finished speaking there was a pounding on the

front door. Mummy went to open it, arriving before her maid. A worried-looking Johnson was standing there.

'Sorry to trouble you, ma'am,' he said, 'but I've just come back from town and there seems to be a police vehicle blocking the entrance to Sir Toby's driveway. I wondered if you knew anything about it.'

'And you are?' Mummy asked, in her best ex-duchess voice.

'Johnson, ma'am. Sir Toby's manservant. I just wondered if something had happened.'

'Yes, it has,' Mummy said. 'Your employer is lying face-down in his swimming pool.'

The color drained from Johnson's face. 'Dead, you mean? Sir Toby has drowned? But that's not possible. He was an excellent swimmer. Besides' – he paused, thinking – 'how can he be here at all? He went out on the yacht today and I saw the yacht in the old port when I was coming back from town.'

'I'm afraid we didn't really know your master,' Mummy said. 'But the police are at the villa. You'd better go down there and see if you can help them with their inquiries.'

'Oh, dear. I don't know how I'm going to do that,' Johnson said. 'My French is nonexistent. I had trouble in town today trying to carry out Sir Toby's various commissions.'

'Doesn't he have any French-speaking servants?' Coco asked.

'Only Marie, the cook, and it was her half day off.'

'So the house was empty,' I said.

He looked at me, as if he was seeing me for the first time. 'Yes, the house was empty for the afternoon. I don't know how or why Sir Toby came back. He knew Marie was off and that I would be kept all afternoon trying to muddle my way through the things he wanted done.' He looked at me again. 'But you were on the yacht with him. You must know of his movements.'

'I left his yacht quite early in the day,' I said. 'A friend came to the yacht to collect me in his motorboat, so I never saw in which direction Sir Toby eventually sailed. It was heading for Monte Carlo at the time I chose to leave.'

'I see.' He was frowning, trying to read the full meaning of my words.

'We all just arrived home,' I said, 'and we happened to spot the body in the swimming pool.'

'It's too bad, isn't it?' Johnson made a face. 'I thought I'd landed myself a plum job for once and I'd be in clover. Now I'm back to square one.' He sighed. 'Oh, well. I suppose I'd better go down and face the music. I hope one of the policemen speaks some English. I don't suppose one of you would like to come down and translate for me?'

'Certainly not,' Vera said. 'Such impudence, talking to your betters like that.'

Johnson flushed. 'I'm sorry, ma'am. I didn't mean what I said. I meant one of your servants, of course. I'm just so flustered at the news. I won't trouble you any longer.'

He hurried out. Mummy closed the door behind him. 'What an extraordinary young man.'

'He was obviously very upset,' I said. 'And frightened of dealing with foreign policemen. I can't say I blame him. He'll have to try to explain his own movements, won't he?'

'Luckily for him he's arrived back in the car to find the entrance blocked,' Mummy said. 'That pretty much guarantees that he was not pushing his master into a swimming pool.'

'Why would he want to, anyway?' I said. 'He's upset that he's lost such a good position. If he had been the one to hit his master over the head, he'd have absconded with some of Sir Toby's art treasures.' As I said this I felt a horrid flush rising on my face, because stealing a treasure was exactly what I had planned to do. Thank heavens I hadn't been caught in the house with the snuffbox in my hand and Sir Toby lying dead in the pool. That would have looked bad for me, wouldn't it?

Suddenly Coco ran to the front door and wrenched it open again. 'Young man, wait,' she called. Johnson was already at our gate. He turned and looked back hopefully.

'We have decided to be gracious and come and help you in your need,' she said.

'Have you gone mad?' Vera hissed. 'We don't want to get involved with the French police. You know what they are like.'

'But, *chérie*, we can't miss out on the chance to witness a real crime scene. Everyone will invite us to dinner to hear the gory details. Come on. Where is your sense of adventure?'

She started off down the drive toward the young man. Mummy's face also had an expectant smile on it. 'I've been dying to see around his place,' she said. 'Come on, Vera. Georgie.'

Vera gave me a resigned look and followed along. So did I. Two conflicting thoughts were going through my head. One was that there might be a remote chance that I could put the queen's snuffbox into my pocket when nobody was looking. It would probably be my only opportunity. On the other hand my more sensible side, the side that took after my austere great-grandmother, was whispering that it might not go down very well with the police if I were caught pocketing an item from a murder scene – especially since it might come up that I had been out with Sir Toby on his yacht that morning. Still, curiosity won out over my qualms and I followed the others down Sir Toby's long, sweeping drive.

# Chapter 21

One of the gendarmes was speaking into a telephone as we entered.

'Yes, sir, I would say that foul play cannot be ruled out. Yes, I suggest that we do notify the detectives in Nice to come to inspect the scene. I have not moved the body or touched anything.' He hung up and turned to stare at us.

'What are you doing here, ladies?' he asked. 'You have something to tell us about this tragic incident?'

'This young man is the servant of Sir Toby Groper,' Coco said. 'He has just arrived home in his master's automobile and found the driveway blocked by your police vehicle. He came to our house and was most distressed by the news about his master. I am sure you will wish to ask him questions, and since he speaks no French, we have volunteered to help him.'

'Four lady interpreters?' the gendarme raised an eyebrow. 'A very fortunate young man.'

'I accompanied Madame Chanel because it was not right that she had to endure an unpleasant situation alone,' Vera said. 'And naturally these other ladies did not wish to remain home alone, knowing there might still be a murderer at large in the area.'

'Murderer?' the policeman asked sharply, glancing at his colleague, who had just come in from the pool area. 'Who said anything about murder?'

'One has to consider all possibilities,' Vera said quickly. 'Men do not often fall into their own swimming pools and die.'

'He could have had a heart attack,' the first gendarme said.

'The water around him appeared to be pink, indicating that he had been bleeding,' Vera said.

'He could have slipped on the wet cement and hit his head,' commented the gendarme who had just entered. His colleague turned to him. 'I think you should stay by the body until the inspector arrives. We should not allow it to be tampered with in any way.'

'Who could tamper with it?' the other gendarme demanded. 'It is in a swimming pool halfway down a cliff, cut off from the world.'

'There are also buzzards and seagulls,' the first gendarme said. 'They will be attracted to this kind of corpse.'

The other gendarme, who looked as if he was fresh out of training school, turned decidedly green. 'I will stay with the body,' he said and retreated again. The first gendarme turned to us. 'It is interesting that you suspect a murder, however. Perhaps you know more about this matter than you are revealing to us. You English know much about the various intrigues that go on when you come to the Riviera.'

'I assure you we know nothing about Sir Toby Groper,' Vera said. 'Only what we have overheard from our own terrace.'

'And what did you overhear?'

'Today, as I told you, we were in Nice all day, so we heard nothing. We were actually at police headquarters in Nice, if you need an alibi for us,' Coco said.

'And what were you doing at police headquarters?'

'A valuable necklace was stolen from us last night. We were attempting to aid the police in its recovery.'

This cheered the young gendarme no end. 'Ah – a robbery took place last night. And today a man is found dead in his swimming pool. Perhaps a second robbery was planned and Sir Toby surprised the thieves, who hit him over the head and threw him into his pool.'

'The robbery took place at the casino on the pier,' Vera said.

'Ah.' The young gendarme looked around as if he were unsure what to do next. His gaze fell on Johnson. 'This young man – is he the only servant in the house?'

The question was translated for Johnson. Coco in turn translated the answer for the policeman. 'He says there is a cook, Marie, but that it is her half day off to visit her family. There is also a local woman who comes in every day to clean, but only in the mornings, and there are two gardeners and a chauffeur.'

'And where are these people now?'

'The gardeners do not live on the premises. I have the address at which they can be found, if you will wait. They usually start early then go home after lunch. And the chauffeur has a small apartment over the garage. I think he was also given the afternoon off, as Sir Toby planned to be on his yacht and this young man was given the car.'

'And what is your capacity in this household?' Johnson was asked.

'He is – he was Sir Toby's manservant, valet,' Coco translated. 'He also acted as secretary when necessary and helped Sir Toby with his correspondence.'

'Why was he not attending on his master, leaving him in the house alone?' the policeman asked.

'Sir Toby went off on his yacht about midday,' Johnson said, addressing the answer to Coco rather than the gendarme. 'I was told to take his car and go into Nice, where I had various commissions to carry out. I had to send a telegram to England, to have his shoes resoled, to obtain more of his favorite cigars and to mail letters. He told me that I need not hurry back as he thought he might sail to Monte Carlo and probably dine there. Therefore I took the liberty of having a cup of coffee in a café and of strolling around, observing the people. This is my first trip abroad, so it's all a novelty to me.'

'And you returned when?'

'A few moments ago, as I told you. The driveway was blocked by your car, so I went to *Madame*'s villa next door to find out what was wrong.'

As this question-and-answer session continued, I found my gaze drifting to the glass-topped table in which the queen's snuffbox reposed. If only they would all go out to the pool, I might have a chance to lift the lid and take it. My heart was racing. This was not in my character, having been brought up with strong Scottish virtues and the Ten

Commandments rammed down my throat by my nanny. But was it stealing to retrieve what had been stolen by someone else? Probably not. The point was that it would be seen as stealing if I were caught, and I wasn't sure that the queen would want me to reveal her little scheme to the French police.

'It will be simple to verify your movements in town today,' the gendarme said, 'if you will write for us the names of the establishments you visited.'

'Certainly.' Johnson went across to a bureau and opened it, taking out a sheet of paper. He wrote swiftly, then handed the paper to the policeman.

I edged closer to the table. They were watching Johnson. I eased the lid up a little. My hand slid inside–

'What is going on here?' a voice demanded in French, and to my horror Inspector Lafite stood behind me. 'What are all these people doing at the scene of a possible crime?' His gaze swept the room, taking us all in. It fastened on me as I tried to withdraw my hand from the table. To my horror the lid had sagged shut and my hand was stuck. I stood there, giving the inspector an inane smile, hoping he wouldn't notice that one of my hands was stuck in a table full of valuable objects.

'We are staying in the next villa,' Coco said, successfully diverting the inspector's attention from me to her. 'Sir Toby's young manservant arrived on our doorstep in great distress, so naturally we came with him as interpreters, as he speaks no French.'

'And we did not want to see him bullied or intimidated by the French police,' Vera added. It was clear she had taken a strong dislike to the little inspector.

'These boys are gendarmes – country policemen,' the

inspector said. 'We town police are of the civility the most great. We do not bully,' Lafite said.

Vera grunted but said nothing. While this exchange had been going on, I lifted the lid and pulled my hand free, unfortunately without the snuffbox in it. The lid closed with a rather loud clack. The inspector spun around. 'Sorry, I bumped into the table,' I said.

His eyes narrowed as he looked at me. 'You are the young lady from whom the jewels were taken last night.'

'That is correct,' I said. 'I am staying at the villa next door with these ladies.'

'Hmmm,' he said, his mind clearly trying to work out an involvement in a robbery and then a suspicious death. 'Please do not leave until I have questioned you. Now, where is this body?'

'Still in the swimming pool, sir,' the young gendarme said, obviously in awe of Lafite. 'I left my colleague to guard it. Nothing has been moved nor the body deranged.'

The inspector gave a curt nod and strode out to the terrace. We followed at a safe distance, although I wasn't sure that I wanted to see the body at close range. As we neared the pool, I could see it still lying on the top step, half submerged.

'Good God, he looks like a pink hippopotamus,' Mummy's clear voice rang out, echoing back from the cliffs around us. 'How utterly revolting. I think I've seen enough. I'll be back at the villa, making cocktails.' And she departed.

Inspector Lafite squatted down beside it, then looked up at us.

'He has been hit on the head,' he said. It came out like "Ee 'as been 'eet on the 'ead.' It was rather an unnecessary statement, since at close range it was obvious Sir Toby's skull had been smashed at the back with considerable force, leaving a horrid matted mess of blood and hair. Lafite turned to his men. 'Telephone to my department in Nice. Tell them we need a team of men and a vehicle to transport the body. In the meantime, begin to search the premises for the murder weapon. The criminal may have thrown it down the cliff or hidden it in the shrubbery.'

The two men began picking their way around the perimeter of the pool. Lafite turned his attention back to us.

'Who discovered the body?' he asked us in French.

'Lady Georgiana did,' Vera said, stepping between me and the inspector in an effort to protect me, I suppose. 'She arrived home to find nobody here, looked over the edge of the terrace and saw the body in the pool. She was just coming up to get help when we arrived home and she showed us the body. We called the police.'

'Why did none of the servants discover their master was dead?' the inspector asked in slow, heavy-accented English as he turned to glare at Johnson, who took a step back. 'They could not have attended to him very diligently.'

'There were no servants in the house,' Coco said. 'Their master was supposed to be on his yacht today. This young man was running errands for Sir Toby in town, using Sir Toby's car. The cook had been given the afternoon off.'

'This is very strange,' Lafite said, looking from one face to the next as if we were the ones concealing something from him. 'Sir Toby sets out on a yacht and yet is found dead in his own swimming pool. If he came back, where is now the yacht?'

'I can answer that,' Johnson said. 'I saw it moored in the old port in Nice.'

'Then how did this Sir Toby arrive here if his car is in Nice, his yacht is in Nice? If he had come from his yacht, would his launch not be at the jetty, when I see it clearly tied to the buoy out there?'

'He could have taken a taxi, I suppose,' Vera suggested.

'Certainly, but why? He owns a car. He owns a yacht.'

'I have no idea,' Vera said. 'We know nothing of this man. We did not mix with him socially.'

'But he was an English milord, like the rest of you, was he not?'

'He was a baronet,' Vera said, 'but he was essentially a self-made man.'

'A what?' Lafite asked. 'He made himself? He is God?'

'I mean he came from the lower classes. His family made a fortune in industry. Therefore he was not one of us and never would be.'

The inspector laughed. 'You English. I shall never understand your snobbery.'

'Your own French aristocrats are just as bad,' Vera said. 'Even more snobbish.'

The inspector nodded as if he had to agree this was true. He stepped back into the house, looking around the room. 'This man was very rich, I think. He had a lot of fine things,' he said. 'Antiques, paintings. I believe I recognize a Matisse, no?'

'Van Gogh,' Vera said.

'Ah, yes, of course. They all look the same, don't they? Me, I do not appreciate this ugly modern art, but I understand it is worth a lot of money,' Lafite said. 'But these old things' – he ran his hand over a sideboard topped with some lovely silver – 'they are very nice. Worth a lot to a thief. Like these silver candlesticks, for example.' He pointed at one of them. 'Heavy silver. This murder was committed during a robbery, I assure you. And Lafite is rarely wrong. Sir Toby swims in his pool. The thief does not know anyone is home. Sir Toby surprises him, and the thief, he hits him over the head with something like this candlestick.'

He lifted his arm up triumphantly but his finger was somehow stuck in the candlestick. It came flying up with his hand. He looked at the dangling object in surprise, then scowled as we grinned. 'They had narrow candles in those days,' he said and tried to shake it loose. The candlestick went flying across the room, struck the little glass-topped table and shattered the glass, which went flying everywhere.

'*Sacre bleu,*' he muttered.

'I think you have rather disturbed the crime scene,' Vera said with a note of triumph in her voice. 'Let's hope you haven't done any damage to the priceless contents of the table.'

Johnson gave a cry of horror and moved toward the table, but I got there first. The candlestick was now lying amid the shards of glass on top of the snuffboxes.

'I think you're in luck,' I said, lifting it out carefully and handing it to Johnson, who put it back in its place with a look of disgust at Lafite. I was not going to let a perfect opportunity slip away. The snuffboxes lay there, exposed, covered in shards of glass. 'The objects in here all seem to be metal, not porcelain or glass. No real damage done.' I started to pick out shards of glass and then the snuffboxes, one by one, dusting them off, then replacing them, with a show of great concern. The queen's box was next. My fingers moved toward it, wishing I had a pocket in my skirt—

'Do not derange those things,' Lafite said sharply. 'My men will take care of it. There may be telltale fingerprints. This manservant shall come with me on a tour of the villa and he may be able to see if anything has been taken.' He spun to face Johnson. 'You weeell observe if any objects are missing,' he said.

'If it was a thief, he left without taking anything, as far as I can see,' Johnson said.

'He lost his nerve after he had killed Sir Toby,' Lafite commented in French. 'Or perhaps he had only come for an especially valuable item. A jewel, perhaps?' And he looked at me, long and hard.

'Perhaps,' Coco said. 'We already know there is a clever jewel thief in the area. Now let us hope your men will double their efforts to catch him and retrieve our missing necklace.'

'Of course there are many reasons for murder,' Lafite went on. 'A rich powerful man makes enemies, does he not?' He turned back to Johnson. 'Who wish harm to your master?'

It came out more like "Oo weesh'arm.'

Johnson looked puzzled. 'Wee charm?' he said. 'What wee charm?'

Lafite scowled. 'What is zee matter? Do you not spick your muzzer tong?'

'He wants to know who might have wished your master harm,' Vera said.

'I hadn't been with him long,' Johnson said. 'And I wasn't privy to his business dealings.'

I was about to suggest that Sir Toby had mentioned a threat from a foreigner when I first arrived at his house, but I realized that would place me at the scene of the crime that morning. My feeling was that Sir Toby probably had upset quite a few people recently, including Olga and his wife. It wasn't up to me to help sort out which of them did the dirty deed.

Snuffbox or no snuffbox, all I wanted to do was to be away from there.

'If you will excuse me, Inspector,' I said. 'I'm not feeling well. The sight of that body – you don't need us any longer, do you?'

'For the moment, no,' he said. 'First I make my investigation of the house. But later I may ask you more questions. You English, you stick together. You may well know things that you have not told me. But do not worry. I shall find out the truth. So if you know something, it would be wise to tell me now.'

'Sorry, but we can't help,' Vera said. 'I've told you, we had no social contact with the man. Now we'd better take Lady Georgiana home. She looks quite white.'

And she bustled me out of the room.

# *Chapter 22*

I tried to push the whole nasty business to one side as I prepared for my date with Jean-Paul that evening. Mummy was reluctant to let me go.

'Are you sure you know what you're doing?' she demanded, sounding for the first time in her life like a mother.

'I told you, he was a perfect gentleman this afternoon,' I said. 'I was only wearing a silk dressing gown and he could easily have tried to seduce me then.' The memory of that kiss flashed into my mind – actually, he was probably in the first stages of trying to seduce me.

'He may have behaved like a proper gentleman this afternoon, but that doesn't guarantee that he'll behave himself once he has you alone in the back of his motorcar,' she said. 'He may have been making sure you let your guard down with him.' She actually came over and put a hand on my shoulder. 'You've lived a sheltered life,

Georgie, and I blame myself for not being a mother to you. Actually, it wasn't entirely my fault – the Rannoch crowd made it clear that I was to stay away from my child in case I corrupted you with my wild ways. Still, I should have insisted.' A frown passed briefly over that perfect face. 'But that's all water under the bridge, isn't it? It's just that – well, I have met plenty of men like Jean-Paul de Ronchard and they only want one thing. He probably sees it as tremendous sport to seduce a virgin – I take it you still are a virgin? Of course you are. One look and one can see. I just don't want you to get hurt.'

I looked at her almost fondly. It was the closest I remember being to her. 'I'm a big girl now, Mummy,' I said. 'And I'm not as entirely naïve as you think. If I go with Jean-Paul, it will be because I choose to.' I saw her face then I laughed. 'Don't worry, I probably won't do anything. That good old Rannoch sense of honor will kick in.'

She pulled my face down and kissed me on the cheek. 'In which case go and have a lovely time. And if you decide to do it with him, I expect the sex will be glorious.'

It was rather a strange conversation to be having with one's mother, but if anyone knew about glorious sex, it was she. I went upstairs to get ready, only to find that Queenie had disappeared down to the kitchen to have her supper, having laid out the strangest assortment of garments for me to wear – a frilly white number that one might wear to a garden party, a full cotton petticoat and a cardigan, in case I got cold, I presume.

'Honestly,' I muttered, 'it would be less trouble to do it oneself.' And I found a shantung evening dress that had miraculously escaped being melted by Queenie's iron. The neck was rather high and the whole thing shapeless, dating back to the waistless days of the twenties, but I added a long string of pearls and anyway it was the best I could do. Oh, how I longed for bright red silk pajamas, preferably backless like the women were wearing at the casino last night. I wished I was small enough to fit into my mother's clothes. I wished Chanel had already had the promised dress made for me. I'd have loved to see Jean-Paul's face if I appeared looking divine. As it was, the best I could say for my appearance was that it was neat and respectable.

Jean-Paul showed no sign that he found me dull and dowdy, however. He gave me that enchanting smile as I came down the stairs to find him waiting in the front hall.

'You look ravishing, my lady,' he said.

'He means worth ravishing,' I thought I heard my mother mutter from the shadows. But out loud she said, 'Have fun, my children. Take good care of her, Jean-Paul. She is under the protection of three formidable women, you know.'

'Don't worry,' Jean-Paul said. 'I shall treat her as if she were your own daughter.' And he gave me a wink that hinted that he had guessed the truth. Then he took my arm and helped me into the Voisin, which still had the top up. I wondered whether to mention the death of Sir Toby to him, but I couldn't bring myself to do so. All I wanted was to put it from my mind.

'I thought we should go somewhere more private than Nice tonight,' he said. 'I know this delightful little place at Beaulieu-sur-Mer. The chef cooks like an angel.'

It was a heady experience to arrive at L'Etoile Restaurant, perched on rocks right over the Med. Lights from moored yachts sparkled on the water, making a fairyland. Jean-Paul was received with the reverence of a royal visit.

'What an honor, Marquis. We have reserved your favorite table.' We were escorted to a table up some steps in an alcove off the main dining room. It was built out right over the water with windows all around. The lapping of waves came up to us, together with the fresh, slightly salty smell of the Mediterranean. Out across the bay, music was playing and the sound floated to us on a gentle breeze. I felt as if I were in a dream – exactly how Cinderella must have felt when she arrived at the ball in the glass slippers and the prince chose her out of all the girls in the room.

A bucket of champagne appeared as we sat down. Two glasses were poured. Jean-Paul raised his to me. 'To the next step on the road to discovery,' he said, his eyes holding mine in that smoldering stare. I felt a strange surge of warmth at the pit of my stomach and recognized it as desire. I had a suspicion that the Rannoch code of honor would not last out the evening, and I wondered how I felt about that.

'Drink up,' Jean-Paul said. 'Plenty more where that came from.' He turned to the maitre d'. 'Now, what do you suggest for such a lovely young lady this evening, Henri?'

'We have acquired some very fine lobsters, so may I suggest one for the fish course? And I presume you wish to begin with caviar as usual? We have had a new batch brought in from Siberia only yesterday. And then a melon filled with port? And for soup – our consommé or would you prefer something more robust?'

'The consommé. One needs a clear palate for the lobster,' Jean-Paul said.

'Naturally. The marquis' taste is flawless as always. And for the main course – breast of duck cooked the way you like it, with orange and ginger? And to finish? I know you like our *baba au rhum* but maybe a crème brûlée for the young lady. She does not want the heavy dessert.'

'Bring both. We'll decide later,' Jean-Paul said. 'And then your fine cheese board and a cognac and we will be content.' He looked up to see if I approved. I, who until recently had suffered Fig's austerities, was so over-whelmed by the thought of all this food that I could only nod dumbly.

'*Excellent, mon vieux,*' Jean-Paul said. 'And I can trust you to select the appropriate wines to accompany each, can I not?'

'Have I ever let you down, Marquis?'

'Never.'

It was a terribly French exchange. I half expected them to leap up and embrace each other. Henri went away and returned almost instantly with a plate with different types of caviar sitting in tiny dishes on a bed of ice.

'Ah,' Jean-Paul said, giving a delighted smile like a child who has been given a present. He scooped some pink caviar onto a piece of melba toast, then repeated the gesture from lunch, reaching across the table to pop it into my mouth. I remembered what he had said about seducing a woman gradually, so in the end it is she who is begging to be made love to. Having dug into the caviar, Jean-Paul appeared relaxed and enjoying himself and started asking me questions about my family and home. I described Castle Rannoch and he shuddered. 'Me, I do not think it sounds very comfortable,' he said.

'It isn't. It's quite spartan and cold.'

'Then I do not think you would find it disagreeable to spend your winters on the Riviera in future?'

'I think it might be very nice,' I said, wondering where this was leading. I remembered Vera saying that he'd have to settle down and produce the heir eventually. Had he decided I would make a suitable marquise?

'Your dear papa – he did not visit his family home very often, I think. He too enjoyed the delights of the Riviera.'

'He might have enjoyed them, but they didn't do him any good,' I said. 'He got through all the family money. He must have been a rotten gambler.'

'Drinking and gambling together are not wise,' Jean-Paul said. 'Your papa – he liked the champagne too much. And the ladies too.'

It was almost a slap in the face to hear that he'd liked the ladies. But then I suppose he was free to do what he liked after my mother had left him. When I was growing up, I'd always pictured him as a lonely man, wandering alone on foreign beaches, and I'd felt sorry for him. Now I thought of Binky, struggling to keep Castle Rannoch going after Father had spent the family money on gambling and the ladies, and I was suddenly angry.

'I hardly knew my father,' I said. 'So I really can't judge him.'

'Very wise,' Jean-Paul said. 'I knew him a little and I think you can say that he was a kind man, but not a wise one.' He leaned closer to me. 'Rather like your cousin the Prince of Wales. He has shown concern for the poor people of your country, he wants to do some good, but he has not demonstrated wisdom in his affairs. I wonder if he will make a good king.'

'I really don't know,' I said. 'I take it you're referring to Mrs Simpson. She certainly seems to have a hold over him, almost as if he's bewitched. One hopes that when his father dies, he'll shape up and do the right thing. We were certainly all brought up to put duty before anything else.'

'Maybe he will,' Jean-Paul said, 'but let us not speak of him or of duty. I thumb my nose at duty. It is boring. Talk to me about amusing things.'

'I'm afraid I don't lead a frightfully amusing life,' I said.

'But you must know some delicious scandals. You are sharing a house with three notorious women, no? What of their love lives? Who goes to bed with whom?'

I felt myself blushing under his frank gaze. 'I know little about such things. Since I've been staying there, there have been no gentlemen in evidence.'

'What of the terrible Sir Toby? He lives next door, doesn't he? Does he never come to call? And the delectably exotic Olga? One hears such delicious gossip about their tempestuous life together.'

I felt a great sob like a hiccup coming up in my throat.

'What is it, *ma petite*? He really upset you this afternoon with his boorish behavior?'

'No, it's more than that,' I said. 'He's dead. After you brought me home, I looked over the terrace and there he was, face down in his swimming pool.'

'He drowned?'

'Worse than that,' I said. 'It looks as if someone killed him. I shouldn't say any more, but it will probably be in the papers tomorrow.'

'How extraordinary,' Jean-Paul said. 'Frankly I'm not surprised that somebody killed him. Such a man makes many enemies. And one wouldn't be surprised if Olga flashed a knife at him in the heat of passion one day.'

'Olga walked out, I believe.'

'And returned for vengeance? How fascinating. I will

follow the case with interest. Quite the thing to lift me from my boredom.'

'You? How can you be bored? You have a wonderful life.'

Jean-Paul sighed. 'I always crave the excitement. And most people I find frightfully boring. Except you – you are a delightful breath of fresh air. But now eat up. We cannot waste good caviar.'

This banquet should have been the ultimate treat for me, but I found that the events of the day had left me so shocked that I could hardly swallow. The rock melon filled with port slipped down easily enough and the effects of the port, mingled with the champagne, gradually started to unwind my tension. I knew I should put Sir Toby from my thoughts. I hardly knew the man and I certainly had no cause to like him. Still, it's always a shock when any human being's life is taken from him.

After we had eaten the lobster and duck, each of them exquisite beyond belief, and a sorbet had been brought to clear the palate, I excused myself and went to the ladies' room. As I entered, the first person I saw, powdering her nose, was Belinda. Her eyes lit up when she saw me.

'Darling, fancy bumping into you here of all places. I didn't see you. Are you with your mama?'

'No, I'm up in a little turret room with Jean-Paul.'

'Jean-Paul?' Her eyes widened. 'You mean the Marquis de Ronchard?'

'The very same. I can hardly believe it, but he seems interested in me. I hope you're not too cross with me. I did nothing to encourage him.'

'Of course you didn't, you sweet thing.' Belinda touched my cheek. 'That's why he finds you so delicious.

A completely unspoiled, unscheming female. What a change. No wonder he is captivated.'

'I know you wanted him for yourself.'

'I have to confess that was the idea, but as it happens I have moved on to pastures new, thanks to you.'

'To me?'

'Yes. Remember the young man who went to buy you a drink last night and returned only to find you had been whisked away by your marquis?'

'I do. His name was Neville.'

'That's the one. Well, I was left to cheer him up after he'd been so cruelly abandoned by you, and we hit it off rather well. To the extent that I've been invited to stay at his aunt's villa. His aunt is Lady Marchington and it just happens that she used to hunt with my papa, so I'm considered suitable and all that.'

'I gather Neville isn't particularly well off, from what I heard at Victoria Station.'

'Not at the moment, darling, but he will inherit a title one day, and a very nice estate. Not that I plan to be around that long, but Lady Marchington's villa is certainly a step up from the little pension near the railway station where I was staying. And Neville actually shows promise as a lover – for an Englishman, that is. So all in all, I'm satisfied for the moment.'

'I'm glad,' I said. 'I was trying to persuade Mummy to have you to stay with us, but it seems that she has to keep a bedroom free in case one of her pals decides to come and stay.'

'So all's well that ends well,' Belinda said. 'I just hope you know what you're doing with your marquis. He has quite a reputation, you know.'

'So I've heard. But he is rather gorgeous, isn't he? And I'm rather enjoying being wined and dined. It's a new experience for me.'

'Poor Darcy,' Belinda said. 'Dropped like a hot potato.'

'Poor Darcy has someone else,' I said.

'No, surely not.'

'I've seen them together,' I said bleakly. 'They have a child.'

'Good heavens. Well, that is a bit of a shock, isn't it? I really thought that you and he . . .'

'So did I,' I said, and I blinked back tears. 'I'd better go back or Jean-Paul will wonder where I am.'

We hugged, and as I crossed the restaurant to return to Jean-Paul, the first thing I noticed was several men standing around our table. To my horror I recognized one of them as Inspector Lafite.

'Ah, there she is now,' one of the men said.

'Inspector.' I eyed him coldly. 'What are you doing here?'

'I have come for you, Lady Georgiana,' he said.

'If you wish to ask me more questions, you can see that this is not a good time or place. I have nothing more to tell you, either about the missing necklace or about the death of Sir Toby.'

'I do not wish to ask you questions at this moment,' he said. 'We will do that at the police station.'

'The police station? I'm not going to any police station at this time of night.'

He took a menacing step toward me. 'I insist that you accompany me, mademoiselle. I am arresting you for the murder of Sir Toby Groper.'

# Chapter 23

I stared at him. My mouth was probably open, which I know is not acceptable for a lady. But you must admit it's not every day that one is accused of murder.

'If you will please step outside, mademoiselle,' Lafite said quietly. 'I'm sure you do not want to cause a disturbance or a scandal in such a place as this.'

Shock does funny things. I looked at his comical face with its exaggerated mustache and I started to laugh as he took my arm.

Jean-Paul, however, had leaped to his feet. 'Are you mad?' he demanded. 'This young lady is the daughter of an English duke. She is related to royalty.'

'Her background is of no consequence,' Lafite said. 'Please come with me quietly, mademoiselle, and let us have no unpleasantness. I am sure you would not wish to cause embarrassment to Monsieur le Marquis.'

One of his men took my other arm. I was conscious

of faces staring at me as I was led through the restaurant and out to the street, where several police motorcars were drawn up.

'Now, mademoiselle. Get in, please.' Lafite opened a rear door of one of the cars for me. I was moving mechanically, like a puppet, but Jean-Paul stepped between me and the police vehicle door.

'This is absurd,' Jean-Paul said, his eyes blazing. 'You know who I am, and I can vouch for her.'

'Forgive me, Marquis. Of course we know who you are. However, we have reason to believe that this young lady is guilty of this terrible crime.'

'What reason?' I demanded.

'I am not at liberty to discuss this here. We will wait until we are in the privacy of the police station. Now, please enter the automobile.'

'I'm coming too, if you are taking her,' Jean-Paul said. He tried to force his way into the motorcar.

'I am afraid that is not possible, Marquis. You must realize this is a very serious matter. You cannot be allowed to interfere with the course of justice.'

'Then I will go immediately to telephone a lawyer friend of mine.' Jean-Paul scowled at him, then touched my arm gently. 'You are not obliged to say anything until you have a lawyer present. Do not worry, *ma petite*. It is all a horrible mistake and we will have you back home in no time at all.'

For the first time I realized the enormity of what was happening to me. 'Please go and tell my mother where I am. Madame Chanel and Vera will know what to do.'

'They will be hammering at the police station door like ravening wolves,' Jean-Paul said with a smile. His hand touched my cheek. 'Courage, *chérie*. All will be well.'

With that, Lafite bundled me into the back seat of the car and we took off, driving along the winding coastal road until the lights of the city appeared below us. I sat with my lips pressed together, trying to look composed and haughty, but under my thin dress I could feel my legs trembling. I was in a foreign country. I knew little of their justice system and I was in the hands of a bumbling policeman. I prayed that Jean-Paul's lawyer and Mummy would arrive as soon as possible.

The police station appeared horribly bright after the darkness of the car. I was led through tiled hallways to a bare room that contained a table and two uncomfort-able-looking chairs.

'Please take a seat, mademoiselle,' Lafite said.

'I am not "mademoiselle,"' I said, trying to sound like my great-grandmother. 'I am a noble lady, a cousin to the King of England, and there will be serious repercussions about this folly when His Majesty learns of it.' At least I think that's what I said. My French might have become a little wobbly at such a moment of stress.

Lafite did not appear to be worried by this threat. 'Believe me, I realize the seriousness of this charge and would not have acted had I not been completely sure of my facts. We have proof, you see.'

'What proof?' I demanded. I was so angry and fright-ened that I forgot Jean-Paul's warning not to say anything until I had a lawyer present.

Lafite looked smug again. He put his hand up and stroked at his mustache. 'You were seen entering the house of Sir Toby this afternoon.'

Oh, crikey. Someone must have seen me making my way down the cliff to his garden. I couldn't think how, unless it was from a passing boat. Our terrace and Sir Toby's swimming pool were not visible to the outside world.

'Well, that's easy enough to explain,' I said, trying to sound calm and in control of this situation. 'I came home, walked on the terrace, looked down and spotted Sir Toby floating in his swimming pool. I called for help, but nobody came from his house, so I made my way down the cliff to see if I could help him. When I was close enough, I could see that he was dead, so I climbed back up and we summoned the police.'

He shook his head. 'No, mademoiselle. You were seen entering his house by the front entrance.'

I sighed again. 'Yes, of course. I did go to visit Sir Toby earlier in the day. But that was in the morning, when I can assure you Sir Toby was alive and well, and his manservant was also there to let me in.'

Lafite's eyes narrowed. 'You did not mention this to me when I questioned you earlier. In fact, you gave me to understand that you did not know Sir Toby. And yes, his manservant tells us that not only did you visit him at his house, but you went out sailing on his yacht – just the two of you. This does not indicate to me persons that do not know each other.'

'I thought it had no relevance to his murder, since there would be plenty of witnesses to confirm that he was alive when I left his boat. And I only met Sir Toby last night. I admired his yacht and he was kind enough to invite me out for a short sail. That was the only time I had any contact with him. I had never been to his house before or after.'

'But again you attempt to deceive Lafite.' He wagged

his finger at me. 'You are not telling the truth, I think. You were seen by a reliable witness entering the house of Sir Toby at around three o'clock this afternoon – which happens to be the time that the doctor has estimated for Sir Toby's murder. What is more, this reliable witness describes your behavior as furtive. He says you crept through the shrubbery as if you did not wish to be seen. And you were carrying something. What have you got to say to that?'

'I say it is nonsense,' I replied. 'At three o'clock this afternoon I was at the villa of the Marquis de Ronchard. He and his servants can vouch for me.'

'And you left his villa at what time?'

I frowned. 'I'm not quite sure of the time . . .'

'You are not quite sure of the time,' he mimicked.

'It was immediately after it started raining,' I said. 'I was certainly home by four.'

'Giving you enough time to pay a visit to the villa of Sir Toby,' he said triumphantly.

'It was pouring with rain,' I said.

'Murders can be committed in the rain, I believe. But my witness does not mention rain. I suspect it was a short, sharp shower and it had stopped by the time you paid your visit.'

'This is absurd,' I said. 'Pray, what would my motive have been, given that I had never met Sir Toby until last night?'

'Who can say? You come to the Riviera and immediately a valuable necklace is stolen from your neck. And the next day you are alone with a man who is murdered. We in the police of France are taught not to believe in coincidences. What do these two events have in common?

we ask ourselves, and the answer to both the robbery and the murder is you, mademoiselle.'

He wasn't going to get the manner of address right, or else he was being deliberately rude to me. I sighed. 'I am a member of the ruling family of England and as such I am hardly like to steal the queen's necklace or to kill a man I had never met before.'

'We have done a little prying into your affairs, Lady Georgiana.' He was looking even more smug by now. 'And we find that, yes, you are related to the king, but that your brother and yourself are in dire financial straits. You have no money, Lady Georgiana. You have no prospect of any money. Maybe you took the necklace, then set up a plan to rob Sir Toby?'

'Utter rubbish!' I said. 'Ask anyone who knows me. They will vouch for my character. I have had plenty of chances to marry for money or to live with a richer family member. I choose to make my own way, living in poverty. I have pride and I have integrity.'

'Very well. I take your word on this for the moment. So let us then say that it was a crime of passion.'

'Of passion?' I almost laughed out loud. 'I felt no passion for Sir Toby, I assure you.'

He leaned closer to me. His garlic breath became stronger, almost overpowering in that small room. 'I understand that you leaped from Sir Toby's yacht into the arms of the marquis. Maybe this Sir Toby tries to have his way with you. Maybe he forces you against your will, and you return to seek vengeance for your honor.'

'You sound like an Italian opera,' I said. 'Maybe people behave in that way in France, but not in England or Scotland, I assure you.'

'Then you please tell me why you crept into Sir Toby's garden, sneaking forward like a thief and carrying something under your arm.'

'The answer to that is that it wasn't I. Your observer saw someone else who may have resembled me. In fact, several people have mentioned that they have spotted someone in Nice who looks like me. I suggest you find her.'

'Were you wearing white trousers today, milady?' He glanced at a sheet of paper in front of him. 'And a dark blue jacket? And a sailor's hat?'

'Yes, I was, but–'

'This is exactly how you were described when seen creeping into Sir Toby's house at around three o'clock in the afternoon.'

'Who exactly described me and witnessed this fictitious event?'

'One of Sir Toby's gardeners. He had finished his work and gone home for the day, but then he remembered that he had left out the good pruning shears and he saw that it was about to rain. So he returned and was looking for the implement among the shrubs when he heard someone coming. He thought it might be Sir Toby and he did not want to get into trouble for leaving his tools behind, so he ducked down, and was surprised to see a young lady – the same young lady that he had seen that morning, in fact, wearing the same outfit she had worn in the morning – creeping furtively up toward the house as if she didn't want to be noticed.'

He got to his feet, coming to stand over me. 'It would be easier for us all if you confessed right away. Crimes of passion are understood in France. If this man violated your honor, the judge will understand that you came to confront him. Perhaps he laughed at you. Mocked you. Boasted about his control over you. And on the spur of the moment you were angry and humiliated. You picked up a heavy object and hit him. You did not mean to kill him, but he pitched forward into the pool. The court will understand this and will not pass a heavy sentence on you, I promise. The jurors have daughters. They will understand that your action was justified.'

'I would be happy to confess if any of this had happened,' I said. 'Fortunately it is all untrue. I did not go to Sir Toby's house and I did not hit him over the head. Now please release me and let me go home until I can meet you tomorrow at a civilized hour with a lawyer present.'

Lafite smiled and shook his head. 'Oh, no, milady. That would not do at all. I am well aware that your relative the Prince of Wales cruises this coast on the yacht of the famous Duke of Westminster. If I let you go, I suspect they would spirit you away on this yacht and you would not be seen again. Lafite does not lose his quarry so easily.'

'But you can't keep me here,' I said. 'I'm innocent. You only have the most circumstantial evidence that just isn't true.'

He leaned down and grinned into my face. His garlic breath nearly overwhelmed me once again. 'You forget that in France we follow the Napoleonic Code. Here you are guilty until proven innocent, not the other way around. If you did not commit this murder, you will have to prove it to me and prove it to the judge.'

'Then I will do so,' I said, staring him in the eye to show that I wasn't afraid.

At that moment there came the sound of raised voices

from outside the door, among them a man saying loudly in French, 'No, *Mesdames*, you may not enter.'

'We demand to see Lady Georgiana. What have you done with her?'

'I assure you she is quite safe, but she is being questioned by Inspector Lafite.'

'By that fool?' Coco's voice had become shrill. 'Let us in at once.'

'I cannot let you pass, *Madame*,' came the worried voice. 'Now please go home before I have you arrested.'

'Then arrest me.' Coco's voice was getting closer by the moment. 'Arrest Madame Daniels. Arrest Madame Bate Lombardi when she gets here. It will only make you look extremely foolish when you have to apologize to us. I should tell you that at this moment a message is being sent to the yacht of the Duke of Westminster, who is a dear friend of mine and related to Mrs Bate Lombardi. And you know who is on that yacht? The Prince of Wales, son of the English king and cousin to the young lady you have locked up in your jail cell. A message has also been sent to the English consul, who is on his way here, and to the ex-husband of Mrs Bate Lombardi, who is a correspondent for NBC – the important American broadcasting network. Soon your chief's foolishness will be known all over the globe and the British ambassador will be hurrying down from Paris with a stern message from the English king.'

I thought I noticed Lafite turning a trifle green. At least his smile had faded. I don't think until this moment he had quite realized my importance or that he may have created an international incident of great magnitude. I don't think I had either.

Then another, richer, louder voice boomed over Coco's, echoing off the tiled hallway walls of the police station. 'My poor baby. I demand that you let me see my child. I demand to know what you brutes are doing to her. You couldn't be heartless enough to keep her mother from her in her hour of need!'

Mummy was playing the part of the bereft mother – and, naturally, playing it awfully well. Miraculously, she was actually acknowledging me as her daughter, but her speech was being lost on the constable guarding the door as it was in English, Mummy's French not being up to dramatics. Lafite went to the door and opened it with a sigh. 'Madam,' he said in English, 'your daughter is safe and unharmed. Please observe her for yourself.'

'My darling!' Mummy cried and threw herself at me, uttering great, heart-wrenching sobs. It was a very convincing performance and I think the younger policeman dabbed his eyes. Then she turned the full force of her gaze onto Lafite. 'You will let me take her home, won't you? If you keep her here, I shall sit on the pavement outside in the cold all night, hoping and praying and waiting.'

'*Madame*, I cannot let her go. She will flee to the arms of her royal cousin and will never face justice for her crime.'

'What crime?' Mummy demanded. 'You can't seriously think that my daughter had anything to do with the death of Sir Toby? Look at her – a sweet, innocent girl. She is in a state of complete shock.'

'Sweet, innocent girls have been known to kill before now,' Lafite said. 'They have even killed their mothers, I believe.'

'But not my daughter. She is the great-granddaughter of Queen Victoria. She has been raised with that code of honor.'

'I remember that your Queen Victoria killed many people as your country tried to rule the world,' Lafite said.

'Yes, but not personally,' Mummy answered. 'She had armies to do that for her.'

Lafite smirked. 'But you are not of royal blood, *Madame*. And you clearly have passion in your veins. Maybe your daughter, she takes after you.'

I was tired and scared and angry. I got to my feet. 'This is silly and it's getting us nowhere,' I said. 'I didn't kill Sir Toby. I did not return to his house in the afternoon. I've made it clear to you that the marquis drove me home, in the rain. He drove me right up to the front door and I ran inside, where my maid greeted me. If I'd gone to Sir Toby's I'd have been wet, wouldn't I?'

'My lady, this does not prove your innocence. Who is to say you did not slip away later, when the rain stopped?'

I decided that a white lie might be in order. 'My maid was with me, helping me prepare for my dinner with the marquis. She would have noticed if I'd left the villa. Why don't you question her?'

'We shall, mademoiselle. Trust me, we shall question everyone. But I would take the word of a maid who is loyal to her mistress with the speck of salt.'

'Then I suggest you question Sir Toby's wife and son, and his mistress, because they all have better motives to want him dead than I.'

Lafite waved these suggestions aside. 'I will decide whom to investigate. And at this moment the cards are all stacked against you, Lady Georgiana of Rannoch. It all comes back to the fact that a reliable man did not see a ghost when he noticed you in Sir Toby's front garden. But trust me, Lafite will leave no pebble not-turned-over to get at the truth.'

Mummy put a protective arm around my shoulders. 'Then it may interest you to know that Madame Chanel has just telephoned to her friend at the Sûreté in Paris, and what's more we have a top man from Scotland Yard arriving any moment. So you had better pray, Monsieur Lafite, that you get it right, because the eyes of the world are on you.'

'You may bring who you like, *Madame.* I have already told you that the Yard of Scotland has no power here. I, Lafite, have the power to send this young woman to trial or not.'

I don't know how long this impasse would have continued or whether Mummy would eventually have worn him down, but once more there were voices in the tiled hallway – men's voices this time – and Jean-Paul stalked into the room, followed by a distinguished-looking man with gray hair.

'I said I would return to put matters right, and I have,' Jean-Paul announced, as dramatically as my mother had done. 'Inspector, may I present Monsieur Balzac, the eminent criminal defense lawyer. Together we have been to the home of Monsieur le Juge and I have placed with him a considerable sum of money to guarantee that Lady Georgiana does not flee from Nice so she may be free to return to her villa.'

I wanted to rush over to him and hug him, but Mummy got there first. 'You are a wonderful, wonderful man,' she said, flinging her arms around his neck. 'I don't know how we'll be able to repay you.' Her actions indicated that she had a jolly good idea of one way to repay him.

Lafite shot a glance at the young policeman. 'Very well,' he said. 'You may take her home tonight. But I send my men to guard the house. Do not even think of leaving Nice, any of you.'

'We wouldn't dream of it,' Mummy said. 'Where else would one want to be in the winter?' She took my hand. 'Come, darling. We're going home.'

And she dragged me triumphantly past the little inspector.

# Chapter 24

*January 26–27, 1933*
*At the Villa Marguerite. Still shaken and stirred.*

We stood together on the pavement in a little group: Mummy and Jean-Paul and the lawyer and Coco had joined us as well.

'So where to now?' Jean-Paul said cheerfully. 'The casino or the Negresco for a late drink?'

'If you don't mind, I'd rather go home,' I said. 'I'm afraid I wouldn't be a very gay and witty companion tonight.'

'Of course you wouldn't, darling,' Mummy said. 'It's been a nightmare for you. I'll take you home straight away. See, my car is waiting over there. If you'll excuse us, Marquis.'

'I understand.' He gave me a wonderful smile. 'Go home and sleep well, *ma petite.*'

'I'm sorry our lovely evening was spoiled,' I said.

He took my hand and raised it to his lips. 'There will be other evenings,' he said, and he looked at me as his lips lingered on my hand in a way that, in spite of everything, made me feel weak at the knees.

'You've certainly made a conquest there,' Mummy said as we reached the car and the chauffeur got out to open the door for us. 'Positively drooling over you, darling. Well, you wouldn't do too badly if you snagged that one. A marquis isn't as good as a prince, I know, but he does have oodles of loot.'

'Mummy, how can you talk about such things, after what has just happened?'

She patted my knee as she climbed into the car beside me. 'I prefer not to dwell on the unpleasant aspects of life. And now the marquis and his lawyer have taken charge, this will all be forgotten in an instant. Especially when our man from Scotland Yard arrives.'

'Who is the top man from Scotland Yard you have coming to help?' I asked.

'Why, your grandfather, of course,' Mummy said.

I had to laugh. 'Mummy, he was an ordinary constable and he's retired.'

'That odious little man doesn't need to know that,' Mummy said.

'Is Granddad really coming, then? Have you heard back from him?'

'No, but I told him we'd booked his ticket. In the morning I'll send a second telegram saying "Georgie arrested for murder." That should do the trick.'

'It would be lovely if he did come,' I said wistfully. Now that I was no longer facing the horrid inspector and safely in Mummy's car, I felt as if I might let myself down and cry. What I wanted more than anything else at this moment was my grandfather's comforting presence, the smell of his old tweed jacket and the feel of his bristly cheek as he hugged me. I didn't dare hope too much that he would come. I knew it would be a huge undertaking for him to leave England and go abroad to a country he mistrusted. But I knew that he loved me too. So I let a glimmer of hope burn inside me.

For once Mummy was a real brick. She pushed Queenie out of the way and helped me undress, then she brought me hot milk with brandy in it and handed me a little white pill.

'What is it?' I asked cautiously.

'Just a sleeping pill, darling. I use them all the time. Take it and you'll sleep like a baby.'

I was too exhausted to resist, even though I had serious misgivings about any pill that my mother took. But she was right. It did work like a charm. I fell asleep and awoke to see Queenie standing over my bed with a tea tray.

'Your mum said I had better wake you up,' she said, plonking the tray down on the side table so that the tea splashed into the saucer. 'That lawyer bloke is here and wanting to talk to you.'

'Oh, golly.' The full memory of the night before came rushing back to me. 'Run me a bath, Queenie, and find me something to wear that looks–' I was about to say 'innocent' but I changed it to 'girlish. Young.'

'Bob's yer uncle, miss,' she said cheerfully and went off. I sat up and drank the rest of the tea. Amazingly, I felt remarkably well, considering everything that had happened yesterday. I bathed and came back to find that Queenie had laid out the same white trousers and blue jacket of the day before. That was one outfit I did not want to be seen wearing.

'No, Queenie. A simple cotton frock. Oh, let me.' I shoved her aside and examined my meager wardrobe.

Simple frocks were actually something I owned. I selected a schoolgirlish check, brushed my hair and went downstairs looking, I hoped, young, innocent and demure. As I neared the drawing room I heard low voices and was mortified to find not only Monsieur Balzac sitting on the sofa, but Jean-Paul standing beside him. I was horribly conscious that I looked like a schoolgirl.

Monsieur Balzac rose to his feet. 'Lady Georgiana. I trust that you slept well,' he said in French.

'Yes, I did. Thank you. And thank you for coming to my rescue last night.'

He shook his head. 'It was the marquis you had to thank. I am just the instrument.'

'My eternal thanks to both of you,' I said. 'If it weren't for you, I'd have been locked up in a dreadful cell, being gloated over by that horrid man.' I turned to focus my gaze on Jean-Paul. 'It was especially nice of you to get up so early for me.'

Jean-Paul laughed. 'But I am an early bird by nature. Ask anyone. Besides, I had to meet the train.' He came across to me and took my hand. 'I just wanted to see for myself that you had survived the night and were well. Now, if you will excuse me, I have matters that require my immediate attention. I leave you in the experienced hands of Monsieur Balzac.' And he kissed my hand lightly before departing.

Monsieur Balzac coughed to draw my attention. 'Please be seated, Lady Georgiana, and I want you to tell me everything.'

He resumed his place on the sofa. I perched on the edge of a chair across from him. 'I don't really know what to tell. I had never met Sir Toby until two days ago at the casino. We exchanged a few words. I admired his yacht because one can see it from our terrace. He invited me to come sailing with him the next day. I went to his house before noon, I think. We went for a short sail. Sir Toby tried to' – I paused, selecting my words carefully – 'take advantage of me, knowing that I was all alone on his yacht. Fortunately the marquis happened to pass by in his speedboat and so I left Sir Toby and went off with him.'

'I see.' He frowned. 'Unfortunately this will not come across well in court. I had hoped that we could claim you did not know Sir Toby. But his crew will testify that he made advances to you and you left his yacht in a state of distress.'

'Yes, but they will also testify that he was still alive when I left, and I never saw him again. I was with the marquis.'

'So he informs me. You ate a meal together on the beach, I believe.'

I nodded. 'Then it started to pour with rain and he drove me home. He actually saw me go in the front door. My maid met me. I rested for a while, then the rain stopped and I walked out onto the terrace and saw the body floating in the swimming pool.' I looked at him and shrugged. 'That's about it, really.'

'So someone was with you all the time after you arrived home?'

'My maid wasn't actually with me all the time, but she was around. So were other servants.'

He frowned. 'So this gardener, who claims he saw you tiptoeing toward Sir Toby's house at around three o'clock? He is lying? For what purpose?'

'Someone has paid him to pin the crime on me,

perhaps?' I suggested. 'Or he saw someone who looked like me. The funny thing is that several people have seen someone who resembles me in Nice. We should try to find this person. Perhaps she had a good reason to go and visit Sir Toby yesterday.'

'We will certainly try to do this,' he said. He leaned across and patted my knee. 'Do not worry. I am sure there is not enough evidence to bring a case against you, especially given who you are and your royal connections. When they look into the affairs of Sir Toby, they will find someone with a compelling motive for wanting him dead. You say you saw him at the casino. Maybe he had gambling debts. Maybe he had run afoul of the mafia – we are not far from the Italian border here. Or maybe he surprised a thief in the course of a robbery. I understand he owned many fine objets d'art.'

'Yes,' I said. 'That's much more likely. And I know from what I overheard that he had quarreled recently with his wife and his mistress. I just hope that Inspector Lafite doesn't think he has found the ideal suspect in me and doesn't bother to investigate any further.'

'We will have to make sure that he keeps on looking,' Balzac said. He got to his feet. 'So have courage, young lady. I think our inspector realizes now that he acted hastily. Let us hope that he will soon be on the track of the real criminal.' He shook my hand. *'À bientôt.'* Then he left the room, leaving me feeling uneasy. I sensed that he didn't really believe I was out of the woods, nor that I was completely innocent.

I went out onto the terrace. The unsettled weather of the previous night had vanished to leave a clear, sparkling morning with the sea so blue that it looked like liquid sapphire. A seagull circled lazily overhead. A small fishing boat chugged past with men in striped jerseys on board. It would have been a perfect day if this cloud hadn't been hanging over us. My mother, Vera and Coco were sitting at the table, looking gloomy. They all attempted to brighten up when they saw me. Mummy jumped to her feet.

'Hello, darling, had a lovely long sleep?' She came to kiss my cheek.

'Yes, thank you. I did. And I've just been talking to Jean-Paul's lawyer.'

'That's good. He'll take care of everything. They'll sort it all out in no time, you'll see,' Vera said. 'Have you had breakfast?'

'No, and I'm starving.'

She got up. 'I'll go and tell Cook to prepare you eggs and bacon. You need a proper breakfast at times like these.'

I drew up a chair at the table, reaching forward to pour myself some coffee. 'Are you going to send Granddad another telegram?' I asked Mummy.

'Already done. I sent Franz into town with it first thing.'

'You're wonderful.' I beamed at her. 'I do hope he comes.'

'He will, after he reads my dramatic rendition of your dire circumstances. I'm almost as good on paper as I am on the stage.'

'But you said telegrams were expensive. You paid by the word, you said.'

She laughed. 'Dear child, I am not exactly penniless. Besides, it's Max's money – at least for the moment.'

'What do you mean?'

'I received a letter from him this morning saying how much he missed me and how he wanted me to return home to him. It was phrased as a request, but it sounded to me like an order.'

'Oh, golly. Will you go?'

She shrugged. 'I don't like being bossed. I'm writing back to tell him that my daughter needs me. And while I'm here I may look for someone to fill his shoes, so to speak. Since you've snagged the marquis, I'll have to cast my net farther afield.'

'Mummy, you are terrible.' I couldn't help laughing.

'Ah, but you have to admit I do have fun.' Her face clouded suddenly. 'Oh, God – you know what just struck me? If that silly little French inspector decides to delve into our connections with Sir Toby, he'll find out that Max and he had a blazing row over Sir Toby trying to steal his designs. Lafite would make hay with that, wouldn't he?'

'At least you have an alibi for the time he was killed,' I said. 'I don't. I think I'm going to visit that gardener this morning and confront him about what he actually saw. That way I'll know whether someone was paying him to say that he saw me. But I can't think why they'd choose me as their scapegoat. I had never even met the man until the night before.'

Coco leaned forward to stub out her cigarette. 'It is all very strange,' she said. 'My money is on Olga. Her type is hot-blooded and does not forgive easily. I would bet that she hired a thug to do the deed for her.'

I nodded. 'She certainly threatened him when she walked out. She told him he'd be sorry. But apparently the gardener didn't notice a big, burly thug creeping into the garden, just someone who looked like me.'

'Breakfast on the way,' Vera announced as she returned to join us. 'And I gather that the Duke of Westminster's yacht has returned to Nice, which is comforting to know. At the very least we could whisk you away–'

'With the Prince of Wales on board?' I said. 'Pursued by French gunboats? I don't think that would go down well at Buckingham Palace. Besides, Mrs Simpson would try to push me back overboard. She loathes me.'

'She loathes everyone who isn't useful to her, darling,' Mummy said, 'but she especially loathes you because you're one of them and she will never be. She sees you as standing in the way of her grand design.'

'She can't really aspire to being queen one day!' Vera laughed and reached across to take a cigarette from Coco's gold case.

My breakfast had just arrived and I fell upon it as if I hadn't had a meal in months. I suppose fear can make people hungry. But I was only halfway through the eggs and bacon when Mummy's maid appeared.

'*Madame*, you have a visitor. I have shown her into the drawing room.' And she handed Mummy a calling card on a silver salver – all terribly proper, which made me surmise immediately that the guest expected that kind of formality. Mummy took the card.

'Good God,' she said, and she flicked it across the table to Vera and Coco. 'Lady Groper has turned up.'

# Chapter 25

*January 27, 1933*
*At Villa Marguerite and later at Sir Toby's villa. Lovely
day. I only wish I could enjoy it.*

Lady Groper was sitting very upright on one of the small
gilt chairs and got to her feet as Mummy entered, followed,
I have to confess, by the rest of us, who weren't about to
miss anything. She was dressed in very English tweeds, in
spite of the weather, and her face looked old and gaunt.

'I realize you don't know me and I have no right to call
upon you,' she said, holding out her hand. 'I'm Margaret
Groper. I only know you as the Duchess of Rannoch,
which title I know you no longer hold. Apart from that
as Claire Daniels, but I presume that is your stage name.'

'Claire Daniels will do perfectly,' Mummy said, 'since
I believe I'm officially still Mrs Homer Clegg – the last
man I was married to, a Texas oil millionaire who found
religion and won't divorce me. Of all the husbands' names
to get stuck with!' She motioned to the chair. 'Please do sit
down. Would you like some coffee?'

'I only take tea in the mornings,' Lady Groper said, perching herself, birdlike, once more on the chair, 'but at the moment I feel more like a good, stiff brandy.'

'Brandy it shall be, then,' Mummy said, turning back to the maid who was hovering in the doorway.

'I wasn't being serious, Mrs Daniels,' Lady Groper said. 'It's only ten o'clock in the morning.'

'If you need it and want it, who cares about the hour?' Mummy shrugged. 'A cognac for Milady, please, Claudette.'

'It's very good of you.' Lady Groper looked inquiringly at the rest of us, who were loitering. 'I'm afraid I haven't been introduced to these ladies.'

'Forgive me. This is Madame Chanel, Mrs Bate Lombardi and my daughter, Georgiana Rannoch.'

'Oh, so you're the one!' Lady Groper's eyes hardened as she looked at me.

'Yes, I discovered your husband's body, I'm afraid,' I said, not sure what she was hinting.

'But they were saying at the Negresco that the police arrested you for his murder. They say you were out with him on his yacht and I know what that generally means.'

Really, I was quite amazed at how quickly gossip spreads among an expatriate community.

'The police have got it wrong, as usual,' Mummy said sharply. 'Georgiana was invited for a sail on his yacht. She was not aware of your husband's reputation, and she left when he began acting boorishly. That was the last time she saw him alive.'

Lady Groper's expression softened. 'I'm sorry. As you can imagine, I'm rather upset. However badly he behaved, he was my husband for over twenty years. I must have loved him once, I suppose. And I wouldn't wish anybody to die like that, bleeding to death in his swimming pool.' She looked down at her gloved hands. 'That pool was his pride and joy. Although a frightful extravagance, if you ask me. What irony that it should cause his death.'

'I rather think the blow to the head caused his death,' I said. 'The pool was just a convenient place to dump the body in the hopes that it would look like an accident. Which of course it didn't. You can't hit the back of your head and then pitch forward into a pool.'

Again she looked at me with narrowed eyes, as if suspecting that I knew more than I was telling. I was glad that Claudette arrived just then with the cognac on a tray. Lady Groper accepted it and took a good swig.

'So you only heard the news this morning,' Mummy said. 'It must have come as a tremendous shock to you.'

'Tremendous.' Lady Groper shuddered again. 'I had been up to visit friends in the hills. I returned to the Negresco very late last night and saw the news when the boy brought in my morning paper. There it was, screaming from the headline: "English Lord Murdered." I couldn't believe it.'

'If you don't mind my asking,' Chanel said in her delightfully French-accented English, 'why were you staying at a hotel when you own such a lovely villa nearby? Had you and your husband had a falling-out?'

Lady Groper flushed. 'It's really none of your business,' she said.

'Ah, but it is. My little friend Georgiana is accused of a murder she did not commit. So I must wonder . . .'

'How dare you!' Lady Groper put down the glass with a

bang on the table. 'Are you suggesting that I had anything to do with my husband's murder?'

Chanel looked not in the least put out. She shrugged. 'I am only curious why a wife chooses to sleep apart from her husband.'

'You know very well why.' Lady Groper almost spat out the words. 'Because I assumed that creature would be in residence. How would you feel, knowing that he flaunted that floozie in public, having her to live with him at the villa? He blamed me – claimed that it was my fault because I refused to come to the Riviera with him every winter.' She looked up, as if asking for sympathy. 'But I hate living abroad. I hate the lifestyle and the constant parties and the gambling and the – carrying-on, if you know what I mean. It's all quite alien to what I stand for. Give me a good old British winter with hunting any day.'

'So why did you come this time, Lady Groper?' I asked, already knowing the answer.

She frowned at me. 'Again it's none of your business.'

'But the police might suspect that you came over here with the express purpose of catching your husband with his mistress,' I said. 'And being the French police, they would go on to surmise that you lost control and hit him with the nearest object.'

She shot me a fleeting look of horror. 'Surely no one would ever think such a thing. That's ridiculous. I have known about his mistresses for years and turned a blind eye, because that's what good wives do.' She sat even straighter and folded her hands in her lap. 'If you must know, I had a small spot of business to attend to with my husband. When it was concluded, I decided to visit an old friend who has a villa in the hills. I was planning to return home by tonight's train, only to hear the news about Toby.' She stood up abruptly. 'I've taken too much of your time. I'd better go to the villa and check whether there are any possessions of mine there – or presents that I gave Toby. I rather suspect he gave that floozie some of my jewels, but I don't suppose she keeps them at the villa.'

'Mademoiselle Olga had left him,' Chanel said.

'She had? When?'

'Only a day or so ago. She stormed out in a rage.'

Lady Groper beamed. 'There you are, then. You have your killer. She was known to be a dramatic, violent sort of person. She came back to kill him. Presumably the police are looking for her?'

'I expect they'll eventually get around to it,' Vera said.

Lady Groper started toward the front door, then turned back. 'I wonder if I could ask a favor – if one of you would come with me to the villa. I don't want to compromise myself in any way – you understand. I'd prefer to have a witness present.'

'I presume you will inherit the property, won't you? So the possessions in it are legally yours,' Mummy said.

'Unless Toby has changed his will behind our backs, my son inherits the estates and the title. I am left a sum of money ample for my needs and of course I own property that comes from my family.'

'Oh, you have a son,' Mummy said innocently. 'How lovely for you.'

Lady Groper's face softened. 'Yes, he is a dear boy and quite devoted to his mother. He's doing well – up at Oxford, you know. His father had high hopes for him. He'll be devastated when he hears this.'

And with that she opened the front door. I watched her

go, then followed at the back of the party. Several things were interesting to me: first, that she had not mentioned her intention to file divorce proceedings against her husband, nor his threats to expose her to scandal, and second, that she didn't appear to know her son was also on the Riviera. Or if she did, she was a very good liar.

There were two policemen standing at the entrance to our driveway. They stepped out to block the way as they saw us.

'We are escorting Lady Groper to her villa,' Coco said to them. 'She has just heard the terrible news and has to see whether anything has been stolen.'

'Very well,' one of the policemen said. 'You will find our men at the villa. You may tell them you have permission to accompany Lady Groper.'

We walked down the driveway. Lady Groper shuddered as the villa came into sight. 'A monstrosity, isn't it? The kind of tasteless extravagance that one of no breeding builds. Toby might have had a title, but he was still a parvenu, a nouveau riche. You've seen the artwork he collected?' She looked back at us. 'He claims it will be worth a fortune, but I find much of it hideous.'

We reached the front door, which was opened for us by another policeman, and stepped inside. Almost immediately Johnson appeared. 'Oh, it's you, ladies,' he said, looking relieved. 'I thought it might be the inspector again. I can't tell you how many times I've answered the same questions, over and over – What time did I go into town? Did I see the young lady from next door?' He looked at me, 'Oh, and I must apologize, my lady. I didn't know who you were before. I must have appeared a bit rude.'

'Not at all. I didn't choose to reveal my true identity at

that moment,' I said. 'People tend to behave differently toward me when they know I have royal connections.'

'I understand, my lady.' His gaze moved on to Lady Groper. She was eyeing him coldly. 'And who is this young man, may I ask?' she said.

'Johnson, ma'am,' he said. 'Sir Toby's new valet. He hired me shortly before we left for the Continent. I take it that you are Lady Groper. May I say how very sorry I am that he met such a tragic end.'

'Another new valet,' Lady Groper said. 'I could never keep up with them. And where were you, Johnson, when my husband was brutally murdered?'

Johnson clearly saw this as a veiled criticism, that he had somehow been neglecting his duty. 'Sir Toby had sent me into town to run errands for him,' he said. 'I saw him set off on his yacht and did not expect him back until evening. In fact, he told me I didn't need to hurry back, so I didn't. I also ran a few errands for myself and enjoyed seeing a bit of Nice. I saw his yacht moored in the harbor, so I've no idea how he came to be back here, all alone. I only wish I had come back sooner – I may have prevented . . .' And his voice wavered.

'Don't blame yourself, boy,' Lady Groper said. 'You did what you were instructed. So I presume that your master was not expecting anybody to call yesterday afternoon? And there is no evidence of anyone having been here?'

'No, my lady.'

'And that woman – Olga?' she asked tentatively.

'She left the master a few days ago. She took all her belongings and moved out.'

'And she didn't come back at all and try to see him?'

'No, my lady. We haven't seen hide nor hair of her

since, and good riddance, if you don't mind my saying so. She was a nasty piece of stuff.'

'And I presume you have checked the villa to see if anything was disturbed or taken?' she asked.

'As far as I could tell, nothing was touched, ma'am,' he said. 'Of course I don't have the keys to his safe or several locked drawers, and I have no idea of their contents.'

Lady Groper moved forward into the drawing room, looking around her with distaste. 'He's acquired even more things since I was here last, and most of them as ugly as sin,' she said. 'Why would anyone want a painting of an old chair? Or that one with all the scribbles and ink blots? Surely he didn't pay good money for something like that.'

'I believe it's a Matisse, my lady,' Johnson said. 'He's a local painter who has gained quite a reputation.'

'I wouldn't give you tuppence for it,' Lady Groper said. 'But I see he's brought out a lot of my family's good silver. That will have to go back home where it belongs. Find me some suitable boxes and I'll tell you which things I want packed and shipped.'

Johnson looked embarrassed. 'I don't think I should do that yet, my lady.'

'Why not?' she snapped.

'The police might not be through with them.'

'What would the French police want with my silver?' she demanded. 'Are they trying to insinuate that my husband received stolen goods or that it wasn't his? The impudence.'

'No, my lady. It's more looking for fingerprints on them – that sort of thing, to try to work out who might have been here and whether they'd tried to take anything.'

'Oh, very well,' Lady Groper snapped. 'I suppose this means I'd better stay at the villa so that some grubby little French policeman doesn't walk off with any of the family heirlooms. You can make a bed up for me in the blue bedroom, young man.' She paused, eyeing him critically. 'What was your name again?'

'Johnson, my lady,' he said.

'And for whom were you in service last?'

'An American gentleman, my lady. I spent the last year living in Los Angeles.'

'And why did you leave him?'

'America was not to my taste, my lady.' Johnson held her gaze. 'But since I am obviously no longer employed by your husband, I think my past history is no longer of any relevance.'

'Impudent pup,' Lady Groper said. 'Go about your duties, boy.'

He gave the slightest hint of a bow and left the room. As they spoke, I had been eyeing the broken glass-topped table with the queen's snuffbox in it. Now I was in a quandary – it was possible that the police had made an inventory of Sir Toby's things. And if they decided to search my room and found the snuffbox in my possession, it would be one more piece of incriminating evidence. I moved away again. Now that Lady Groper had announced her intention to stay in the villa for a few days, I would wait for a suitable moment and then tell her the truth – well, maybe part of the truth – that Her Majesty maybe lent the snuffbox to Sir Toby for a special display . . . ? And at the very worst, I'd tell Johnson the truth and have him acquire it for me.

Lady Groper made her way out through the French

doors and stood looking at the pool. 'So it was here,' she said. 'He lay here, bleeding to death, poor stupid man.'

And surprisingly she started to weep. While the others were comforting her, I went in search of Johnson. He was standing at a linen cupboard, taking out sheets. He looked up at me.

'That's the last thing I need right now,' he said in a low voice. 'Her bossing me around. I only went into Sir Toby's employ because I knew he wasn't one of those toffee-nosed snobs. But she's the worst.' He leaned closer to me. 'I'd like to walk out and take the next train back to England, but then that might look suspicious, mightn't it?'

'Definitely,' I said. 'But at least you've got nothing to worry about. You can prove you were in town when he was killed.'

'Why would I want to kill him?' Johnson shook his head. 'That's the same as killing the goose that laid the golden egg, isn't it? He was paying me well. He was a baronet – a step up in the world for me. Now I'm back to looking for a new position, like everyone else.'

I watched him as he took out matching pillow slips then closed the cupboard. 'If you don't mind my asking, Johnson,' I said, 'you sound as if you've had an education. Why are you in service?'

He turned back to me, eyeing me critically for a moment before saying angrily, 'I don't know if you've noticed, but there is a depression going on. There are no jobs for people like me – grammar school boys with no family connections behind them. Domestic service gives me a roof over my head, three good meals a day and a decent wage, if you're lucky enough to latch onto someone like

Sir Toby. That's why I'm so angry he's been killed. I'd like to throttle the person who did it.'

I moved closer. 'Do you have any idea who might have done it?' I asked. 'You've been close to him recently. You must have some suspicions.'

He was silent for a while. 'I've thought about it. Believe me, I've wondered. Sir Toby wasn't the best-liked man in the world. And I know some of his business dealings were – what would you say – shady?'

'When I was here yesterday morning and Sir Toby was in the bath – he said something about "that slimy little toad" and some German-sounding name. And he said he'd be sorry. What was that about?'

Johnson closed the cupboard door, holding the sheets draped carefully over one arm. 'I'm not quite sure. Some business Sir Toby was doing with an art dealer. He claimed Sir Toby had cheated him.'

'Any chance that the art dealer came here yesterday afternoon?'

'Possible, I suppose. Frankly anyone could have come here and we'd never know, would we? The place was deserted. We don't even know what Sir Toby was doing back here.'

'I'm just wondering,' I said, as the thought formed in my head. 'What if Sir Toby had arranged a secret meeting with somebody? He sent you away, he gave the other servants the afternoon off and he left his yacht very visibly moored in Nice. Doesn't that seem suspicious to you?'

Johnson frowned. 'Now that you mention it, it does.'

'Then I think you should suggest it to the police, and mention this German fellow too,' I said. 'At least it would remove the suspicion from me and from you.'

He looked up, amused. 'From you? Why on earth would the police suspect you?'

'Haven't you heard?' I said. 'I'm suspect number one. In fact, they arrested me last night on the charge of murder. I'm only out on bail.'

'Good Lord,' he said. 'Because you went out on his yacht yesterday? That's absurd.'

'Not only that,' I said. 'One of the gardeners claimed he saw me creeping into the house around the time Sir Toby was murdered.'

'You didn't come here yesterday afternoon, did you?'

'Of course not. It's utter rubbish, of course. I never came near the place, so I'm thinking that maybe the intruder was someone who looked a lot like me. Several people have thought they'd seen me around town when I was nowhere in the area. So either I have a double or the gardener is being paid to incriminate me.'

'One of our gardeners?' Johnson looked surprised. 'But they don't work in the afternoon.'

'He saw it was going to rain and came back to get a tool, I gather. I rather think I'm going to pay him a visit and try to get the truth out of him.'

Johnson frowned. 'Be careful, my lady.' He lowered his voice, looking around to see if anyone else was within hearing distance. 'If someone is paying this man, he may well be in league with some kind of gangsters. There are plenty of them on the Riviera, so I hear, including the mafia.' He paused, considering. 'But don't you have an alibi for yesterday afternoon?'

'Yes, I do. I was at the villa of the Marquis de Ronchard and then he drove me home, where the servants saw me.'

'There you are, then.' He gave me a relieved smile.

'I told the inspector that, but it doesn't seem good enough for him.'

'He doesn't seem too bright to me,' Johnson said. 'I'll let him know about Schumann and the threats. Although I find it so hard to get through to him, what with me speaking no French and his awful English. He may end up thinking I'm trying to confess myself.'

He gave me a grin as he carried the bedsheets toward the back of the house. I stood watching him, wondering if I had an ally.

# Chapter 26

**January 27, 1933**
***A hectic day on the Côte d'Azur.***

As we came out of the villa, Mummy slipped her arms through Coco's and Vera's, marching them up the driveway like a brisk governess with two reluctant schoolgirls. 'God, how terribly dreary, wasn't she? I suppose one should feel sorry for her–'

'Sorry for her? But no,' Coco said. 'She is rid of a bad husband and she has plenty of money to enjoy life.'

And she doesn't have to go through an ugly divorce case, either, I thought but didn't say out loud. If only there was a sensible policeman I could share this knowledge with. Or someone like Granddad or Darcy, who would know whom to tell. I found myself wondering if Lady Groper had orchestrated the whole thing perfectly – the alibi of being in the hills, far enough away from Nice, of not finding out about the murder until she read the morning papers. Or – an even more chilling thought struck me – the coincidence of their son, Bobby, suddenly turning up, but not wanting to be seen. Was it possible that Lady G and Bobby had planned this between them? I had seen from her face that he was the apple of his mother's eye. Was it plausible that he had not made contact with her and she had really not known he was here? If the police had decided that I was the guilty party, then I'd have to seek out Bobby for myself and see if I could get to the truth.

'She could lead a delightful life if she chooses,' Chanel continued. 'But I do not think she will do so. She will certainly not buy herself a decent wardrobe. She will hunt and fish and live in the boring English countryside.' And she gave that delightful laugh.

'I know,' Mummy said suddenly. 'Let's have a party. Things have been all too gloomy around here and we haven't had a party in ages.'

'Is that wise, with Georgiana under suspicion of murder?' Vera asked.

'Darling, that's the very best time to do it. Georgie needs cheering up, don't you, darling?' She looked back at me, trailing behind them up the driveway under the eyes of the watching policemen. 'And we'll show these horrid little men that they've got it wrong and they can't intimidate us.'

'When do you propose holding this party?' Vera asked.

'Why not tonight? I'll get on the telephone – invite a few people and they'll spread the word.'

'Tonight, Claire!' Vera complained. 'We need food and drink and decorations.'

'Simple, darling. I'll telephone my favorite restaurant for their lovely hors d'oeuvres platters, cold lobster, that kind of thing, and I think you'll find that my wine cellar

is well stocked. So we just need ice and lemons and a few
fun things like paper lanterns – the shops are full of fun
stuff ready for carnival. I'll pop into town. No problem.'

'Let me go,' I said.

They turned to look at me.

'I want to show them that I'm not their prisoner.'
Another thought had also come to me. I wanted to speak
to the crew of that yacht and find out exactly what happened yesterday afternoon and how Sir Toby came to be
back at his villa.

'That's the spirit, my sweet,' Mummy said. 'Of course.
You go into town and enjoy yourself. I'll make a list of
things to buy.'

We went into the house and Mummy sat at her pretty
little secretary desk, scribbling at a list that got longer and
longer. 'Oh, and fireworks,' she chirped. 'We must have
fireworks, don't you think? And masks? Do you think it
should be a fancy dress do? Or just carnival masks?'

'Aren't you going a little overboard?' I asked, picturing
a day ahead of me of trying to find these items in a town
I didn't know.

'Nonsense, darling. What's the point of a party if you
don't go overboard?'

I sat on the sofa watching her, admiring her. Not only
was she beautiful, but she had a wonderful way of shaking off life's little problems like water off a duck's back.
Nothing seemed to upset her. I just wished I had inherited
that trait. Then I noticed that while we had been at the
villa, someone had delivered the morning papers. There
it was – the big, black headline, *English Peer Found Dead in
Swimming Pool*. My eyes scanned down the article. Then
I looked up, frowning. Lady Groper had said she'd found

out about her husband's death from the morning papers, but in this particular article there was no mention of the blow to the back of Sir Toby's head or anything about him bleeding to death. I went through the rest of the papers. Again no mention of details.

'Here you are, darling.' Mummy waved a long list at me. 'Just a few things to pick up in town. I'd better get busy making telephone calls or we'll have no food, no ice and no guests.' And she was off, yelling instructions to servants.

Franz was summoned to bring the motorcar to the front door. But as I came out, a policeman stepped to block my way. 'Excuse me, mademoiselle, but you must not leave.'

'Must not leave Nice,' I corrected him. 'I'm not leaving Nice. I'm going shopping.' And I showed him the list.

He looked very worried. 'I do not think my chief would want you to go into the town alone. It would be too easy for you to board a train or the boat of a friend and thus escape.'

'I have no intention of escaping,' I said. 'But nobody said I had to remain a prisoner in my house. My mother is giving a party and I am helping her. So if you want to come with me to keep an eye on me, you're welcome to do so. In fact, you can help me find the right shop for these items.' I waved the list again. I could see indecision on his face. He knew he couldn't let me go alone, but the thought of shopping with a young woman was daunting. Duty won out.

'Very well. I shall accompany you. But I warn you – if you try to make an escape, you will be returned to a jail cell.'

'No escape, I promise. I wouldn't want to miss the

party tonight,' I said and climbed into the backseat of the Mercedes. The young policeman got in beside me, ignoring the dirty look he got from Franz.

One thing I realized as we drove into town was that I probably wouldn't have time to seek out Bobby Groper today, unless I happened to bump into him. In fact, I rather suspected that by the time I had fulfilled Mummy's commissions, I'd have to rush back to deliver them for the party. Oh, well. It was better than sitting around at home all day. The weather was perfect, the sea was blue, the sky even bluer, and a walk along the Promenade would be enough to raise my spirits.

With assistance from my poor policeman friend, whose name turned out to be Marcel, I located lemons and paper lanterns and even fireworks and a selection of carnival masks. It really was rather fun shopping in the market and having someone to carry the stuff back to the car. I got some funny looks from people as I strode ahead with a uniformed policeman in tow, loaded with my packages. When we had finished, I treated him to a coffee at one of the little outdoor cafés, then told him I was going to walk along the seafront to get some fresh air. He didn't have to accompany me, I said. He could sit on one of the benches and watch me. He agreed to this, obviously not having enjoyed the indignity of the shopping.

I stood for a while in the fresh breeze blowing off the sea. After the previous day's rainstorm, the sea was still choppy, and waves hissed and crashed, rattling the pebbles. I found myself scanning the beach to see if I could spot Darcy. *If only*, I thought, and I reminded myself that Jean-Paul was filling his shoes quite admirably. He had rescued me twice – once from Sir Toby's clutches and then again, obviously having paid a large amount of bail money to have me released from jail. And he was gorgeous and rich and everything a girl could want – except that he wasn't Darcy. However much I tried to fool myself, I still cared horribly about Darcy, and thinking of him produced an almost physical hurt in my heart.

But the day was too windy and even the hardy types were not swimming in the sea. I turned away to continue my walk when I heard my name being called, and there, coming toward me, were the two elderly princesses from the night of my modeling disaster. The spry little French princess was walking beside an old-fashioned wicker bath chair in which the large Russian princess sat, being pushed by a formidable woman dressed in black.

'Lady Georgiana. How lovely to see you,' Princess Marie said in English, holding out her dainty hand, clad in a gray silk glove, to me. 'I trust you suffered no lasting injury from your tumble the other night?'

'No, thank you. I am fully recovered,' I said. 'And I hope that the princess also suffered no ill effects.'

'She did not, I am pleased to say.' She smiled at me, patting my hand now. 'So all is well, and we take a nice stroll and enjoy the good weather.'

I didn't like to ask whether the princess might have come upon a pearl and diamond necklace hidden about her person when she undressed that night. But I did say, 'Of course, we're still frightfully upset about the missing necklace. We can't imagine who took it.'

'There are clever thieves in the world,' Princess Marie said, while the dour Russian lady nodded in agreement. 'Princess Theodora here had her jewels taken from her compartment on a train, when she fled from Russia.

The brazen thief climbed in through the open window, removed the jewel case as she slept, then climbed out again.'

Princess Theodora sighed, but still said nothing. I wondered if she spoke English.

'I am sorry to hear about the loss of your jewels,' I said in French.

'Tragic,' she said, sighing again.

'The princess has known much sorrow,' Princess Marie said in a low voice. 'We live a simple life in Paris. We do not move in society anymore, so I bring her here to cheer her up.'

From her face it didn't look as if it was doing much good.

'But you are a young thing.' Marie smiled brightly at me. 'You should not concern yourself about a stolen necklace. You should be out dancing and having fun, and meeting interesting men. But never an Irishman, remember. They make wonderful lovers but poor husbands.'

A sob rose unbidden in my throat and I forced it into a hiccup, then remembered my manners. 'My mother is giving a party tonight at her villa,' I said. 'Perhaps you would like to come? I suspect it will be quite informal.'

She smiled, a little sadly. 'Oh, no, my dear. We do not go into society any longer. We allowed ourselves the indulgence of the fashion show the other evening, but we rarely go out at night. And all our friends are dead.'

I nodded in commiseration.

Suddenly her face brightened up. 'You must come to lunch,' she said. 'If you have time in your busy social schedule. It would brighten the day of two old dinosaurs.'

'Thank you, I'd love to,' I said.

'Come tomorrow,' she said. 'Any day you like. You'll find us at the Hotel de la Méditerranée. On the Promenade. Not the quality of the Negresco, of course, but a high class of clientele, and they take good care of us.' She reached into a tiny silk purse. 'Here is my card. I will tell the hotel receptionist to expect you.'

I thanked them again and watched them making their slow way along the boulevard. And I realized that they knew nothing about the murder or my arrest. As the princess had said, they did not get out in society much. Would they feel so happy about inviting a suspected murderer into their rooms?

I met up with my policeman again and went back to the motorcar. As we passed the port, I remembered that I had planned to interview the crew of Sir Toby's yacht and asked Franz to stop the car.

'I wish to speak to the crew of Sir Toby's yacht,' I announced to my policeman.

'I am not sure . . .' my policeman began, but I cut him off. 'Can you see any reason why I shouldn't talk to the crew? They are not under suspicion, are they? I am. I have to do everything I can to clear my name.'

With that, I got out of the car and strode down the dockside to the yacht. The gangplank was lowered and I went on board.

'Hello!' I called, and almost immediately a face appeared from belowdecks.

'Oh, it's you, miss,' he said. He was a young Englishman with a trace of Yorkshire accent. 'I'm sorry, the police said we weren't to leave and nobody was allowed on board.'

'They don't think Sir Toby was killed here, do they?'

'The police don't let us know what they're thinking,' he

said. 'We told them that Sir Toby was alive and well when we docked here.'

'Why did you come into the harbor here instead of sailing back to the villa?' I asked.

The young crewman shrugged. 'Who knows? He was the boss. He said "sail into Nice" and so we did. He told us to take the afternoon off and that he'd take a taxi home later and we were to await instructions. That's all I can tell you.'

'And you told the police that?'

'We did.'

'He didn't say where he was going or whom he planned to meet?'

'People like Sir Toby don't have to tell their crew anything. We were paid well to keep quiet and say nothing.'

'I presume Sir Toby entertained other young ladies on his yacht. Do you remember another young lady who resembled me?'

'No, miss. I can't say that I do.' His face was so impassive that I couldn't tell if he was lying or not.

'So you couldn't tell me whether any other young lady might have had a reason to want Sir Toby dead?'

'No, miss. I couldn't tell you.'

'And you also told them that I'd been on the yacht that morning and left rather abruptly?'

He looked uncomfortable now. 'We had to, miss. He asked who else had been on the yacht. We didn't say anything to incriminate you, miss. We knew what Sir Toby was like, and I can't say I blame you for jumping overboard to your friend's speedboat. Although I have to say it took guts. Not many young ladies would have jumped into the water like that. . . .'

'It doesn't matter,' I said. 'The inspector has still put two and two together and come up with a motive for murder, so the sooner this is solved, the better.'

I started to make my way back to the gangplank.

'I'm sorry I can't be of more help, miss,' he said. 'But frankly there's nothing else to say.'

I walked slowly back to the motorcar. So either Sir Toby had an assignation in town and had taken a taxi home after his meeting, or mooring in town had been a smoke screen so that he could take a taxi home for a meeting that nobody else would know about. I could hardly question every taxi driver in Nice, could I?

We drove home. I stared out the window, not really seeing the spectacular scene below me – the white boats bobbing on blue water, the pastel villas perched on the hillsides. All I felt was frustration, and a hint of fear. What if they found my fingerprints on that little table, for example – even on the objects inside that table? Would that add to the weight of evidence against me?

By the time we arrived back at the villa, I had come to a decision. Danger or no danger, I was going to confront that gardener. I wanted to hear from his own lips exactly what he had seen that afternoon. Surely I'd know if he had told a lie. I helped Franz unload the motorcar, carrying the packages in to oohs and aahs of delight from my mother, who had already done an amazing job decorating the terrace with fairy lights and white-clothed tables. Ice buckets stood ready, as did small plates and forks and serving dishes.

'The food is all ordered. We've got masses of champagne on ice and more arriving any minute. Forty people have already said they are coming,' she said happily, 'and they will all tell their friends, so we'll wind up with a good crowd.'

I had a sudden thought. 'Can I invite Binky?' I said. 'I know it will mean Fig too, but he's having such a dreary time at that awful villa, and he is such a good soul at heart.'

'The more the merrier, darling. You know how fond I am of him,' Mummy said.

I telephoned and the dragon agreed to pass on the message to the duke. Well, I'd done my part. Now for something a little more difficult. I went upstairs and deliberately put on the blue and white sailor outfit. Then I told the policeman standing outside our front gate that I wished to speak to Sir Toby's gardener. He conferred with the policeman guarding Sir Toby's gate.

'Not possible, mademoiselle,' he said. Why couldn't these Frenchmen get the concept of 'my lady' into their heads?

'And why not? This man's evidence has convinced your inspector that I am guilty. I want to find out for myself what he really saw. One of you can come with me, if you like.'

The two men exchanged glances, then gave that Gallic shrug. 'Why not?' one said. 'I will accompany her.'

The address was obtained and we walked up the road until we came to a row of cottages. A woman answered our knock, wiping her hands on her apron.

'But my husband has not come home yet,' she said. 'I thought maybe you police have required him to give his testimony again at headquarters.'

'Possible,' my policeman said. 'But I know nothing of this. I will ask.'

So we walked back to Sir Toby's property. An impressively high wall of rough stone bordered the road, cutting off any view of the villa, but I noticed that there was a small door in the wall. Presumably the gardener entered the property this way, rather than through the impressive main gate. I tried the door and it swung open.

'This must be how the staff come to work,' I said to the policeman. 'I'm going to see whether it is possible to get a good look at someone entering from the main driveway.' And without waiting for approval, I pushed open the door and stepped inside. A narrow flagstoned path wound between mimosa trees in full flower and black cypress trees. On either side of us were fountains and flower beds and gracious lawns. It was truly a lovely garden, especially as we were in the middle of winter. The scent of the fluffy mimosa flowers was sweet in the air. Birds were chirping gaily. A skinny cat crossed the path ahead of us, stalking something – presumably one of the birds. Suddenly its fur shot up and it bolted away as if burned. I looked to see what had spooked it so violently and saw the foot, sticking out from under a large oleander bush.

I grabbed the sleeve of my young policeman, who gave a horrified yelp and rushed over to part the foliage. Underneath the oleander bush, a burly man with tanned skin and grizzled gray hair was lying with a pair of what looked like gardening shears sticking out of his back.

# Chapter 27

**Villa Marguerite**
**January 27, 1933**

One might have thought that the discovery of yet another dead body in the next-door shrubbery would have put a damper on my mother's party plans. Not a bit of it.

'Well, at least you're off the hook, darling,' she said. 'You were in town all day and accompanied every step of the way by one of that silly inspector's own men.'

This much, of course, was true.

'I do see Georgie's point,' Vera said. 'I mean to say, do you think it's – well – proper to hold a party when people seem to be dropping like flies next door?'

'All the more reason to cheer ourselves up,' Mummy said. 'After all, nobody that we know is doing the killing, so let's enjoy ourselves and leave the Gropers and their murderers to sort themselves out.'

As you have probably realized, my mother was one of the world's truly self-centered women.

'But what about Lady Groper?' Vera pointed out.

'How will she feel if there's a party going on right next door?'

'Then send Georgie over to invite her,' Mummy said airily. 'She'll need cheering up too, won't she? Now, do you think these flowers go well in this niche?' The dead gardener, for indeed it was he I had stumbled upon, was put from her mind and she was back in full party preparation.

Vera suggested that I pay a courtesy call on Lady Groper. I saw her point – she may not have been fond of her philandering husband but a violent death is a terrible shock to the system. So I had a policeman let me into the Gropers' estate. The door was opened by Johnson, who was beginning to look rather haggard.

'Lady Groper's not here,' he said. 'She decided that she didn't want to spend the night here after all. She said it was too unsettling to be in this house and headed back to the Negresco. I gather she's coming back to resume cataloging her stuff tomorrow.'

'I don't think I'd want to stay here either,' I said.

'I'm not exactly enjoying it myself.' Johnson made a face. 'But I've been asked by the police to stay on and keep an eye on the place. And there's still a policeman stationed outside if I need help.'

'There was a policeman stationed outside when the gardener was killed,' I said. 'Be careful, won't you?'

He gave a grin of bravado. 'Who'd want to kill me? I'm not worth anything to anybody. As soon as this is over, I'll be out on my ear.'

'You don't think Lady Groper will keep employing you?'

'She made it clear that she had no intention of doing so.

She said she never approved of her husband's choice of servants. Besides, I bet she'd be a cow to work for.'

I felt sorry for him. He was a bright young man forced into this kind of work by circumstance, and now he was jobless again. I walked slowly back up the driveway. Truthfully I wasn't anxious to be roped into more party preparations. I just wasn't in the mood. I told myself that I should be happy that I would no longer be suspected of the first murder if I couldn't have committed the second, but I kept seeing that poor man lying there with those shears savagely driven into his back. And I thought back to the wound on Sir Toby's head. Surely it would have been simple enough to have knocked him out and then dragged him into the pool to drown. These were crimes of great savagery committed by a violent and angry person. As I went about my tasks – blowing up balloons, setting out candles and ashtrays – I wondered why it had become necessary to kill the gardener. I could come up with two reasons – one, that he had been part of the original plot, including the need to incriminate me, and his conscience had gotten the better of him, or two, that he knew who had committed the murder and was attempting, foolishly as it turned out, to extract some hush money from the murderer.

I had just pondered these things when Inspector Lafite turned up, the last person any of us wanted to see.

'Lady Georgiana. We meet again. And do I understand correctly that you were the one who discovered this body?' he asked. 'I find this most interesting.'

'Yes, your man was with me. I saw the foot sticking out and he parted the branches to reveal the man lying there.' I made sure he knew that his man was part of this equation.

'And how did you come to be strolling through the garden of Sir Toby Groper? Was this a usual occupation for you? You had done it before, perhaps?'

I tried not to let my face show annoyance. He was so clearly trying to trap me into confessing that I often took a short cut across Sir Toby's property.

'That's simple to answer,' I said. 'I wanted to meet this gardener for myself. I wanted him to have a chance to see me face to face and realize that I was not the one he saw sneaking into Sir Toby's house. Since I was under the supervision of your men, I took one of them with me. The gardener's wife said he had not returned home from work. On our way back to Sir Toby's house we noticed the small door in the wall, found it unlocked and followed the path. That's when we saw the foot.'

'A second murder,' he said. 'One must ask oneself why this man was killed.'

'Presumably because he knew who the murderer of Sir Toby was,' I said.

His eyes narrowed. He stroked his extravagant mustache.

'Precisely, young lady. And if he was the only witness to the murderer entering the house? Why, he must be silenced forever.'

I looked at him and had to laugh. 'Surely even you cannot suspect me of this second crime,' I said. 'For one thing I was in town all day, in the company of one of your men, and for another, I just don't think I possess the strength to kill a man of his size by stabbing him with a garden tool.'

'Perhaps yes, perhaps no,' he said. 'My men will be examining the murder weapon for fingerprints. And do not think you are in the clear because you went to town. I am told that this man had been dead for some time when you found him. Perhaps since before you took your nice little trip to town to create your alibi.'

I could feel my anger rising. 'May I remind you, Inspector, that your own men are standing guard outside our house? And outside Sir Toby's house too. How do you think I got past them?'

That smug look returned to his face. 'I understand it is possible to make one's way down the cliff from your terrace to the terrace of Sir Toby. In fact, my men tell me that there are indications that somebody has climbed down that way recently.'

'Yes, I did,' I said. 'When I first arrived at the villa I wanted to see if I could get down to the beach from our villa. I realized I would be trespassing on Sir Toby's property, so I went back. He was still alive at the time,' I added. 'And he had a lady called Olga with him. They were arguing, loudly.' I paused, staring eye to eye with Inspector Lafite. 'Have you looked for this Mademoiselle Olga, Inspector? I am told she is a passionate and violent person. The kind of person who might stab someone with a pair of garden shears.'

I used this as my parting blow, turned my back on him and started to set out ashtrays again. In the end he admitted defeat and left.

Deliveries started – trays of food and sacks of ice, extra champagne in case the cellar ran dry.

'Heavens, are you planning to feed the five thousand?' I asked my mother, who was flitting around in her element, bossing the staff, as well as some extra local women she had acquired for the evening.

'The biggest crime in all of society is to run short of food,' she said.

'But what if nobody comes? It was rather short notice, wasn't it?'

She smiled and patted my hand as if I were sweet but silly. 'Darling, people drive for miles for free food and drink.'

'But not our crowd, surely.'

She turned to rearrange an enormous vase of spring flowers. 'In case you haven't noticed, the world is in a depression. Our crowd might be putting on a brave front, but they are struggling to keep up appearances, and hurting like everyone else.'

'Except for you, apparently.'

'Ah, well, I'm enjoying Max's money.' She gave a naughty smile.

'I thought Germany was in a worse state than everywhere else,' I commented.

'It is. Absolutely terrible. The mark isn't worth the paper it's printed on. People are using their life savings to buy bread.'

'So how is Max doing so brilliantly?'

'He's not stupid, darling. His money has always been in Switzerland, and he owns factories around the world. And now he's working with the German government to develop new military vehicles. Of course, you're not supposed to know that.'

'But that might all come to an end for you, if you don't return to him as commanded,' I pointed out.

'It might. We'll see how I feel about him, and what else turns up. Something usually does. Now let's go and see how they are getting on with those oysters, shall we?'

I went upstairs to change, wishing that I had smart silk pajamas or a slinky backless dress like the other guests would have. My dresses looked hopelessly unsophisticated and old-fashioned. And I didn't have the heart to wear the dress I had worn the evening before. It now reminded me too strongly of the police cell and my current predicament. And as far as I could tell, Inspector Lafite still wanted to find me guilty. He was probably working hard at this moment to come up with another piece of incriminating evidence.

So I was hardly in the mood for a party when I went down to join my mother and the first guests. It appeared that she was right about food and drink enticing people and that those original forty she had invited had all told their friends. More and more people kept arriving. What's more, they all appeared to know each other, and there were scenes of embracing and murmurs of 'darling' this and 'darling' that. And it was amazingly informal after the parties I was used to at home. On the rare occasions we gave parties at Castle Rannoch, the guests would be announced by the butler and then greeted formally by the hosts before they were allowed to mingle. It seemed that on the Continent the British really did let down their stuffiness. People came, grabbed drinks from trays and generally made themselves at home without even introducing themselves to the hostess.

'Do you know all these people?' I whispered to Mummy.

'Haven't a clue who they are, darling,' she whispered back, then stretched out her arms dramatically. 'Darlings! How lovely that you could come!' she cooed and rushed to greet the newest arrivals.

I overheard the words 'Toby Groper,' 'next-door villa'

and 'murder' and realized that as well as food and drink our place had the added attraction of being next to the murder site. But I didn't hear any whispers mentioning my name or any quick glances in my direction, for which I was truly grateful. So nobody outside my immediate circle knew that I had been arrested and was the prime suspect. I eavesdropped shamelessly as people speculated who might have done it. The interesting thing was that Toby Groper was clearly not among their set – in fact, he was regarded as a bit of a bounder. Also so rich that it was vulgar.

'Kept the place absolutely stuffed with bloody antiques and pictures. Like a bloody great mausoleum or art gallery,' I heard one man say. 'And didn't even play a decent game of tennis.'

I broke off my eavesdropping as someone tapped on my shoulder and was pleased to see Belinda, looking rather stunning in a figure-hugging emerald green dress that made it perfectly clear she was wearing nothing beneath it.

'What a nice surprise,' I said. 'I didn't realize you were invited.'

'Of course I wasn't. But when has that ever deterred me from anything? I overheard some people talking about it in Galeries Lafayette this afternoon. All that lovely free food and drink, darling. One could hardly pass it up, could one? But I'm awfully relieved to see you here, yourself. Last time I saw you, you were being dragged off by a horrid little policeman with a ridiculous mustache. What on earth did he want with you? Was it about the missing necklace?'

'Worse than that. He thinks I killed our neighbor, Sir Toby.'

'I heard a rumor that someone had been murdered. So that's who it was. Toby Groper, eh? Horrid man. Pinched my bottom once. But what in God's name would make that inspector think that you did it? It's too ridiculous for words.'

'I know. It is, but he's not very bright and extremely pompous and it's a case of "I'm guilty until proven innocent" to him. I'd still be in a jail cell if it weren't for Jean-Paul, who bailed me out and found me a lawyer.'

'How awful. You poor darling. But don't worry. I'm sure your heavenly marquis knows how to bribe the right people and they'll sort it out soon. If not, you can simply start waving the royal standard and they'll have to back down.'

'I hope so,' I said. I looked around. 'Did you bring Neville?'

'Still parking the car, I believe. And yes, I am with him, unless and until something better turns up.'

'So he's not quite as wonderful as you thought he was?'

'I never said "wonderful,"' Belinda muttered, looking around to see if he was approaching. 'And frankly I think I overestimated his prowess in – *that* area. It is so off-putting if one is asked if one "fancies a spot of the old rumpy-pumpy," and even worse when he has his teddy bear sitting on the bed beside us.'

'Belinda!' I exclaimed, not knowing whether to laugh or be shocked.

'It's too much boarding school,' Belinda said. 'It makes them all strange. I'm on the lookout for a nice Continental type with oodles of money, like your marquis. He's still in pursuit, is he?'

'He appears to be.'

'Great catch, darling. I'm mad with jealousy.' She leaned closer. 'So do tell, how far have you got with him? Is it positively blissful?'

'Not very far yet,' I said. 'I might have had more to tell if I hadn't been hauled off to a police station last night.'

'Is he here? Perhaps you can carry on a little later from where you left off.'

'I hope so,' I said. 'I haven't seen him yet, but I'm sure Mummy invited him. She fancies him herself.'

'Oh, Lord.' Belinda grabbed my arm suddenly. 'Isn't that your brother just coming in the door? Don't tell me the dreaded Fig is going to be here.'

I spotted him through the crowd and his face broke into a big smile. 'What-ho, Georgie. It's good to see you, old thing.' And he barged his way toward me.

'Where's Fig?' I asked cautiously as he put his arm around me.

'Sends her apologies. Doesn't think that the noise and all the standing would be good for her. But Ducky and Foggy are here.' I turned to see Ducky in an outfit even more dreary-looking than mine. In fact, she looked as if she might have knitted the evening gown herself from an unwashed brown sheep. She nodded a greeting to me. Foggy came up, and he greeted me more effusively. 'Hello, old thing. Splendid to see you again. I must say, you're looking rather pretty. And what a splendid place this is. You must give me a private tour later.' He gave me a little nudge, and was that a wink?

Yes, I know what your idea of a private tour is, I thought, and I directed them toward the champagne while I made my escape.

'Where does the money come from for all this?' Ducky's

brittle voice carried as they moved away. 'I mean, it's not as if she's an actress anymore, is it?'

'Talk about biting the hand that feeds you,' Vera muttered in my ear. 'How are you surviving, old thing?'

'I'm all right,' I said.

'It can't be easy, knowing that dreadful inspector is lurking,' Vera said.

'Or that a murderer is lurking,' I said.

'That too, of course. I wish they'd find the blasted man so that we can go home. We've got work to do. It's not good for Coco to sit idle. She smokes and drinks too much. She's the type of person who needs to be busy all the time or she self-destructs.' She looked up just then. 'I think your marquis is just arriving.'

# Chapter 28

*The night of January 27, 1933*
*Party at the Villa Marguerite.*

I felt my pulse quicken as I saw him scanning the crowd. He spotted me and came over. 'You don't have anything to drink,' he said. He snatched two glasses of champagne from a tray and handed me one. 'If you don't mind my saying so, that is a perfectly terrible dress. It does nothing for you and makes you look about ten years old.'

'I know,' I said. 'My wardrobe is positively hopeless. Everyone's so smart here.'

'I thought Madame Chanel was designing you a dress,' he said.

I shrugged. 'Things became a little crazy around here. First a stolen necklace, and then the murders. She's probably forgotten.'

'Then we must remind her again.' He looked around, then spotted Belinda hovering just behind me.

'Hello,' he said, his eyes traveling over her. 'I believe we've met before, but I'm afraid I can't remember your name.'

'It's Belinda. Belinda Warburton-Stoke,' she said.

'Delightful. Another English rose.'

'In full bloom,' Belinda said in a way that only Belinda or my mother could say it.

'And are you enjoying all the delights the Riviera has to offer?'

'I've yet to experience all the delights,' she said, with an emphasis on the word 'all.'

'I'm sure you will experience them all, given time.'

I watched this exchange, feeling uneasy and angry. Were they flirting, or was this normal fashionable society talk? Jean-Paul turned back to me. 'You two are friends?'

'We were best friends at school,' I said.

'Ah. But I think that this young lady has led a more adventurous life than you since leaving school, *ma petite*.'

'Oh, absolutely,' I agreed. 'My life has been rather dull.'

'Until now,' Jean-Paul said. 'At the moment you must agree it is far from dull.' And he smiled at me, removing some of those fears. Neville joined Belinda, putting a protective arm around her shoulder and thus making sure that the flirtation with Jean-Paul didn't continue.

'Awfully glad to see you here,' he said to me. 'The last time we met you'd just fallen off a stage and been robbed. I was frightfully worried about you.'

'I'm fully recovered, as you can see,' I said. 'I wish I could say the same for the necklace.'

'Lots of thieves and crooks on the Riviera,' Neville said. 'Damned foreigners don't have the same moral code as we do at home.'

'If you'll excuse me, I should greet our hostess,' Jean-Paul said and melted away.

I was about to follow him, but a thought had been

nagging at the back of my consciousness. I remembered
Neville saying that he'd seen me before. And Coco and
Vera thought they'd seen me too. Even Belinda. I needed
to locate this mysterious double who had been seen entering Sir Toby's house.

'"Remember you said you'd seen me before?' I asked
Neville.

'Riding your bike up near our villa,' he said.

'Where exactly is that?'

'Up in Cimiez, very near where Queen Victoria used to
stay when she came here.'

I had never known that my austere great-grandmother
enjoyed the delights of the Riviera. 'She came here?'

'Every winter during the 1890s, I believe. Rented a
whole wing of the hotel. They even changed the name to
Regina to make her feel at home.'

'Goodness,' I said. 'She must have been awfully old
then.'

'Oh, she was. She thought sea bathing was good for her
rheumatism.'

This went against the picture I had of the spartan life
she led and the palace more freezing even than Castle
Rannoch.

'So how does one get to Cimiez?' I asked.

'There's a little bus that takes you up the hill from the
Place Massena – you know, the big square in the middle
of town? There are Roman ruins at Cimiez, and the view
is delightful, so people take picnics up there.'

'I must go and see for myself,' I said.

'Do come up and visit anytime,' Neville said. 'We're on
the Boulevard Edouard VII. Villa Victoria – aptly named,
what? I'm sure my aunt would be glad to receive you.'

'Thank you,' I said. 'I hope to.'

'And thank you for hitching me up with Belinda,' he said, squeezing her shoulder as if testing a ripe melon. 'She's a corking girl. Absolutely spiffing. Even my aunt likes her.'

Oh, goodness, I thought. He sees Belinda as a future wife. I didn't see her staying with him beyond the end of the week. In fact, I noticed she was watching Jean-Paul's back as he joked with Coco and my mother. This time she's not going to get him, I thought, and I was just moving to join him when a stir went through the crowd. It parted as if Moses had just arrived at the Red Sea, and there was Mrs Simpson, with – miraculously – Mr Simpson in tow and no sign of the Prince of Wales. I watched, absolutely bewitched, as Mummy came forward to greet her. As these two had been involved in mutual loathing since they had met, I couldn't imagine what might happen next.

But Mummy, ever the actress, held out her hands. 'Wallis, how simply sweet of you to come.'

'Wouldn't have missed it for the world, honey,' Mrs Simpson said and the two ladies kissed, about four inches from each other's cheeks.

'How nice to see you, Mr Simpson,' Mummy said, holding out her hand to him. 'Do help yourself to a drink.'

This suggestion was met with a grunt, which was about all I had ever heard Mr Simpson say. As he moved off, Mummy asked, 'So might we be expecting a visit from a special friend later this evening?'

Mrs Simpson gave an annoyed little shrug. 'One never knows which friends will turn up,' she said. 'I have so many friends.'

'You know the friend I am referring to,' Mummy said. 'I just wondered . . .'

'Was summoned home to England unexpectedly,' Mrs Simpson snapped. 'Apparently his daddy wasn't happy that he was enjoying himself on the Med while his subjects were suffering. I told him it was nonsense. His subjects would still be suffering whether he's in England or not. But he said his father's health hasn't been the best lately, so he felt he should be a good little boy and run home.' She smoothed back her hair, which was not out of place to start with. 'And how about you? I don't see any burly Germans in evidence.'

'Making money back in Germany,' Mummy said. 'Germany's simply too depressing, so I escaped.'

'Things should be looking up there soon,' Mrs Simpson said. 'I understand this new guy, this Hitler, is a little firecracker. David says he's got lots of splendid ideas to put Germany back on its feet.'

'I'm not so sure I want it back on its feet,' Mummy said. 'I'm fond of Max, but it's hard to forget that Germany was the enemy and all the awful things they did . . .'

'That was just the old Kaiser,' Wallis said. 'This new regime will be more forward-looking. David thinks we'll get on splendidly.' She looked around expectantly. I thought she might have been seeking out a particular person, but then she said, 'So I understand you can actually see the swimming pool where the dead man was found.'

'Yes, from our terrace,' Mummy said.

So it was only morbid curiosity that had made her sink to attending Mummy's party. How screamingly funny. I couldn't wait to tell Belinda.

'I must take a look for myself,' Mrs Simpson said. 'Dying of curiosity. Such a strange murder, don't you think? Personally I'd put money on his wife. A sour-faced creature if ever there was one. These English aristocrats are so repressed – all that bottled-up tension and not enough sex. It's not healthy.' She smirked as she looked at my mother. 'I suppose you should be glad you're lower class.'

'Ditto,' Mummy said. 'Although I was a duchess, which is more than you can say.'

'Ah, but who can say what the future may bring?' Mrs Simpson replied with an enigmatic smile. 'Come and show me the murder scene. I find murders most fascinating, don't you?'

Others followed them out to the terrace, talking excitedly about murder. I stayed behind. I had no wish to be reminded. In fact, I wondered if I would be missed if I slipped away. So the Prince of Wales had left Mrs Simpson to return to England. It was encouraging to know that he did still feel the call of duty and she didn't have a complete hold over him. But for me it meant that I didn't have a royal relative in the vicinity, should Inspector Lafite decide to proceed with prosecuting me. I wondered if the Duke of Westminster would appear at the party and whether I was actually related to him.

I jumped when I heard what sounded like gunshots from outside the open French doors, until I realized that the guests were already letting off fireworks. I happen to love fireworks, so I went outside and watched rockets and Roman candles shooting up into the night sky to fall sparkling over the dark sea, while the sophisticated crowd greeted each firing with oohs and aahs.

The fireworks obviously put everyone in a party mood. They started playing parlor games, harmless ones at first, but then progressively more risqué.

'Let's play statues,' someone suggested. There were giggles as ladies were selected to stand as statues in the middle of the room. A male volunteer was called for and Foggy Farquar stepped forward. He was blindfolded, spun around and then put among the statues. The object of the game was then revealed – he had to feel the statues and guess the women's identities. What followed was a lot of groping and bawdy comments. I was so glad I hadn't been picked as a statue; I'd have died of embarrassment. But the women actually seemed to enjoy it. I noticed Jean-Paul standing in the doorway, chuckling. His eyes met mine and he winked at me.

Then the band arrived and the activity turned to dancing. After a few dances, Jean-Paul claimed me and held me close as we drifted around the floor in a slow fox-trot. 'I want to say something to you,' he muttered, steering me toward the edge of the crowd. My pulse rate quickened. Was this a proposal?

'I think you should go home,' he said, eyeing me seriously. 'As soon as the police give you permission, go home. This place is not right for you. You do not belong here.'

'Why not?' I asked.

'You're a nice girl. A decent person. You don't belong with a crowd like this.'

I didn't know what to say, because I knew that what he was saying was true. I didn't feel comfortable with them. 'So you don't care if I go?' I dared to ask.

'Of course I shall be sad, but I care about you more. I don't wish you to wind up like them. There have been many women in my life and most of their names I have forgotten by the morning. But your name, I do not think I shall forget.' He put a finger under my chin and lifted it up toward him. 'If things had been different . . .' he said and didn't finish the sentence. But he pulled me toward him and kissed me gently. 'I have to go,' he said.

A little later Neville came up to me. There were beads of sweat on his forehead and he was frowning. 'I say, you haven't seen Belinda, have you?'

'No, I can't say that I have recently.'

'Damned rum do. She seems to have hopped it.' He scanned the room hopefully as he spoke.

My stomach lurched. It wasn't long since Jean-Paul had whispered, 'I have to go.' It didn't take too much imagination to suggest that Belinda had gone with him. I felt sick and angry and more than a little confused.

Midnight passed and people started to drift away. The die-hard few had become mellow. Large amounts of liquor had been consumed. The air was hazy with cigarette smoke. The band had stopped playing.

'How about dustman's knock?' someone said, laughing.

'What's dustman's knock?' I asked.

'Like postman's knock, only dirtier,' he replied.

Everyone was chuckling now. I wasn't sure if I was having my leg pulled or not.

'Capital idea. Do you have keys, Claire?' one of the men said.

'I never lock anything,' my mother said. 'We'll have to write numbers on slips of paper. We can put them in this bowl.'

I knew what postman's knock was, as I'd played it at parties. A boy was chosen to be the postman and was then

sent outside the door while the girls drew their numbers
from a bowl. He'd knock, then announce that he had a
package for, say, number twenty-one. That particular girl
would go outside to receive the parcel, and she'd get a
kiss. It was a fun way of pairing up. Fun, but harmless.
So I could imagine what this version might entail and I
had no intention of being part of it. Maybe if Jean-Paul
had stayed . . . I was still perplexed about his behavior
to me. Perplexed and more than a little disappointed.
When nobody was looking, I slunk away and went to my
bedroom.

    I shut the door behind me with a sigh of relief.

    'I'm glad to see you're alone,' said a voice and there was
Darcy, sitting on the end of my bed.

# Chapter 29

*Villa Marguerite*
*January 28, 1933 – early next morning*

Darcy was sitting on my bed, wearing an open-necked shirt. His dark curls were unrulier than ever and those alarming eyes flashed dangerously when he saw me. I felt my heart give a giant lurch. If I had thought I was getting over him, I was hopelessly wrong.

'What are you doing here?' I asked shakily.

'Keeping an eye on you,' he said. 'I just heard what happened last night. You've got yourself into a bit of a pickle, haven't you?'

'I'm sure it will all be sorted out soon. The police will realize they've made a stupid mistake. And Jean-Paul has found me a first-class lawyer.'

He got up and came over to me. 'That's another thing,' he said. 'Your marquis. I want to warn you about him. He's a dangerous man, Georgie. I can see why you're attracted to him, but he's not to be trusted. I'm afraid there are things you might not like to know about him.'

'Oh, that's rich, coming from a man like you.'

'What do you mean by that?'

'That there are so many things you've conveniently forgotten to tell me. Important things.'

He shrugged. 'As for the secrets, I admit that there have been things I can't tell you. But I have always cared about you. I care about you now – that's why I'm warning you to steer clear of the marquis.'

'Are you jealous?' I asked. 'Or are you upset that I got over you so quickly?'

'I just don't want to see you get hurt, that's all.'

'Funny, but Jean-Paul said the same thing to me, about an hour ago.'

'Then perhaps he is finally developing a conscience, at least about some things,' Darcy said, 'although I doubt it. All I can tell you is that you'll find yourself in even deeper trouble if you stay with him.'

'I'm a big girl now, Darcy.' I faced him defiantly, trying to sound more confident than I felt. 'I can make my own decisions and take care of myself.'

'Hardly.' He looked at me angrily. 'You go out alone on Toby Groper's yacht? You hitch up with one of the most notorious men in Europe? You're arrested for murder? That doesn't sound much like taking care of yourself, Lady Georgiana.' He grabbed my shoulders. 'Georgie, what are you doing? What has happened to you?'

I wished he hadn't touched me. I fought to stay calm. 'Nothing has happened to me, except that I've discovered the real reason you're here.'

'Oh, you have, have you?' He was staring hard at me.

I nodded, biting my lip. I waited for him to say something, to apologize for deceiving me. Instead he said,

'In that case, all I can say is that you shouldn't spread it around too much in certain circles. Not if you're wise, that is.'

'I don't know why I'd want to spread it around.' I shook myself free from him, bumped against the bed and sat down heavily.

'Careful,' Darcy said, grabbing at me. 'You don't want to sit on your pearls.'

'My what?' I stood up as my hand touched something sharp. There, lying on my bed, was the missing pearl and diamond necklace.

I stood staring at it as if it had been magically produced by a genie and might vanish again at any moment. 'How did it get here?' I asked. 'Did you put it there?'

'Me? Of course not. What would I be doing with a necklace like that? Is it yours?'

'It belongs to the queen,' I said. 'It was stolen when I fell off the stage at the fashion show.'

'Fell off the stage?' He looked as if he might grin.

'You didn't hear about it?'

'I've been rather occupied with – other things,' he said. 'So it was stolen and then returned?'

'It's amazing,' I said. 'Someone at the party must have taken it, then their conscience got the better of them and they returned it.'

'Really?' He was frowning, staring at the door.

'I must tell the others. They'll be thrilled.' I made a move toward the door.

Darcy grabbed my arm. 'Maybe it might be wise to say nothing at this point.'

'You don't understand. They've been worried sick,' I said. 'At least I must tell Vera and Madame Chanel.'

I opened the door and stepped out onto the landing. It was unnaturally quiet after the loud noises of the past few hours. I looked around and at that moment Vera walked across the foyer below. Obviously she wasn't one of those playing naughty games. I ran to the railing and leaned over.

'Vera. Look! It's been returned. The necklace has come back!' I shouted. I suppose I had been drinking rather too much champagne all evening because I know a lady never raises her voice. The effect was instantaneous. Bedroom doors opened and people in various stages of undress looked out.

I waved the necklace. 'It's come back. It was on my bed.'

Vera's face lit up. 'Thank God,' she said. 'It's a bloody miracle.'

'Yes, isn't it?'

'How on earth did it get there?' she demanded.

'Someone must have deliberately put it there, knowing I'd find it when I went to bed.' As I said this it did cross my mind that Darcy might somehow have been involved. Had he in fact known about the stolen necklace and managed to recover it for us from the thief? Had he done this for me – as a peace offering? I glanced back at my bedroom, expecting him to come out and reveal himself, but there was no sign of him.

I started to come down the stairs toward the small crowd that was now gathering in the foyer. Halfway down I caught my heel somehow and grabbed at the banister to stop myself from falling. The pearls slid from my hand and fell to the marble floor below. Vera and several others darted forward to grab them. But they were too late. The necklace hit the ground with a light, high, tinkling crash.

'I'm so sorry. Are they all right?' I asked.

Vera was on her knees, staring down at the floor where the largest of the diamonds had shattered into a hundred pieces.

'Oh, no.' I joined her on my knees. 'Vera. I'm so awfully sorry. I know I'm clumsy. I've ruined it.'

She looked up at me, grim-faced. 'Diamonds don't shatter, Georgie.'

'But—' I looked down at the floor then back at her face. 'You mean it wasn't a real diamond?'

She nodded.

'So the queen didn't lend us her real jewels after all.'

Vera looked around the room at the faces now staring down at us. 'It appears that the person who stole the necklace has replaced it with a clever fake. If Georgie hadn't dropped it, we might not have found out for ages, if ever.'

'Damned clever,' one of the men muttered. 'Should we call for the police?'

'Not tonight,' Vera said. 'I don't think I could handle another round of Inspector Lafite. Besides, if the thief is that clever, I doubt the police will have any chance of catching him.' She started to pick up the remains of the necklace. 'You have to admit it was slickly done, and obviously planned. It's unlikely that such a necklace could be created in a couple of days.'

'So the thief went to the fashion show with the intent of stealing the necklace,' I said. Somehow that made me feel a little better. It wasn't only my clumsiness that had caused the theft. I was intended to fall.

'But how did it get into your bedroom?' the same man

asked. 'The thief must have climbed in through your window.'

'Or been among us,' Vera said.

'One of us? That's ridiculous,' the man said. 'Implying that somebody English is a thief. Some damned Frenchie, you mark my words. Slippery chap who crept in through the window and then out again – while we were watching the fireworks, probably.'

I decided to keep quiet about Darcy. One thing I knew about him with absolute certainty – he was not a thief. If he had brought the necklace back, it was because he believed he had recovered the real one for us.

'We should take a look at your room,' the man insisted. 'See if the blighter left any clues, don't you know?' He stomped upstairs before I could stop him and flung open my bedroom door.

The room was empty. The window was wide open and the net curtains flapped in the breeze.

'There you are. What did I say?' the man said, nodding at us triumphantly. 'Some damned Frenchie or Italian crook climbed in this way. You should take a look at the flower bed in the morning, see if the blighter left telltale footprints. Not that the French police will be much use. Useless bunch.'

I just prayed that Darcy hadn't left a footprint in the flower bed. I didn't know why I wanted to protect him so much, but I did. You can't just shut off love, I suppose, and he did come to warn me, which was rather sweet. 'If only,' I found myself muttering. Did he still love this woman who was the mother of his child? He clearly adored the child. Did his appearance tonight mean that he still loved me? It was all so complicated and so hard to handle.

'There's still a policeman stationed outside the villa,' Vera said. 'We can ask him if he noticed anyone suspicious slinking in and out.'

The guests were now caught up in the excitement of the hunt. They streamed out the front door. I followed, rapidly trying to decide how I could vouch for Darcy, should the occasion arise. But the weary policeman at the gate just shrugged. 'You have a party,' he said. 'That means many people come and go. Am I supposed to recognize if one of them is a thief?'

As the noisy revelers streamed back into the house I managed to slip away and went to my room. I checked the wardrobe and under the bed just in case Darcy was still there, but he wasn't. I closed the shutters. Tiredness overcame me and I fell into bed.

# Chapter 30

*Villa Marguerite and later at Sir Toby's*
*January 28, 1933*
*Wonderful news for once. Feeling much happier.*

Queenie had clearly forgotten to bring my morning tea, because I awoke to brilliant sunlight streaming through the slats in my shutters. Down below I could hear animated men's voices. Oh, no, please don't say that the inspector is here, I prayed silently. I opened the shutters and peeked out cautiously. What I saw was a taxi and beside it an attractive gray-haired man in an immaculately cut dark suit and next to him a shorter man in a scruffy old raincoat – a man with a bald head who was saying, 'What 'ave they done with my little girl? Where is she? I told her not to go gallivanting abroad. No good ever comes of it.'

I gave a great whoop of joy and rushed down the stairs, not even aware that I was still in my nightgown. 'Granddad,' I cried and flung myself into his arms. 'You came! I'm so happy to see you.'

'Oh, there you are, my love. You're safe. You're all right,' he said, his voice choking as he spoke. He hugged me tightly in a display of affection that was not considered seemly in the circles I normally moved in. There was no way Fig would ever have hugged anybody – even if they'd wanted to hug her, which wasn't likely.

Then he released me and stood there, holding my hands with a look of concern on his face. 'Ever since I got that telegram I've been worried sick. They said you'd been arrested for murder. I didn't believe it for a minute, but–'

'I have,' I cut in. 'I've only been released on bail. The French police inspector is horrid and won't listen. But now that you're here – you'll know what to do.'

'I don't know what I can do,' he said, 'never having had no experience of foreign courts, but this bloke what came with me, well, he's the cat's whisker.'

I looked up to observe the elegant gentleman standing beside him. 'Who is that?' I whispered.

Before I could answer, there was an exclamation of delight and Madame Chanel came flying out the front door. 'Jacques!' she said. 'You came. I knew you would.'

'My angel. As if I could resist you,' the man said, and there followed an embrace that only the French can do well.

When they had broken apart, both a little breathless, Coco turned to us. 'He has come. All will now be well. This is my dear friend Commissaire Jacques Germain of the Sûreté in Paris. I pleaded with him to come, as a little favor to me.' She was beaming as if she had just produced a rabbit out of a hat. 'I could see that something needed to be done and Jacques is the man to do it.'

'I thought Inspector Lafite made it quite clear that

the Sûreté would not be allowed to step on his toes,' I reminded her.

'But naturally,' Jacques Germain said in cultured English with only a slight French accent. 'I have decided to take a little holiday. And if I happened to take a small interest in a case that was in progress down here – well, that would be quite understandable, no?'

He smiled, the most charming, sexy smile. I could see that Frenchmen had earned their reputation. 'And with my dear friend from Scotland Yard here, we will make a formidable team.'

'How did you meet?' I asked Granddad. They seemed a most unlikely pair.

'I met this delightful gentleman on the train,' Jacques Germain said. 'He needed assistance in finding the dining car and then in ordering. We dined together, and when I discovered that he had worked for the famous Scotland Yard and he actually knew men I had long admired, we became instant friends.'

Granddad was beaming. 'I didn't say I'd actually worked for Scotland Yard,' he muttered to me. 'At least not like that. Just an ordinary copper. But he's a good bloke, and, what's more, he speaks English.'

'So all is well,' Coco said. She took Jacques' hand. 'Come. Let us go and have breakfast. And you, *ma petite*,' she said in an aside, 'you should probably put on something a little more suitable before you join us at the breakfast table.'

'Oh, yes.' I realized for the first time that I was in a flimsy nightdress. I caught Jacques' amused look. Like any Frenchman he was appraising me, enjoying the sight of my bare legs.

We walked together into the cool marble entrance hall.

Granddad looked around him. 'And this place belongs to your mum?'

'Yes, it does. Her French racing driver gave it to her.'

'Blimey, she ain't done badly for herself, I'll say that for her – not that I approve of her morals, as you know. So where is she?'

'Sleeping off a hangover, I suspect. We had a rather wild party here last night. You go through to the breakfast room and I'd better change.'

I went upstairs to find Queenie standing in my room with a tea tray.

'The one time I remember to take you up your tea, you're not blooming well there,' she said and plonked it down on the side table.

For once I wasn't in a mood to reprimand her.

'Do you want me to run you a bath?' she asked, as if this might be a huge imposition.

'No time for a bath,' I said. 'My grandfather has just arrived. Help me into the new linen suit.'

A few minutes later, smartly dressed for company, I went downstairs to join them. I found that Vera was also at the table. There was no sign of Mummy, but plenty of evidence of the previous night's party – empty glasses and full ashtrays all over the terrace, streamers, masks. The local women were bustling about clearing up and sweeping, chattering to each other in their shrill voices.

'Now, tell them everything,' Coco said. 'About the necklace and the murder. Every detail.'

I tried to tell the whole thing logically. They listened, asking the occasional question.

'I don't know about you, old friend,' Germain said to my grandfather, 'but when two crimes occur so soon in an otherwise peaceful area, I have to wonder whether there is a connection between them. This stolen necklace – was the murder of the neighbor also during an attempted robbery? You say that Sir Toby went out on his yacht, therefore the thief would not expect to find him at home. The thief is startled and reacts by hitting Sir Toby over the head.'

'The only thing against that is that there was no sign of any disturbance in the house,' I said. 'And Sir Toby's servant and wife noticed nothing obvious missing. There were valuable objects all over the place. If Sir Toby was lying dead, why didn't the thief help himself before he got away?'

As I said this I realized that I was using the pronoun 'he' when the person seen slinking toward the house had been someone who looked like me. Not only that, I realized, someone who had taken the trouble to dress like me, to pin any crime on me, essentially. I explained this and the men listened.

'But a young woman like you – would she have the strength to kill a big man like Sir Toby?'

'If she caught him unawares,' I said. 'What if he came home, changed into his bathing costume and went out for a swim? She was startled to see him so she grabbed a heavy object, crept up behind him and hit him over the head?'

'You know what I'm thinking?' Granddad said. 'I'm wondering if we're not looking at this the wrong way round. You say this bloke's house is chock-a-block full of valuable things. He's a real collector, you say. What if he's the one what's been nicking the stuff himself – or at least had other people working for him to nick the stuff?'

'But then how do you explain the necklace, or at least a fake version of it, being returned to me after he was dead?' I asked.

'Because whoever was working for him got cold feet, or decided to make off with the real necklace themselves?'

'It's possible,' I agreed.

'On the other hand,' Commissaire Germain said, 'if a fake necklace has been substituted for a real one, it is possible that Sir Toby had similarly been a victim of such a switch. You say the young woman was seen carrying something beneath her jacket, no? What if she was replacing a stolen object with a replica, so that nobody would ever know?'

He looked at us and we nodded agreement.

'Then the first thing to do is to try to find this mystery girl,' Vera said. 'Someone who looks remarkably like Georgie.'

'It may not be so easy. She will surely have been in disguise – wearing a wig and maybe having made up her face to look different too,' Germain said.

'I know that she was seen on a bicycle in a particular section of Nice so I thought I might find myself a bicycle and wheel it around the neighborhood. If she lives nearby, then maybe someone will recognize me.'

'Capital idea,' Germain said, 'and you know what I would wish to do first? I would like to take a look for myself at the crime scene. Can you show me the way?'

'I'm not sure,' I said. 'There are police stationed outside the house to guard it. But perhaps they would let you in if you told them who you were.'

'I would prefer that they not know at this moment,' he said. 'Let us gain entry with a little subterfuge.'

'Breaking and entering, you mean?' Granddad asked. 'I don't know about that. Not with the Frenchie police.'

'We will think of something,' Germain said. 'Perhaps—' But before he could finish the sentence there were raised voices in the hallway and a flustered maid announced the arrival of Inspector Lafite. The little man swept in, looking around like a bloodhound on a scent.

'You English – is it your wish to keep me on the toes, as you say? First the necklace is stolen and now it is returned, but no – it is not the same necklace, it is a forgery.'

'That is correct,' Vera said coldly.

'And how do I know that the first necklace was not an imitation?' he said. 'And you English try to fool Lafite so that you can collect insurance money?' He tapped his nose. 'I know the English are not rich anymore. They wish to pull the wool over the eyes of Lafite. But they will not succeed.'

Vera stood up, staring at him eye to eye. 'I can tell you that the first necklace was real because it came from Buckingham Palace from the Queen of England, and Her Majesty does not wear glass and paste,' she said.

She stared at him so hard and fiercely that in the end he shrugged. 'So maybe the clever switch has been accomplished. Maybe not.' He seemed to realize for the first time that he was speaking in front of two men he didn't know. 'And these two gentlemen?' he said. 'They are your friends? Your guests?'

'Art experts,' Coco said smoothly. 'Art experts from London and Paris we summoned to examine the necklace.'

'And we wonder if maybe a similar robbery and subsequent replacement took place at the home of Sir Toby,' Germain said in French. 'And that maybe this was the cause of his death.'

'The young woman you thought was me was carrying something under her jacket,' I said. 'Perhaps it was a forgery she was bringing to replace a piece of art or an antique.'

Lafite seemed to be considering this as if it might make sense to him. 'If there was indeed another young woman who was not yourself, then perhaps yes, perhaps no,' he agreed.

'So we wondered if you would like us to take a look at the house of Sir Toby and give you our expert opinion on his art and antiques,' Germain said, getting to his feet. 'You would be welcome to accompany us, of course, because I realize that you are still working to unravel the mysteries of a complicated crime scene.'

Lafite looked noticeably puffed up by this. 'The crime scene, it is not so complicated, monsieur. A simple blow to the head and, poof, the poor man falls into the swimming pool and drowns. But I would appreciate the impressions of an art expert like yourself.'

Granddad shot me a quick glance and tried to look like a distinguished art expert. 'Blimey,' he whispered as we came closer together. 'I never thought it would come to this. I thought your mum was the only ruddy actress in the family.'

'Just play along and nod occasionally,' I said.

We walked together to the Gropers' villa. Johnson opened the door. By now he was looking decidedly white-faced and ill at ease.

'Your mistress is here?' Lafite asked.

'No, sir. She hasn't shown up today yet. It's just me. I'm all alone here and frankly I don't like it. Can you tell me when I can leave? I'd just as soon go back to England.'

'Soon, my boy. Courage. You are doing a splendid job,' Lafite said. 'These gentlemen are art experts. I asked you before whether anything had been stolen from this house and you said you noticed nothing missing. Now it seems possible that something was replaced with a forgery. These two men will look around and you will assist them.'

'Very good, sir,' Johnson said, 'although, as I say, Sir Toby might have kept the most valuable stuff locked away.'

'We shall see,' Lafite said. He indicated that Germain and my grandfather were at liberty to look around.

'He appreciates the modern art, I can see,' Germain said. 'Matisse, Renoir and two Van Goghs. He was an astute man. These paintings are growing in value daily.' He paused beside one of the paintings, put his face close to it and sniffed. 'Interesting,' he said. 'The paint on this one appears to be fresh, but that is not possible because Van Gogh has been dead for forty years.'

We gathered around to look. It was a very ordinary sort of painting, not something I'd have wanted in my own drawing room – a crudely executed kitchen chair. That was all. Just one chair done in bold, uneven strokes. Next to it the painting of some sunflowers was a little better – more cheerful if not more skillfully done. I couldn't see why anyone would want to steal or forge such a painting when there were some exquisite classical landscapes on other walls. I walked away and joined Granddad, who was staring out through the French doors at the pool.

'Anyone could have clambered down that cliff and clobbered him,' he muttered. 'Or come up from the beach. And you say nothing was touched in the house?'

'Not that I could see.'

'Then I don't know why we're wasting our time looking at pictures. It obviously wasn't a burglary in progress. It was someone who wanted him dead and knew he'd be alone.'

'I don't know who that could be,' I said. 'Everyone thought he was on his yacht or in Nice.'

'So it probably wasn't planned then. Someone showed up, found him alone and took their chance. Or someone followed him here. Do you have any ideas about suspects?'

'Well,' I began, looking around to see how far away the others were, 'my money would be on his mistress. A flamboyant Russian who left in a huff and swore vengeance.'

Granddad smiled. 'That type is usually all bark and no bite. Who else?'

'There is Sir Toby's wife. She wanted to divorce him, from what I overheard, but he was threatening to expose her liaison with someone important. And there's his son, who didn't want his father to find out—'

I broke off as Lady Groper herself swept into the room. She looked around in annoyance.

'What on earth is going on here now? Surely you men have done everything there is to be done here!'

'I've brought in art experts to examine your husband's possessions, *Madame*,' Lafite said. 'It appears that someone may recently have substituted one of your husband's paintings with a forgery.'

'Good God. Which one?'

'This one, *Madame*. The painting of the chair.'

'That awful thing? Who'd possibly want it? I was going to have the lot of them thrown on a bonfire.'

'But no, *Madame*,' Germain said. 'The impressionist painters are becoming more desirable for collectors every day. Mark my words – these paintings will be worth a fortune, given time.'

'Really? So it would seem that my husband was killed while someone switched the real painting for a forgery? How extraordinary.'

'You left your bag in the car, Mama.' Bobby Groper ambled into the room, wearing an open-necked check shirt and white flannels. He started visibly at finding the drawing room full of people. 'Oh, hello,' he said. 'What's going on here? A party?'

'This is my son, Bobby,' Lady Groper said. 'He arrived on this morning's train. Came straight from England as soon as he heard the news. He's devastated, poor boy. Worshipped his father.'

Bobby looked around and caught my eye. I saw him swallow hard, his Adam's apple jerking up and down, then he shot me a warning glance – presumably to keep quiet.

'I'll go and find somewhere to put our bags,' he said.

I followed him into the hallway.

'For God's sake don't tell them I've been here a while, will you?' he whispered to me.

'Why not? Why are you lying?'

He glanced in at the open doorway, then put his lips close to my ear. 'Because it wouldn't look good for me, would it? Son gets sent down from Oxford in disgrace. Skips off to Riviera. Tries to keep disgrace from father for as long as possible.'

'But surely people don't kill their fathers because they've been sent down from university?'

'I've also accumulated a large pile of debts,' he said. 'It's actually quite convenient that the old man is out of the way. Now I inherit the money and the title. Ergo, the slate wiped clean. You could say that's a pretty good motive for bumping someone off.'

'You aren't sad your father's been killed?'

He shrugged. 'I expect I will be, when I've had time to think about it,' he said. 'At present my only thoughts are about saving my own skin. Not very honorable and all that, but then I'm not the honorable type. Take after him too much, I suppose. He didn't care whom he walked over. I don't want to walk over people, but I do tend to put myself first.'

'Did you hear that the necklace that was stolen from me showed up last night?' I asked.

'No – did it? That's a stroke of luck, isn't it?'

'Only it was a forgery. A clever duplicate. And it appears that one of your father's paintings has been substituted with a forgery.' I watched his face as I said this. He was, after all, the only person who helped me up and then slipped out of the room before the police searched everyone at the casino. But did he have the skill or the contacts to create a perfect replica of the necklace so quickly? And as for the painting . . .

Bobby grinned. 'I can tell what you're thinking. But I'd hardly be likely to steal one of my father's paintings, would I? Especially since I've now inherited the whole bally lot.' He picked up a bag he'd left in the foyer. 'I don't know why you suspect me of anything,' he said, looking back over his shoulder as he made his way down the hall. 'I'm a perfectly nice chap, actually.'

# Chapter 31

## January 28, 1933

We made our way back up the drive again, leaving Lafite with the Gropers.

'So that painting really was a forgery?' Vera asked. 'You didn't just say that?'

'No. I've actually had quite a lot of experience with art forgery,' Germain said, 'and one can still smell the odor of fresh paint on that one. Maybe I am wrong. Only a true expert could tell if the brushwork was not that of Van Gogh, but I am not usually wrong.'

'Then we must find the girl who posed as me,' I said.

'I agree,' Germain said. 'But do we have any other suspects in this case?'

'Georgie suggests his mistress, who left in a bit of a two and eight,' Granddad said.

'A what?' the others said in unison.

'Sorry.' Granddad chuckled. 'A two and eight – that's rhyming slang for "a state." She left in a bit of a state.'

'And this mistress might be found where?'

'I've no idea,' I said. 'Her name is Olga and she was a dancer.'

'Easy enough to locate, then. And who else?'

'His wife and son both had reasons for wanting him out of the way,' I said, 'and his son just lied about arriving on this morning's train. He's been here a few days.'

'Interesting.' Germain nodded. 'So we have enough to keep us busy.'

'Apart from his family, who do not seem to be mourning his death,' I said, 'everything one heard about Sir Toby suggested that he was a man who was ruthless, who didn't play by the rules and who made enemies.'

Granddad nodded. 'I remember his name now. I was wondering where I'd come across it before and it's just come to me. It was that big trial.'

'He was involved in criminal activity?' Germain asked.

Granddad shook his head. 'No. It was a civil suit. Made all the headlines.'

'What was it about?'

'If I remember right it was a motorcar engine,' Granddad said. 'Some bloke took Sir Toby to court, claiming that they had designed a motorcar engine together and then Sir Toby had claimed the whole thing as his own and cut the other bloke out. Sir Toby hired a top-notch barrister who proved that the other bloke had been driven off his rocker by being in the trenches and had delusions. Might have been true, of course. The war did strange things to a lot of blokes. Anyway, this bloke lost the case and hanged himself.'

'Do you remember what his name was?' I asked.

Granddad sucked through his teeth as he did when he was thinking. 'Some German type of name. That's why there was little sympathy for him, even though he'd been in the trenches like all the other poor blokes. Sherman? That's what it was. Johann Sherman. He was a Jew, I believe, who'd left Germany as a young man.'

'Then that's it. The man who was threatening Sir Toby. I think his name was Schumann,' I said. 'That's close enough, isn't it?'

'Which man was this?' Germain asked sharply.

I told them about what I had overheard and how Johnson had said it was some kind of business deal gone wrong.

'Again he should be easy enough to locate – businessman or crook, perhaps. I will have a private word with the commissioner down here and maybe put some of my men from the Sûreté on to tracking this Schumann.'

'Hang on a minute,' Granddad said, making us all pause in our tracks. 'When that necklace was stolen – you said the flashbulbs went off, right?'

I nodded.

'Before or after you fell?'

'Both, I think.'

'If someone took a picture of you being helped up, then it's possible that one of the cameras caught the robbery.'

'Excellent,' Germain said. 'Why don't you and Lady Georgiana make a tour of the newspapers and press services here, while I confer with my colleagues and decide how best to intervene here without it looking like intervention.'

'I'm anxious to find the girl who impersonated me,' I said. 'Don't you think that should come first?'

'I will take your charming grandfather,' Coco said. 'It will help to have a person like me who is used to dealing with these photographers. I know many of them and I am known to them all.'

'Bob's yer uncle,' Granddad said.

'What has my uncle got to do with this?' Coco asked, looking bewildered.

He laughed. 'Sorry. Another bit of Cockney slipped out. It means that it's all right with me.' Granddad blushed as Madame Chanel slipped her arm through his. 'I never thought the day would come when I'd be escorting a charming French lady around the Riviera. Me, of all people.'

'I am delighted to have such a debonair Englishman to protect me,' Coco said gallantly. 'Let us go and ask Claire if we may borrow the car and the delightful Franz.'

Mummy had just surfaced as we entered the house and she looked decidedly the worse for wear.

'Remind me not to drink gin,' she said. 'It doesn't agree with me. I should stick with champagne.' She frowned to focus on the men in our party. 'Good heavens, Daddy. You came.'

'Wasn't going to let my little girl get into trouble now, was I?' he said. 'And now that I'm here, I can't say that France looks as bad as I thought it would. Quite nice, in fact, especially after gray old England.'

Mummy gave me a knowing smile. 'So what's the plan then?'

We told her.

'If you don't mind, I'll bow out of this morning's activities. I'm really not at my best. Maybe after a few cups of coffee I'll feel human again. So run along and play, children.'

Franz brought around the motor and we all piled in.

This time there were no police guarding our villa and the gendarme at Sir Toby's gate saluted as we drove past. At least it seemed I'd been removed from the role of number one suspect. When we reached the center of Nice I asked Franz to drop me where I could ride the bus up the hill to Cimiez.

'I don't know if I like you going alone,' Granddad said. 'You're looking for someone who might have committed two murders. You're putting yourself in harm's way. Come with us to the newspapers first and then we'll all go with you up to this place.'

'No, that wouldn't work at all,' I said. 'I want to see if anyone mistakes me for this girl. I'm going to try to borrow a bicycle and wheel it around the neighborhood. At least I might be able to find out where she lives.'

'Well, be careful, then,' Granddad said. 'And let's arrange to meet back here at a certain time. That way, if you're not there, we'll come looking.'

We arranged to meet at noon, which gave me an hour and a half to begin my search. I joined the other passengers on the bus and we bumped our way up the windy road, the little bus belching out smoke and groaning as the hill became steeper. We saw glimpses of the bay as the town spread out below us. Then we were in an area of impressive villas. A great white curved building loomed over us. So that was the Hotel Regina, where my esteemed great-grandmother had stayed with her retinue of one hundred. I didn't think somehow that they would rent bicycles.

I got off with the other English tourists, who made straight for a ruined Roman amphitheater, their cameras at the ready. I asked for directions to the street where

Neville's aunt's villa was situated. It was actually not far below that great hotel. Since I could find no businesses here that might be willing to rent me a bicycle, I set off on foot, surveying the area. To one side was an olive grove and a monastery and beyond them the terrain fell away sharply, down to a river below. There was no way down that I could see. So I had to think. If this girl had been riding, not wheeling her bicycle, she could not have come from down below. The climb was simply too steep and she would have been wheeling it and out of breath. And above us seemed to be vineyards and small farms. Which must mean that I had to find a road that wound around the hill.

I started from Neville's villa and continued westward as the road hugged the hillside. At times I glimpsed a spectacular view of the city and the Baie des Anges sparkling in the sunshine. There was no traffic and the only person I saw was an occasional gardener, working outside one of the villas. I sang out gaily, *'Bonjour,'* in the hope of seeing recognition on their faces, but a polite *'Bonjour'* was all I received in return. So the girl was not known in this quarter. Which made me wonder why she had ridden her bike here. It certainly wasn't a short cut to anywhere. Which must mean that she had wanted members of the English community to see her and to notice her – to think that she was I. It was all so horribly and thoroughly well planned, and the worrying thought came to me that she had known exactly what I was wearing that day, when I had only bought the outfit hours before. Someone had been spying on all my movements.

There was something else that was worrying me, and I tried to think what it was as I stared at the spring flowers growing in those gardens. Something to do with flowers. Something I had heard that morning – at Sir Toby's villa. Suddenly I stood stock-still in the middle of the road. The two paintings, one of which had been forged. The sunflowers and the chair. And I remembered where I had heard those words spoken together before, in French. It was in the bar on the Channel steamer and the speaker had been Jean-Paul. Not the *tournesols*, he had said. Much simpler. The chair.

I found it hard to breathe. With this realization more things became obvious. Jean-Paul knew what I was wearing and had kept me nicely occupied all afternoon while someone dressed like me entered Sir Toby's house, put in a forged painting, presumably taking the real one, and killed him. I shook my head, trying to shake out the thoughts that whirled around it. Stupid. Impossible. He was a fabulously rich French aristocrat. Why would he want to steal a painting when he could buy what he wanted? I started to walk, faster and faster. I examined his reactions to me. At first anger, surprise at seeing me. Then appraising, curious, pleasant; then flirtatious. He thought he recognized me, but he must have seen the resemblance to someone he knew – and realized what an opportunity he had.

So he had used me. The flirtation had been an act. He hadn't been in the least interested in me, as he had demonstrated the night before, when he had probably gone off with Belinda because I was no longer any use to him. I recalled his frank appraisal of my dismal dress. A man in love does not notice the cut of a dress, but rather the face of a beloved. I felt hot tears of anger and embarrassment welling up in my eyes. The angry blare of a motorcar

Klaxon brought me to an abrupt halt. I had reached a wider road, on the other side of which was a more ordinary neighborhood with shops, apartment blocks and smaller houses. I crossed the street, now absolutely determined to find this woman and turn her over to the police. I pictured my triumph when I brought Lafite to her. You didn't believe me. There she is. She was the one who killed Sir Toby and do you know who made her do it?

I choked back a sob as the truth sank in. Jean-Paul. Beautiful, wonderful Jean-Paul had used and betrayed me. No wonder he had been so eager to find me a lawyer. He probably hadn't counted on murder. At least he had a speck of conscience.

'How could you?' I said out loud.

*'Eh, Jeanine. Toujours la blonde?'* a voice called as a young man sped past me on a bicycle. It meant 'Still a blonde?'

*'Attendez!* Wait!' I called and started to run after him but he was moving fast and was gone. But at least I knew something now. The name was Jeanine and she was known around here. I wished I hadn't promised to meet Granddad and Coco at noon. I had no time to search properly now. But I'd come back as soon as I'd checked in with them and I could tell them exactly where I'd be. Maybe they could tail me at a distance, just in case. Or better still, maybe Commmissaire Germain could tail me. Thus reassured, I made my way back to the bus and came down the hill.

Granddad and Coco jumped up excitedly as they saw me.

'You've found the thief?' I asked.

'Not exactly,' Coco said. 'But we've established one thing. Look at this.' She held out a glossy photograph. It showed my back, being led away from the stage, with the Prince of Wales and Mrs Simpson muttering something to each other in the foreground. And around my neck . . .

'The necklace is still there,' I said.

'Precisely,' Coco replied. 'Which means it was taken when you were helped to a seat. But I thought your mother and I helped you to the seat.'

'And the marquis,' I said flatly. 'Remember he got me a brandy and he put his arm around my shoulder as he handed it to me. And that's when he took my necklace.'

'The marquis? Jean-Paul?' Chanel laughed incredulously. 'But that is absurd. Why would he steal a necklace?'

'I don't know,' I said, 'but the more I've thought about it, it all points to him. He orchestrated everything – the necklace and Sir Toby's villa the next afternoon, sending someone who looked like me to pin everything on me.' I could feel a lump in my throat and swallowed it back hastily.

'You are trying to tell us that Jean-Paul killed Sir Toby?'

I shook my head violently. 'He was with me. By the time he drove me home, Sir Toby must have been already dead. It was the young woman who must have killed him – or maybe they had a third coconspirator we don't even know about.'

'This is absurd,' Chanel said. 'Jean-Paul is fabulously rich. Everyone knows that. And he comes from an old family. Why would he want to rob people?'

'For the fun of it, maybe?' I was trying to stay calm and detached. 'Look, I have no idea why. But someone must be told. Can you go and find your friend Jacques Germain? He will know what to do.'

Coco shrugged and threw her scarf around her

shoulders. The wind had picked up and it was chilly so near to the sea. 'We did not arrange a time or place to meet, but we will do our best. But what about you?'

'I want to keep on looking for the girl,' I said. 'I think I'm in the right area now. Someone recognized me, or thought he recognized me, up on the hill to the left of Cimiez.'

'University quarter,' Coco said, nodding.

'That makes sense. There were young men sitting at a corner bar. I'm going right back there.'

'Half a mo,' Granddad said. 'Do you think that wise? I mean this girl – well, she's an all-around bad lot, ain't she? What's more, she's dangerous too. I don't want you going after her alone.'

'But I'm the only one who can find out who she is and where she lives,' I said. 'One chap already recognized me. I'll find out her name and address then I'll come and find you and we can pass the information over to the police.'

Granddad sucked through his teeth before nodding. 'All right, but you be careful. I know what you're like – rushing into the middle of trouble.'

'I don't rush into it,' I said. 'Trouble seems to come and find me.'

He gave me a reassuring pat. 'You come straight back as soon as you find out her name, got it?'

I nodded and watched them get into the motor, wishing I could go with them and that this horrible thing was over and done with. I was about to retrace my steps when I heard a woman's voice calling me. I saw a bath chair bearing down on me and recognized the two princesses.

'How lovely. You are coming for lunch. We're just on our way home from our walk now,' Princess Marie greeted me. 'Come along. It's not far.'

There was nothing I wanted less at that moment than lunch with two elderly princesses. I was about to make my apologies when I saw their expectant faces and I realized at the same moment that a lunch with them might not be wasted time, if I could escape at a reasonable hour. I allowed myself to be led along the Promenade des Anglais and into a hotel that was not the quality of the Negresco but more like the seaside hotels one encountered in England. It was pleasant enough, respectable, comfortable, but not glamorous. It reinforced to me that the princesses lived very simply.

Their suite on the first floor was not opulent but pleasant, with French windows leading out to a balcony and a lovely view of the seafront and the blue water beyond. The wind was whipping up the water into impressive waves and we could hear the hiss and slap of water on stones through the open windows. The furniture was old-fashioned but good quality, with the obligatory gilt-framed landscapes of the Romantic era on the walls.

'Tell Antoine we will take our meal in our suite today,' Princess Marie said to the black-clad maid who was divesting Princess Theodora of her bonnet and cape. 'And tell him we have a guest, so maybe a little extra wine?'

She led me over to a table in the window. 'The food is really quite good here, and so much cheaper than renting a whole villa that one doesn't really need. Do sit down, my dear. This is such a treat for us. You don't know how much the old yearn for the company of the young.'

Even if nothing came out of this I was glad I had come. They were so nice and normal and this was a world I was used to – manners and polite conversation and standards that would never be lowered, in spite of lack of money.

Almost immediately a young man wheeled in a trolley containing a tureen of soup, chicken salad, desserts, bread and white wine. He served us the soup – an herby tomato concoction that was delicious. All that walking and worrying had given me an appetite. The princesses both tucked in well too, obviously enjoying every morsel. We talked, in French for the sake of Princess Theodora, about things we had in common, my family, the Prince of Wales – they had heard rumors of Mrs Simpson and wanted to know if they were true.

'He has just gone back to England, summoned by his father,' I said. 'And she is still here, so hopefully that's a good sign.'

'Let us hope so,' Princess Theodora said, shaking her many chins. 'It would kill his father if the son does not do the right thing.'

The maid now waited on us at table, pouring wine into our glasses and serving us cold chicken in a cream sauce. I tried to protest the wine, but my protests were dismissed.

'So good for the digestion,' Princess Marie said. 'We would not be alive today without our wine, would we, *ma chère*?' Princess Theodora nodded, already munching a great hunk of bread.

We worked our way through the chicken salad. It was only when the desserts were put in front of us – delicate floating islands with strands of crystallized sugar all over them – that I dared to ask, 'Highness, you said you are acquainted with all the great families of Europe–'

'Not any longer,' she replied. 'We do not entertain anymore, nor are we often invited out, so I am woefully behind on my gossip.'

'But you know of the Marquis de Ronchard?' I asked.

'Of course. I knew his dear mama well,' she said. A soft, wistful look came over her face. 'We were girls together. We were introduced into society about the same time.'

'And what can you tell me about him?'

'It was such a tragedy. His poor mother never recovered.'

'What was such a tragedy?'

'His death,' she said. 'He died so young.'

'He died? The Marquis de Ronchard died?'

'It was years ago now.' She wiped her mouth delicately with a napkin. 'And yet I still feel the sorrow. I was close to his mama, you know.'

'How did he die?' I could hardly make the words come out.

'In the great influenza epidemic. They were out on their estates in the West Indies. They had gone there to escape the war and when his father was killed in the fighting they stayed on because France was not an agreeable place to be for a long while after the war. Then the epidemic reached even far-flung corners of the world and the young man succumbed. The influenza, it targeted the young, you know. The young and healthy. They were the ones stricken.'

'So he died in the epidemic. Did his younger brother inherit the title, or a cousin?'

She shook her head. 'The title died with him. He was an only child and soon after his death we received word that his mother had died also. Of grief, if you want my opinion. She worshipped that boy. And now they are both buried in a foreign field, so far from home. Life is full of such tragedies, is it not?'

Theodora nodded vigorously but didn't stop munching on her dessert. Coffee was served. As soon as possible I made my excuses of an urgent appointment and took my leave.

'You will come again soon?' Princess Marie asked expectantly as she clutched my hand between her bony fingers. 'Such a treat for both of us.'

I promised I would return and made my way down the broad curved staircase. As I came out the front door, blinking in the strong sunlight, someone came running up the steps toward me. I looked up into the face of Darcy.

# *Chapter 32*

**January 28, 1933**
*In Nice. But really not very nice.*

It was all I could do not to fling myself into his arms.

'Georgie?' His face showed concern. 'Is everything all right? What are you doing here? Did you come to find me?'

'I didn't know you were staying here,' I said.

'Oh, yes, we've been here a couple of weeks. They'll probably stay on another couple but I have to leave soon.'

'I see.' The desire to hug him faded. 'Darcy, I want you to do something for me. The Marquis de Ronchard – you warned me against him. Was it just because you thought he had a bad reputation with women or did you suspect something more?'

He was still frowning. 'Let's just say that certain people wanted me to check up on him. He may not be what he seems, Georgie.'

'I know. He's not.' The words burst out. 'Darcy, he's not a marquis. I suspect he's a clever thief who stole the queen's necklace and is probably responsible for the death of Sir Toby Groper. You must go and arrest him.'

'How did you come by this knowledge?' he asked.

'I worked it out,' I said. 'I put together the pieces of the puzzle.'

'Then you are very astute, my dear. But arresting him – that won't be so easy. The gentleman is more slippery than an eel. There have been incidents before when his name was implicated and every time he walked away smelling like a rose. But this time we have someone who might be willing to testify against him.' He looked hard at me. 'If we can just come up with one damning piece of evidence.'

'I heard him on the Channel steamer speaking to a man in French. They were discussing whether it was to be the sunflowers or the chair. At the time I thought this sounded like nonsense but then in Sir Toby's villa it was determined that the Van Gogh picture of a chair had been replaced by a forgery while the picture of sunflowers beside it was unharmed. And I realized that his attentions to me were only to set me up as the suspect.' It really hurt to confess this to Darcy but I forced the words out, feeling my cheeks burning with embarrassment.

Darcy nodded. 'I thought you weren't his usual type. But I suppose he would turn any girl's head. He's handsome and rich and has a good title.'

'Which is a lie,' I said.

'It is?'

I nodded. 'I've just been speaking with two elderly princesses upstairs. They knew the real marquis. He died abroad right after the war. His mother died soon after, so there was no one in France left of that line.'

'And then this man appears several years later, and

nobody disputes his claim. If we could prove that, it would be a step in the right direction.' He touched my arm. 'Look, Georgie, I want you to go back to the villa where you're staying and don't move. The place is guarded by police still, isn't it? It was last night.'

'They're still outside Sir Toby's villa next door,' I said. 'You will put a watch on the marquis, won't you?'

'I'll pass along your information through the correct channels,' he said. 'You may be required to give evidence, but for now I want to make sure you are safe. I told you before that this is a dangerous man, and you really have no idea how dangerous.' He stopped and put a tentative hand on my shoulder. 'Take care of yourself, won't you? Don't do anything brave and stupid.'

'I'll try not to,' I said.

'Good girl.' He leaned forward as if to kiss me, then looked into my eyes and disappeared into the building. I stood on the steps with the wind blowing in my face, wanting with all my heart to call him back. Then I jammed my hat down on my head and forced myself down the steps and started walking. I knew I should go home as he had told me, but I also knew that only I had a chance of finding Jeanine, so I made my way back up the hill to begin my search in earnest. The streets to the left of the boulevard were lively with students and housewives shopping for the night's meal, which reassured me that I was relatively safe. And on the way up the hill I had developed a plan. I would go into every café and bar and shop. If I got a flicker of recognition from anyone, I'd tell them I was Jeanine's cousin, looking for her. If nobody recognized me, I'd ask for directions to the Roman amphitheater and act the part of a lost English tourist.

I put my plan into action at the café on the corner where
the bicyclist had called out Jeanine's name. No reaction
but several helpful patrons came out and seemed as if
they wanted to direct me in person to the amphitheater,
which was quite in the wrong direction. I had to wait
until they'd gone back inside again before I could sprint
back across the street and continue my quest in the right
direction. I went into the next shop and then the next.
Then the next street, and the one after it. After a while
I felt a prickling at the back of my neck, as if I were
being followed. I spun around but saw nobody that I
recognized among the passing pedestrians. I continued,
but the feeling didn't go away. I had almost decided that
I was being foolish to be hunting down a killer alone,
when a young man, dressed in a shabby jacket and wearing a student's cap, gave me a glance as he walked past
me, then a rapid double take. I turned and ran to catch
up with him.

'Excuse me,' I said, 'but I noticed that you thought you
recognized me.'

'My apologies, mademoiselle,' he said, 'but you resem-
ble a young woman I know.'

'Would her name be Jeanine?'

'Ah, so you know her too? You two are related, perhaps? The resemblance between you is strong.'

'Yes, we're cousins,' I said, 'and I've been trying to find
her.'

He glanced at his watch. 'It's a little early but she may
already be at the club.'

'The club?'

'The Black Cat. She is one of the dancers there. You
knew that, didn't you?'

'Oh, of course. I heard that she was now working at a club.'

He looked at me strangely. 'You are not French,' he said.

'No. The English branch of the family. It's a complicated story. So how would I find the Black Cat Club?'

He was still staring at me. 'It's not the sort of place a young woman would go to alone,' he said.

'And if she is not already at the club? Do you know her home address?'

He gave an apologetic shrug. 'I have never been one of those lucky enough to be invited back to her apartment, but she has rooms in one of the buildings around here. Not that she sleeps at home much, if you get my meaning.'

'I'll try the Black Cat,' I said. 'At least I can leave a message for her. How do I get there?'

'It's down by the port,' he said. 'One of those buildings below the castle. Ask anyone. They'll know.'

So it was back down the hill again. By now I was feeling rather tired and ready to give up for the day. A long cool drink and a good dinner awaited me at my mother's villa. And tomorrow I could set out again with Commissaire Germain and my grandfather. That made a lot more sense. But I decided just to have a look at the Black Cat Club before I found a taxi to take me home. I didn't think my legs were up to the mile walk to the villa this evening.

I could see at once why it was not recommended as a place for young women like myself to go alone. It was discreet enough, but outside there were framed photographs of young women in provocative poses. The front door was firmly shut. As I turned away, someone came clattering over the cobbles toward me. Her head was down against the strong wind that now blew from the harbor and she wasn't looking where she was going, so that she almost bumped into me. She realized at the last second I was standing there and looked up. A look of surprise and then recognition crossed her face. We stared at each other for a long moment without speaking.

'You,' she said at last. 'It's you. You really do look like me. He said you did.'

She was not as fair skinned as I and lacked my freckles, and her hair was reddish brown, but a face with my features was staring back at me.

'It's unbelievable,' I said. 'We could almost be twins.'

'Not so hard to believe,' she said, still staring at me. 'We are sisters, after all.'

'Sisters? What on earth do you mean?'

She looked around. The street appeared to be deserted but she tapped on the door of the club. 'You had better come inside. It would be a serious mistake to be seen together.'

The door opened a few inches. 'It is I, Robert,' she said. 'I have someone with me. Let us in and then leave us alone. We want to talk.'

We stepped into the nightclub. The chairs were still on the tables and it smelled of cigarettes and old wine. Along one side there was a mahogany bar with leather-topped bar stools and at the back was a stage with red velvet curtains. The only light came from a dirty window on one side that looked out onto an alleyway. One half of the window was open and the cold breeze stirred the curtains. The person she had called Robert had vanished.

Jeanine took down two chairs. 'Sit,' she said. 'Do you want a cognac or Pernod?'

'Nothing, thank you.'

'I think I need one,' she said, and she poured herself a glass before sitting opposite me.

'I don't understand,' I said. 'How can we be sisters? My father's first wife died soon after Binky was born. My mother certainly only had one child.'

She looked at me, her lip curled in scorn. 'You think all children are born on the right side of the blanket?' she demanded. 'Our father came to the Riviera after his first wife died. He was enchanted by my mother, who was a famous dancer at the time. I was born. For a while he was enchanted with me too. He set us up in a nice little house and came to visit us often and all was well. Then he met your mother and he married her – although she too was not of his station. We heard that he had a proper daughter now – a legal daughter. He hardly came to see us anymore. You were now the apple of his eye.'

She was looking at me with undisguised animosity. I didn't know what to say. I was still stunned by the word 'sister.' A small voice inside me whispered that I had a sister. I who had longed for a sister during my lonely childhood was now presented with one and she was looking at me with hate.

'And then the war came,' she said. 'And France was occupied by Germans. The English did not come to the Riviera anymore. There were no millionaires, no clubs. It was a hard time for my mother. She needed someone to take care of us, you see, so there were several new "uncles" in my life. A German officer once, and then an Italian who was probably a smuggler and a crook. When the war ended, our father came back to visit us, but my mother was with this Fratelli at the time. I was no longer the adorable little girl but an angry, awkward twelve-year-old. So

Papa went away. He did not think he was welcome anymore – which was perhaps true.'

She looked at me for understanding now. I nodded.

'And then my mother died in the influenza epidemic. I was essentially on my own from the age of thirteen onward. I saw my father at times on the Riviera. Sometimes he gave me money, but I understand that he had lost most of his fortune by then. He didn't have much money to give. Then I heard he had killed himself.'

There was a trace of sympathy now in the way she stared at me, never taking her eyes from my face, but then the scornful smile returned.

'But I have survived. I am not a great dancer like my mother was, but men find me attractive.'

'One man in particular?' I asked. 'He employs you to be much more than a dancer. You were impersonating me, so that I'd be the one suspected of theft and forgery and murder.'

'Murder?' she asked, her face suddenly wary. 'Who said anything about murder?'

I shifted uneasily on the chair, which creaked, the sound echoing through the empty room. 'You must have heard that Sir Toby was found dead in his swimming pool. You didn't expect to find anybody home, did you? And so you had to kill him.'

'No!' She shook her head angrily. 'This is not true. I do not kill.'

'At the very least you can come with me to the police and let them see that they have made a mistake in arresting me.'

She laughed. 'Are you quite stupid? I don't want to go to jail. And why should I do anything for you? You are nothing to me. You robbed me of my father. You took away our life. I've had to suffer. Now it's your turn.'

'Jeanine,' I said softly. 'That is your name, isn't it?' She nodded. 'I can't believe that you're really bad. I can't believe that your conscience would let someone else be punished for your crimes.'

'Crimes? How are these crimes?' Her voice had risen now. 'I help to take from those who have so much money that the loss of a valuable item is a mere inconvenience. They care nothing for people like me who know what it is like to be starving and beaten and raped. No, rich lady. I do not think I'll be helping you.'

'Did it mean nothing to you when you saw your sister standing before you? Had you never dreamed of the day when you would be with your sister?'

The angry look faltered. 'I always imagined—' she said. 'That great big castle and pretty dresses and enough to eat, and no more men.'

'Then come with me now, Jeanine,' I said. I stood up. 'We have a very important policeman staying with us. I'm sure he can help. He can show that you were forced into what you did. And I'll take you to the castle.'

'You are foolish,' she said slowly. 'You don't think he'd let me get away, do you? Or testify against him?'

She looked past me suddenly and I saw confusion and then terror in her eyes. 'No!' she shouted and tried to grab me and drag me down to the floor. At the same moment there was a deafening explosion and we fell together, knocking over a table and chairs.

I got to my knees, shaking. 'Jeanine, are you all right?' I looked down at her. She was lying sprawled like a rag doll. Her mouth was open in surprise and her eyes were staring. And blood was spreading across the floor. 'I'll go for help,' I said.

A small smile spread across her face. 'My sister,' she murmured, and she reached out a hand to me. Then the light went out of her eyes.

I was on my feet. The shot had to have come from the slightly open window. 'Help!' I shouted. 'Help. She's been—' In my state of panic I couldn't remember the French word for 'shot.' Or for 'gun.'

Nobody came. I ran outside. I knew the shooter might still be waiting for me in the alleyway, but there were people in the street now – coming home from work, going for an evening stroll. Some had gathered, looking around nervously after the gunshot.

'Help!' I shouted again. 'She's hurt. Get a doctor, quickly.'

Some people hurried past or backed away from me, but then I heard a shout from inside the building and Robert appeared at the doorway behind me. 'She's dead,' he shouted. His gaze focused on me. 'You killed her.' He pointed at me. 'This woman killed Jeanine.'

A crowd was gathering. 'No,' I shouted back. 'I didn't kill her. She was—' Why couldn't I remember the word for 'shot'? I tried desperately to think of hunting and shooting expeditions – had I ever had to speak French at one? I didn't think so. 'Somebody through the window . . .' I said. 'Bang. One time and—'

I looked up and there was Jean-Paul de Ronchard at the edge of the crowd, making his way toward me.

# Chapter 33

***In Nice and beyond***
***January 28, 1933***

I didn't hesitate another second. I turned and ran. I heard shouts behind me. Someone grabbed at my sleeve but I felt the fabric rip and I wrenched myself free. Feet were running behind me, the footsteps echoing from high buildings in the narrow lane into which I had turned. I said a silent prayer of thanks that I had chosen to wear the linen trousers and not a long, fashionable skirt that would definitely have slowed my progress, but even so, I couldn't outrun the whole of Nice. Soon there would be police on my tail. Maybe they'd believe that I had nothing to do with Jeanine's death, that I had never owned a gun and that she was not shot from close range. Maybe not, if they didn't want to. I wished fervently that the Duke of Westminster's yacht was still in port, with my cousin on board. They would have transported me to safety.

My breath was now coming in ragged gasps and my side

was hurting. I heard the sound of a car engine approaching – and a car slowed beside me.

'Hello. You're in a hurry. Are you going somewhere?' an English voice called. I looked at the racy little Fearless Flyer and at Johnson behind the wheel. 'Do you need a ride, my lady?'

I leaped in. 'Drive as fast as you can,' I said. 'People are chasing me.'

'Good heavens,' he said, already revving up the motor. 'What on earth for?'

'They think I shot somebody.'

'Well, then, let's get out of here.'

He changed gears and the little car sped forward, screeched around a corner, then took another one. We started to climb the hairpin bends of the Corniche. I looked back but nobody seemed to be following. I breathed a sigh of relief. 'You saved my life,' I said.

'All part of a day's work,' he shouted back, and he swung us around the next bend.

We went on climbing until I could see rooftops below us. 'Aren't you taking me back to the villa?' I asked as I clung onto the armrests, bracing myself for the next turn.

'I thought the upper road would be better,' he said. 'They won't suspect we'd take this route. We can drop down before Monte Carlo.'

'You're a really good driver,' I commented, raising my voice over the rush of the wind and the roar of the engine.

'One of the few things I inherited from my father,' he shouted back. 'The love of motorcars. He'd have approved of the way this handles. I'd have been a racing driver if I'd been born in different circumstances. But that's a sport for the rich, isn't it?'

We had left the town behind and the road became a narrow strip of asphalt cut into the side of the cliff. Above us was scrub and rocks. Below us the land fell sheer away to the sea far below, dotted with white yachts. The whole scene was glowing gold in the winter sunset. It was breathtakingly beautiful. Any other time I'd have loved to stop and enjoy it.

'So why do they think you shot someone?' Johnson asked.

'I was alone in the room with her. I think someone shot her through the open window.'

'Alone with whom?'

'A young Frenchwoman.' I couldn't bring myself to say 'my sister.' 'She was the one who impersonated me, who went to the villa that afternoon. I thought she killed Sir Toby but she swears she didn't.' I paused. I hadn't had much time for thought recently. 'Or I suppose she might have seen his killer. She might be the one witness. I never thought of that.'

'So she didn't tell you that she'd witnessed the murder of Sir Toby?'

'No. But we'd only just started talking. She confessed she was at the house.'

The tires screeched as we negotiated yet another hairpin bend, a little too fast for my comfort. I looked back.

'You can slow down now,' I said. 'I don't believe we're being followed.'

'You can't be too careful,' Johnson said, speeding up if anything. 'Besides, how often do I get the chance to drive fast? Only when one of you lot lets me. Take chances while you can. That's my motto.'

Something was stirring at the back of my consciousness.

Love of motorcars. *One of the few things I inherited from my father. He'd have approved of the way this handles.* Of course he would, because he designed the engine for it. I gripped the armrest harder as we swung around the next bend. The engine that Toby Groper stole and claimed as his own. Johann Schermann. A German Jew. Johann – the German word for John. And this was Johnson: John's son. He had been waving his identity in Sir Toby's face and Sir Toby had been too blind to see. We'd all been too blind until now. Because nobody pays attention to servants. They do their job. They are just there, in the background, and they don't matter.

'Where are we really going?' I asked, trying to sound calm and interested.

'I don't want to hurt you,' he said. 'You've been kind to me and you've treated me like a person, which is more than the rest of your lot. But you're my insurance, I'm afraid.'

'So where are we going?' I repeated.

'To Italy. I'm banking on there being plenty of ships that sail out of Genoa and don't ask too many questions. And I hear there are opportunities to make a fortune in South America. The perfect place for a bright chap like me. Away from the snobbishness of the English class system.' He glanced across at me. The wind was in his hair and his eyes were alight with – what? Danger? Excitement? 'You suspected me for some time, didn't you? I saw it in the questions you asked me. Why didn't you turn me over to the police?'

I didn't like to say that I had only just twigged to him. It would be better to let him think that I may have confided in other people. 'Those two men you saw at our house this morning,' I said slowly, not sure if this was playing with fire or not. 'They were not art experts. One of them was from the Sûreté in Paris and the other from Scotland Yard.'

'The Sûreté and Scotland Yard? Just for me? I didn't think I was worth that much.' He sounded pleased and then he laughed out loud. 'Well, Georgie – that is your name, isn't it? – we seem to have left the opposition behind.'

'But if you killed Sir Toby, how did you do it? You were in town.'

He was still smiling. 'Pure luck. One rare bit of luck in my life. I'd gone into town as he commanded. I'd finished his errands and I was about to do my own when he saw me driving down the street. He flagged me down and got in. He was in an awful mood. Apparently his day had not been going well and he'd changed his mind and didn't want to stay in Nice, so he told me to drive him home. As we drove, I realized that we'd have the house to ourselves and I wondered if I'd have the nerve to do it. And how I'd do it. I'd gone through the scenario in my mind many times – stabbing him, shooting him – but they all seemed so risky. There was only a point in it if I got away safely, wasn't there?'

I didn't answer so he went on. 'We got to the house. I didn't put the car away. He was annoyed about it but I pointed out he'd given me the afternoon off. I still had things I wanted to do in Nice.

'"You're not going anywhere. I'm here now, aren't I?" he said. "I'm not going to cook my own damned supper."

'Then he said he was going for a swim. He peeled off his clothes and dropped them all over the floor as he put on his bathing suit. He looked disgusting, like a great walrus.

'"Pick up those things," he commanded.

'"Have you not guessed who I am yet?" I asked him, and I told him. And do you know what? He laughed. "Oh, dear me. The family has come down in the world, hasn't it? Your father was such a clever chap too," he said, "clever in some ways, but really stupid in others. Not a businessman, and apparently neither are you." Then he looked back at me. "I presume you knew who I was when you applied for the job?"

'"Yes, I did,' I said. "I took this job for one reason: to avenge my father's death."

'He looked at me and laughed again. "How melodramatic. And how do you plan to accomplish this? Steal the plans for the car back from me?" He actually walked ahead of me out toward the pool. I picked up a rock and I hit him hard over the back of the head. "Like this!" I said. Then I pushed him into the pool. And you know what? I'm not one bit sorry. He was a poor excuse for a human being who deserved to die. I am sorry about the others, though. I'm not a born killer. But they were sure to have remembered something if the police questioned them, something like the motor being parked that gave away that I was there.'

He looked in my direction again. 'It seemed so easy. I waited until the road was empty then drove back into town again. Made sure people noticed me at all the shops. Perfect alibi, wouldn't you say? Except that you were determined to find the girl who looked like you.' He stiffened suddenly, glancing in the rearview mirror. A large sleek sports car had swung into view. It was still far behind but gaining on us.

'I think we're being followed after all,' he said. 'It's not the police. Who can it be?'

The only person I knew who drove a car like that was the marquis. Hope was tinged with fear. If it really was Jean-Paul, was he coming to save me or to finish me off?

'No problem. We can go faster.' He put his foot down. The engine whined in protest. The rocks shot past us as a blur. The big car was keeping pace. A rock wall loomed up ahead of us. I think I screamed as we shot into the darkness of a tunnel and then out again the other side without slowing at all. We approached a small hamlet where a stream tumbled down to the sea below, its course marked by a line of greenery. Suddenly a farm cart, pulled by a great yellow horse, lumbered out from between two buildings. Johnson shouted and jammed on the brakes. Tires squealed as the car skidded, hit the low wall and bounced back into the road again. Johnson cursed, jamming the car into a low gear as he tried to steer around the terrified and rearing animal.

I had been waiting for the slimmest of chances to escape. Even though the car was still moving, I saw the bushes beside the road, instead of that forbidding wall. I threw open my door and fell out, rolling onto the spiky plants beside the asphalt. I had expected it would hurt but I hadn't anticipated how much. I felt stones cutting into me and the breath knocked out of me as I hit the ground and rolled. I came cannoning into the bushes, which yielded under my weight, then I felt myself sliding down into nothingness. I grabbed wildly as branches slipped past me, scratching at my arms and face. Somehow my hands managed to hold on to a small branch and I came to a halt, half suspended, half dangling out over the most horrendous of cliff faces.

My position was so precarious I wasn't sure what to

do next. Leafy branches were in my face. Some kind of stump was sticking into my back, holding me out from the cliff, as my hands clutched at a branch that was bending with my weight. When I looked down all I could see were rocks, hundreds of feet below. At any second I expected to feel the thud of a bullet into me, or to feel the slender branch finally yield and crack beneath my sweaty fingers. Instead I heard a great boom far off, then I spotted a fireball somewhere below me. Fire raced up the cliff, consuming the scrub it met. As it came upward it spread. Through the leaves and twigs below me I could see orange flames licking their way out toward me, like a hungry dragon devouring everything in its path.

I was hanging facing out, away from the cliff face, and I couldn't work out how to turn myself around to use that stump that was digging into my back. I wished I had been more diligent in gymnastics classes at school. The fire was directly below me now and I certainly didn't relish the prospect of being burned alive. This spurred me into taking the leap of faith and letting go with one hand. The branch bobbed dangerously as I swung myself around. I thought I heard the sound of a branch cracking over the crackling of the fire, but I managed to turn enough to grab hold again, with my body now facing toward the cliff. I pulled up my legs and struck out in all directions, trying to find something firm enough to take my weight. My right foot hit a rock. I scrabbled madly and it held firm. Holding my breath, I transferred some of my weight to it, then inched my way back up the branch until I was standing on the rocky outcropping. There was another branch above me. I made a grab for it and tried to haul myself upward. Pebbles showered down around me. I found a clump of grass or weeds growing from the face and dug my other foot into it. Then inch by inch I was making my way upward. I could see the road above. A big racing car had stopped.

'Help!' I yelled, in English. I suppose it would have been more sensible to have shouted in French but one tends to forget logic at times like this. Two men had been walking ahead of me, presumably hurrying toward the site of the fireball. At the sound of my voice they spun around and ran back to me. Hands grabbed at me and I was yanked back up to the road just as the bushes below me burst into flame.

'*Merci, monsieurs.*' I remembered my French this time, and I looked up at my rescuers. They were the Marquis de Ronchard and Darcy.

# Chapter 34

'My God, you look terrible,' Darcy said at the same moment as the marquis said in French, '*Mon Dieu*, you look terrible.' He ran back to the car.

'Of course I look terrible,' I snapped, the tension of the past hour spilling out. 'So would you if you'd been kidnapped by a murderer and nearly fallen down a cliff and been singed to death.'

'I didn't mean that.' Darcy had dropped to his knees beside me. 'I was just horrified by what had happened to you. But you're safe. That's the main thing. Rather, it's not the main thing. What was the last thing I said to you when we parted? Was it not "go straight home and stay there"?'

'Yes, but—'

'No buts,' Darcy said angrily. 'What were you doing in that man's car in the first place?'

'I didn't realize he was the murderer until I was in the

car with him. I tracked down Jeanine – the one who looked like me – and someone started shooting at us and . . .' I looked up at the marquis. I still wasn't completely sure that he hadn't fired that shot.

'Jeanine is dead,' he said flatly. 'That brute shot her. I wish I could have caught up with him. I'd have strangled him with my bare hands.' He handed me a silver flask. 'Drink that. It's cognac,' he said. 'And we should try to move you. The fire is getting rather too close.'

Other people had gathered around us – the carter from that farm wagon, and various inhabitants of the cottages. At a word from the marquis they picked me up between them and trundled me across the street into the nearest open door.

'I'll go for help,' Jean-Paul said.

'I'm sure you don't have to,' Darcy replied, looking up at him coldly. 'There will be a telephone somewhere around.'

'I don't want to risk those flames coming too close to my car,' Jean-Paul confessed. 'And Georgie needs a doctor right away.'

He came over to me and bent to kiss me gently on the forehead. *'Adieu, ma petite,'* he whispered. I didn't take in until later that he had not said *au revoir.* He was not planning to see me again.

People fussed around me, tucking a rug around me, offering coffee, soup and hot water and a cloth to clean up my wounds. It wasn't until then that I noticed the extent of my injuries. My arms and legs looked as if I had been wrestling with a tiger. Blood was trickling down my face. But I moved my hands and feet experimentally. Nothing appeared to be broken. The warm water stung as an old woman dabbed at the worst of the cuts and scrapes, making clicking noises with her tongue at what she saw.

'What happened to her?' someone asked.

'She fell out of a motorcar,' Darcy said.

'I jumped out,' I corrected. 'I had been kidnapped by a murderer. He was taking me as a hostage. When the horse and cart came out in front of us he had to brake. I took my chance and flung myself out. I thought those bushes would break my fall. I hadn't realized they were growing over the edge of the cliff.'

Darcy shook his head as if nothing I could say would surprise him.

'Who was that man?' he asked.

'Sir Toby's valet. He called himself Johnson, but his real name was Sherman. His father was the one Sir Toby cheated out of his share in the design of the Fearless Flyer. He came to get revenge. Did he get away?'

Darcy shook his head. 'His car went over the cliff,' he said. 'That was what caused the fireball. He lost control, swerving to miss that horse. Ironic, isn't it? He has no qualms about killing people but he wasn't about to hit a horse. How typically English.'

I was shivering. I pulled the rug up around me and accepted the coffee someone was offering. Another thought struck me. 'What were you doing with the marquis?'

'As you knew, I'd been keeping my eye on him for a while. We finally thought we had enough to bring him in, but just as I caught up with him, someone was shot. He'd been coming to spirit her away, apparently. He saw me and yelled that you were in danger so we hopped into his car and gave chase. Another irony, don't you think? Life seems to be full of them these days – like the man you chose over me turning out not to be a marquis but a slick international thief and forger.'

'I didn't choose him over you,' I said hotly. 'I chose him because I was flattered that he'd be interested in someone like me. . . . And because I knew I wasn't exactly number one in your affections.'

He frowned now. 'What made you think that?'

'I found out about your secret family – well, not so secret, since I saw you playing with the child on the beach. And I heard two women talking on the train about how much you adored him.'

'Well, of course I adore him. He's the only nephew I've got so far and he needs a man in his life.'

I stared at him. I don't think I fully took in the words for a moment. 'Your nephew? That woman with you . . . ?'

'My sister, Bridget. Her husband was an officer with the British army in India. He was killed last year in the North-West Frontier. Bridget's had a hard time of it – suddenly having to cope with life in England on a small pension after having had all those servants in India. So I've been helping out when I can. Since I had to come to the Riviera on a small matter of business, I suggested she come along too and give the little chap a holiday.'

'Your sister.' I stammered the words. 'Of course.'

'You saw her once with me in London, didn't you?'

'I only saw her back.' I felt my cheeks burning.

Darcy was looking at me strangely. 'Wait, you didn't think–?'

'I thought she was your mistress and that he was your child,' I said. 'I feel so stupid.'

'You could have asked me,' he said quietly. 'Do you think I wouldn't have told you about something as important as a child?' Then that wicked grin spread across his face. 'Besides, I don't make enough money to keep a mistress. They're an expensive proposition.'

'My father had one,' I said, staring at the steam rising from the cup of coffee. 'Here on the Riviera. And we never knew. I had a half sister I never knew about until today. We looked so alike, Darcy. We might have become friends, but she was shot.'

I felt the tears welling up again. Darcy nodded and put a comforting hand on my shoulder. 'Maybe it was better that she died,' he said. 'Better than spending years in prison.'

'Will the marquis spend years in prison?' I asked.

'If we can make any of his crimes stick,' Darcy said. 'That's why I was sent over here – that, and to recover a few valuable pieces of artwork that had vanished from British stately homes.'

'Then we were sent on similar missions.' I actually laughed. 'I was sent by the queen to recover a snuffbox that Sir Toby took from her.'

'Sir Toby? Then they were all as bad as each other, weren't they?'

I nodded.

'And we're well rid of them.' A long pause followed in which he looked at me with those dangerous bright blue eyes. 'And you and I – well, should we start over from square one, do you think? If you can trust me not to have more mistresses hidden away.'

'All right,' I said slowly. 'Let's start over at square one.'

He held out his hand. 'How do you do? I'm Darcy O'Mara, or rather the Honorable Darcy O'Mara, since your type cares about such things.' He took my scratched and battered hand in his and then slowly brought it to his lips. 'I'd kiss you properly, but I don't want to do more damage to such a bruised and battered face.'

There was a squawking outside as chickens scattered at the arrival of a big black car. The police had come.

The next hours were an unpleasant mixture of interrogation by the police and examination in the hospital. Luckily I came out of both unscathed. No serious injuries, miraculously, and the police interview was made easier by the arrival of Jacques Germain and my grandfather.

'Too bad that car went over the cliff,' he said, looking at me with concern. 'I'd have liked to wring his ruddy neck for him. Doing that to my little girl.'

Later that evening I was safely back at my mother's villa, my wounds cleaned and still feeling sore but relieved. Queenie made an awful fuss of me. She insisted on standing at the foot of my bed and looking at me with those big cow eyes as if I were about to expire.

'Please don't go and die on me, my lady,' she said. I was rather touched until she added, 'If you go and die, nobody else will employ me, as you bloody well know.'

I hadn't seen Darcy again since he left me at the hospital. I lay back and closed my eyes. I wondered if Jean-Paul had been arrested or if he'd managed to slip away. I sort of hoped the latter. In fact, I learned next morning that he was nowhere to be found. Much later it transpired that he'd taken the choicest pieces of his art collection, chartered a yacht and gone to America, where presumably he'd do very well for himself.

Chanel and Vera moved out to Coco's own villa, and Jacques Germain went with them. Granddad, Mummy and I spent some pleasant days together as I recovered. Darcy stopped by to visit every day. When I had sufficiently recovered he brought Bridget and little Colin. As I lay there, I thought a lot about Jeanine. I grieved for her and for what might have been. She and I shared the same father, but had led such different lives – mine full of hope and expectation, hers full of disappointment and the struggle to survive. Would I have fared as well if our situations had been reversed? It simply didn't seem fair. Our father could have done more, I thought. He could have brought her to stay with us. We could have become friends. But even as these thoughts passed through my mind, I knew that they could never have happened. In our world, a piece of paper made all the difference, dividing the legitimate from the illegitimate.

At the end of the week, Granddad came to sit beside me on the terrace and told me that he was thinking of going home. 'If you're well on the road to recovery, that is,' he said.

'How about you?' I replied. 'You seem a lot better already. Why not stay until you're completely well?'

'Don't you worry about me, ducks. And it's not that I don't like it here. Smashing, isn't it? But it's like living in a dream world, and I miss my little house, and I like to keep busy, and I don't feel right here. This is a place for posh people and their servants. So I don't really fit anywhere, if you understand.'

'I do,' I said. 'Do you need me to come home with you, so that you find the way?'

'Find the way?' He chuckled and gave me a pretend punch. 'I've found my way through plenty of London fogs and a person who can do that can get around anywhere. No, you stay and recuperate properly, ducks. I'll be just fine.'

'I'll miss you, but I'll never forget that you came to help me when I needed you.'

'I didn't do much, did I?' he said. 'Didn't exactly earn my keep.'

'Yes, you did. You were the one who told us to look at the photos and that was the first time I realized that the marquis had to have taken the necklace.'

He stared out the window, out to a blue, choppy sea. 'I just wish I'd spoken up sooner about that young man,' he said.

'Which young man?' I asked sharply.

'The valet. The one what bashed Sir Toby over the head. I saw it, you see.'

'Saw what?'

'In his face. When we were taken to the house I took one look at him and I knew right away he was guilty about something. Well, after all my years on the force you learn to pick up little signs like that. He had that look about him – wary but cocky that he'd got away with something. At the time I thought he'd probably nicked something from the house after the bloke was killed, and it didn't seem worth mentioning. If only I'd spoken up. Trust your gut instincts. That's what my old inspector used to tell us.'

'We'd never have suspected him of the murder, even then,' I said. 'We thought he had a cast-iron alibi. And he didn't seem to have any motive.'

'Always the quiet ones,' Granddad said thoughtfully. 'And we never found out how your marquis managed to spirit the necklace out of that room, did we?' he asked.

I shook my head. 'He was very clever. All that talent wasted.'

'Hardly wasted. He was a bloomin' millionaire, wasn't he?'

'But you know what I mean – turned in the wrong direction.'

Granddad nodded. 'I know what you mean. You and I, we were both raised with a conscience. We could never be happy doing what was wrong. But other people just aren't made the same. They take what they can, and if they get away with it, then they give themselves a pat on the back.'

That reminded me of one task I still had to do. I decided to approach it straightforwardly and went to visit Lady Groper. When I'd told her the story she sniffed.

'Frankly, I'm not a bit surprised,' she said. 'That was the sort of man he was. Not the easiest to live with, made more enemies than friends. Now it's my job to make sure that Bobby doesn't turn out like him. He was sent down from Oxford, you know. I'm going to take a firm hand with that young man from now on. Keep him on a tight rein.'

I felt a little sorry for Bobby as I returned to the villa holding the precious snuffbox.

As Granddad prepared to go back to England I considered how long I'd like to stay and of course my thoughts turned to Queenie. I didn't really need a maid and Mummy's Claudette could help me in a pinch, so the kind thing to do would be to send Queenie back with Granddad. I broached the subject as she brought in my morning tea, miraculously on time.

'Queenie, my grandfather is going back to England,' I said. 'I know you haven't been happy here, so I wondered if you'd like to go back to England with him.'

She looked shocked. 'Oh, no, my lady. I wouldn't dream

of it. My place is here with you. You need me to take care of you and help you on your road to recovery. . . .'

'Queenie!' I interrupted sharply; but she went on, 'I know I haven't been up to scratch in the past, but now I'm going to work bloody hard to be like a proper lady's maid . . .'

'Queenie!' I said again; but she still kept talking, 'and you'll be so proud of me and . . .'

'Queenie!' I said for a third time. 'You're slopping the tea onto my bedspread.'

'Oh. Sorry, miss,' she said, looking down at the brown splashes. 'Well, never mind. It blends in all right with the flower pattern, don't it?'

I sighed. I was stuck with her whether I liked it or not.

So Granddad went home and a few days later Mummy announced that she was going back to Germany. She'd had a letter from Max. 'Such a lovely letter,' she said. 'All about how much he misses me and that life has no meaning without me. He wants us to get married. He promises that if I don't like living in Germany we can have a château in Switzerland instead. On a lake. That sounds nice, doesn't it? And he's even hired a tutor to give him English lessons so that we can talk to each other more.'

'But you said he was boring,' I reminded her.

'I know, but one does want so much to be adored, and he does adore me,' she said. 'And all that lovely money is rather nice too.'

'And will you really marry him?'

She wrinkled her pretty little nose. 'I'm not quite sure about that part. We'll have to see how it goes, won't we?'

'So I presume that means you want to close up the villa and turn me out.'

'Madame Chanel says she'll be delighted for you to come and stay with her,' Mummy said. 'And I understand that the Duke of Westminster has said you're always welcome on his yacht.'

Darcy came up with the best suggestion. 'I have to go off again,' he said, 'but the hotel suite is booked through the end of the month. I wondered if you'd like to take my place and keep Bridget and Col company.' When he saw my face light up he added, 'It might be a good idea if you got to know the rest of my crazy family – just so that you know what you're in for.'

It was the closest he had come to hinting that we had a future together. I thought it wise not to pursue it. 'So you have another little assignment to carry out?'

'Something along those lines.'

'Darcy, will I ever find out who you work for?'

'Whoever's willing to pay me, my darlin',' he said in a broad Irish brogue. 'And you know what your grandfather would say, don't you? Them that asks no questions don't get told no lies.'

He put his finger to his lips, then to mine. Then without warning he drew me into his arms and was kissing me hungrily.

'Darcy,' I protested feebly as things began to heat up, 'I already have enough bruises for now.'

'Then we'll save the next installment for when you're fully recovered,' he said. 'So hurry up and get well, or I might have to take a mistress.'

Then he dodged as I flung a cushion in his direction.

# Chapter 35

***March 2, 1933***
***Back to jolly old England. Sad to leave France but***
***actually keen to be home.***

At the beginning of March I took the Blue Train back to
England. Belinda came with me. It turned out she hadn't
run off with the marquis that night, but had developed
a simple headache. And, being Belinda, she had made
the most of her time on the Riviera. She'd struck up a
friendship with Chanel and gone to stay at her villa. She'd
plucked up the courage to show Chanel her dress designs
and Coco had said she had talent and had given her tips
on running her own design business in London.

'She's helped me to overcome my biggest obstacle,'
Belinda confided. 'How to make society women pay for
the gowns. You know the trouble I had collecting money
from them.'

'And the secret is?'

'I make myself look absolutely stunning and threaten
to go to their husbands to collect the money.' Belinda

laughed. 'And if that doesn't work, I make sure I've acquired a juicy tidbit or two about them that I might just let slip at the wrong moment.'

'That's blackmail.' I laughed.

'Done very discreetly, of course. But Coco says it works every time.'

The crossing was smooth. The white cliffs of Dover looked welcoming. There were snowdrops and early primroses growing along the rail embankment and white clouds scudding across a blue sky. Binky and Fig had returned to Rannoch House ahead of me, since Fig wanted to be back in England in good time for the birth of the new little Rannoch.

'There's a package waiting for you, my lady,' Hamilton said as he helped me out of my coat and hat. They were, incidentally, a new fur coat and matching hat, courtesy of my mother, and in my cabin trunk were several Chanel gowns. I'd no longer be the worst dressed at any social gathering. Jean-Paul would have been proud of me.

I went up to my room and opened the brown paper wrapping and out tumbled the queen's necklace. There was a note with it. *I didn't want you to incur any blame for this,* it said. *And, yes, it is the real thing.* It was signed with a line of kisses, and underneath, in smaller script: *And in case you're wondering – the brandy decanter. I was holding it all the time.*

I stood looking down at the note and smiled in spite of myself. There was no mention of the sticky stuff on the sole of my shoe, I noted. Had Jean-Paul left that part to Jeanine? Or was it possible that I had only imagined the sticky sole and the fall had been simply a result of my usual clumsiness? I supposed I'd never know now.

I delivered the necklace to the queen the next afternoon, along with the snuffbox. She looked awfully pleased. 'I never thought I'd see these again. How strange some people are, to get pleasure from things not rightfully theirs.'

'Especially when both men already owned so many beautiful things, ma'am,' I replied. 'Their houses were full of paintings and antiques.'

'I gather you put yourself in considerable danger to recover these for me,' she said. 'It was wrong of me to have asked you. One should never put things before people.'

She looked at me appraisingly. 'You are a splendid girl, Georgiana,' she said. 'A credit to the family. What do you plan to do now? It isn't good for a girl like you to be idle. I wish we could find you a suitable husband.'

'I'm sure I'll find one soon enough, ma'am,' I said hastily. 'And in the meantime I'm open to suggestions to keep me busy.'

I didn't add that Darcy was due back in town by the end of the week.

# *Historical Note*

It is always exciting to discover where research might lead. Of course, most of my characters are fictitious, but I enjoy bringing real people and events into my stories. So I tried to find out who might have been on the Riviera with Georgie. It turned out that Coco Chanel was there, in a nearby villa given to her by her lover, the Duke of Westminster. Then I discovered that she had held a fashion show, combining the masculine and the feminine – tweed jackets borrowed from the Duke, coupled with fabulous lace and jewels.

And then I hit pay dirt: The jewels had been graciously lent by Queen Mary, who was related to Coco's business partner, Vera Bate Lombardi. The queen's jewels, Coco Chanel and a few wicked men around . . . how could I go wrong?